The Sam Evans Collection

By

Sam Evans

Copyright © 2012 Sam Evans 2020

Contents

The Headmaster's Office

By

Sam Evans

Copyright © 2012 Sam Evans 2020

The Headmaster's Study

It was Friday and James Hunter was heading to a meeting. It was not a business meeting but one he'd set up a week before with Charles Willis. Charles was his strict headmaster, or that was the role he played. The journey time ahead was over two hours, time to think about what lay ahead and just as important, what had gone before in his life. James knew Mr Willis, or Sir as he would be called; would answer the door on his arrival and invite him inside, knowing he would have prepared for his arrival. Willis lived in a secluded period cottage with a thatched roof and upstairs was a room where he knew he would soon face corporal punishment. Willis always dressed in a traditional master's gown which sent shivers down James's spine. It was a reminder of his own headmaster back in the 1950s when corporal punishment was the norm.

He joined the motorway, but James didn't rush, it was just like the long walk to the headmaster's study; he'd drag his feet, knowing he'd get there eventually. Today his appointment was at 2pm, his satnav had predicted an arrival time of 1.45pm which left just fifteen minutes to spare. Willis hated bad timekeeping, but even so, he didn't wish to arrive too early, then have to sit around and wait as the clock ticked slowly by. James was wondering, as he did on every trip, why he was making the journey at all? Didn't he, after every return trip, vow to make it his last? Weren't the canings getting more prolonged and severe? Was he a masochist? Did he really enjoy pain? Those were questions he'd asked himself countless times and he knew the answer was an emphatic no! The next question seemed to naturally follow. Why had he made the trip? He knew this went back to his childhood and his time at school. He shivered at the memory, especially as his mind went back to 1960, he was just fifteen then……

James had looked forward to school with the same lack of genuine enthusiasm most boys felt at the end of a long summer holiday. This was always the longest of the year, lasting a full six weeks and although he never admitted the fact at the time, he was looking forward to getting back, if only to get away from the boring routine each day and doing the same old things with a small circle of friends he had grown up with.

At fifteen, James had been tall for his age, fair haired and slim. He hadn't gone out with girls then, although a good number had tried dropping the hint. He'd been painfully shy and still preferred members of his own sex for company. Quite often, when the mood took him, he'd preferred his own company as he liked the solitude that walking alone in the open fields and woodland areas would bring. James had been the younger of two brothers, the elder having gone to university some three years earlier, much to the delight of his parents who he'd felt had forgotten his very existence as they'd thrived on the continued reports of his older brother's success.

James had grown used to this however, and he hadn't let it bother him unduly but, without realising, it had had the effect of making him something of a recluse? It had become the norm to be on his own and seek out a solitary existence. It had been during the school holiday that James heard of the sudden death of his school's headmaster. This had come as a tremendous shock to the whole community because he had always been seen as a very fit man who could only have been in his late forties. James recalled vividly the last time he'd had contact with the late Mr Forbes, but probably not quite as vividly as a boy of his age, who had been in a different class to him. He had received a caning behind the closed doors of Forbes's study while James had waited outside to see him on another matter.

Thinking back, James realised he'd always kept out of trouble generally, except for minor issues when lines or detention were the prescribed punishment. James had always been aware the cane had its place in the school where all the teachers had the power to resort to its use. He remembered Mr Forbes's use of the cane was always evident however and it had stood out like a beacon from the rest of the teachers in the school, because he was the only person allowed to cane an errant boy's bottom and the vivid stripes were plain for all the world to see in the changing rooms or shower where it had become something of a status symbol to show other boys the results of their misdeeds.

The boy had already been inside the headmaster's study when James had arrived to see him on a matter relating to a career opportunity, he was interested in. The door had a sliding sign, which signalled whether it had been vacant or otherwise whenever the door was closed. The voices inside had been quite clear which at the time he felt made the ENGAGED sign unnecessary. He was looking at the various staff announcements on the nearby notice board at the time. He recalled the shock he'd felt hearing a swish followed by a crack and a howl of pain and this had certainly brought him to his senses; this was quickly followed by another and two more. He'd felt a strange sensation, a quickening of his pulse, his thoughts then concentrating entirely on the subject. It had felt very similar to how he'd felt when he'd seen the marks on the rears of boys of all ages and sizes from time to time.

The door had opened and a tearful boy, who would never forgive him for being there, left the room and disappeared out of sight down a side corridor. James then entered and stood by the headmaster's desk, upon which lay an open book listing scores of names and misdeeds; across it a cane, some three feet in length, which had assumed was the cause of the cries of pain he'd just heard. He'd felt a strange sense of excitement having been there at that time, knowing an event had occurred only minutes before which he wished he'd witnessed. As he stood waiting, he had seen the evidence of the punishment was being placed aside for another time and the reason for being there was about to be explored further. Afterwards, James had wondered if he'd ever commit an unmentionable crime needing such retribution.

Back on the busy motorway James saw ahead the annoying spectacle of two heavy trucks blocking two of the three lanes. The road was quite steeply inclined, and an overtaking vehicle struggled to make much headway, while the truck being overtaken seemed to deliberately ensure things remained that way! James signalled, eventually managing to get into the fast-overtaking lane and then get past himself. He soon resettled and his mind drifted back sixty years.

It was a Tuesday when he'd started back for the first term of the new school year. It always seemed strange to him why this day was chosen and not the Monday instead. He hadn't dwelt on it as he'd loaded his books onto the carrier at the rear of his cycle and prepared for the twenty-minute journey that would take him to his final year at school. He'd arrived with about ten minutes to go before assembly was called and it had become obvious the overwhelming thought on everybody's mind that day was the new headmaster. What was he like? Had it been true he'd come from one of the toughest schools in the midlands. A special school for delinquents with a reputation for harsh discipline!

James had been at the rear of the hall where the school's six hundred mixed pupils had been gathered: awaiting the arrival of Mr Walker to take the morning service. His arrival had caused a ripple of shock as he'd burst into view walking down an open veranda along the side of the hall before entering at a side door which had led to the steps of a raised platform.

'We will sing hymn number one hundred and sixty-two'. He'd spoken in a clear voice.

Those had been the first words spoken by this tall man to the hushed audience before him. Walker had been dressed in a dark suit over which he'd wore the draped black gown which needlessly indicated his rank. The service had been short and just as he was last to enter, he had chosen to be the first to leave. He'd made his way to the main exit where he had stood almost threateningly as children filed past and on their way to new classrooms and curriculums for the year ahead.

It had been a first term which saw much change in the school; the most obvious one, from his point of view, was the sharp increase in striped bottoms in the shower rooms, where previously it was something only seen infrequently. Now boys with white buttocks, clear of the marks left by the cane, were becoming the minority. He'd seen boys carrying the marks from a fresh beating even before older markings had died away. No boy had been really safe, as the head had taken to prowling the corridors with cane in hand, where he'd dished out instant justice to any boy who had been sent out of the classroom for bad misbehaviour. It had often applied to anybody he'd found not in their class with an insufficient reason for not being so.

James smiled as he remembered smoking, which had always been the number one punishable offence! The rate of detection had grown rapidly as Walker made it a personal crusade to stamp out the habit. Thankfully, by the second term, things had settled down a little, or so it had seemed, although more likely, the school was growing used to the institutionalised brutality which had become his trademark since he'd arrived.

James had known he was finding the thoughts of punishment entering into his thinking on a growing scale. His dreams and fantasies had been centred on the cane and the effects of it on the smooth, rounded bottoms of young boys. This had produced a yearning to be involved; to take his share, to find out how painfully those marks he so regularly saw were earned? He'd found the effects had always given him an erection, often resulting in an uncontrolled climax. At least that had then eased the thoughts playing in his head which had enabled him to sleep and put his troubled mind to rest. His fantasies had grown more strongly as the weeks moved on; the most reoccurring one taking place in the shower surrounded with boys all carrying the marks of their misdeeds, he having been the only exception.

James had one particular fantasy; he'd imagine his name called out and stepping out from the wet and steam finding himself confronted by Walker, cane in hand. James was naked, that is how he was to be as the head then called the boys to form a circle with James at its centre bending over a

13

vaulting horse placed there for that purpose. He knew he'd always wake at this point, sweating and shaking with a mixture of fear and excitement, having wet the bed as the result of a savage climax which had left him cold and breathless for several minutes afterwards.

It had been lunchtime when James, together with three others, having left the confines of the school, had become involved in an incident which was to put some of his nighttime thoughts into a savage reality and start a chain of events which would cause tragic consequences and shake the community to its roots. James had only tagged along for the ride that fateful day, normally he would have had nothing to do with the sort of company with which he was then associated. James had worn a school uniform blazer, while the others had more casual clothing. In fact, two of the boys had knitted pullovers of such outrageous colour and design that they were easily identifiable; something they'd regret later.

They were a boisterous group as they took to an alleyway near the town centre, most of their energy was now taken up with a game of football where the ball had been substituted by an old paint tin. Over the top of the din, they were making came the sounds of play, the happy laughter of infants in a nearby school playing during the lunchtime period. James never saw which member of the group picked up the heavy metal milk crate and hurled it over the high wall into the midst of the tiny children the other side; miraculously it had missed everyone there, but the thought had haunted James even then as he drove that day. The terrible tragedy that could have happened because of the mindless act performed in the name of fun.

The group had run off. James, finding himself alone, had casually turned around and giving the impression of being an innocent bystander, walked away back towards school having completely disowned his so-called friends. It was the following day during morning assembly when the full wrath of the headmaster was brought to bear on the hapless culprits. A boy wearing school uniform, as yet unidentified, had been seen at the time of the incident, the rest was a formality with the multicoloured attire of two members group still giving them instant recognition that morning. Another boy too was normally associated with the pair, so it became his problem to prove he'd not been involved.

The scene at the morning assembly was one of swift retribution. While the actual punishment was not carried out publicly, the interrogation was and the whole school assembled knew the fate of the three identified boys before they were dispersed en-masse to take their lessons. By coincidence, games had been a feature in the afternoon and James was able to see first-hand the effects of the Walker cane on each of the boys picked out and harangued so publicly earlier in the day. The shower room became a focal point to show off their painfully earned trophies, their buttocks a mass of livid weal's where the cane had viciously left its mark. Each boy had received six strokes, the maximum permitted by law, it was obvious Walker would have preferred many more as told by the deep bruising left behind to ensure the meagre pittance doled out would not be forgotten quickly. The sight of the marks was emblazoned on James's mind all that night, giving him a strange feeling, a knowledge that he himself could, or more probably should, have been similarly punished. As he'd dropped back into a deeper sleep, his old fantasy returned, only now it had moved from the shower room to the headmaster's office where he'd stood naked while Walker fetched the cane and prompted James to take position over the conveniently placed vaulting horse.

He'd felt the coolness of the cane as it was measured across his buttocks…. He'd then awoken with a start, shivering and sweating under an enormous climax as the cane swished through the air and landed with its fearful and searing pain seconds later. James had realised the dilemma he was in; he'd tried to imagine the pain levels attached to the stripes he'd so often seen emblazoned across the buttocks of boys as they showered. Then, he realised he'd had the knack of avoiding trouble and it was likely he would never find out, unless he took the golden opportunity he now saw presented before him?

Back on the road, making steady progress, James recalled his last visit to Charles Willis. He'd arrived on time and walked up the path to his front door. He'd knocked and as always, a voice called out 'Wait!' He knew it was symbolic, his means of prolonging the wariness James always felt, very much like that memorable day back at school.

It was just before lunch when James had knocked on Mr Walker's door the following day, it was answered with his normal brusque manner typical of the man, which had instantly filled James with a foreboding which made him instantly regret the course of action he was now committed to.

'Yes Hunter, what can I do for you?' Walker had asked aggressively as soon as James had entered his study.

'I've come to own up sir; I was with the other boys in the group that threw the milk crate'. He'd felt relieved he had said it, got if off his chest at last! Unless there was some overwhelming sense of forgiveness or compassion, he knew then he would soon have the same emblazoned pattern as he'd seen on others so often before.

'So why are you here then Hunter, I don't normally associate this school with courage and chivalry, is this some joke'? He had risen menacingly from his seat and stood over James whose previous lack of fear had all but vanished now and replaced by an increasing sense of dread.

'No sir, it's no joke, I was with the other boys, but I didn't run off with the others, it was me wearing the school uniform'.

'Did you throw the crate?'

'No sir, in fact I didn't see who did, it happened so quickly.'

Walker had delayed any further questioning, spending the next few seconds deliberating over his next action, all the time keeping his gaze fixed upon James as if it had been some trial of strength to ensure the truth was being told before having come to his decision.

'You were out of bounds, going into town in the first place, while I appreciate you might not have prevented the incident at the infant's school you were there and must be accountable for that'. There had been brief hesitation before delivering his verdict

'You will receive six strokes of the cane. Come back here at the end of school this afternoon, you may go'. Walker had turned away and returned to his desk leaving James to ponder on the situation facing him. He hadn't discussed the matter with anybody during the three or so hours that followed, time as always in these circumstances dragged by and as a result James's mind had been unable to focus on his work or events going on around him. Twice during that long afternoon James had been reprimanded for his lack of attention, but nothing was going to make him attentive with what he had on his mind.

At four thirty that day, when the bell rang to signal the end of the day, James had risen from his desk, collecting his things together and prepared to make his way to Mr Walker's study and take what was inevitably coming to him. The school had been more less empty as he visited the toilet first, and in a moment of pure fantasy he'd imagined being ordered to remove his clothes and take his punishment naked; just as it had been his dream. It had been in such a mood that his inspiration had taken him into a locked cubicle where he removed his underpants and carefully rolled up his shirt such that only the absolute minimum protection existed. To satisfy an aim which he'd realised could never be fulfilled.

The door had been open when he'd arrived outside the headmaster's office a few minutes later. Just as on a previous occasion, a cane lay across an open punishment book, and this had been the first thing he noticed as he'd walked in. This time, HIS name had been entered on the latest line to be completed. There had not been too much time for ritual; just a request that James should remove his blazer and hang it on a hook behind the door. He had then found himself standing in the centre of a space which had been cleared at one end of the room. James had remembered the next words spoken as if it were yesterday.

'With your legs apart, I want you to bend over and touch the floor with your fingertips.' James had obeyed and soon he'd found himself adjusting his vision to the upside-down world he then found himself in. He'd watched as Walker had picked up the cane which he'd flexed in both hands before taking up position to James's right, giving him plenty of room for a full swing.

'For the record Hunter, you are to receive six strokes of the cane, as rightful punishment for leaving the school without permission, and later, for your involvement in activities likely to bring the schools good name into ill repute'. He had hesitated very briefly before continuing.

'Have you anything to say before I carry out the punishment as specified?' James had then given his expected answer.

'No sir, other than to say how sorry I am'. He'd wondered then how sorry he was about to be.

'I will call out the number of the stroke as it is delivered.' The next few moments had been noticeable for the excitement he'd felt as he sensed Mr Walker adjusting his stance. He'd yearned to have his master request him to loosen the belt holding up his trousers so he could remove them for him, but he'd always known it was not to be as he felt the cane touch his buttocks halfway up on their fleshiest part and waited after it was removed for the pain he'd only imagined up till now.

He didn't have long to wait as 'One' was followed by a swish and followed instantly by the most excruciating pain he had ever felt! Then there had been a long delay which James hadn't expected. The next words had become immortalised, etched on his brain even as he overtook another vehicle in the slow lane.

'What are you wearing under your trousers Hunter?' Walker had quizzed James then bending before him. Immediately suspicious of the tightness of the target before he had even started, he'd become more so by the staccato crack as the first stroke landed and then even furthermore so seeing the line formed by the weal growing by the second under James's thin flannel trousers. James felt growing arousal as he relived the event in his head. When he hadn't replied instantly Walker had made him stand upright and had given him a request which made his heart pound almost to the point of missing a beat.

'Undo your trousers and slip them down to your ankles - quickly boy' His request had been sharp but without the usual venom he'd normally reserved for wrong doers. James had felt his mind was all at sea as he'd fumbled with the awkward belt of matching material which supported his thin grey flannel trousers. Once they were undone, he'd lowered them, just as he had done on endless occasions in his dreams. James's shirt tail had fallen like a flap as his trousers fell silently to his ankles, but it hadn't concealed for one moment the way it had been folded and the absence of underwear was more than mere coincidence.

'Do you normally come to school without underpants Hunter?' He'd asked

'I took them off for the beating sir' Those words came back instantly, as if he'd only just spoken them...

'Why, when most boys do their utmost to increase their protection do you choose to wear less, do you enjoy being beaten?' That had been a question he was still asking himself as he made the journey to visit Charles Willis that very day. His stammering, almost incoherent reply still haunted him.

'Please sir, I know you cannot for a minute understand why, but I needed you to ...... sir. I cannot explain it's all too difficult.'

Walker then put down the cane and had moved forward to the door which he'd locked. Outside, this would have instantly displayed a 'Do not Disturb' notice. James had watched as Walker had pulled the curtains across at the window, obviously realising the position he could find himself in if seen in such circumstances

'Take off your shirt James' Walker had completely changed his approach, now bringing the conversation onto less formal Christian name terms. 'How long have you had these strange feelings then'? He had then asked as he continued to look at the boy whose adolescent maturity must have quickened his pulse as James had now stood naked before him preparing to answer. He would have noticed a vivid red stripe carved across his tight plump bottom, and an erection indicating the excitement the experience was giving him.

'Ever since I saw boys in the shower with marks across their bottoms sir, and since you came here everybody seemed to have them - except me sir'.

'That just goes to show how misbehaved boys are at this school James' The head still persisted with his Christian name address.

'Do you like pain?' He paused, then seeing his obvious erection continued. 'Does the thought of being punished excite you?'

'Yes sir .... I mean no sir, I don't really know sir, I just can't stop thinking about it sir'. James had never forgotten his confusing answer.

'What do you hope will happen now?' The head had just asked the one question James dreaded having to answer.

'I don't really know sir'

'You must know, you had things all worked out when you arrived, therefore you must have wished something to happen, quickly boy give me an answer'.

'I want you to cane me as I am sir, really punish me, make an example of me' He'd finally blurted out his response.

'Impossible, it's totally out of the question, I would be prosecuted'. Walker had relished the thought of carrying out James's wishes but was totally unable to contemplate the consequences if his actions were ever brought to light.

'Please sir, I am very sorry for letting the school down I deserve to be punished or are you going to let me off'.

Walker had stared at the boy before him. He'd realised he couldn't drag out the issue all night, it was not unusual for him to work late, in fact the cleaning staff always left his office until last for that very reason, but this was a difficult and dangerous situation.

'As you wish, bend over boy, I will give you two further strokes instead of the five you had left'. He had contemplated asking the boy to dress again but reconsidered as the time he had available was limited and he had chosen the more pleasing option from his point of view.

James had bent forward as commanded, his lithe young body able to stretch and meet the demands made upon it with consummate ease. His buttocks had been stretched to an eye pleasing rounded fullness, a single red line diagonally bisecting them where the first stroke had landed in what now seemed an age ago. Walker had then landed the second stroke with some force, the swish and crack filling the room with a sound that had never been present before. Another weal swelled, white at first where the blood under the surface skin was squeezed out under the force of the blow, before returning red. James had cried out in pain, but he'd remained in position for the last stroke which had arrived an inch below the last causing another agonising cry and another red mark to explain in the days if not weeks to come.

'Stand up James, get dressed, you must go home now, thank you for being brave.' Walker had watched fascinated as James had withdrawn the underpants from the pocket of his blazer and climbed into them one leg at a time, before putting on his shirt and trousers. Two minutes later he had been gone, the punishment book and cane had been put away for use another day. The timing had been perfect too, just before the friendly face of the school cleaner had put her head round the door unaware of the scene which would have confronted her only minutes before.

It was the following day when James had met Walker again. Earlier still, in the morning, James had felt it was no coincidence for him to arrive in the changing room while he and other boys of his same year were taking a shower after a games period. Walker had stood talking to the master in charge on some matter, but even through the strained silence his presence evoked, James knew it was he that the head had come to see. Wantonly, he'd provoked and taunted him by ensuring he gave Walker the fullest opportunity to study his still striped backside as he went through an exaggerated ritual of drying himself, bending over frequently to ensure his handiwork was made a constant reminder. Their eyes met, communicating a truth only they knew. James had still been able to recall the searing yet beautiful agony he had felt the previous late afternoon as Walker had succumbed to his wishes and risked everything on a craving to cane his beautiful bare arse. It was later that day, just before school finished, that James received the instruction to

24

go to the head on some undisclosed matter. He'd found Walker sat at his desk as he entered the room again, still steeped in fond memories of the last time he had been there.

'Sit down Hunter, are you well?' Things were formal today

'Yes sir, I feel fine.'

'Not too many problems with the marks left by the cane then?' Walker had seen the effects of the beating he had administered earlier in the day but decided to seek James's comments on other people's reaction to them.

'They hurt for a long time afterwards sir, and it has caused quite a stir amongst the other boys because they are so pronounced.'

'What did you tell got them, I hope you didn't tell them how you really got them?' Walker spoke with a note of anxiety in his voice underlining his concern about his moment of weakness.

'Oh goodness no sir, I told them I bruise easily, that I had finally become one of the boys sir'.

'You have no regrets then'?

'No sir, none at all, in fact I wish you could find fault with me so you could do it again sir.'

'What if I invited you to my house for some more, would you come?'

'I think so sir.'

'You could come during the half term holiday, then your stripes would be gone before you returned to school.'

James had hesitated briefly, 'What would you do to me sir?'

'That depends on you really James, it really depends on what you would wish me to do, and how well you could keep our little secret.'

'Oh, there would be no problems sir, honestly I wouldn't say a word.'

'Is it just a good caning you want James, or would you like me to do other things as well?'

'Such as what sir?'

'Now that would be telling wouldn't it, now you run off and give it some thought, just think of some nice things I could do as well as giving you a caning.'

'I would like to visit sir, but will the cane hurt a lot sir?'

'I expect so, you will be stripped naked and restrained across apparatus specially designed for the purpose, are you frightened at the thought of that James?'

'Yes sir, a little, the cane hurt a lot the other day and it was only three strokes so I'm not sure if I could take much more sir.'

'You won't have much choice if you are restrained, so you had better think on that.'

'I will let you know before we break up sir.'

'Very well James, that is all, you can go.'

James had risen and left, closing the door behind him; he recalled walking away in a daze of terror and excitement, overwhelmed by the unusual offer that had been made; an offer that at last would once and for all turn into reality all the wild strange dreams which had ravaged his sleep night after night over the last few months.

James had now reached the halfway point of his journey to visit Mr Willis. His reflections had only re-emphasised the need for his visit, where on so many occasions what had taken place in his large house copied the event which he was about to run through his mind yet again. He knew now the actions of Mr Walker had been that of a sexual sadist and one, who worst of all enjoyed hurting young teenage boys. James knew now, if not then, Walker was committing a serious offence, punishable by law even then. Today, it would have seen him imprisoned, placed on the sexual offenders register too. Possibly, it had been the shame and realisation of what he was to face which had caused him to take the action he'd eventually take. He reflected back once again.

The next couple of weeks dragged by slowly. James had had a lot on his mind as he considered the proposal that had been put to him. He had yearned to take a beating such as he had received from Walker. But it had hurt far more than he had ever expected; he vividly remembered the pain which had made him call out involuntarily; a searing, stinging pain which didn't take effect immediately, but one which had grown and grown uncontrollably to a peak which was only reached long after he had called out in his agony. His time at school had become more and more difficult. Similar to the day he had gone to Walker, had owned up and been rightly punished. He had realised he'd have a similar choice that time too. He could choose to lay in bed at night wondering what the ordeal would be like but always knowing he could also walk away from the challenge never knowing if he could have met it.

James had always enjoyed soaking himself in the bath when he lived at home as a child, the water, hot as he could bear, up to his shoulders as he would lay for almost an hour before clambering out and drying himself in front of the full mirror which ran from floor to ceiling down one end of the bathroom. He had taken to turning his back to the mirror and just as Walker had instructed, he'd bent forward, legs slightly apart and would look at the view his tight buttocks presented anybody who might have been there behind him. At night he would lay in bed naked, his hands running over his bottom exploring its rounded smoothness feeling imaginary ridges left from his latest dream where the thrashing received had left its mark.

He recalled the day vividly. It had been before the end of term break when James had gone to see Walker to tell him of his final decision. When he had arrived, it had come almost a strange sense of relief to find he was out for the day and not expected back for the rest of the term. Even so, he was worried, particularly as he had given his word to Walker that he would advise him of his decision, and now he would not be able to. James had packed his books as usual and walking to his cycle undid the saddlebag in which he always carried them while cycling to and from school. He was just about to load the bag when he noticed a plain envelope lying in the bottom.

He had removed it, before placing his books inside. He'd sat astride his cycle and ripping the flap open before removing its contents, a single sheet of paper. It was typed and read;

*'Dear James, I haven't heard from you, so I have no idea of your final decision. However, the offer still stands. If you wish to visit, come to my house **next Monday evening** at seven, if you come, make arrangements to stay overnight, I will be expecting you anyway'.*

There had been no signature, obviously, the note was intended to be anonymous, in case of accidents. James had intended telling Walker of his intention to accept the offer, now he knew all he had to do was to turn up. He now realised the harsh psychological pressure which had been exerted at every juncture by his headmaster; where every decision was placed on him and every obstacle was quickly removed before it could be used as any form of excuse.

James had always enjoyed fishing and spent the greater part of most weekends at his chosen hobby. It had been a deliberate action, as staying out all night, fishing for a mighty carp in a nearby lake, was something he'd often done. He'd quickly realised this would give him the perfect excuse to be out the following Monday night without involving anybody else who could later break his alibi.

James had set off to meet his fate just after tea on the following Monday, with eating having been a little difficult with the thoughts of the likely events of the next few hours firmly on his mind. With his fishing gear packed to cover his absence that night, he'd climbed aboard his cycle and ridden steadily the four miles from his house to that of Mr Walker who was no doubt expecting him and had fully prepared for his arrival.

Walker's house was huge in comparison to the much more modest one he lived in then with his parents, it was detached, and set well back in its own grounds, which consisted of mature trees and rolling lawns, broken up into flower beds, through which early spring flowers were even now beginning to show. James had ridden up the gravel path which led up to the house and after parking his cycle well out of sight, he'd walked nervously up to the front door and rang the doorbell.

'Good evening, James, I am glad you came, come inside' Walker had spoken in a friendly manner, and in no way having indicated any form of authority in his voice. James had entered a large hall which had opened up in front of him immediately he'd entered the house. He'd been aware of

Walker closing the door firmly behind him without any form of ceremony, then ominously locking it! Next, he had been shown into a large room where he was invited to make himself comfortable while Walker himself left, returning a few minutes later with a tray containing tea and an assortment of biscuits.

'What reason have you given for being away tonight, James'?

'I told my parents I have gone fishing and to not expect me back until late tomorrow, it's quite normal'

'No second thoughts I hope?'

'Obviously I'm nervous sir, I have given it all a lot of thought and I intend going through with whatever you think suitable'.

'Good lad, I expected you would attend all along, but I began to have my doubts when you didn't come back to me as you had indicated'.

'I did come to see you before term ended but you were not there, then I found your note.'

Both parties had finished their tea and realising time was pressing on, Walker had risen. James realised how much more formal and stricter he'd become than previously. 'Well Hunter, you know why you are here, you can leave now, and in fact there will be several other times when you will be quite free to go, do you understand?'

'Yes sir.'

'I would like you now to go upstairs and take the first door on the right which is the bathroom, take a hot bath, off you go.'

James had left the room and climbing the stairs and seeing the door in question, he'd entered a bathroom in which towels and soap had been placed ready for use. It didn't take very long to run a bath and stripping off his clothing he'd soon found himself basking in the warmth of the hot water and relaxing just slightly, forgetting briefly the real purpose of his visit. His relaxation was short lived as Walker entered after about five minutes and going to a nearby cabinet had taken out a safety razor, brush and soap.

'Out you come then James, time to have your bottom shaved'. He'd demanded.

'Why sir, you didn't tell me about this, besides I don't have very many hairs on my bottom'. James had become just a little alarmed as to why this act was necessary.

'Don't worry James, you have left the proceedings to me, and part of the process involves you being shaved, anyway I am sure you will enjoy it, now get out of the bath like a good boy.'

Gone was the formal Walker he knew at school, instead this had been replaced by a fatherly man and somehow, with the wetness of the bath, he began to relive his fantasy of the shower room scene where he was publicly beaten after being ordered out of the shower. Without any more questions, James rose naked from the comfort of the bath and stepped out into a welcoming towel which was held outstretched before him. James had then dried himself as Walker fitted a new blade to the razor and moving a flat bathroom stool, he had invited James to lay across it and bend forward giving the fullest access to accomplish his work.

The sight of James's beautifully rounded bottom had excited Walker, he knew it would not be long before those pale white globes would be reddened with the spanking and caning, he had waiting for him in the study below. Until then his intention had been to prolong the build-up ritual; he then proceeded to lather the brush and transfer the soap mixture to James's taught buttocks, working the creamy substance into every crevice likely to need the attention of a razor. He'd found, as James had stated, he didn't have a lot of body hair, in fact the exercise was quite meaningless other than for the mutual enjoyment each had felt.

James never forgot the feel of the brush working its way between his legs, and he'd felt a particular sense of excitement as Walker gently parted the cheeks of his bottom and had run the soapy brush across his anus. The razor had felt cool and smooth as it took off any hair that did exist, then just as his master had parted his buttocks to apply the soap to his anus, those same fingers had opened up this area again exposing it to the rasping effects of the razor, as any miniscule trace of hair was quickly removed from James's most intimate and sensitive region.

James had felt his headmaster's hands wander during the

exercise, a probing finger touching his anus, which contracted instinctively at the contact.

'Don't you like me touching you there James?' He'd asked as a result.

'Yes, I think so sir, it's only those boys aren't supposed to let themselves be touched there, are they sir?'

'That rather depends James'. Walker had replied

'Depends on what sir' James had queried.

'It depends on whether you would mind, if nobody were ever to find out'. Walker had then moved his hand lower and probed between James's thighs.

'I see you have an erection James, could that mean you really do want me to do this?' Walker was milking James's aroused mind, leaving confusion in its wake.

'Please sir, it does feel really nice, but I'm not too sure I should be allowing you to touch me like this.' Walker had withdrawn his hand and stood up, then leaving James still bending over the stool spoke over his shoulder as he left the room.

'I will be in the room facing you when you leave the bathroom, dry yourself and join me as soon as you can.'

James, slightly more apprehensive now, had done as he was requested and risen before taking up the warm fluffy towel and drying himself in those regions that had been smoothed so gently only minutes previously. He had then turned about and followed his master into a large bedroom whose centre piece was a large double bed with a rubber sheet laid along its length. Walker had taken a seat at the bottom of the bed and beckoned James, still naked towards him.

'Bend over my lap James, legs slightly apart and get your bottom up good and high'.

'Yes sir' James quickly moved forward standing legs apart, slightly on tiptoe, before leaning forward and presenting his smooth rounded buttocks to Walker.

'You really do have a nice firm bottom James, so nice I am afraid I am going to have to smack it' He'd replied which had left James feeling decidedly nervous.

'Yes sir' James felt his headmasters' hand slowly running over his smooth bottom, softened by his period in the bath.

'Now James, this is only a warmup, then it is downstairs for the cane, I assume you still want me to give you a good caning'.

'Yes sir'

'Well then, we had better get down to business hadn't we, now keep very still, and stay in position until I say you can get up'.

James had felt a hand circle his bottom once more before it lifted off; after a brief delay it came sharply down with a resounding smack. James felt his right buttock sting and the burning sensation increased as the hand remained in place for several seconds before it rose again and was brought down on the other cheek with an even louder crack.

'Ouch' James had never forgotten those smacks and he'd been surprised how much those blows stung and he'd responded accordingly.

'Did that hurt James?'

'It did a bit sir, it stung quite a lot sir'

'Wait until you feel the cane James'.

'Yes sir, I realise that that will really hurt.'

His hand had again been brought down hard and James winced as the pain really burned across the middle of his bottom. Walker had really got down to work and slightly shifted the boy to allow more access to his left cheek. He began to quicken the pace as smack after smack landed on the boys ever reddening buttocks. His cheeks had burned, and they'd felt hotter and ever hotter; gradually the skin darkened and several deeper purple streaks appeared which looked suspiciously like finger marks where the man's heavy hand and landed. After a countless number of hard smacks James's ordeal was over, at least for a while as he lay face down on the cool rubber sheet. While he laid there, Walker had placed a cool wet towel over both buttocks and gently rubbed his own burning hand over the outside.

'Stay as you are James, I haven't finished with you just yet' 'Walker disappeared briefly and James had found himself alone, enjoying a strange mixture of fear and pain which was mixed further with a pleasing throbbing sensation, together with a coolness from the wet towel which made him shiver slightly. Walker had returned shortly after, and sitting next to James on the bed removed the towel and squeezed a generous quantity of white cream through the nozzle of a tube. The master's fingers had then smoothed out the cream and soon his gentle circular rhythmic movements kneaded the hot burning flesh in a way which began to cause strange sensations to grow deep in James's groin. A straggling finger had found his anus again and then gently gained entry causing James to groan and ask a pointless question.

'Why are you doing this sir'?

'Because it is necessary James, and because you know you really want me to, don't you?'

'Please stop sir you are starting to make me feel very strange.' James relived that moment now, he didn't know what a climax was then, although he'd unwittingly had many before. James was now speaking with a voice which had urgency and truth etched within it. Walker had stood up and had spoken with a mixture of firmness and kindness in a way James had liked and respected deeply.

'The time has come James for you to decide whether you wish to leave my house or receive the caning I have organised for you downstairs.' James had known this moment would eventually arrive. He'd stood up, an erection standing hugely before him, the tip moist where his excitement had been obvious and further evident by a damp patch left on the bedcover.

'Put on this bed robe James, go downstairs and wait in my study which is second door on your right down the hall.' Walker's instruction had been clear.

Back on the road as the distance between himself and Willis was closing mile by mile, James realised that instruction had been very similar to those uttered by the man he was about to become re-acquainted with again. He had little doubt he'd hear an almost identical instruction as soon as the door was closed and escape denied.

'Upstairs Hunter, you know where to go. Prepare yourself and wait to be called!' The instruction was barked before James could even draw breath. He knew the man was impatient to get started. James knew he had to enter a room to the left after ascending the stairs. He knew he'd find a large double bed inside upon which was often a pair of folded and pressed pyjamas. Beside it was the cane which was the be used that day. Both were evident that day, so he knew he was in for a hard spanking first. He was always in two minds about this. A cold caning really hurt, with the first six strokes so painful he was often just a whisker away from begging Willis to stop. He'd never had to test whether he would stop which was always a concern, especially when he'd been restrained across a caning bench which James had already glimpsed in the room Willis set aside for corporal punishment. He would strip. If the pyjamas were not on display, he would then stand in a suitable corner with his hands on his head and wait for Willis to arrive, collect the cane and request he followed him. Today he separated the pyjamas, putting on the bottoms first, then getting himself into the jacket top. He still got into the corner and waited. Back again to the present as the miles slowly ticked off, is mind went back in time.

James had vivid memories of leaving the bedroom that evening, his bottom still smarting from the spanking, but it had been somewhat lessened by the cream which had been carefully rubbed into the wounded area. He found Walker's study as it had been described, a door opening into a large, darkened room, lit only by a blazing fire which gave it a somewhat ghostly appearance with shadows leaping in a variety of directions on the surrounding walls. The room seemed somewhat empty, but only because it had been cleared to form a space for a long bench to be placed directly in front of the fire, a bench with padding along the top and several straps placed at strategic points.

Directly beside it on a nearby table, he'd noticed was a cane, he guessed it to be around three feet long, and quite straight. It had looked distinctly different to the one he'd remembered had been used at the school and he had wondered why? James found his eyes riveted to the instrument which was intended for his torture, and he was about to look still closer when Walker had followed him into the room, beckoning him to sit in an armchair beside the fire.

'James, you can still stop this from happening, I will leave you to think it over for ten minutes and when I return you will either be dressed and gone, or you will be in position bent over the bench in front of us, do you understand?'

39

James had found difficulty in replying, as always at these times his throat tightened, and his answer came in the form of a croak. Regardless of whether he had been understood, Walker rose from his seat and left the room leaving James to contemplate his fate. Walker himself, having retired temporarily to an adjacent living room, had poured himself a drink and sat staring ahead, his eyes blank and unseeing as his mind churned over. He realised the position he was in, and while the moment he had yearned for all his adult life had finally arrived, he was at the same time fearful something was very wrong, and his reputation, all that was dear to him, could be lost very soon. Deep down he had hoped the boy would be gone when he returned; he had enjoyed touching James's young smooth flesh, enjoyed even more smacking his plump rounded bottom. Wasn't that enough, surely it had to be? Wasn't now the time to return to the study, and send the boy packing before further damage was done? Another five minutes passed before Walker rose from his chair and with his mind made up, he had proceeded to the door and the room directly in front of him.

James could still remember pacing up and down the room, his gaze rarely moving from the cane which lay beside the padded bench. He too had realised things were going too far, but feared going back, more because he'd so wanted to test himself and fulfil a thousand nights of frustration! He had never forgotten the pain resulting from the brief but sharp caning he had received at school some weeks earlier, surely only the lightest of punishment compared to that which the instrument on the table facing him would cause if he were to give Walker his chance. He had found himself looking at his clothes carefully folded and hung up on hangers by tidy hands. He'd reached up and taking his briefs he'd quickly stepped into them. He had reached up again for his shirt, but stopped short thinking about the finality of the decision he was making? He had removed his dressing gown and still leaving his briefs in place he'd walked to the bench, standing astride its front and leaning forward as far as he could. He'd bent over the cool deep cushioned bench having finally decided to go through with whatever agonising ritual his tormentor was likely to put him through. He had deliberately left his pants on; these would offer some protection from the cutting effects of the cane without them affording much respite from the searing pain it would cause. Surely, Walker would relent and allow him to keep them on during the punishment. James had waited as he lay full length along the bench, it seemed an endless wait, the fire frequently spitting in mock displeasure at the quality of the wood which fed it. There had been shadows continuing to dance around the room, just as they had earlier; a gentle warmth had radiated from the blaze, which James felt on the backs of his legs and across the entire surface of his buttocks. Finally, after he had almost given up hope the door opened and Walker had entered rather sheepishly, before moving forward and coming to a halt by his side.

'I am surprised you are still here James; you really should go.' He had spoken almost with regret at seeing the boy in position and ready to be beaten.

'I gave it a lot of thought sir and decided to stay.' James had replied

'Why are you wearing underpants?' He'd asked

41

'I didn't think you would mind sir' James had hesitated if only to put on a more reassuring voice.

'They will not offer very much protection' Walked had reminded him.

'I imagine they won't sir, but it will still hurt I'm sure', James agreed

'Recently you took your underpants off when visiting me for the cane, now you wish to keep them on. Remove them!'

'But sir' James had pleaded.

'I really think you should go James, if you insist on wearing this pointless garment, then I insist you get dressed and go.' An ultimatum had just been issued.

Walker had hoped James would take his advice, but in almost dismay he'd watched him rise from his comfortable position, and with the athletic nimbleness associated with youth, step out of his briefs and hand them to him.

James's turn was indicating a mile ahead. He signalled and pulled into a slow lane, finding himself hampered by a slow-moving truck just ahead. His focus was back to the present and the likely mood Willis would be in when they met soon. He'd never forget the last visit; it was on a stinking hot day. He was in pyjamas, as ordered, when Willis had entered the room. He made for the bed and picked up the cane which he furiously swished through the air several times

'Fifty strokes of the cane on your bare buttocks today, Hunter. But first let's warm you up – follow me!' Fifty fucking strokes James had muttered under his breath! He trailed behind and waited as Willis took a seat at the chair, he always placed in the room next to his caning bench. 'Due to the harshness of the flogging I plan to inflict, you will be under restraint, do you understand?'

'Yes sir,' James had replied, his voice shaking with trepidation.

'Remove your pyjama bottoms then get over my lap!' Was his next barked command. James obliged leaving them in a crumpled mess on the floor.

'Did you find them like that boy!' Willis snapped. He loved to call James a boy despite his near fifty years of age.

'Sorry Sir.' James apologised stooping to pick them up before carefully folding them and placing them in a neat pile on a nearby table. His mind went back to another time he'd had to remove a similar thin covering to his buttocks.

James had felt quite dejected having lost out in a minor power battle with such dominating man who had driven him forward to destruction at that moment of time so many years before. He'd felt awkward standing there naked, the bruising redness of his previous encounter still vividly portrayed on his buttocks in the half-light afforded by the still blazing fire to his rear.

'Bend over the bench James' Walker had commanded in a soft voice which now seemed to accept the situation and all its obvious dangers. James had found himself hesitant for an instant, then having resigned himself to his fate he had bent forward as he had been commanded to do.

Walker, then moved to the front before he had time to change his mind. He'd taken James's arms one at a time and secured them at the wrist to the straps which had been put there for this very purpose. Two more held then held his ankles to the feet of the bench, thus causing his legs to be placed apart a couple of feet, while a larger strap round his waist ensured he was unable to move in a lateral position while the blows were being inflicted. At length he was ready and as a final act of humiliation James's underpants had been pulled over his head to form a hood, thus blinding him from seeing what was taking place to his rear. James shivered as he recalled that moment; he was terrified, his world had been almost blanked out by the briefs which had filled his nostrils with a pungent musky body smell from his own intimate regions. This had been emphasised even further by the high state of excitement he had been in since he had first put them on several hours earlier.

Walker had picked up the cane, it felt quite at home in his hands as had many before James had found out, when he had run the approved school in his native Derbyshire, before he'd fallen foul of the local authority over his excessive use of brutal discipline to ensure the one hundred and sixty inmates placed in his care, each toed the line. The situation he faced now was quite different; in front of him was a boy, who had wanted to be flogged, not at all like the whimpering wretches who had shivered and cried out in terror as they also lay trussed and helpless before him.

James had become aware Walker had picked up the cane, with his sense of sight having been removed, his hearing had become far more sensitive as he strived to understand what was happening. He had tensed and stiffened when the cane had been measured across the full breadth of his bottom. It had felt cold against his burning flesh as the rod seemed to search for its own particular area of skin and mark out a territory to sear and mark as soon as the full force of the big man's arm was brought to bear. Only someone who has been caned could ever describe the sound a cane made as it whistled through the air prior to contact. James never forgot its singing noise, the echo from every corner of the room, as the prelude to an indescribable pain James had likened then, to red hot wire searing his bare flesh. The swish was deafening as the supple cane sped downwards to find its target.

James was just aware of a slight rush of air cooling his back just before the explosion of pain struck him in a broad swathe across his lower regions. First a form of numbness followed by wave after wave of increasing agony as nerve ends, gradually recovering from their initial starvation of blood, did the job for which they were intended.

James was getting closer now, his satnav suggested he had five more miles to travel before he arrived at the Willis residence. His mind went back to when he leaned over his master's lap. The first smack was hard, it stung like mad. Willis had a very large, hard hand, like a paddle it had felt! Another smack made him wince and he fought back a cry of pain. Willis shifted his position and then he really started. Blow after blow had landed, and once he had reddened both cheeks he'd moved down to the tops of James's thighs.

James was hanging in; caning was painful, but he hated flat objects even more, always struggling when Willis used a thick broad strap, another, split with twin tails and even worse a wooden paddle! God, he loathed that object with a vengeance. Eventually, the spanking had stopped, and James had dropped to his knees. Willis was up on his feet and instructing James to get to his feet, he'd led James downstairs to a rear door which he opened.

'Outside, sit on the wooden seat. I'll call you when I'm ready!' James hesitated. He was to be shut outside, naked and made to wait? All manner of thoughts went through his head. True, he lived in a remote area, but there were other houses around, although not overlooking Willis's home. 'Out!' Willis pushed James who promptly slammed the door. 'Sit on the bench or I'll increase your punishment!' James found the bench with its hard-slatted seat. He sat and he immediately saw why it had been chosen. The sun had baked the seat, so it was hot, it was hard too! James was thankful the weather was cooler now with a threat of rain. He wouldn't, would he? The Satnav was busy now as his mind returned the that first stroke of Walker cane.

James had screamed loud and long, as the vicious arc of the cane had already searched for as yet untouched parts to torment. Walker had decided not to prolong the ritual any further, it was too late to turn back, he knew he had to whip the boy stretched out before him and get the gristly business over with; then hope no long-term price would have to be paid. He had touched the boy's comparatively unmarked buttocks with the cane and had seen immediately a tensing of James's whole body as he had prepared himself for the next stroke. Without more hesitation he'd raised his arm and brought the cane down centrally across the middle of James's bottom. The hiss and crack as it landed was followed by a shriek of pain as it had forced its way from the boy's mouth hidden by the plain blue underpants he had quite needlessly and cruelly had the boy remove.

Instantly a second broad weal was raised on the boy's flesh. Already Walker had been thinking of the further pain he would inflict and was searching his beautiful athletic buttocks for the next area to attack as he'd raised the cane for the third time. Even before the boy had settled from the second stroke, he had followed it with a third, then a fourth. Each time the scream coming from the muffled end had been more intense, the flesh of the boy's buttocks had become more marked, as vivid stripes had appeared, some turning a darker red where welts criss-crossed as his tormentor continued his cruel work. James had found himself totally immersed in a tidal wave of searing pain, everywhere from the waist down burned and as each second had passed this was further increased as even more agony had been piled on top of what had gone before.

James had even then, at his tender age, quickly learned to mentally count the strokes but this had soon got lost as he had attempted to survive in a cruel uncertain world. By the eighth stroke James's buttocks had been a mass of raised welts. His screams had subsided, and they were now replaced by loud shouts, begging Walker to stop.

'Please stop.' He'd implored.

'No more, please stop.' He'd begged.

The cane had still whistled through the air as it continued to find its mark, until the twelfth, after which all had fallen silent except for the sobbing of a broken teenage boy, who's naked buttocks had been one mass of striped and swollen flesh. James had very hazy recollections of being removed from his restraints. Unable to walk, Walker had carried him over his shoulder to his bedroom where he'd laid him carefully face down onto a clean white sheet.

'Hunter!' A load voice had called out. James was back to the present day, not recalling what had taken place thirty-three years before. He'd looked up and saw Willis looking down from an open window. 'Get up here now!' The voice commanded. James had nervously made his way up the stairs once again and upon entering the room set aside for punishment was told to get over the bench - just was Walker had done all those years earlier. Twelve stokes later, wincing, James had found himself outside once more, again with the instruction to sit down on the same hard, still hot, slatted bench seat. This time a lot more gingerly. Two more similar visits upstairs had taken place and to his complete amazement Willis had appeared in the garden, cane in hand and had inflicted the final twelve, plus two, to the round up the fifty strokes - outside, bent over a garden table with the instruction to not awaken the neighbours!

Janes could see Willis's house now; his thoughts were on Walkers actions as he slowed to enter the gated property and park. The cries of pain had gradually subsided as for another half hour, the painful stripes and bruises were treated with cool soothing water which was carefully applied with cotton wool, followed afterwards with more cold cream. Soon, the area so disastrously damaged, had taken on more normal appearances, the marks from the cane were only superficial mostly, although in some places, where the rod had criss-crossed a little too often, the skin had almost broken, marks which James knew had taken many weeks to heal.

Later, put to bed, James had lain awake, his night had been one where he had kept thinking, recalling events which had taken place the previous evening. He'd felt his buttocks and was excited by the marks which covered them, no great pain now, just warmth and a burning sensation which had produced an erection. He had wondered where his master was at this moment, he'd yearned for him to come to his bed and instead of inflicting pain, to continue the pleasant things which had proceeded a caning which had hurt him far more than he had expected? After some time, James, who had still been unable to sleep, decided to solve the problem, and had risen from his bed, walking naked to the door of his room and moving tentatively onto the broad landing where he had then made his way to the bedroom he had visited shortly after his bath the previous evening.

James had been surprised when he entered the room to find Walker was still awake and reading a book, the shadowy light from a small bedside lamp assisting the process.

'I wondered if you would come James' Walker spoke gently, as he rose in his bed before placing his book carefully on the table beside him, but only after ensuring he had marked his place before he did so.

'I couldn't sleep sir'. James had explained.

49

'I can see why James' Walker had looked at the boy's hard erection and leaning forward he had carefully grasped his penis and drawn him slowly but firmly towards him.

'That is a nice erection James, do you often have this problem'? He'd asked softly.

'Quite often sir'.

'What do you normally do about it James.' The boy had looked downwards, unable to meet the older man's eyes. 'Bend over my lap James, I want to look at your bottom.' He'd requested when James's reply wasn't forthcoming.

'You won't smack me will you sir, I'm really sore.' James had almost begged.

'No James, you have had all you're getting for one day' Walker had meanwhile shifted position to accommodate him, and James had responded and taken up position over his headmaster's lap.

Walker had been pleased with his handiwork as he had gazed down at the boy's previously unmarked buttocks, now red and swollen, with weal's criss-crossing in angry lines across both cheeks.

'Did it hurt very much James?' He'd then asked.

'Yes sir, it was very painful'. James had given his honest reply.

'One or two of these welts look a bit sore, does this hurt?' Walker had then touched a raw spot where at least three strokes had intersected, and this had brought a sharp intake of breath from James as he winced in pain.

'I am sorry James, I didn't mean to hurt you that much, but sometimes these things happen, and the skin gets marked where the cane hits too often in the same place'. Walker had then soothed a cooling hand over each cheek, then he'd gradually found his way between them, seeking out his anus which he'd fingered before moving his hand further down between his legs and groping for his erect penis.

'It's getting late young man, now turn over and let's have a look at what I can do about your problem at the front'. Walker had given James a sharp playful smack on his right cheek, and James had risen, then, as Walker had made room, James had laid on his back, his head resting on the soft cotton pillow waiting for the attention he sought. The older man had sat level with James's knee and soon he was stroking the boy's hard penis, pausing at the tip and running his finger in a circular movement helped in no small way by the slippery liquid which had flowed in profusion from its opening.

'Will you come here for more punishment James; I haven't put you off I hope?' Walker had asked

'No sir, I mean yes sir, I will come back and no you haven't put me off'. James had felt a thrill he'd been asked to return.

'Did you enjoy the cane James'? Walker had then asked.

'Not really sir, I found it very painful, but the rest was all worth it'

'Was it how you imagined it would be'? Walker had slowly begun to masturbate James, who had then laid back on the pillow with his eyes closed, his mind now at peace and feeling contented, as he'd enjoyed the attentions he was receiving.

'I have always wanted you to cane me naked sir, but I never imagined it would be like this.' James had found himself confessing.

'You like what I am doing to you?'

'Oh yes sir, it feels wonderful.'

'You will tell me when you are about to come won't you James, I don't want you spurting all over the place'. Walker had quickened the rhythm, James had felt his breathing gradually increase in tempo with it, then he'd felt his knees began to rise and quiver before he'd called out urgently for action as the involuntary feeling had risen within him.

'Quickly, I can feel it coming sir'

Walker was just in time to smother the torrent of hot white fluid which burst forth in a solid stream, and he continued to cover the end as spasm after spasm brought forth more, until it subsided, and the boy turned on his side and curled up in contented peace of mind. So ended his first meeting, an event which would be repeated often over the coming months, as the occasion arose.

On the return trip, sore from the thrashing he'd just received from Willis, James again wondered about the wisdom of continuing. Hadn't he done this with Walker? Each time, after leaving, vowing never to return? At least his trips to Walker's home had been curtailed abruptly. Walker, it seemed had crossed a line with another boy, unbeknown to James. He shivered at the thought he'd walked up the same staircase where, after those who knew Walker, hadn't seen him in days and seeing his Triumph Mayflower motor car parked outside his home, had eventually been concerned enough to call the police, where his lifeless body was found hanging from a rope. James had been very upset by this and the local community had been shocked, especially when his secret room was found, with the same bench he'd been secured to the centre of speculation as to who had been Walker's victims? James knew he'd been one, but he doubted he had been the only teenage boy to have been voluntarily strapped to it and caned.

James had struggled with the loss of a man who had become a huge recent influence in his life. It had moulded his future of which Willis was the latest example in his attempt to re-enact what had taken place
so long ago. The overriding question firmly in his mind was would he make this trip again?

The Appointment

By

Sam Evans

Copyright © 2012 Sam Evans 2021

The Appointment

James turned into a narrow tree lined road; he'd arrived. The trees were mature and like so many across London, they were leafless pollarded London plane waiting on the advent of spring to burst into life once more. Either side, tall, narrow terraced houses faced each other, each with steps leading up to a wide main door, set back under an ornate porch. As he searched for the number, James realised this was the culmination of a month of searching and brief correspondence between himself and the man who probably even now was pacing up and down expectantly waiting for a ring on his doorbell.

James parked up. He was just past the house, it's green front door unmistakably identified by a large, polished brass number 27. He wondered who kept that polished. His hands

57

were on the steering wheel, and he stared ahead sightlessly. Most of the forty mile drive he'd had plenty of time to question the wisdom of his action that day, heading to work in the morning and taking the afternoon off. It was a Thursday and Mr Burrage's chosen day to receive him. Arrive at 2pm, not a minute later was his instruction; he looked at his watch which showed he had five minutes to go, although the clock in his car said he had longer. He now wished he'd checked the accuracy of either before he'd left, maybe both were wrong, and it was 2pm already – he was late! What then?

A month earlier, after a week of troubled thinking where his mind cast back twenty-two years to fifteen, his last year at school, he'd had a yearning to revisit the last time he'd found himself in the headmaster's office to receive the cane. What had taken place in there had troubled him on and off ever since and he'd even sought men since then to relive the event. He'd tried to put it out of his mind, but it always returned to haunt him, especially at night. Then, he'd seen a magazine on a newsagent counter. It was stuffed full of articles about corporal punishment and within the classified advertising on the last pages he saw something which excited him greatly.

Former headmaster from the Welsh Valleys. Seeks errant boys over 18 in need of corporal punishment. Serious applications only – no timewasters.

He'd read and reread the brief but very concise wording. It was 1986 and corporal punishment had just been banished from state schools. This man was "Old School" when such abolition delicacy was unheard of. James tried to imagine his age, maybe a man in his late sixties or early seventies? It was before any such arrangement could be put in place instantly via the internet. This was seriously slow. A box number and an accommodation address to forward mail. James procrastinated. He was good at that. He'd think about it, sleep on it, revisit it later. The words were still the same, nothing had changed, it was down to him to decide. The following morning, he put pen to paper, it felt like he was about to write an essay, one to be handed in and marked!

Dear Sir,

I read your advertisement with interest. I think I'm the sort of boy you seek, I am lacking discipline, and I need to arrange to visit you as soon as it can be arranged. Weekdays are the only time I have available so I hope I can be fitted into your schedule. I can assure you I am genuine, and I certainly won't waste your time. I look forward to your reply.

Yours sincerely

James Hunter.

Later, James's hand had hovered over the slot of the post box. Once again, he wasn't sure whether to release the envelope and hear the satisfying clunk as it hit the metal bottom. When it finally did, he realised it was too late now and he'd await the postman bringing his reply; assuming he got one. The reply came a week later. The envelope was handwritten, and it had a London postmark. He knew instinctively it was the reply he was hoping for. James made tea; he placed the envelope against a vase containing flowers picked from his garden which stood on his kitchen table. He'd normally be watching the news, but the presence of the as yet unopened envelope prevented this. His mind was in overdrive trying to imagine the contents, which by its feel was probably a single sheet. The handwriting screamed at him as he took a mug of tea to the table and sat down - OPEN IT! Eventually he took action, his neat, OCD, nature took over as he quickly rose to his feet and selected a thin bladed knife from a block. Rather than tear it open, he slid the sharp pointed object under the flap and ran it along until the contents were revealed. It was a single folded sheet which he removed, opened flat and read.

Dear Hunter,

Thank you for contacting me. I never enter into exchanges of correspondence, there lies the path to time wasting and fantasists getting an unintended thrill from discussing subject matter best dealt with in person, face to face.

Please attend at the address shown at the head of this letter on Thursday – 2pm sharp. No later or there will be consequences. Reply confirming your intention to attend.

Yours sincerely,

Raymond Burrage

Headmaster (retired)

James looked at his watch, the time showed he had a minute to go, while his car clock said four. He decided to err on caution, which was his nature, and go now. To lock up and make the short journey to the house and announce his arrival. There were eight stone steps leading to the door, weeds sprouted from the edges of several which suggested neglect, or, if as he suspected the property was split into separate apartments, who was responsible to keeping nature at bay.

He reached the top and with surprising confidence he knocked. He then saw an illuminated bell push button to his right, it said simply "BURRAGE" – his first mistake; at least he wasn't late! He heard movement and the door was pulled open.

'Yes?' A large black woman answered the door and glaring at James she presumably wanted to know why he was there?

'I'm here to see Mr Burrage.' James replied meekly. Just then there was movement, and a small, sprightly man appeared out of nowhere.

'I'll take this thank you Mrs Brown.' The man spoke firmly in an unmistakable Welsh accent that was hard to miss. He turned to James as soon as the woman was out of sight, but not before she'd looked back at them both in judgement. 'You obviously can't read young man, we can discuss this upstairs – inside now, don't just stand there!' James realised Mr Burrage was cross and that wasn't a good start.

'Yes sir.' James crossed the wide threshold, he imagined being given a clout round the head as he walked past his host, like his own father would have done when he was a child. He walked to the wide staircase and started to ascend. He sensed movement a couple of steps behind, knowing immediately Mr Burrage was following him. He waited, somehow expecting to feel his hands fondling his buttocks through his trousers but it didn't happen. James assumed a degree of sexual contact would take place during his stay, but the short correspondence hadn't shed any light on that likelihood, so he waited to see what transpired. He reached the top and Burrage spoke once more.

'Turn to your right, continue into the room facing you.' James looked back and saw the man who was soon going to inflict pain, he was wiry, his hair grey and he wore round, wire rimmed glasses which gave him an owlish appearance. The room he entered was large, ahead were two windows which James knew would overlook the street outside, where he'd parked his car. 'Wait here! I will be back soon.' Burrage barked his request in an unfriendly way, he was clearly annoyed about something.

'Yes sir.' James decided to get into role immediately. He felt it would be expected and he had no wish to be reminded to adopt a suitably passive and submissive tone. He looked around. The room was spotless with an unmistakable scent of lavender furniture polish he could imagine having been frequently used on the dark wood furnishings set around the room. It had a look of the 1940s and he could see the man he was visiting was a traditionalist by ornaments and paintings which adorned the room. James was about to look out of the window when Mr Burrage returned, he was carrying a metre length cane which he swished through the air for effect.

'Bend over and touch your toes!' James gulped. He'd barely arrived and yet his punishment was about to commence. His frown of confusion was quickly picked up by the small man who James realised was wearing a one-piece track suit. 'The last thing I needed was that nosy woman answering the door to you Hunter. All I ever see is Baptist church judgement written all over her face, every time I entertain a guest, that is usually from her own front door, but it's far worse just two feet away! Bend over!' James now knew why he was angry and resigned to his fate, he found a clear space, parted his legs and leaned down until his fingertips were touching the carpet. 'Toes I said!' James looked back at an inverted Mr Burrage who was taking up position just to his left. He made the adjustment which stretched the material of his thin trousers still tighter.

THWACK!

'Ouch!' James grunted. God, that fucking hurt he really wanted to say!

'I spent a fortune having that bell installed, I had it illuminated too, yet you still couldn't see it.'

THWACK! The second stroke landed, it was just slightly lower, and it hurt even more.

'Get up and stand in that corner.' James rose, he felt the heat of embarrassment as he looked back at the man who was pointing to an empty corner in the room with the implement he'd just used. James moved over and stood where instructed, rubbing his sore bottom vigorously. 'Wait there until I return!' Then, as silently as he'd arrived Burrage left the room.

Five minutes later Burrage returned. He carried a tray with bone China cups, a matching teapot and milk jug. There was sugar too in the same service. James imagined a full set somewhere, three sizes of plates, plus serving dishes and a gravy boat. He wondered if Mr Burrage had ever hosted a party. He took the tray over to a low table next to a sofa. He invited James to join him.

'Come and sit over here, it's James, isn't it?' Gone was the strict tone. James imagined it would have been like that from the beginning had he not made a mess of his arrival. He could see Mr Burrage's frustration, fed up with pious judgement from a religious woman who would disapprove of his lifestyle and the guests who would no doubt frequently arrive. He was annoyed with himself for being so careless, although the stinging pain he felt as he walked across was a reminder of the price, he'd paid for being so thoughtless.

'I apologise sir, I should have thought. I was nervous, in fact I still am.' James replied as he reached the sofa. Burrage patted the seat beside him.

'Well, that matter has been dealt with, a couple of good strokes of the cane quickly wipes the slate clean. Get used to it young man, there's plenty more coming your way soon and we'll have those trousers off for those – pants too of course.' James shivered at the prospect. The two strokes he'd just received were the hardest he'd ever been given, and he'd had the protection of clothing. He couldn't imagine similar on bare flesh.

'It hurt sir! I deserved it.' James replied meekly.

'How do you take your tea?' He asked, seemingly moving the conversation on.

'Just milk sir, no sugar.' James replied.

'That's how I take mine.' He then got to work pouring milk into two cups then picking up the rose patterned teapot he started to pour. 'Call me Ray, there's plenty of time for formality later. I baked a Dundee cake especially; we'll have a slice with another cup of tea when I've dealt with you.' So, he had a first name. Raymond Burrage, shortened to Ray. James moved to take an offered cup, and he winced as he pinched a raised welt, something Burrage noticed.

'Does it hurt; I'll have a look at that in a moment. Goodness knows what face you'll be pulling later young man, I'm afraid you're going to be very sore!' He picked up his own cup and moving slightly back he continued. 'Why did you answer my advertisement, James. Most young men who visit me have their reasons, what is yours?' James had expected such a question, and he'd put some thought into his reply.

'I have very low esteem Ray. I was bullied at school, and I should have achieved more. It's hard when you can't understand what you're being taught, and nobody seems to be around who can help. I suffered terrible humiliation during PE lessons where I was singled out and exposed as a coward. I was picked on by older boys. I was glad to leave school, and my life hit rock bottom when my father told me I was a failure!' James stopped at that point, feeling a huge lump in his throat, knowing he was on the verge of bursting out in tears.

'It's okay James, you're in good hands now. I hear similar stories twice a week when I take to the phones as a Samaritan. A lot of young men, many younger than yourself, call as they sit on a station platform trying to resist the urge to throw themselves under a train or jump off a high building. They too have suffered humiliation, felt judged, left isolated.' James looked up; surprise written all over his face.

'Really, I've obviously heard of that organisation, I know the work they do, but I've never met anyone who admits to being a Samaritan.' James responded.

'It's something you do, few admit it. If you feel the need to boast about it then you're probably unsuited to the role.' Mr Burrage put his cup down. He'd finished and James sensed it was time to move on. 'We'll have plenty of time to discuss your lack of esteem and its source later James. Meanwhile, I have an important question to ask.' James put his cup and saucer back onto the table and replied.

'Please ask anything. We didn't correspond, so I assumed you'd wish to ask questions of someone you hardly know?'

'A lot of what we do now rests on what your expectations are. I can take you to a room at the end of the house and give you a good thrashing and we can have a longer chat afterwards or we can extend your visit by engaging in other activities while we talk. You will be thrashed but you will be better prepared for your thrashing when the time comes.' James had wondered how the session would go; he'd lain in bed thinking about this meeting and he knew he'd hoped for more than a sound caning.

'I've thought about this too Ray, I decided when I entered your home, I'd place myself entirely in your hands and let you do anything you wished. I'm submitting to you; I will obey you. I will tell you if I don't want you to do anything' James waited for a response.

'That was what I hoped you'd say. I didn't enter into long exchanges of words. Many who call me expect this, but their interest is in the thrill of reading the written word and there is enough masturbation material around without me adding to it.' He stopped then made an immediate request. 'Up you get lad and loosen your trousers. Then lie face downwards over my lap.' James felt exhilaration. What he'd hoped for was about to be fulfilled. He stood and loosened the buckle of his leather belt and hung onto trousers which otherwise would have slid to his ankles. Burrage moved centrally and then moving to the far end of the sofa James placed himself full length so the area he knew would interest Burrage most was directly below his line of sight.

'Is this how you want me Ray?' James asked, knowing it was precisely how he was meant to be.

'Right young man, we are in role now, so you will revert to sir. I also suggest you don't ask silly questions otherwise you'll feel my cane across your backside again and this time it will be bare.' Burrage instantly changed his tone. Strict had returned. James felt a hand slide under his loose trousers, it continued until it reached his underpants. It went still further until it reached his buttocks where it started to caress its plump outline. 'You have a very nice bottom James; I'm looking forward to having a look and especially at the effects of those two cane strokes.' He paused and asked a question. 'Did they hurt?' James didn't hesitate.

'Yes, sir they hurt a lot.' James felt an erection forming which he sensed Burrage had noticed. This was confirmed when his other hand slid deeper and was feeling him from outside his underwear.

'Do you get aroused a lot James's - do you masturbate?' James was unsure if he should admit that he did, probably more than he should.

'Yes sir, I probably shouldn't but I've thought about this moment for a long time.' His response saw both hands removed.

'I think it's time we had those trousers, down, don't you?' Burrage tugged at them and James lifted his lower body to allow them to be pulled down to his knees. 'White underpants, that might be a problem later, but I'll let you find out why, instead of explaining.' Burrage was drawing this out and next his hands slid under the elastic of his pants, quickly followed by his other hand which sought his erect penis. His hand gripped it, not tightly, using his thumb to encircle the leaking, slippery tip. 'You are an excited boy aren't you.' He removed his hands from above and below and joined them either side on the lower sections of James's full underpants and then pulled them in unison tight between his cheeks, exposing his buttocks across which were two thick red welts. 'Nice to see the business end at last James. They look sore, shall we have a closer look?' With that Burrage's attention then moved to the elasticated waist band which he gripped and pulled until his pants had joined his trousers at his knees.

'You have a very nice bottom young man.' Burrage started to slowly stroke both cheeks. 'Pity I had to mark them so early. I like this introduction to a new client, which is what you are James. I'm here to help.' He then placed his hand on both cheeks and pulled them gently apart, leaning forward to peer down. 'All seems in order down there too, although I like to make sure. We'll give you a good wash before I take you into my kitchen and shave off all that nasty hair you've accumulated.' James had said nothing for a while and he reacted when a probing finger found its way down to his anus and slowly encircled it. 'You like that don't you?' He asked.

'Yes sir, very much sir.' James replied breathlessly.

'When I found you erect, I wondered what had caused that? Was it the thought of being caned that excited you, or the hope I'd be touching you there?' He then left James to supply the answer.

'It's both sir. I tried to explain earlier. I often fantasised about being caned, I always became erect although then, as a teenage boy, I had no idea what it meant or why I got stiff. I'd sometimes have wet dreams where I woke up and found this slippery mess on my bed and a very pleasant feeling while it happened. But I was also fascinated by that place you are touching, and I always imagined one day someone doing what you are doing?' James replied, hoping his explanation was sufficient.

'Are you married?' Burrage asked.

'Yes sir, I have young children too.'

'So, you have been hiding this desire for over twenty years?' He concluded and waited for James to confirm it.

'Yes sir. I have often wondered if I was gay, but I've never felt the need to explore this with a man?'

'Isn't that what you're doing now, and aren't you rather failing your test of denial?' Burrage continued to stroke James's anus causing audible ripples of pleasure to escape from his lips.

'It's nice to be touched sir, I don't mind that, but I have no desire to engage in any overt sexual practices, I couldn't kiss a man, I'm sure of that.' Burrage offered a surprising response to that.

'I'm glad to hear you say that James, you make any attempt to touch me or even kiss me and I'll flay the skin off your bottom!' James shook his head vigorously.

'No sir, I wouldn't I swear I'd never even try. I'm just not interested that way, although it seems selfish for the enjoyment to be one way.' Burrage laughed, still stroking his tight crinkled bud.

'Don't imagine for one minute I am not enjoying myself young man. I can't wait to put you across my knee and smack that bottom hard!' He became serious again. 'Do you scream and cry when you are caned? I noticed you reacted a little to those two cane strokes earlier, you do realise I will be caning you very hard quite soon and it will be inflicted on your bare skin?' James paused briefly then gave his response.

'I never cry out sir. All my time at school I got into lots of scrapes. When you're bored, because you cannot grasp what is being taught, or the only friends you make are those who lead you into trouble, you realise the only thing you are good at is taking a good beating. I have been caned bare bottom several times sir, and I've never once cried out in pain. I refuse to allow the person carrying out the punishment the satisfaction of knowing he is hurting me.' As soon as he'd uttered the words James regretted what sounded like a challenge. Something Burrage picked up on.

'We might have to test that resolve James. I've had lots of young men visit me and once I get to work on them with my canes, they all break down. It's necessary you see.' James was puzzled by that remark.

'Necessary in what way sir?' He then asked.

'I told you earlier about my role as a Samaritan. I'd frequently have boys at the end of their tether on the phone. Almost always they were gay or uncertain about their sexuality, a bit like you, I imagine. They were being bullied, picked on, beaten up. The biggest problem always was the reaction of their parents. They'd finally come out to mum and dad who imagined them meeting a nice girl, getting married and presenting them with grandchildren. Instead they found he had a boyfriend who'd had the same issue when he told his parents. How did you overcome your issue James?' It was something he'd never considered himself until a couple of years before.

71

'I was never interested in boy's sir. I did get erect in the showers at school but only when I saw a boy with cane marks on his bottom which wasn't unusual. The cane was used a lot at my school.' He paused and turned his head and looked up at Mr Burrage who continued his activity between James's cheeks. 'I was very shy; I never imagined any girl interested in me. I had quite a few girlfriends, but I never tried anything on. A girl becoming pregnant before marriage was frowned upon and this was before the pill became widely in use. Then I met someone, and I got married, I've never been totally sure ever since. Whether I should have married her, even got married at all.' James realised Mr Burrage hadn't answered his question.

'You didn't explain why it was necessary to break a man's resolve. I imagine that will be your intention with me?' The question was out, and the reply didn't take long to arrive.

'Many of these boys who ring up the help line, yes, they still ring, are desperate. They have to wait to sit down with some counsellor or even psychiatrist who won't understand. They can't help these young men from a course they took, or something read from a book. The only person who can help them is someone who does understand, who has been where these men are. Someone who has suffered like they are suffering.' James nodded his understanding, but he wasn't prepared for what came next. 'I'd invite selected men, those I suspected I could help more directly, to contact me privately. I'd invite them here and most ended up exactly where you are James, lying across my lap with my finger stroking their anal region. Then I'd take them down the hallway to where you will be going soon, and I'd cane then to the very limit of their endurance. Afterwards, I'd comfort them back here on this sofa. They'd be like babies, naked and snuggled up, their faces red from tears they'd shed. They'd open up and tell me everything. I'd masturbate them and make them realise who they were made no difference. I'd give them attention; I'd listen to them while I rubbed cream onto their sore bottoms. They'd leave here relieved in more ways than one. They return James, just as you will.' James was like a fish gulping air, his mouth open with surprise bordering on shock.

'That's incredible, and nobody knows, where you carry out your Samaritan work?' He asked.

'If they do, they're not saying anything. This is why you've got those stripes on your bottom. I like to keep that judgemental woman out of my business. Those men are thriving James, I know my method is unorthodox, but it seems pretty effective as a way to get everything out of their system, their guilt and shame and to realise there are many others like themselves, which is the greatest comfort. Knowing they are not alone.' Burrage now slapped James on the bottom. 'Let's get going. We've got lots to do. Up you get, pull your trousers and pants back up and follow me.'

Mr Burrage walked towards the door. A glance through the window showed James it was raining outside: this meant a drive home later in the wet, which didn't bother him although the run to his car parked further down the road might mean he got wet before he'd even set off. James followed the man past a bathroom on the right which his host pointed to without comment. Then, stopping at a door, the last but one on the left-hand side, Mr Burrage opened it and invited James to enter.

'The next room is the punishment room, that's where you'll be going next time. Meanwhile, I need you to undress completely, that means total nakedness and very importantly, I want you to fold your clothes properly.' He paused as he removed a coat hanger from a hook which he handed to his guest. 'Put your trousers on this with your tie placed equally and centrally. Put your shirt over the top and your jacket over that. Your shoes together, exactly underneath your hung-up clothing, with each sock folded and carefully placed over the rear of each shoe. Finally, fold your underpants and place then behind your shoes. I will check, if you are sloppy, I will give you extra strokes of the cane.' He looked up at a bemused James. 'Is that clearly understood?' James thought he'd taken it all in and replied in the affirmative.

'Yes sir.' Mr Burrage went to leave, standing centrally in the open doorway.

'I require you down in the bathroom we passed. Three minutes James, no more, or that will result in further caning.' Then he was gone, closing the door behind him. James quickly removed his shoes, then undoing his trouser belt, he stepped out of his trousers and slid his pants down too. He felt panic as he undid his tie and then started to feverishly work on the buttons of his shirt. He was naked, as instructed. He started with his trousers which he folded along their creases before slipping them over the central bar of the hanger. This was followed by his shirt, which he assumed didn't need all its buttons done up. He just chose the top button and hoped that would suffice. He took his tie and folded it along its length and carefully placed it centrally.

James wondered if Burrage would use a tape measure to check centrality. Finally, removing his watch, he placed that in his jacket pocket and then fitted the hanger inside. He put it on the hook and stood back. He made a couple of minor adjustments before placing his shoes side by side on the floor, looking up to check if he'd positioned it where he'd been instructed – directly below. That left his pants which he neatly laid flat in front of the shoes. He was done.

James left the room. He had no sense of whether or not he'd overrun his time. He saw a light on to the left-hand side as he walked back. He instinctively knew it was coming from inside the bathroom where he'd been instructed to go, as soon as he'd finished undressing and tidying the clothing he'd removed. He felt vulnerable as he made his way down and stood outside the open doorway waiting to be invited inside.

'Come inside.' Mr Burrage spoke. He stood back away from a wash hand basin to his right with a bath to his left. He noticed the bath had several inches of water and initially he thought he was going to be bathed. 'Turn to face the bath, part your legs wide, bend forward and grip the side of the bath.' James turned. He took a wide step to his right and then moved his left leg too and when he felt he was in the requested position, he leaned down. That was when he saw something which sent a cold shiver down his spine. Directly below and submerged, were two long canes soaking in the water. He looked up at Mr Burrage.

'They have been soaking since six pm yesterday; they are reed canes which are soaked before use. They are quite heavy as a result. You'll find them excruciatingly painful.'

James had no desire to contradict, and he turned his stare back to the long objects which were honey coloured with brown rings equally spaced along each length. They had a strange beauty, despite their intended use. 'I think they will test your fortitude young man.' James was starting to get cold feet; he'd had two hard strokes from Mr Burrage and that had been through clothing. He couldn't imagine the pain he'd suffer from the objects lying at the bottom of the bath, especially as he had no idea how prolonged his punishment would be? Mr Burrage turned on the taps to the wash hand basin. James remained in position, in fact parting his legs still further and leaning down even more to open up the area he knew Burrage was intending to wash. The sound of slippery rubbing told James soap was being applied to hands, he knew the action about to take place wasn't necessary, but he realised the older man needed to have his pleasures too.

'Let's give this area a good wash shall we.' Raymond Burrage spoke in his soft Welsh valleys voice as his hands found their way between James's legs. He'd worked up quite a lather which he then transferred to his balls and around to James erect penis. Both hands were in action now and the feeling was so exquisite he feared his arousal would soon spill over as boiling milk did in a pan on the stove. 'You still have an erection I see; I suspect that will quickly subside when you feel that cold, wet cane being measured across your buttocks!' James shivered at the thought and he sensed his erection had dropped slightly as the words sunk in. 'That's nice and clean, let's move to your cheeks, shall we?' The words were expressed as a question and James was beyond being able to reply or express an opinion. He realised he was in a position of total submission and nothing he said or even attempted to say was going to change that.

Mr Burrage re soaped his hands and these were both transferred to his plump cheeks. He rubbed them and kneaded them, squeezing his fingers together but unable to pinch due to the slippery nature of the soap. Then a hand went between and ran up and down the cleft before settling in the middle at a spot James knew was set for attention.

'We'd better make sure you're nice and clean up here don't you think?' That was a question which needed a reply and James quickly supplied one.

'Yes sir.' The words he spoke were made with a trembling voice. When he'd left work to travel and meet Mr Burrage, he hadn't in his wildest dreams imagined some hours later he'd be bending over a bath, staring at two vicious looking canes, while a much older man fingered his anus with a soapy finger. He knew there was only one direction of travel now and that quickly followed as the finger sought the centre of his sphincter and entered him. James closed his eyes. He'd dreamt of this moment and masturbated at the thought of it being done more times than he cared to even think of counting. In and out the finger pumped slowly. Then it was withdrawn before more soap was applied and it was reinserted.

'One cannot be too sure; I might have to give it a third go young man.' Burrage was true to his word and the finger was withdrawn again and more soap applied. So much so he felt a warm, slight burning effect taking place inside him. Another hand came around and gripped his cock, a thumb rubbing the tip and with the effect of the finger working inside him at the rear he felt his sap starting to rise.

'Please sir I'm starting to cum!' James called out in alarm to which Mr Burrage stopped instantly.

'I've a good mind to bring you off young man and let you face the cane with all your ardour gone!' James shivered at the thought. He knew from endless masturbation that his need melted like ice dropped into a boiling pan once he'd released a slippery mess into a waiting tissue. 'No young man, I'll keep you on the boil until I've finished dealing with you. I think you'll have a climax like none you've had before. Let's dry you off and take this further in my kitchen.' James was intrigued, he wondered what could possibly await him in a kitchen, although he did know what lay down at the end of the long corridor. He stood legs apart while Mr Burrage dried him off and after hanging up the towel, turned off the bathroom light and invited James to follow him to the next stage.

The kitchen was small, at its centre was a table on which there was shaving equipment at its far end. To the right was a working surface overhung by mugs on hooks ready for making tea. The tray on which Mr Burrage had earlier delivered tea was now refreshed by clean cups and saucers of the same pattern as before. Obviously in readiness for tea and discussion after......? That was James's overriding thought now – after what! He realised the main reason he'd travelled to this man's home was drawing closer and while his sexual arousal had reached new heights, he was soon to receive levels of punishment undreamed of in his thirty-seven years. One prominent and unmistakable object lay next to the tray on a plate, a Dundee cake which looked home-made. It gave James the means to open a new conversation while he awaited instruction.

'Did you bake the cake?' He nearly used his first name Ray, but quickly stopped himself, knowing he was still in submissive role. His eyes looked round at racks of herbs and spices and recipe books standing on their edges.

'I did, I baked one especially for today, I'll cut a slice later when we have more tea, unless you want to rush off?' Burrage replied, moving centrally into the room.

'No sir, I needn't rush away. It looks delicious and at least that is something to look forward to.' James's last comment reflected his growing apprehension over what was soon to happen.

'I cook a lot, I've never married, my interests have always laid in men so there was no woman in my life who might traditionally have taken on that role. I've never eaten out, or purchased ready-made food. If I want an Indian curry, I make my own. I'm quite adept at cooking, I particularly like baking cakes.' With conversation concluded Burrage now gave an instruction. 'Okay, time is pressing, let's have you up on the table, kneel, legs apart and get your head down.' James hadn't been sure what the next stage of his visit would entail, but now it was clear, and he was about to adopt the most lewd and embarrassing position he could imagine. He hesitated just briefly, then climbed up and obeyed.

'I didn't expect this sir, it's rather humiliating for me.' James replied as he moved his legs apart helped by Mr Burrage hands who wanted them even wider. He then leaned down until his head touched the table with his arms folded on either side. As he lowered himself, he felt himself peel

79

open and cool air invade his most private areas. Burrage came closer and inspected the sight before him closely.

'That is a beautiful sight, James. The only thing spoiling it is nasty hair, which if we are revisiting your schooldays, and I suspect we are, you would have been much smoother then. Burrage placed both hands on James's stretched cheeks, sliding a hand down past his hanging testicles and running finger and thumb up and down his erection. 'I get great enjoyment looking and touching a man like this. I don't like very large penises or muscular bottoms. Yours is perfect size!' James closed his eyes again, he loved being touched and, in many ways, he now wished what was taking place could continue and the painful next stage omitted. Burrage now got down to business. He filled a bowl with warm water and taking a shaving brush he wetted it and rubbed it onto a block of shaving soap until he'd created a frothy lather which he transferred directly onto James's pouting anus, causing a reaction of shear bliss which was signified by a noticeable sigh and shiver of enjoyment.

'Oh my god that's nice!' He exclaimed immediately afterwards. Burrage then went to work, rubbing the brush into every crevice and forming a coating which covered his bottom completely.

'Tell me more about yourself James. Tell me about your schooldays and your home life?' The conversation was moved away from the work about to get underway as Burrage reached for the safety razor. James wondered how he was going to be able to concentrate and remain coherent as Burrage got to work. He knew much of the surface area was already hair free but he also knew other areas were like a bushy undergrowth and once he arrived there, he'd probably lose focus. He started.

'I actually had a pretty happy early childhood. Initially there was just me and my older sister. We didn't play together much but I had friends in the street where we lived. It was an area where there was a lot of open ground, and we climbed trees and made dens and camps out of branches we found. During the summer I'd be out at dawn and except for lunch my mother wouldn't see much of me till the evening when it was time for dinner.' James paused and closed his eyes. 'Oh my god sir, that feels nice.' Mr Burrage was running the razor down between his cheeks and he had to stop talking briefly. Burrage broke in.

'Sounds idyllic James, so good I can't really understand why you struggled so much with self-esteem, something must have happened to change that?' It was a good question, and one James had thought about for a long time.

'Things went wrong from the age of thirteen. I had a younger brother, and he was the clever member of the family. My parents doted over him and indulged him far too much. I began to feel excluded from my parent's affection in favour of him; left out. Then I took an exam which put me onto a different stream at school and from that moment on my success at school melted away. I was pretty hopeless at gymnastics. I couldn't bear to be turned upside down it made me feel odd. I found out later I have low blood pressure and even now leaning down is something that can make my head swim. All this and having my brother rammed down my throat made me feel worthless. It's never really left me and the reason I'm here is because I want to be beaten for

81

existing!' James stopped; he could feel tears pricking his eyes.

'You're not alone young man.' Burrage responded. He then moved his attention to James's hanging balls, transferring soap and pulling them taut so he could run the razor down their rear. 'I don't think I've ever had anyone visit me who felt the need to be punished for wrong doing. Everyone has come to be to be punished for who they feel they are or how they feel about themselves. Usually it becomes a very emotional experience. Pain has a way of cutting through pretence. It's why it has been used for centuries to reach the truth.' He'd finished and now wetted a flannel and wiped the soap from where he'd done his work. He followed it up with a fluffy towel. 'I'll have you turn over next but first I will rub some cream into your skin.' He took a jar and opening it he dipped two fingers into the soft, scented contents and transferred it to James's cheeks. He started to spread it and then work it in. 'It stops razor rash young man, but it also softens the skin. I want to see you marked as I apply the cane and leave a reminder which won't disappear for a couple of weeks. I'm not sure how you are going to hide it at home!' It was a question James quickly answered.

'That won't be a problem sir, I'm afraid things don't happen very often in that area. It won't be hard to hide.' Burrage had a new request.

'Turn over, let's deal with your front.' James was pleased to raise his head, he did it slowly and sitting up he turned and then lay down, parting his legs to allow access.

'I want to see you once a month James. Your caning will be severe, and it will test your fortitude to the limit. I'd prefer you don't hold back. It's no shame to show emotion and having a good cry will make you feel much better. Being stoic isn't going to help you at all. I'm going to talk to you throughout your punishment which will consist of a warmup over my knee, six strokes of the slipper, and six more with a twin tailed strap. You'll get your bottom smacked too. Then the cane.' James felt a shiver go through his body. He hated the slipper. He'd had it enough times over his gym shorts for not trying or that was the excuse of the gym master who carried it out, with James bending over the vaulting horse while the rest of the class watched and laughed.

'Will I have to bend over for the cane sir?' James asked, then added. 'How many strokes can I expect?' Burrage was now applying soapy foam to James's pubic area. He lifted his still erect penis and rubbed the brush down the front of his balls and down the sides he hadn't reached while he was kneeling.

'No James, not the cane. You will go over my knee to have your bottom smacked, then you will bend over for the slipper and strap.' He started to strip the main source of hair, running the razor up the stem of his penis which Burrage held firmly with two fingers so it could be moved into position for the razor. 'For the caning you will lie flat on your front, over a raised mound, your wrists and ankles will be secured to the bed frame. Burrage saw fear form on James's face. 'I said your caning will be severe, I intend giving you fifty strokes and the benefit, at least for me, is I can apply the strokes from each side of the bed. Twenty on each buttock and ten applied diagonally.' He stopped talking and continued his work, waiting for James's reply.

'I'm not sure I can take fifty strokes sir, that is very harsh; severe!' He responded looking up beseechingly.

'That is up to you James, when we're done, you are quite welcome to get dressed and leave. I won't see you again of course and I suspect you will regret your action as soon as you climb back into your car.' There was silence. James's mind was in turmoil. What was happening was what he'd always dreamed of, even the severity of caning, but reality beckoned, and he didn't have long to decide. Burrage had nearly finished, and he was putting the final touches to his testicles at that very moment. It was done and as before he was wiped clean and dried.

'It feels so brutal sir, I've never had more than a dozen and even those hurt like hell. You hurt me earlier and that was over two layers of clothing, but four times that number bare – I couldn't possibly bear that?' He ended his answer as a question, one which Burrage intended to answer as he poured away the hair covered water and tidied up.

'You will be under restraint, you'll have no choice, the first six to twelve are the worst and I'll make sure they are! But nature will kick in at some point after that and with some stimulation such as you've had already, the rest won't seem too hard at all. Some actually enjoy the sensation, the careful mix of pain and pleasure. The thing is James, you've got to let this out, express your emotions, all that hurt and humiliation needs to be gone and you can only achieve that by lowering your defences and to let someone in – me!' James had another question.

'Won't someone hear? I've never really cried. I've been knocked down so often, but I always got up, I never fought back. I never let anyone have that pleasure of knowing they'd hurt me. The slipper in the gym, the countless times I visited the headmaster for the cane. I grew to believe it was the only thing I was good at, taking a beating. Otherwise, I was worthless.' James was now sitting on the edge of the table, his feet just inches off the ground.

'Nobody is worthless, and you obviously left your place of work. You wore a business suit so even there you are of use to your employer. As for giving any pleasure or satisfaction, I'd like to think we can become friends. Someone who understands you better than anyone, someone you have confided in. I will enjoy beating you, I get pleasure out of inflicting pain and seeing the multitude of reactions, but I like helping people too and I know you need my help; someone you can trust, and you can feel comfort you are in safe hands. I've had boys half your age stretched over my bed, and I know how far to go. If I sense you're at you're limit of endurance I'll stop, I'll untie you and help you recover. The aftercare is more important than anything.' He stopped, then realised he'd left a question unanswered. 'I've chosen a room at the end of the house. You will have a rolled handkerchief across your mouth, and you can scream into a pillow. I will break you James, but probably more through conversation than pain infliction, that is there to drive you on.' He was finished now and moved to the kitchen door. 'Come, it's for you to choose now James, turn left and wait for me to collect you in the lounge, or turn right to where you left your clothes.' James moved forward. His erection had drooped, and his penis was dangling down. He looked across at the bespectacled man who was waiting for an answer and without a further word he turned to his left and walked towards the lounge.

The lounge seemed a haven of peace and solitude, somewhere for James to gather his thoughts while he considered the decision he'd just made. He moved over to the window overlooking the street, taking care to stand well back because he was naked. He looked down onto the windowsill where a Christmas cactus was in bloom, a title wrongly bestowed as it was still early November. He saw the rear of his car further down the road and wondered if Mr Burrage's words would have been true, had he turned right instead of left, got dressed instead and exited the building. He knew he'd never know; well not now. All he did know is soon, the door would open, and he'd be called to follow a self-confessed sadist down a long corridor to a room he had yet to enter. What was to take place in there was unimaginable, but even so, James had made his decision. He knew he needed and deserved what was soon to happen and he hoped he could get through it with dignity.

As he stood looking out, a salmon pink flower dropped from the flower, James stooped and picked it up, fascinated by its delicate beauty. Movement along the far pavement outside, saw a black woman, probably of Caribbean heritage, walk past with a little girl, unmistakably her daughter. It had been raining and the girl had boots on which she wore to good effect as she splashed through puddles which created a reprimand from her mother. James looked at the scene. Family life in action. Hadn't that been the reason she was happy, like he'd been in his early years? Wasn't it a stark contrast, him upstairs in the shadows, hidden from view awaiting corporal punishment while a woman with her beautiful, well-loved daughter with a yellow bow in her hair walked by below without a care in the world, other than splashed legs? James stepped away, he looked over to the sofa where it had all started. He waited.

'I'm ready for you now James, follow me.' The door had opened suddenly. Mr Burrage stood in the doorway; two long canes were tucked under his right arm. James felt a long shiver run through his body, the wait was over and soon he was to face an ordeal he could barely imagine.

'Yes sir.' James left the room and waited while Burrage overtook him and marched ahead, obviously eager to get proceedings under way. At the far end he stopped and turned at an open door of a room James was invited to enter. He walked inside. The room was bare, it had just a small window high up, otherwise it would have been in darkness except for lighting above and to the end from a table lamp. Bare except for a metal framed bed in the centre. It had a blanket covered mattress and in its centre was a low padded box which James realised he'd soon lie over to offer his raised buttocks for caning. He realised he was to be caned in a downward position and James looked up at the high ceiling which gave plenty of clearance for an unimpeded swing. His eyes moved to leather straps fixed to each corner of the bed. He knew these were to secure him in place while his punishment was inflicted, and it was then the finality of his directional decision earlier really hit him hardest.

'Nervous? I can see you are. Let's get down to business,' James snapped out of the almost trance like state he'd found himself in and turned back to Mr Burrage who had placed the two canes down on the floor, so they leaned against the wall.

'Yes sir, very.' James quickly replied.

'I see your erection has gone, I suspected it might. The sight of those two canes puts off every naughty boy who comes in here and there have been quite a few.' James had no doubt he was the latest of many who had stood where in was standing, having made a similar decision.

'You've been a naughty boy haven't you James?' Burrage opened what was to be a brief question and answer session.

'Yes sir!' He replied in a soft voice.

'What happens to naughty boys?' James stood submissively before Burrage who now took a seat on the bed.

'They get punished sir.' James was getting more and more nervous now, he placed his hands together in front of himself, covering his limp penis.

'They do indeed. They get their bottom's smacked – bare! They get worse, the slipper and the strap too!' Burrage was enjoying James's discomfort. 'What happens to exceptionally bad boys James?' There was only one answer expected and he delivered it.

'They are caned sir!' James replied. He felt his penis shrink further into his groin, he'd felt this sensation before as a schoolboy, he likened it to a tortoise pulling its head into its shell, as its own method of protection. James didn't feel his natural protective instinct was any different.

'You are correct young man, and I shall be using one of those canes on your bottom quite soon. Do you have anything more to say before I commence your punishment?' James knew there was little point in prolonging the agony of uncertainty he shook his head and waited for further instruction. 'Come here boy, let's have you across my knee.' Burrage pulled the sleeves up of the track suit top and patted his lap to reinforce his command. James moved to the seated man's left and was about to lower himself when Burrage stopped him. 'I want you the other way. I'm right-handed you stupid boy, how on earth do you imagine I can smack your bottom if you lie across me from that side.' James realised his unforced error and quickly walked to the other side where he dropped to his knees and scrambled across. It didn't take long and soon both hands were touching the carpet, his feet remained planted firmly the other side and his bottom was placed directly below Burrage's line of vision. 'Legs apart!' Another command which James obeyed with question. Mr Burrage started to stroke James's cheeks, he slid his hand deep and fingered his anus. A hand reached for a tube which was placed nearby, and the cap was removed before a generous amount was squeezed onto his tightly closed, crinkled opening. Immediately Burrage started to distribute the slippery contents in a circular movement to which James felt a stirring commence.

'I know you like that; I can feel you. I'll come back to this later.' His right hand now transferred to his right buttock which he stroked gently before lifting it and bringing it down sharply.

SMACK!

'Ouch!' The action took James by surprise and his hand striking bare flesh made him jump. Burrage ignored the cry of pain and quickly delivered another and yet another. The hand spanking continued, he stuck to James's right cheek which became increasingly sore. James was starting to complain and the words "Ow!" and "Ouch!" were becoming more frequent and he started to wriggle about. 'Keep still and stop complaining. You know you deserve this and you've had it coming a long time. His open hand now moved round the side of his buttock and lower down to his thighs. His bottom, or half of it was getting very red. Then after what James felt was around eighteen smacks Burrage stopped and pulled his cheeks apart. He stroked his anus before inserting his finger deep.

'I spoke of pain and pleasure young man. Here is one example.' He started to move his finger in and out and James's arousal increased. Finally, Mr Burrage removed it and leaning over selected a short string of black balls which he inserted slowly one by one. 'This is another, do you like me doing this?' He asked what was plainly a stupid question, because James was purring with enjoyment, the pain forgotten and his bottom almost pushing against Burrage's hand to force the next round object in. With them all inserted he slowly rubbed James's sore bottom which was hot to the touch. 'We must raise your self-esteem young man. Think about pleasure, all the nice things you can accept if you allow someone in who cares. I'm going to hurt you soon but remember I will inflict pain with love and without any sign of anger. You need to let out all the hurt you have bottled up and just look at the caning as a vehicle of release.' He paused, then continued. You have two cheeks, and we haven't touched the other yet.' With that he pulled out the beads in a ripping sound which had James crying out in undisguised pleasure.

'Oh my god, how did you do that!' He grunted and flopped down helplessly. Burrage quickly shifted his position, turning his hidden left cheek into the firing line.

SMACK!

The first blow landed and as before Mr Burrage built up momentum until he got back into rhythm. James's cries of pain became more pronounced until something different started to emerge, distress and for the first-time tears. He started to sob which Burrage ignored until he was done.

'Up you get, into the corner and put your hands on your head.' James clambered up, he was crying, and tears stained his face. 'That's what we need to see, that's just the start, I think any chance of you thinking you were going to hold out on me is just not going to happen is it?' It was a question which James answered as he almost ran to the corner and placed both hands on his head. Burrage watched as James slowly sobbed, he knew his emotional situation hadn't been caused by pain but by words expressed during the break, he decided it was time to increase the tempo. He picked up the slipper and walked over using his spare hand to stroke

James's sore bottom. He moved clover and spoke softly into his right ear.

'You're going to get the slipper next, just like that PE teacher did in the gymnasium. Do you remember that lad, all those boys standing there laughing?' James replied with emotion in his voice.

'Yes sir.' Burrage followed up.

'You didn't cry, though, did you?' He asked knowing full well he hadn't.

'No sir.'

'But those boys aren't here now are they and the nasty bully who beat you isn't either. So, you'll cry for me won't you James.' He burst into tears which prompted Mr Burrage to take his hand and lead him gently to the centre of the room. 'Bend over boy, part your legs and touch your toes.' James looked at him, his eyes were red with tears. Burrage let go and watched him go down. He patted the inside of James's legs as an indication he wanted them wider and when he was nicely positioned Burrage moved back and taking aim at a point where James's left cheek was open, he swung his arm and stuck his bottom with some force.

WHACK.

James's reaction was instant, he was up and hopping on one leg his hands clutching his bottom

'Owwww!'

'Get back down. That doesn't count, you got up and touched your bottom without permission!'

'That really hurt you hit me between my cheeks!' Burrage knew he had but showed no regret.

'Touch your toes otherwise I'll do it lower.' James went back down; he was openly crying now.

WHACK

'Ouch!' James called out but stayed in position as the next swing of Mr Burrage's arm brought the slipper down fully on his right cheek. Four more times the slipper found its mark and each time this was met by a cry of pain.

'Back in the corner but open your legs wide.' James shuffled over now, his bottom extremely red and burning. Burrage put the slipper down and moved across the room to where James stood nose pressed hard into the corner of the room. 'Take two steps back and keep your hands on the wall.' James could see what his tormentor had in mind as his backwards movement meant he had to lower his hands and lean forward into a bending position. He stood there expectantly and soon he felt a familiar finger probing his anus. 'How is the self-esteem now James, are you feeling better towards yourself; ready to like yourself perhaps a little more?' James didn't answer right away, in fact he was a little confused over what he was supposed to say.

'I don't think I feel any different if I'm honest sir?' Burrage stopped stroking him and moving away picked up the strap.

'In that case you'd better bend over, touch your toes as before.' James wasn't as compliant as before.

'I can't be something I'm not and I refuse to say something you just want to hear.' He replied, sensing that reply was something Mr Burrage definitely didn't want to hear.

'Obviously I'm not reaching the parts of you I need to change. I need to hear you tell me you like yourself. I'm not expecting you to love yourself.' James was defiant, he knew how he felt, and he didn't see any point in pretending otherwise.

'I'm not going to lie, I don't even like who I am. I'm far from loving myself. I feel much better having met you and having someone who is interested in who I am and makes me feel needed and wanted will create the change you are looking for; I just need time sir.'

'At least that's a start young man but I haven't finished with you yet, not by a long way.' Burrage raised the strap and lashed it across James's buttocks. Gone were the tears. Resolve was back. James grunted and remained in position. Five more lashes were applied without a sound coming from James. Burrage wasn't impressed.

'Looks like we're going backwards James. In that case we'll see if a good caning has any effect. Up on the bed.' James rose he gave Mr Burrage a look of defiance and just for the briefest of moments it looked like he was about to refuse. In the end he clambered onto the bed, then placed himself across the raised padded area and stretched out in a spread-eagled position ready to be secured. Burrage grasped James's nearest ankle and secured it with a strap. He walked around and did likewise to the other. He then pulled the bindings tight which ensured James's legs were stretched wide apart. He now moved to the front and tied his wrists to the front corners of the bed frame. He pulled on these too which stretched James taut across the padded box. Burrage placed a pillow under his head, then rolled up a handkerchief and invited James to bite on it and keep his head pressed into the pillow. 'Let's see how brave you are now young man, keep your head down, we don't want half the street hearing you.' He walked over the wall and selected a cane which he swished through the air, which caused a thin spray of water to shower James's prone body.

'We'll start with a dozen from this side, then I'll move across and give you twelve from the other side, I won't be rushing it, I want you to feel the benefit of every stroke.' Burrage moved centrally to face James's marked, red bottom. He moved position until the cane slightly overlapped his furthest cheek, then after a couple of practice taps which caused James to clench his buttocks tightly, he lashed the cane down in a fearful whooshing sound.

THWACK

James's whole body went taught and his outstretched arms fought against their secure bindings. He made a noise and turned his head towards Burrage, his face wracked in pain. Burrage waited a full ten seconds before he brought the cane down hard in unerring accuracy which saw a second raw looking welt appear next to the first.

THWACK

The beating continued and anyone standing near the stairs leading onto the lounge would have heard the rhythmic sound of a cane being applied to bare flesh. Each stroke followed by a muffled cry of pain. A sadist was at work and his victim was swimming in a sea of pain. After twelve delivered strokes the noise stopped – briefly.

In the room, Mr Burrage carefully examined his work. He took pride in his accuracy, twelve raised welts, side by side without any overlap. He put the cane down and moved to the end of the bed where James's wide-open legs offered a pleasing view. Burrage had a plan which started when he picked up a one-inch paint brush. There was no intention to dip this into paint, it was a soft bristled brush and was to remain dry for a totally different purpose. James's balls hung down over the leather mound he laid across, above it, a short distance away, his anus pouted and contracted as James fought against the stinging pain from the caning. Burrage leaned down and stroked the brush down along the now hairless, facing side of his balls which saw an immediate reaction of surprise. He continued to stroke the brush up and down. James was groaning now, but not from pain. Burrage moved upwards, trailing the brush along his perineum to his anus, which he stroked instead. Burrage reached forward, sliding his free hand up under his body until he found James's penis which was erect once more.

'It doesn't matter how hard I cane a naughty boy, they cannot resist the application of my brush, applied where it matters. Burrage found the tip of his penis which was

96

slippery. He used his thumb to encircle this, causing James to groan even louder. 'Pain and pleasure James, that is the key, I'll give you another twelve then I'll turn you over and sort this little issue out, after that we can have tea and a nice slice of cake.' He stopped, then moving over to the other side of the bed, picked up the cane once more and as he had before measured it across the relatively unmarked furthest cheek.

THWACK

The punishment restarted and immediately James's sounds changed from pleasure back to pain. This continued until after twelve more strokes had been delivered. Burrage moved further up the bed and lashed the cane down twice more diagonally, before moving down to James's feet he gave two more in the opposite direction. Blood appeared now from several raw spots which had now formed where the cane had been deliberately overlapped. He had intended more, far more, but Burrage felt his work was done today. He picked up the brush.

Five minutes later James was groaning for the same reason as before, twisting and turning as far as his bonds would allow. Burrage had pulled the rolled handkerchief from his mouth and James lay, looking back at Mr Burrage as he applied the brush to where it mattered most. Inside James's thighs, his groin too, soft rhythmic strokes, some even applied to the tip of his again erect penis.

'You like this don't you James?' Burrage asked.

'You won't believe how much sir!' He replied, closing his eyes when once more the brush found his anus.

'Let's untie you, time is pressing and I'm on the phones again this evening.' First, with a tissue, Burrage dapped the sore areas where droplets of blood had formed, then he quickly released James who was able to lie on the bed after the raised padded structure was removed. Burrage encouraged him to lie on his back and with oiled, practised hands Mr Burrage clutched James's balls gently, then gripped his erect penis which he started to work up and down. He looked down at a very contented man as he worked and watched his face intently. When he saw obvious signs, his excitement was growing, he stopped, prevented the sap from rising up the stump. Having edged him, he restarted the process. 'I like a boy I can control, some boys can't, I've even had to put them over my knee again when they make a mess. Do you like being taken to the edge and pulled back.' James couldn't answer, he was being brought to climax once more and each time he sensed it was only a matter of time before the milk would boil over past the point of no return.

'Oh god that was close, there was a point I didn't feel I'd go back; I just managed it sir.' James finally replied, far too busy concentrating to answer before.

'It builds like that, rather than have you cum because you can't return, I'd sooner wank you off with the intention of making you cum at the end, I can bring you to a peak and let you go when you're ready. Shall we?' He asked finally. Burrage came closer, first pulling James's far left leg over so he could reach his anus where he inserted his finger. Then, with it still in place, he started work on his erect penis, working his hand more purposely up and down, increasing its tempo. James lay back, his eyes closed. His breathing became faster and deeper and Burrage knew he was close. Burrage wigged his finger buried deep and then slowed the strokes making then deliberately long. 'Tell me when you're ready, I want to catch you on the peak.' He replied, watching James's face which gave everything away.

'Now sir, I'm cumming, I can't stop this time!' Burrage now speeded up and watched as James's penis went even more erect and then with his back arching upwards with the effort, a long stream of white fluid shot out of the end and up into the air. He went down and a second wave spewed out, the translucent ejaculation dropping back onto his belly. One more much reduced amount spurted out, then James lay back spent.

Thirty minutes later, James was seated on the sofa. Amiable Mr Burrage was back together with another pot of tea; bone China cups and saucers and two plates with generous slices of Dundee cake placed on top. After a period where no words were spoken, Mr Burrage opened the inquest.

'I expect you're pretty sore?' He asked.

'Very, I've never experienced pain like that sir.' James replied.

'Let's revert to Ray again shall we. The session is over and so we can relax more now.' James replied immediately.

'I'd like that, Ray.' He paused before continuing. 'You're like the father I never had.' He added.

'Thank you, that's a huge compliment. I hope what I did hasn't stopped you returning?' He replied.

'Not at all Ray, obviously there is a bit of damage that needs to heal, but when you feel I'm ready to return just drop me a line.' James hoped he hasn't sounded too eager.

'I stopped short of what I had planned. A couple of dozen has left you with plenty to think about as you drive home, next time wear black pants, you'll have some blood on those which might have some questions raised when you get home.' James had a solution.

'I'll put them in the washing machine myself, that way they won't get seen.' Mr Burrage put his cup down and offered James some cake.

'Tell me what you think, it's my mother's recipe, she loved baking cakes, I guess it rubbed off on me.' James held the plate which he then carefully rested on his knee. Burrage moved the conversation on. 'You need to move on with your life James. Stop dwelling over things you can't do anything about. Your tormentors can't touch you now, but you can prove they were right if you continue to allow them into your head. Cast them out; look at what I did to you as the means towards achieving that. Both ate some cake and James picked up some crumbs which dropped from his mouth. 'I'll ask you this now and again when we meet next time. Do you still hate who you are?' James shrugged.

'Will you feel pleased if I say I don't hate myself.' Burrage looked back with a serious look on his face.

'If you mean it and you're not just saying that, then it's progress. I need you to say you like yourself, or at least you are starting to. We'll discuss this next time.' He then asked a question which James initially found hard to answer. 'Did you ever think about taking more drastic steps?' James stared ahead, then placed the remainder of the cake in his mouth, a deliberate ploy to give him time to answer.

'I often thought about it. The problem was the means. So yes, it did enter my thinking, but I never did anything about it.' This reply seemed to satisfy Burrage who now sat back and looked at James as he washed down any remaining cake with what was left of his tea.

'Good, you must talk to me if you get down or have those feelings again. We made a good start today, I enjoyed everything although I suspect there were bits you weren't so keen on?' James smiled.

'You could say that. I found the whole visit a hugely emotional experience and I haven't actually cried for twenty-five years. Strangely it wasn't even the pain, it was your words. You made me confront those areas I've avoided facing. I just broke down and the pain just kept it there. My old self came back briefly but I think I learned a lot about myself today.

'When you get back, wait a day or two and write to me. Tell me what worked or didn't, tell me what could have improved the session. Tell me what you learned about yourself.' He stopped and took a deep breath. 'You are gay James, homosexual like me. I think you were in denial which is why you married; more I suggest for image. You also have strong masochistic tendencies too. You respond well to the mixture of pain and pleasure, and I feel you are going to need someone like me in your life longer term. Still, the good news is you've got me and I'll write to you in three weeks' time and set up another visit. Thursdays are good for me, but so is a Saturday. We could make a day of it, stay over even if that could be arranged?' He then stood up, signalling the visit was over and it was time to depart. 'I need to get ready. There will be people needing my help tonight, almost certainly a confused young man trying to cope with who he is, a boy who has deeply disappointed his parents who expected different outcomes.'

James rose too, he looked out of the window and saw street lighting on, the scene outside was now bathed in darkness. Mr Burrage moved forward, and he placed his arms around James, he nuzzled his head against James and kissed him gently on the cheek.

'Drive safely young man. I think we will become close friends, and you'll spend a lot of time here. I like good open conversation as well as smacking a nice firm bottom.' He patted James on the rear to reinforce his point.

At the door, Mr Burrage stood watching as James walked to his car. Looking back and waving before he got in and drove away. As he drove, he felt tears rolling down his cheeks, he recalled everything that had happened as he weaved in and out of busy traffic. Soon he felt something else, his arousal had returned. He thought he was spent but he was far from that. His erection grew as did his excitement and pulling into a lay-by he unzipped himself and masturbated.

102

A Tale of Corporal Punishment

Caning as you've never read it before....

By

Sam Evans

Copyright © 2012 Sam Evans 2023

My name is Henry Billings. I'm in my 60s and I provide disciplinary services for young men between the ages of 18-25. I advertise in magazines and websites which specialise in corporal punishment and surprisingly I get a lot of responses. I say surprisingly, because there was this belief that later, into adulthood, interest in corporal punishment stemmed from experiences at school when administering the cane was the norm. That it opened unhealthy thoughts, created an addiction that had to be satisfied later. Now, when such punishment no longer exists, one would have expected very little response to my adverts, but that isn't the case at all. Most of the young men who visit me find their "beware what you wish for" moment comes home to roost rather quicker than they imagined. Many just want to exchange email. Sadly, very few meet the profile I have now set out in a small leaflet I send to each person who contacts me. It explains what they can expect, if and when they visit my home.

When I received an enquiry from a young man named Timothy, I felt he stood out from the rest, it seemed he was looking for something rather special.

Dear sir,

I read your advert with interest. I am just 18 and I've had a lifelong interest in corporal punishment. I've never received it but feel now as an adult, I'd like to. I need someone who will help me explore its depths in a practical way which opens up every aspect of how it is administered and everything that is associated with this activity. I don't want to rush into this, I need to be gilded by experience, to leave no stone unturned. I hope you can assist.

Sincerely,

Timothy

I was astonished. At first, I thought it was a scam. I wasn't used to replies like this which did make me suspicious. What 18 yr old writes a reply like that? I decided to be cautious, to assume the worst and hope for the best. I'd send my standard response and take it from there. My gut feel was I'd never hear from him again. But I was wrong, I was looking at his reply now and the plot deepened. Timothy had replied to say he was interested in a meeting, but not to rush straight into a session he might not enjoy which could destroy his overall hope and impressions formed about the scene. He lived 200 miles away and it was his wish to travel to see me, to meet on neutral ground and discuss in detail the content of the leaflet I'd sent. I was warming to Timothy. I decided to reply suggesting he came by train, had an open return, just in case our meeting was positive, equally to bring an overnight bag and stay over because any session, should it take place, would be long and pretty heavy. Travelling back the following day on a train would give him a chance to relax and consider what had taken place in relaxed comfort at least. I decided not to use the term discomfort, which was the most likely end result, I wanted him to at least come, and not be put off by my wrong choice of words. I penned a reply and sent it, whether he took up my suggestion or not would now be for him to decide.

A week went by, I'd heard nothing, then when all hope seemed to have disappeared, I got a reply. He'd like to meet me off the train the following Saturday, then find a quiet pub, and we could take it from there? Sounded good to me so I replied and suggested he give me his train time. I added the description of what I'd be wearing so he'd have some idea it was me as he exited the train. I had plenty to do in between so I didn't dwell on his arrival, assuming he didn't change is mind.

Saturday came, I woke up as normal. I had no other planned visitors that day and I'd kept Sunday clear, just in case. Timothy's train was due it at midday, I'd leave soon to ensure I wasn't late for when his train arrived.

I'm looking out the window as the train speeds its way into Reading. It's where Mr Billings, Henry, said he'd meet me. I'm unsure where we'll head off after that, he had suggested a riverside pub if the weather was fine and as there didn't appear to be a cloud in the sky, I guess that's the option he'll choose. I'm nervous, as I sit with my overnight bag on my lap, unsure if it will be used or even should be. I know this venture I've embarked upon has its risks, many will even suggest reckless, but I must understand something which is troubling me, something, no matter how hard I try, will not go away.

I've had what many might describe as an unhealthy interest in corporal punishment since my early years. I've read up on it but that only takes one so far; there comes a time when words alone, or the written word at least, isn't enough. I've now decided to take it to the level of spoken word and in Mr Billings, I'm hopeful he can bridge the gap between the spoken word along to the next stage, that of the practical. That is the part that makes me nervous, especially after reading the leaflet he sent with his reply. There seemed a lot to discuss. I've never been thrashed, although I've long wondered about exploring it. My greatest fear was visiting someone for that sole purpose; I needed someone I could talk to, someone I could share my most personal thoughts and feelings with. Someone I don't know and someone who doesn't know me. I realise I'm young, I can see Mr Billings only specifies contact with young men my age and a little older. He has requested I bring my ID and my birth certificate. I'm barely 18 and I know I look much younger. He may decide not to risk going any further. I hope not because he looks the best option I've seen so far. I guess I'll have to wait and see, my stop is next and the butterflies are lifting off.

I'm on Reading station, Timothy's train has just pulled in and screeched to a halt. Suddenly, what had been a relatively empty platform is now a mass of people. I'm looking ahead but overlook the part of the train behind me. It's only when I hear a voice behind, I suddenly realised I had been looking in the wrong place.

'Mr Billings?' A young, still maturing voice asked. I turned quickly.

'Timothy?' I asked a small fresh faced young man who certainly didn't look the 18 yrs of age he'd described.

'Yes, I'm pleased to meet you sir.' He replied formally and held out his hand.

'An honour shared.' I replied, taking his hand and shaking it warmly. 'Shall we?' I continued, using my arm to guide him to the stairs leading to the exit. We walked out and headed to my car which was parked in a short-term passenger pick up carpark. As soon as we were seated, I got down to business. 'Now I've met you it's even more important I see your ID and proof of age.' He opened his bag and extracted an envelope which he handed to me.

'I hope this allays any fears you might have over dealing with an underage person sir.'

'I have to be sure; you do look more like 15 than 18 and bearing in mind the activity we may possibly engage in, I cannot possibly take the risk.' I replied, then opened the envelope which contained a birth certificate, an ID card and a student bus pass, both of which displayed his boyish face.

'I understand sir.' He responded.

'I see you are barely 18, you must be keen to immerse yourself in this activity?' I asked.

'I've wanted to for a long time, but I sensed anyone genuine would have questioned my age and not wished to proceed. I've had plenty of offers from men who wanted someone underage, but I decided to wait and hopefully meet the right person.' I fully understood and I admired both his honesty and his maturity.

'I'm happy.' I handed the evidence back. 'I know a nice pub not far from here. It's a beautiful day and one suited for an outdoor lunch, just sit back and relax and we can talk more seriously when we arrive.' We made small talk during the twenty-minute journey and soon we were at an old country pub, possibly a coaching inn which dated back to horse drawn transport. We exited and I suggested Timothy found a table some distance away where we could have a frank and open conversation without our voices being overheard. I took a drinks order and entered the pub.

'Tell me about your interest in corporal punishment and to what level you wish it to proceed?' I asked immediately upon my return after placing large glass of sparkling water with ice and lemon down in front of each of us individually. I then sat back while Timothy explained his passion for a subject most wouldn't understand, and many would worry a man of just eighteen would have such a morbid interest. He

111

was interrupted by a waiter who took our food orders but afterwards having concluded, he picked up his drink and waited for me to respond.

'I assume this arouses you sexually, you get an erection, and you masturbate?' I asked my first question.

'Yes sir, I do, usually nightly, sir'

'That is good, I place a lot of emphasis on the sexual side of sadomasochism. Are you a masochist, do you think you enjoy pain?' I asked, continuing.

'I don't think so, but until I feel pain inflicted, I cannot judge, sir.' I hadn't asked him to address me so, most young men I met had to be taught such respect, I was impressed it was something that came naturally.

'I exclusively use the cane, does that bother you?' I asked.

'Not theoretically sir. I realise this is a classic implement, just as much as the birch, which was used within the public school and penal systems. On a practical sense I'm obviously nervous, perhaps even fearful because I've never experienced it and I have no notion of how I might react to its application sir.' I loved this young man's choice and use of words. It was refreshing and heartening to know he respected the English language and used it so articulately.

'Tell me what you hope will have happened by the time we return here tomorrow, that is if you decide to return with me to my home after we have finished.' His answer was delayed by our food, which consisted of two BLT ciabattas, arriving.

'A lot depends on what you plan to do to me. At the very least I imagine I will be beaten, so I expect to be sore from that, anything else is rather out of my hands sir.' He answered my question.

'Nothing is out of your hands Timothy. Almost, without exception, you are free to leave at any time and anything you are unhappy about engaging in will not take place.' His face indicated he was considering his next question.

'Such as?' A not unexpected question under the circumstances.

'Being restrained, especially during the application of corporal punishment?' I saw a flicker of fear sweep momentarily across his face.

'That places a huge amount of my trust in you to reside entirely in your hands sir. Anything else?' There was and it needed to be mentioned.

'How do you feel about a man having access to your anus? It's a very private place for a man and during a session of corporal punishment it is hard not to touch around that location although any diversion towards that part of your body would be a deliberate act?' I clarified.

'Would you wish to penetrate me?' He asked.

'There is penetration and penetration Timothy. An inserted finger or insertion of some not too intrusive object which cannot get lost is totally different to being fucked, if I may use that term to be clear about what I meant. Whatever, I do will always be consensual.' I am sure I saw relief spread across his youthful face.

'My greatest fears were being hurt very badly, because I found myself in a position where I was unable to stop a sadist expressing himself with no regard to my safety and being raped. I know you will look after me, so I am going to tell you now I am happy for you to do as you please. Sir.'

'I'd wait until I tell you what I do have planned before you hand me a signed blank cheque.' Timothy smiled.

'Should I be worried, is this how you treat others who visit you?' He asked.

'Do I treat everyone the same, yes, I treat everyone with respect, and everything is consensual. I'd say the only person I am treating very differently is you.' I now saw puzzlement.

'How so, sir'

'Most young men come for a thrashing. A hard caning which I gladly apply. Afterwards, I care for them while they recover their composure, and they leave. All done and dusted in a couple of hours, three at the most. They had what they came for, some more than they bargained for. They leave and few return. You are different.' I saw a grateful smile appear briefly before the inevitable question.

'How am I different sir?'

'Everything about you suggests a young man who has thought very carefully about this. You've probably wrestled with this decision for years and your heartfelt explanation as to why you are seated facing London's main river on a beautiful sunny day, is what has brought you here. The decision you make, one way or the other, is going to be potentially life changing, so I have a responsibility towards you to ensure you make the decision knowing all the facts and if you choose to proceed, I will make the event so special you will wish to return again and again.' I watched him stare back in awe.

'You'd do that for me?' He asked.

'Yes, of course. I've done this a while and I've never met anyone quite like you before, so for me, if you proceed, it will be particularly rewarding, or I'll do my very best to ensure it will be.'

'I can't believe I met you Mr Billings, sir.'

'Let's hope when you're strapped down and I'm applying the cane to your bare buttocks you do not regret saying that.'

'Bare?' He asked in shock.

'Yes Timothy, I only do hard caning on bare skin. The buttocks are the historic place to apply corporal punishment. Is that a problem?' He shrugged.

'I guess I have to wait to find out. Do I have to be restrained too?' He asked. I knew it was time to change the direction of the conversation. Just then the waiter reappeared to collect plates, we took the opportunity to refresh our drinks.

'Why don't I explain in detail what happens if you decide to return to my home. That having meant you have accepted what I am about to describe and explained anything you then wish to ask.' Timothy nodded his agreement.

'You return with me, whereupon upon arrival, I take you to my bedroom where, in my presence you strip naked. You follow me back downstairs into my kitchen. Are you shaven?' I saw confusion.

'Yes, sir I shave, I thought that was obviously visible?'

'Actually, I meant where I cannot currently see, but I will as soon as you are stripped.' I saw immediate recognition.

'Ah, you mean – there?' I nodded 'No sir, I don't keep that part of me devoid of hair.'

'At this point you will clamber up onto the table, which is stout and heavy, and kneel on the towels I have set out. You will then part your legs wide apart and rest your head down on the cushion I have placed especially for your comfort.' Again, I saw wide eyed amazement appear on his face.

'My god, that won't be leaving anything to the imagination sir.' He replied.

'No Timothy it won't, I see this as a wonderful way for me to acquaint myself with you intimately. Will you object to being touched, penetrated even?' I decided to cross off the first consensual request should this become a reality.

'No sir, it would be expected I imagine.'

'Even the penetration?' I asked.

'I've never experienced it so I cannot judge.' He replied. I looked around at other lunchtime diners and wondered if any conversations being held came close to matching mine.

'It would be gentle if it took place, I wouldn't insert anything painful?' I suggested.

'As it was you, I probably wouldn't have any problem with it.' He replied. I decided to try and move on.

'You'd be shaved from navel to the tops of your knees, front and back and all between. I don't use creams or waxing; I like to rub shaving soap round your sensitive bits and use a razor. It's very intimate and we can talk throughout. Turned over I will shave your pubic area and carefully shave your balls, and around the stump of your penis. I will pull your cheeks apart and shave each side and around your anus. Even if you have no visible hair, you'll rather enjoy the intrusive experience. You'll end up like the day you were born.'

'I've got an erection just thinking about that, but why shave me?' He asked.

'Let me explain the next two stages. It will help you understand my mindset, okay?' He nodded.

'Yes sir.'

'Following this you'll be led upstairs to the bathroom where you will adopt a kneeling position, similar to that you adopted on the kitchen table.'

'Why?' He asked.

'To offer me your anus for your double enema.' I replied. He looked confused.

'What's an enema?' It was now my turn to show surprise.

'Seriously, you don't know?' I asked with a smile.

'I've heard the word, of course but I don't know what it means?' He replied.

116

'Let's leave that for later, assuming there is a later. It'll be a nice surprise for you. It doesn't hurt, in fact I think you may enjoy it?' I watched as he nodded.

'Okay.'

'After that you take a shower, you'll be hairless and clean inside and out, ready to be punished.' I paused briefly. 'Earlier you asked why I felt it necessary to shave you? Now, two steps further, I'd have a young man clean and pure in body, ready to atone and show remorse for actions he now regrets and for which he is to be punished. This is how I wish you to be presented to me, ready to be restrained ready for your caning.' I watched Timothy's face turn to open mouthed shock. I was then surprised by the words he then expressed.

'Oh my god, I cannot believe what you just described. I've had this same scenario running through my mind for years. Maybe not the same details you expressed, but the end result certainly. It is where I hoped I would be with someone eventually and it seems I have met my perfect match.' It wasn't the reply I expected.

'In that case from this moment onward, I need you to think of three events in your life where your action was something you have always regretted and for which you still feel the need to atone, because one of your first actions on returning to my home will be to sit in private and write this down on paper to be presented to me. You will be caned for these offences. At the same time, you will write a disclaimer, giving me permission to inflict corporal punishment on your naked person. Can you do this?' I asked, finishing.

'Yes, sir I can.'

'In that case let's move onto the punishment itself.' He nodded. 'After your shower you will present yourself for inspection. It's all part of the ritual of judicial punishment. You will be taken to a room, and centrally placed, is a leather bench with restraining straps. It slopes downward and its rear legs are angled apart. You will quickly realise that if restrained to that bench you will adopt a downward open legged position with your bare buttocks ideally presented for me to cane.' I watched Timothy swallow hard as brutal reality quickly took effect. 'Before this, you will stand before me and I will sentence you formally, using your prepared words. I will describe the offence for which you will receive twelve strokes of a medium weight rattan cane. It is flexible and it curves through the air as it arrives with force across your bare buttocks.' I waited and saw real fear appear for the first time. 'I will then inspect your body carefully, intimately, and at length. You will bend over legs apart for anal inspection. I will inspect your penis and scrotum. Satisfied, you are fit for punishment I will invite you to place yourself over the bench, whereupon I will fix straps to your wrists and ankles, your upper arms and thighs with one final strap over your torso. You will have one final opportunity offered to cancel and walk away. I'll offer you one quite soon when I've finished this description. There will be one further after I leave you with a period of reflection prior to the punishment commencing. I will leave you retrained and naked. I will show you the cane I plan to use, and I will exit, turning off the light. This will be your time to prepare to atone or walk away with your sins remaining a burden. You will give me your final decision on my return. Walk away and you will have the restraints removed, you will dress, and I will return you to the station. To accept and the full punishment of twelve cane strokes will be applied without mercy. No matter how hard you scream, and I anticipate you will inside this soundproofed room, the punishment will be completed. Do you understand?' I now waited for the moment of truth to be faced and the answer given which would mean Timothy returned with me or we parted company for ever.

'I do understand sir.' He replied after a period of deliberation.

'Okay, before you make your final decision. I should point out there will be post punishment after care, and even during the punishment I will seek to arouse you sexually. Even before the first cane stroke you will be brought close to climax. You will be edged throughout the punishment. I will introduce you to pain and pleasure as an integral part of your punishment. Finally, you will be taken to my bed and masturbated to a climax. I will be naked too and I will hold you while you recover. What takes place after, we will just have to wait and see but nothing will be off the table.' I rose to my feet. 'Now, really is decision time young man. I'd like you to go for a walk along the river and reflect on everything I have described. Take your time and when you return, I will be in my car. I will either take you with me to my home and I will enact fully what I have described, or I will return you to the station. You cannot pick and mix, what I described, together with a few extras I have not, will be your fate. If I return you to catch your train instead, we will part, and we'll never meet again. Off you go.'

I'm alone now. As I look around, I see an idyllic landscape, with a huge famous river as its centrepiece. It seems a bizarre backdrop to the decision of such huge magnitude I now have to make. I watch a swan, surrounded by its cygnets just ahead and I stop and stare and wish my life was so simple. Mine has reached a point of impossibility going forward. Dare I walk away, return, thinking I could just blank out a life I knew I had to explore? Remain in denial, like so many men in the past had done. Pretend the life they were leading was

119

their chosen path when all the time it had been chosen as a result of not facing up to the truth. So much of what Henry had described in that so memorable paragraph had matched my own desires. Not the detail, especially one I had to await in surprise. It was the concluding part that hit me with such force. That I would go through a cleansing ritual which led up to atonement, I hadn't considered the "cleansing" in the purest form or indeed any form of what Henry had described, but it matched my own thoughts in general and he'd just filled in the blanks, the details.

That, and the aftercare ticked every box! But there were some extra boxes I'd never considered, some that hadn't been there to even tick. They were ticked now. There was just one large, ticked box I now had left to consider. I'd often wondered about corporal punishment. I'd looked at it from every direction. The historical angle, which was plainly documented in some detail. I'd looked at porn and seen it from that perspective too. All too often it featured women in ridiculous scenarios which were only ever intended to arouse and titillate. Few, if any, featured a man beating another man in the situation I faced. Graphic, judicial caning. What I did find was worrying. I'd never been punished. This wasn't going to be a mere slap or a spanking. This was going to the top floor of a high-rise block of flats! No stop off points on the way. From zero to max in one step – what if I couldn't take it? Hadn't that been solved though? I wasn't going to be given a choice. Once I'd agreed and my fate sealed, it was going to happen - end of! Hadn't Billings said the room was soundproofed and no matter how much I screamed and begged him for mercy the sentence would be carried out in full? That brought up another thought, just as a pleasure craft went by with an attractive looking young woman laying on its cabin roof sunbathing. Sentenced for what? Didn't I

120

have to be considering this too? A regretful event in my life, maybe more, for which I needed to atone? There was one. There was a man who lived down an adjacent street. I had an issue with him which led to him coming around my home and complaining. I was grounded for a week, but hadn't I climbed out of my bedroom window and taking a box of matches from a kitchen drawer, hadn't I set his shed on-fire, which was bad enough, but hadn't it spread to his chicken coup and killed his laying hens. Obviously, I had kept quiet, I was never even a suspect, after all how could I have done it, I was grounded? I'd always felt sorry for those hens. I had to atone. I would tell Mr Billings in my confession. He had said three. I'd been a good boy, never got into serious trouble. Okay, I'd briefly smoked and drank alcohol underage. I could mention that. I decided to take a huge risk and question his motives. I'd provoke him. That I believed he was deep down a paedophile, and he really wished I was underage so he could get inside my pants and play with my cock, touch my bum! Of course, he'd make extra effort when he caned me. I often wondered if smoke rose when a cane struck struck bare flesh. I'd likely find out with those accusations! I'd reached the end of my deliberations. Any longer and I'd be procrastinating. I was back at the car now. I opened the door and got in. Mr Billings looked across and asked the key question of that moment.

'Well, Timothy, have you decided?'

'Yes sir, take me to your home.'

The journey to my home didn't take long and we didn't engage in detailed conversation. On arrival I set Timothy the task of writing his confession. I asked for detail as I would interrogate him during the punishment and extract replies under duress. I also asked for a handwritten disclaimer too. I gave him a legal draft which would stand up in court if it ever got to the stage of anyone, I had beaten deciding afterwards to report me what what would be termed an assault, physical, sexual or even emotional. I covered all bases and so far, this hasn't occurred. While Timothy was working, I prepared lunch.

Timothy was completed just inside an hour, and he handed me three sheets of lined foolscap filled with his neat handwriting. I decided to eat first, suggest Timothy took a nap and then reconvene around 6pm to commence a session which if played out to its end, would finish around 3am. It was around 5.30, I poured myself a stiff whisky and chose the time before Timothy's arrival to read his confession. I smiled at the shed burning, a typical schoolboy prank, perhaps one which then got out of hand with the unexpected spread to the hen coup. Some discussion while I administered four hard strokes of my cane would quickly drag the necessary level of remorse from his lips. I'd then arouse him, get him to within an inch of climax before stopping. Then, move on to the next misdemeanour. Smoking and underage drinking. We'd all done that, and I'd been caned myself at school when caught with a smoking cigarette in my hand. Another four strokes and certainly more edged milking of his penis! Onto the next and unlike the previous two this so called "confession" left me angry and in a state of shock. It wasn't a confession at all, it was more an accusation and had it been true it might have been MY confession. No, I was beyond angry, this was crossing a line, and it changed everything. Instead of the "follow me" command which would have taken young Timothy to my bedroom to remove his clothes before a trip to my kitchen table, this was to be more of a direct confrontation!

'I read your confession; it makes interesting reading.' I opened the conversation when Timothy appeared on time as and where we agreed to meet at 18.00 hrs.

'Does it meet your requirements, sir?' He replied.

'Most of it yes. I think burning down a neighbour's shed and killing his chickens is worth putting four stripes on your arse. Smoking and drinking another. It was the accusation of sexual activity with a minor which rather broke the mould. Now, that wasn't a confession, unless you were seeking one from me. Problem is, I cannot work out in my mind how many strokes of the cane to apply for that slur.' I looked at the young man who stood quaking with fear and embarrassment before me.

'Sorry sir, I couldn't think of anything more, I was trying to wind you up, it was a misplaced attempt at humour. Can I retract it?'

'You can, but the damage is done. For you to even imagine I'd do such a thing after requiring you to prove your age, suggests I have made a grave error of judgement in selecting you. I'm afraid I am calling off the session. I need you to gather your things and I'll return you to Reading station.' I saw horror spread across Timothy's face.

'Please sir, don't send me away. Beat me harder, increase my punishment. Anything, but don't reject me.' He begged; I could see tears flooding his eyes.

'I never beat anyone in anger and that is what I'd be doing, so no, I can't increase your punishment even though I'm tempted. I've made my decision. You are leaving.' Ten minutes later we were heading towards the station. I had a distraught passenger, and I had decided not to reengage in conversation. On arrival he went to leave. I decided to speak. 'I need a period to reflect, days certainty, it might be weeks. I'm not saying never, that is a long time, but I need to think more about you Timothy and if I decide to proceed, I will contact you. My advice do not contact and engage with anyone else. You don't understand the scene and what is out there. I fear you'll get seriously hurt if you do. Goodbye Timothy, have a safe journey home.' I watched a young man in tears walk away. I didn't dwell but put the car in gear and drove away.

A month went by, I'd heard nothing from Mr Billings. I was very upset at the start, I really felt I'd met someone very special, someone who understood my needs, understood me? Then I blew it big time. I got cocky and tried to be smart and it backfired hugely. Much as I'd have dreaded the aftermath, I was willing to be severely punished for my unforgivable insult, but Mr Billings had refused. I can now understand why, he'd have been angry, thrashed my arse raw, then thrown me out. Hadn't he said his ambition was for me to revisit him again and again, my wish too. That would have now been impossible. Even so, despite my heartache, I missed Henry. We had connected. I was within touching distance of learning all that I needed to know about ME! Now it seems I'll never know.

I took his sage advice. I'd made one huge mistake; I decided to listen and not make another. I'd written to others, but their response had all been similar. To come and be punished! End of! I did trust Henry, totally. He said he'd look after me. I tried to imagine that post punishment aftercare he'd mentioned. I tried to think what it would feel like later, still sobbing but being held in that man's safe arms while he comforted me, allowing my tears to dry naturally, to fall asleep and wake up still being held. I wouldn't get this from the others. It would feel like that trip to the headmaster's office, to be thrashed, then told to leave – get out!

124

'I'd given up hope when my tablet pinged. Messenger had received a message. I opened it routinely, but my heart leaped when I saw the contact was from Henry. He asked me to attend the following weekend. To book my train and as before he'd collect me from the station. I was asked to make a new confession. Just one which outlined the biggest mistake I'd ever made. I knew I wouldn't have to spend much time considering this!

'What have you been doing since we last met?' Henry asked as we headed to his home.

'Nothing in particular. I've applied for several jobs; I'm waiting on interviews.' I replied.

'No visits?' I knew what he meant.

'No sir, I hoped for forgiveness. At least you contacted me, forgiveness is another thing, but that is outside my control.' I replied unsure what his response would be.

'I forgave you as soon as you left my car, forgetting is another thing.'

'I am truly sorry sir.'

'I'm sure you are Timothy, now you must atone, display remorse.' I expected this.

'I accept that sir, what I did is the biggest regret of my life. I have been very open about that.' I replied.

'I assume I will read this in detail soon?' He asked.

'Yes sir, I haven't spared myself sir or tried to make excuses or sought mitigation.'

'I'm glad to hear that. I've purchased a new cane, especially for you Timothy. It's a reed cane, hollow and it's been soaking in my bath overnight, I've been told it's excruciatingly painful.'

'Use it sir, I deserve it.' I replied, nervously.

'Brave words Timothy, I'll remind you after a couple of strokes – see if you still feel that way.' He responded. My reply was simple.

'Yes sir.'

On arrival Henry got down to business. 'Hand me your words. I'll read them while you strip. Present yourself down here in 30 minutes. The bedroom is along the landing, first door on the left. I suggest you peer in the next door; it is where you will be flogged!' He'd never used that word before. It sounded so judicial. Felons and mutinous sailors and those in the British army were flogged. That was savage and brutal. Was I to join their ranks?

I left Mr Billings reading. I ascended the stairs and at the top faced an open door to a bathroom and toilet. Further along in the opposite direction was a door that did indeed lead to a bedroom. It was dominated by the largest bed I'd ever seen. I noticed a large towel had been spread over the top. There were tubes of what looked like gel, but others unmistakably used to soothe battered skin! There were objects laid out which I assumed were designed to enter the human body and I could only imagine one place their owners might have in mind. I stripped, leaving my shirt and underwear until last. I found myself naked for the first time in a stranger's bedroom. I left the room, but as I still had more time left, I decided to explore the room Henry had set aside in his home, solely for the purpose of punishing young men of my age. I entered. The door was much thicker than normal doors. I recall Henry describing them as soundproofed. There were no windows, it was dark, and it had the mixed scent of leather and the sweat given off by straining naked bodies. I sensed it had been recently used. I turned on the light and fear took over when I saw the bench in the centre of the room. My eyes then fixed on a cane leaning against the wall, it sat in a pool of liquid where I assumed it had drained excess water. I picked it up and I was surprised by its weight, I bent it in both hands, and it moved into an arc shape with minimal effort. It had the same flexibility as rubber. I shivered as I realised this was intended for use on me. I looked at a clock on the wall, it showed it was approaching the 30-minute deadline. I turned off the light and left the room before heading downstairs – naked.

'This make's interesting reading Timothy. A perfect match to what I requested this time. Here, read it to me.' Mr Billings opened the conversation shortly after I arrived. I didn't try to cover my private parts, he was going to see every mole or dimple on my body, besides, I wanted him to see me. I wanted him to own my body, and I really didn't care what he did to me – I welcomed it. I didn't expect to be reading my words though, that was unexpected. It seemed odd standing naked in in a kitchen I'd only ever entered briefly as a guest. I watched as Henry took a seat and after pouring himself a glass of neat whisky, motioned me to commence.

"Dear Sir,
Recently I made a huge mistake. I believe in life, everyone makes mistakes, I've learned to my cost such mistakes should be minimal and once made, to ensure they are never repeated. Making mistakes in life should be a learning exercise. I have learned the hard way, and I believe I will be required to atone for my actions. I had sought a type of person all my young life. Through childhood and then into adolescence I needed a strong male role model who would understand my needs and meet those with firmness, even strictness. A month ago, I felt I had met that person. I had

quickly bonded and in doing so I became blasé. In jest, hoping to add a third confession when I could only think of two, I suggested this wonderful man was a paedophile. I actually wrote that he wanted to get inside an underaged boy's pants and to touch him intimately.' I stopped at this point and started to sob.

'Don't stop Timothy, I know this is painful to say in actual words, but you must see how this felt for me too. Continue!'

'I'm sorry sir.' I continued after a brief pause while I sipped water.

"I knew this amazing man wasn't the man I described. He'd insisted I brought proof of my age, two forms of identification too, I was writing a false narrative, and I knew it. I was stupid and I didn't consider his feelings for a minute. I have been given a second chance for which I am eternally grateful. I will accept any punishment deemed necessary for this cruel and offensive accusation. I will be loyal to him, return to him because I know instinctively, I need him in my life. Sir, if you are reading this, I will never repeat my action. I'll never let you down.

Sincerely yours

Timothy ❤️

(PS – the heart is my display of affection towards you sir)

I stopped and handed back my written sheet. Mr Billings stood and stepping back spoke clearly.

'Get up on the table Timothy, kneel, spread your legs wide and place your head on the pillow.' I closed my eyes with relief. I was chosen, forgiven too. Obviously, I had to atone but I hadn't been cast aside despite my error of judgement.

'Yes sir.' I climbed up onto the table I crawled forward onto the towel and after parting my legs wider than I'd ever done in my life I put my head down onto the pillow and thrust my bottom out to him. I wanted to enjoy what was about to start, but just as importantly I wanted Mr Billings to enjoy me too.

'Has anyone told you what a nice bottom you have, it's small but firm in going to enjoy playing with it.' Before I could answer I had shaving foam squirted on my anus which was a surprise and created a massive shiver which ran down my spine.

'Oh god that is so nice!' I murmured as searching fingers started to spread this over my bottom, those same fingers probing each and every crevice. Then a scraping sensation as the safety razor worked its way around.

'You have some hair further away, along your perineum. Most men of your age have hair along there, but it quickly disappears once my razor gets moving. Another time, assuming you return I'll get my open razor out. It creates a bit of fear and tension knowing something so sharp it could slice off your balls in a single act, is in use at such a sensitive place.' I'd often wondered how I'd feel knowing I had someone working with a lethally sharp blade in such an intimate place. Now I had more than a clue.

I was turned over; I had a huge erection, and my cock stood vertical. Henry covered my pubic hair with more soapy foam, and this was spread up as far as my navel and down to my knees before the shaving began again. Soon, I was hairless, and the final part saw him holding my penis while he shaved its stump. A quick rub down with a towel displayed skin but not a trace of hair down there. The shaving equipment was moved, and Henry returned. He gripped my cock, pulling my foreskin down to its limit, then to my astonishment he leaned down and took me in his mouth. I could feel his tongue feeling it way around, a sensation which began the first signs of a climax starting to form.

'Please sir, I'm starting to cum.' He stopped, sucking hard on my cock as he withdrew, leaving it wet and glistening.' He smiled.

'You can do that to me later, in fact we'll do mutually in the classic position. I assume you'll like to?' He then asked.

'I'm rather innocent sir, I've never tried it.' I replied.

'Then it'll be your first time won't it.' I nodded, still wondering if I was dreaming this. Then he got up and walking over to a cupboard opened the door and reached inside and brought an extraordinary object towards me. It was a dog's collar. 'On the floor, now please.' I jumped down, whereupon he leaned in and fixed the collar round my neck. I didn't react, I waited to see what happened next. 'Down on the floor, on your hands and knees, we are going for a walk.' He then turned and reached out for a dog's lead which was hanging on a hook nearby. I dropped down. I was resigned to do anything he requested. As soon as I was in position he leaned down and connected the lead. He gave it a tug and I started to crawl, leaving the kitchen and heading to the stairs. I didn't complain, even though I was being treated like his pet dog. I just wondered what he now had planned for me. The stairs were difficult, but he was patient and once at the top I was led onward until we moved from carpet to the tiled flooring of the bathroom. I was taken to a position near the shower where the lead and collar were removed. 'Legs open and get right down onto your elbows boy!' Was his next command. I complied and I felt cold air invade a place now gaping and exposed to his gaze.

'Yes sir, thank you sir.' I replied, unsure why I was thanking him at all, something he picked up on.

'I've no idea why you are thanking me, Timothy. Can you remember what I have planned for you now?' Since my hair removal everything felt more open, my skin slid deliciously too. I realised what part of my body he must now be studying, even so I still wasn't sure.

'No sir, I've forgotten some of the detail. I imagine it had something to do with my bottom?' I answered.

'It does indeed, did you ever Google enema?' He asked.

'No sir, after being banished, I assumed knowing its meaning was rather irrelevant. Is that what I'm to expect now?' The answer came in a strange way, as a leather hood was pulled over my head and fixed by straps from behind. I felt a degree of panic spread over me. His calming voice then eased my fear.

'Calm down Timothy, I'm not going to harm you, I've just removed your ability to see what I'm doing that is all, this next stage is all about the sensation of touch and feel.' My pounding heart eased, I think my fear wasn't helped by the sense of a sudden enclosed world, and the invasive scent of leather from which the hood was made. 'You will retain this hood from now on until your punishment is over.' I shivered, it was worrying to know I'd be unable to see my surroundings or what was to take place. This was sadism of a different kind; just retaining a sense of sound and feel. My buttocks were now pulled apart and the sensation of coldness felt as what appeared to be a wet substance was pressed and smeared around my opening. I heard water running, next followed by virtual silence. I knew somebody was moving around behind me, then something was pressed against the centre of my bottom and slowly inserted. I panicked.

'Please sir what is that?' My answer came in a sensation of something being pumped inside me, it felt strange but rather nice, I was filling up. A hand slid along my erection as

131

the liquid continued its relentless journey inside me and Henry milked me; again, I felt arousal beyond anything I'd even felt before.

'That is your first, one more to go.' He updated me. The object was removed, his hand gently gripping my cock released too, much to my relief. More water was run, something was being filled and soon, whatever it was being used, was being reinserted.

'Oh my god.' I mumbled as the sensation of being filled continued. The hand was back around my penis too and this slowly masturbated me. I was now getting very bloated, I wondered how much more I could take in before it began to hurt. 'Is there much more sir?' I asked.

'About a pint, was his answer.'

'Are you sure I can take that sir?' I asked nervously.

'You must and you will.' I sensed he did something because the liquid invasion quickened, and my bloating was becoming a worry. Then it stopped the object removed causing a dribble to run down my inner thigh.

'Hold it, grip your sphincter boy! Any leakage will mean an additional six cane strokes.' I gripped as hard as I could. 'Stand up!' Was his next command. I did so carefully, ensuring I didn't leak. The next request made me unsure. 'Hands on your head and stand feet astride.' I panicked.

'I can't sir, I'm struggling to hold this in as it is.'

'In that case I'll have to resort to this.' I sensed movement, then the sound of water dripping. There was a loud swish followed by a spray of cold-water droplets. 'I brought the cane back for refreshing. How about I lash it across your bottom.' I felt something cold and wet tap my cheeks and I clenched them even tighter expecting pain any instant.

'Please sir, I'll try harder.' I bleated.

'Good boy. I'll leave you now. I'll return in five minutes. Keep it under control.' Then it seemed he was gone, and I was left with what had been pumped into me trying to force its way out. I struggled; I knew closing my legs would ease the problem, but I dare not. What if he returned and found I'd disobeyed him. I continued the fight. Eventually, Henry returned, and I was led to the toilet where I was eased down into the seat. Wait until the door closes. I leave boys to do what comes next in privacy. Take your time. I'd suggest fifteen minutes until you are clear, then flush the toilet. Wipe yourself and stand. Wait until I return.' I heard the door close. I then let the deluge loose.

I left Timothy and closed the door. I didn't wait, I knew what would happen next and it wasn't part of anything I wanted to be present to witness. I had brought the cane with me so I took it to the next room which was becoming closer to becoming the main feature of the session. I had a sadistic plan for Timothy, this long before my reed cane played any part. I just checked it was ready to come into play and I shivered as I wondered how Timothy would react when I brought it into play. I made myself a drink and sat at the table watching the clock tick by. I gave it an extra five minutes before I made the journey back. When I did, he was standing, hands on his hooded head waiting. I ran the shower, lowering the head so it just washed him from shoulders down. I guided him in then proceeded to clean all his parts downward.

'I see you're still erect, are you always like this?' I asked.

'I haven't masturbated for a month sir, I felt self-denial was penance for my actions.' I nodded as I lathered my hands and cleaned around his penis, his balls and up deep between

133

his cheeks. He was clean now and there was just one more thing to do before I flogged him.

'Let's dry you off.' I took a fluffy towel and rubbed his body vigorously. Timothy had a nice firm body which wasn't muscular. His weight was perfect too. I then led him to my bedroom where I bent him over the bed. I took some soothing, moisturising cream and rubbed it into his fleshy cheeks. 'It seems bizarre to soften your skin for caning but while it will raise delicious welts, it should help prevent bleeding.'

'Bleeding?' He asked.

'It's quite possible, probably not during the application of eighteen strokes but it is possible.' There was a quick response.

'Eighteen strokes, I thought I was to be given twelve?' He queried rather loudly.

'That was then, this is now!' I replied.

'That's a lot!' Timothy concluded.

'It's what you deserve. We can stop this now if you feel you cannot proceed?'

'No sir, I'm frightened because I know what comes next, but I must know myself. Besides, I like you a lot and I want you to be proud of me.' He replied.

'Don't do this for me Timothy, I've become very fond of you too and regardless of what happens next I'd like to think we have so much in common we can become more than just friends.' I replied. I was looking at his gorgeous little bottom, my oily hands were pulling his cheeks apart and I was lubricating far more than the target area for my cane.

'I want that too sir, but I need you to carry out the sentence you have imposed. I need to be known to you sir, I need to also be known to myself. I need to be taken far beyond my pain threshold, I need to atone fully, totally, completely.' He responded softly and calmly.

'Those are mere words dear boy. I'm now going to divulge something I had intended keeping as a rather cruel surprise. I caned a young man of nineteen in the room down the hallway the day before your first visit. I hadn't had a chance to air the room, you might have smelt his sweaty exertions when you had your peep. He took his thrashing very badly. I've never heard anyone scream and beg me to stop so loud before. Thing is, I recorded it and I had intended securing you then leaving you alone to listen to his suffering.' I paused, I was unable to see his face or his reaction. 'I had planned to play this after you finally agreed to proceed, an attempt to break you before I'd even started. You will scream and beg me to stop. It's inevitable you will, however as a concession I'll let you hear this first then give you that final opportunity to get into my bed instead, or go next door and take the severe caning I have planned?' I patted his bum to indicate the treatment for over. The rest would take place next door.

I was led from the bedroom. The option to remain felt so enticing. To make love with and to this older man who I desperately needed to kiss. I knew I would anyway, but continuing along the path I was heading meant not only later, maybe in two hours, but I'd be recovering, and my rear would be a mass of raised welts. We reached the room, and the door was opened. The light was put on but I couldn't see much more than a dim glow through the hood. Then I felt movement behind and sensed it was being removed.

'Let's get this hideous thing off. I'm not sure I can do this now?' Immediately I sensed I'd gone back a month, I'd done something wrong, and it was my fault, again.

'Are you rejecting me, are you sending me home again – why?' I asked. Panicking now.

'No Timothy, quite the opposite. I want to take you to bed instead, spend the rest of the evening exploring you, tasting you smelling you. I want to be inside you. I just can't bear the thought of hurting you.' Oh my god. I didn't expect this. After all we had done so far, and when the main event came up, he was backing down.

'What if I want you to continue. I can't go through my life wondering what I can endure. I have to know, if you can't or won't, I'll only eventually find someone else who I fear won't look after me the way I know you will?' I replied, trying to adjust my eyes to the light again after the rather strange and bizarre decision to hood me.

'I've never loved anyone in my whole life, those I felt I could love didn't love me in return. The reverse when people expressed their love of me, and I felt unable to return it. Then you came along, and you turned my world upside down. I know if we continue, I will fall in love with you and I sense you feel the same, how can I strap you down on that frame and beat your bare buttocks until they inevitably bleed. To hear you scream as Gerald screamed, to hear you beg me to stop. How can I do that to someone I love.' He replied.

'But you must Henry, even if it's just once. I beg you to let me live this experience, something between just us, you, and me. It won't take long, carry out the ritual you planned and do it, we have all night afterward and you can kiss my bottom better.' I watched as he digested my words. He seemed to make a decision but not quite the one I'd hoped for.

'Listen to Gerald's beating. It makes for hard listening, but this will probably be you soon if we do proceed. Give a thought to how this will make me feel? After, depending on your reaction we can decide. It's the only way I'm prepared to proceed.' Henry walked over to a player, he turned the sound up, started the recording and left me to listen to it alone.

I was in the kitchen when Timothy came down. I'd opened my single malt, something I did when I was troubled. I'd caned, often brutally, young men for years, so why was I so hesitant, especially as he clearly wanted me to beat him? I decided to remove the hood, it wasn't a necessary prop. Now I'd left him to listen to Gerald, probably the most vocal boy I'd ever beaten. It had even shocked me how upset he'd got; I almost stopped the caning, clearly, he'd had enough, and I couldn't imagine anything on earth that would now convince him to return for more of the same as he had before. Possibly, it was hearing those screams, the begging and imploring me to offer mercy, that made me reconsider? What if this was a prelude to Timothy being likewise. I'd have to stop for him, I couldn't bear the thought that he'd leave, disillusioned and to never return. He'd become part of my life now, even during the month I'd waited before contacting him again, I'd nearly made contact early. I could say to draw a line under what had happened and start again with a clean slate.

'Well?' I asked him with a single word. The naked boy sat down, and I reached up and grabbed a glass which I slid across. I pushed the bottle in his direction too.

'It was horrible, is all this because you fear that will be me soon?' That was a good point.

'Certainly, but not totally. Maybe I've reached a point in my life where things have to change, perhaps meeting you has shown me I don't need a whole succession of young men of legal age passing through my hands: that I just need

137

someone special?' I replied, sensing I'd hit the nail on the head. Timothy poured a drink which he got up and watered down. 'You've drunk whisky before then?' I added.

'I might not have known what an enema was, although I do now, but I have been to college, and I have had the occasional drink.' Timothy delivered his riposte with a smile. I decided there was only one way forward.

'I'm supposed to be the Dom and you the obedient submissive, but this sounds like a case where the sub actually calls the tune. I know what I'd prefer to do, that is to take you to my bed, suck your stiff cock and fuck your arse! I sense you have a slightly different agenda?' I looked across and put the ball neatly in his court.

'I've never been fucked Henry. When you sucked me earlier that was a first. I want to have a full sexual experience with you and be an integral part of it too. I've never sucked a man's cock; I've never had as much as a finger penetrate me either. I'd like to wake up tomorrow having broken my duck on both counts. But I also want wake with a very sore bottom. I do have a suggestion.'

'Why don't you share it.' I replied, now rather intrigued.

'Why don't we make the caning a sexual experience rather than punishment? Yes, restrain me, go through the ritual, and most certainly cane me as you planned, but instead of it just being punishment why don't you stop at key stages and make the sexual arousal you had planned far more interesting. You'd be naked too and while my hands won't be in play, my mouth could be. You can gain access to my cock with my legs apart, I've seen the frame, its intention is to force one's legs apart. Dare I say my anus is exposed too. Putting it bluntly sir, you could fuck me and in turn I could suck you!' I looked at this young man in a totally different light. He'd come up with an amazing solution. It was one I could accept and while I'm sure he'd cry out in pain, that would be allayed by internals of a highly sexual nature. It would then continue until the allotted strokes had been applied.

'You're really serious, aren't you?' I asked.

'Of course, I get to find out how painful a hard caning is, while at the same time we both get high levels so sexual pleasure, it is kinky beyond belief. We don't have to stop there; we can move onto even greater pleasure in your lovely bed. I get to wake up with a sore bum too!'

I'm in the room now, Henry said he'd catch me up. I wondered if his delay was for the reason I'd hoped for when I made the suggestion we then agreed. It seems Henry had tired of bringing a succession of men my age into this room and thrashing them so hard few would ever return. I wondered if I would if the event was purely that of pain and of minimal pleasure. I'd long dreamed of enacting the scenario I'd described, one of meeting a much older man and engaging in sadistic sexual abuse on this scale. There was one specific area yet to be explored and I decided to throw this into the mix on his arrival. I still couldn't believe I'd taken charge. I'd read, amongst a lot more, of something described as "topping from the bottom", a strange description but put simply where the submissive controls the dominant party? Hadn't I just done that? Henry Billings was going to dance to my tune. I really didn't intend to; I didn't want that. I wanted Henry as my rock, my strict mentor, the father figure I'd never had in my life. I couldn't submit to a submissive, it just wouldn't work. Wasn't the truth that we had both seen a different direction and all that I did was guide the conversation in a direction we both wanted it to go? The door opened, I stood in the centre of the room with my back turned, I knew I'd soon find out if my hunch was true.

'In the time-honoured way, prior to flogging, felons are given a medical inspection, are you ready for yours?' Henry - Sir, whispered into my ear as he leaned into me. He was naked. My hunch had come true.

'Yes sir, I am ready for my inspection.' I felt a hand slide down between my cheeks while another grasped my erect penis.

'Your erectile function seems to be working young man.' He continued.

'Yes sir, sometimes it works too well, if gave me problems in the school showers, especially if I imagined a boy with visible cane marks on his bottom.' I replied truthfully.

'So, that activity has always aroused you?' He asked.

'Oh my god yes. I'm sure in years gone by this scene must have existed, especially if the boy has new stripes alongside fading ones. That always suggested caning didn't work as a deterrent or that boy enjoyed it so much, he came back for more?'

'I can confirm the situation you describe did happen; I saw it myself at first hand. You might have too if the do gooders hasn't wrecked school discipline by abolishing corporal punishment back in the 1960s. Do you think you'd have been one of those boys, proudly showing off their trophies?' He had asked a question I'd often put to myself.

'Undoubtedly sir and if I didn't misbehave, I would have engineered that event.' Henry then came round, and I saw him naked for the first time. He was lean, quite muscled for a man of his age. He has a large cock which like mine was erect. He moved to the end of the room and brought a wooden chair across whereupon he sat down directly in front of me.

140

'Let's have a really close look shall we.' He leaned down and took hold of my cock which he went through a rather exaggerated routine of examining. He pulled my foreskin back then moving in closer took it into his mouth and started to suck while his tongue massaged its tip. He grabbed both cheeks invasively deep, fingers meeting at my vent which he pulled open. I found myself gasping.

'Is this how inspections were really carried out sir?' I asked, starting to struggle to find words.

'This is my new method, if you find it unpleasant, I can just go back to a formal, visual inspection?' He answered.

'No sir, this is fine. Have you come to any conclusions yet?' I knew if he continued, I'd cum in his mouth.

'I'm doing a taste test, so far my findings are positive.' He replied.

'I hope you conclude your examination soon sir, I'm starting to cum!' I warned him whereupon he pulled me off his mouth, sucking long and forcefully as he seemed to relish every drop.

'Turn around and bend over, legs apart.' He then instructed me. I did so and without delay his hands pulled me even further open and then to my astonishment I felt his tongue lick my balls and work upward until it stopped at a place, I never imagined anyone would wish to lick. He did and his tongue pursued a circular rimming motion.

'What are you testing for now sir?' I asked, any thought of formality having left the station. This was just plain dirty, kinky sex and I loved it.

'Taste comparisons. Smell too. Your scent here is musky, while around the other side it had the very recognisable scent of cum. I hope you don't even consider farting!' I hadn't, but I suspected once his cane got to work, I'd lose my discipline in holding any back which might result. I wondered what this room would smell like the following morning after what we had planned was completed and the room shut up for the night. The licking over, my vent was lubricated and his finger inserted. 'You are very tight; I think you'll have a shock when I insert what I have planned quite soon.' He continued.

'Would that be what I saw when you walked toward me sir, you're much bigger than me, I hope it'll go in?' I teased knowingly. I'd never been fucked and while the size of his penis and especially its length did leave me feeling nervous, I was looking forward to it being inserted all the same.

'It's all about lubrication dear boy, I'm sure it'll be fine. You'll know I'm inside you that's for sure.' He finished. He then had me walk one step forward.

'That is a very fine bottom Timothy, it seems a shame I must decorate it. I'm trying to work out how and where to place eighteen strokes. I might break it up. Four on each cheek. Six across both, then the rest on the sweet spot. You'll feel those every time you move sitting down, a reminder on the train tomorrow.' I'd read about the sweet spot, the most excruciatingly painful place to be caned, under the cheeks where it met the upper thighs. I then decided to up the tempo still further.

'Sir, ever since we met, you have discussed spanking me OTK, but you haven't. Don't you want to?' I knew it would provoke a reaction.

'I think you feel a good hard spanking will be a pleasant interlude. A moment of grace to savour before I use my cane on your bare bottom. I think you are misguided and having reminded me I suggest you get over my knee – NOW!

'Yes sir.' I placed myself over his knee, he parted my legs with his knee after rubbing my right cheek which was uppermost.

'I normally concentrate on one cheek; I won't alter my routine this time either. Trust me after I've finished with this example of curved perfection, you'll be begging me to smack the other one. Believe me Timothy, you'll prefer the caning after this.

SMACK SMACK SMACK.... It started. It stung like I couldn't have ever imagined, and it was relentless. After a dozen, I swear were on the same spot and getting more and more painful, he spread me around to ensure there was no place missed. He worked on my flanks, then smacked my thighs. I started to cry out in pain.

'Ouch that hurts!' I screamed eventually.

'It's meant to!' Henry shouted back, smacking even harder if that was possible. I'd lost count, whether he of the large horny hand had I couldn't tell, it just wouldn't stop. Then it did, but only to reposition me so my other cheek was now put into the firing line. The spanking continued as did my squeals of pain. Then it was done.

'Get up, stand in the corner and place your hands on your head, no rubbing!' I didn't argue, even the running through the room seemed to create a soothing breeze to fan my red hot, burning cheeks. Then I stood and slowly sobbed, yearning for Henry to rub my bottom.

'I love to see a well spanked bottom, it's red all over, I didn't miss a spot! All that it needs now is a damned good caning!' I heard some activity going on behind then the moment I was dreading. 'Time for your caning. Come here and place yourself over the frame. I've opened the legs wider to ensure yours are wider too!' I turned and made my way back. The cane I'd last seen, even felt measured across my bottom, was back on display leaning against the wall, it looked wet, suggesting it hadn't been out of its soaking bath very long. I noticed a large tube of gel nearby too and I had no doubts where that would be used, especially as my legs were to be widened to provide easier access. I stretched forward and found myself leaning down. I stretched out my arms to allow my wrists to be secured tightly by straps. Then my legs were moved to rest on the outstretched rear legs. Straps secured my ankles too. Further straps secured my thighs just above each knee and if that wasn't enough a wide strap secured my torso just above my waist. My buttocks were parted so I could imagine Mr Billings target for entry was fully displayed too. I was now totally at a man's mercy, and I hoped the complete trust I'd invested was not a decision I'd live to regret. I felt his hands running over the contours of my bottom before he picked up the cane which he swished through the air causing droplets of water to hit my back in a cold spray.

'As promised Timothy, I'm going to give you one final opportunity to call this off. If you do not, I will commence your caning immediately. There will be four strokes then a break while I take my pleasure from your body as I have already described. I must now ask you to give me your decision.' This was it. Every minute for my thinking, researching, and reading about being whipped, flogged with a cane on my bare bottom had come to this moment. To say no meant continuing that uncertainty, wondering what this would be like to experience would continue; could I have taken such pain or was it to be left as a theory only and certainly not something to put into practice. 'Well?' He pressed; he needed an answer.

'Go ahead sir, beat me!' I called out. I closed my eyes. I wasn't sure when the sound of a cane whistling through the air would come, or the searing and possibly unbearable pain that would surely follow. Instead, a hand went between my legs; it grasped my erect cock and started to masturbate me.

144

Then a finger smeared my anus with lubricant before being inserted too.

'Let me know in plenty of time when to stop. I want you right on the edge, then I'll introduce pain. Climax and you will lose the pleasure, and it will all be pain.' I did feel my climax building, I let it continue. I knew how far I could go before I'd have to call out. I was staring ahead now. My level of sexual arousal was reaching new peaks. It was time.

'Stop sir I'm cumming!' I shouted. Everything stopped and silence became invasive. I was just wondering what was going on when the sound I had dreaded filled the room.

THWACK! I felt very little at first, possibly my hold on the reality of time had disappeared because it felt like ages before the searing pain caught up with me. I soon realised that this period of time was an instant measured in milliseconds, but it had arrived now, and I found myself stifling a scream of pain. I stared down at the floor, breathing heavily, trying to find anything to distract my thinking away from what felt like a rod of red-hot metal having been placed across my exposed skin. I waited, I knew there would be more, and it would be soon. I'd just taken a deep breath when that sound arrived again THWACK. This time there was no delay, my right buttock was on fire again. I then remembered Henry describing the distribution of the promised eighteen strokes. I didn't hold back but cried out in pain.

'Let it out, don't hold back – express yourself.' I heard a voice, recognisable and unmistakably male speak behind me. I didn't reply but looked down at the floor which was tiled. I followed its regular pattern to the skirting, then there was nothing to distract me further. Another stroke took any potential distraction away as I screwed my eyes closed and fought for control. I started to cry. All those weeks, leading into months and then years, I never imagined this. The term beware what you wish for formed large in my thinking and this was worse than even my worst nightmare suggested. I was just about to cry out in pain once more when the fourth stroke arrived and my whole body stiffened, and I strained against my bonds in a vain attempt to protect the target of my abuser's sadism. I cried like a baby as rough hands now pulled my cheeks even wider as a contrasting coldness took my breath away before something cold and wet was smeared across my anus. Something was being pressed against its centre and a new sensation of splitting pain gave me more to fight against. I was being stretched; something was being forced into me. Then I remembered Henry's large stiff cock. I realised I was being entered, I was being fucked and hands on my shoulders further confirmed this as I was being pulled in and onto him and this sensation of being torn apart continued until I felt his warm body pressed up against my bum where it stopped because Henry Billings was now fully inside me. He fucked me slowly, a very filled and burning sensation replacing the searing pain from the caning I'd just received. A hand now moved between my legs; it stroked my limp hanging balls on its way to something that certainly wasn't limp. My own erect cock which was now being milked but not beyond a point from which I couldn't recover and prevent an eruption of cum that was being held back and waiting to shoot out in streams from its tip. Then it all stopped, and one slow and final withdrawal meant my sphincter could close and retain its original closed seal. There was more silence, broken only by my occasional sob, then a couple of loud swishes and a sadist, my sadist, prepared another assault.

THWACK. I cried out immediately, this time my left cheek burned. Three more times that cane was brought down hard and true and each time I howled in pain. Then movement came from the front. My hair was grasped, and my head lifted, I saw Henry's erect cock, still glistening from its previous use waiting in front of my mouth.

'Open!' Henry ordered. I complied.

'Yes sir!' I sobbed as he thrust his penis into my mouth, and I sucked my own tasty juices from its length. He didn't cum, Henry made it clear he'd return to his first port of call for that and cum inside me there when my beating was completed. I was now informed I was bleeding.

I was sadistically flogged afterwards, with little respite. Six further strokes, with most placed horizontal and accurately. Two were placed diagonally, creating a cross and the point where this intersected was pointed out as the exact position where the ordeal would end. I realised that meant where he'd enter me to climax. The last two hideously painful strokes were delivered upward and under my cheeks where they swelled to meet my upper thighs. Henry reminded me of that placement name – the infamous "sweet spot", a place for pain to linger long afterwards, often days and showing up particularly when sitting down or moving position. 'You'll remember this on the train young man.' he again reminded me.

Then he returned to finish the job completely. I was again entered. He fucked my arse while masturbating me and I let out a scream of ecstasy as my month of pent-up store of semen sprayed the floor below. Then calm. I was unstrapped and lifted bodily up into strong caring arms and carried along the corridor and laid over the towel where Henry licked the blood from open welts before returning to my anus to lap up the remains of that which had leaked.

147

'How are you feeling?' I asked Timothy the following morning. I had woken some time earlier and lay watching Timothy, sleeping peacefully. That was in sharp contrast to the young man I'd carried to my bed late the previous night after the conclusion of the hot, erotic orgy of sadistic sex we'd engaged in.

'Sore!' He mumbled.

'You couldn't be otherwise, the question is how you feel about what took place, I'll be dropping you back at the station in a few hours and I am wondering if that will be the last time, I'll see you?' I asked the question I dreaded asking above all else.

'Would it bother you if I joined the ranks of those who have never returned, like Gerald?' He asked.

'Is that what you have decided. I think you found the ordeal much harder to bear than you expected?' I persisted, still unsure what conclusions he'd made.

'Would it be a surprise if I said what you did hasn't changed anything. So yes, I hope my return home is only temporary and in a few day's time I'd return, this time hopefully for good?' I wasn't expecting that. Timothy was so upset at times. So many young men like him were equally so, I'd seen it so often. He matched all the classic signs of someone for whom that experience would never be repeated.

'You'd engage in such brutality again?' I asked.

'Yes, why not? Maybe not every week, I'd have to let my bum heal but otherwise, I'm happy to repeat it, so long as I still get everything that went with it?' He expanded.

'I don't have to beat you to achieve that, we can do this again any time, minus the painful part.' I smiled.

'My rear end is still burning from you enjoying yourself and I think I'd need a day or so before I could recover to even

148

climax again. My god I've never been as aroused as that before. Do you need to beat me regularly?' Timothy put a question to me I had been thinking about for some time.

'I was quite prepared to never beat you at all, but you insisted. I think it's something we can do occasionally or when I feel you need it. I'm your Dom remember, and you will be my masochistic sub and you won't top me from the bottom again. I know you took advantage of my uncertainty when I was briefly vulnerable.' Timothy asked a very interesting question now.

'Will you still advertise for young men to visit you?' I'd given a lot of thought to my answer.

'No Timothy, but with one exception – Gerald.' I saw his eyes open wider.

'Gerald? I thought he'd gone never to return. I heard his screams remember.'

'I heard yours too, I didn't record yours of course. No, Gerald visits me two or three times a year. He needs what I give him. It doesn't become sexual. It's a beating, I patch him up and when he is emotionally stable, I return him to the station just like I will you soon. He'll never be part of my life as you are, but I'm an important part of his life and with your permission I'd like that to continue?' I asked, wondering how he'd react.

'I wouldn't mind, but maybe on one condition?'

'What is that?' I needed to ask.

'That I take part in the session. I could comfort him, maybe he lies over me while you beat him. To feel another human being suffer at such close quarters, to share his pain through direct physical contact. God, that must sound the ultimate in sexual perversion, sadomasochistic depravity.' I'd heard some bizarre suggestions, but Timothy always seemed one step ahead of me in landing surprises on my lap.

149

'I could ask him but that seems a small concession to solving a dilemma you moving in here would create. I'd feel I was letting him down and you know yourself how important living the experience you engaged in last night meant to you. Gerald is nineteen and he is a troubled young man. I'd hate to cast him out into the cold.' I couldn't believe he'd made the offer which was so generous of him.

We pulled up outside the station. Henry had showered me and given me more well received aftercare. I'd seen my lacerated bottom for the first time, and I was horrified I'd marked his sheets with steaks of my blood. He didn't use surgical spirit but something far more soothing. We had earlier made love one final time before I left to return home to pack. I'd never properly kissed a man before and we'd exchanged kneeling positions to allow access to each other's dangling appendages. I'd heard of the 69 position of course, but it took my breath away to engage in it for the first time. After breakfast I left Henry's home. Knowing I'd be back in a few days. I felt whole, totally complete in body and mind and as I walked into the station, turning to wave one final time, I knew he'd be on the station platform waiting for me on my return. One thing throughout the journey, was the sharp sting of my underwear chafing the sweet spot where Henry had struck as a constant reminder. I doubted that would leave me any time soon.

Reunion with the Devil

By

Sam Evans

Copyright © 2012 Sam Evans 2023

Reunion with the devil

When I was at school, I feared the man in the next room. I wasn't alone, everyone was terrified of him and to be sent to him for punishment was a mission of dread. I visited him a few times in his office and each time when I left, I limped out of the room. I'd been severely thrashed but only to a limit prescribed by law. Meeting someone privately was a different matter. That's what I'm doing today. It's horrible waiting, not knowing what is going to happen when he enters the room. At school it was different, he'd be there waiting. Sitting behind his desk. This time it's different. True I have chosen to visit him this time but now I am waiting for him to arrive. I have been sent to an upstairs room and told to strip. Then wait for his arrival.

I can hear movement; something has been dragged across the room. The waiting is torture, but I suspect this is all part of the plan to instil fear and uncertainty. I've just heard a cane swished, not once but three times. I know he's winding up the fear as I so often heard that sound the other side of his closed office door. Now there is silence, then, after each swish was the sound of it hitting the soft coverings of a schoolboy's stretched trousers. That in turn was often followed by a howl of pain and a boy in obvious distress. Everyone knew he enjoyed this and the louder the boy howled the harder he would hit. He loved the sound of suffering and as such his reputation grew. But didn't this leave an uncomfortable question – why was I here?

The door opened and he entered. Mr Banford stood before me. He was 6 feet in height and despite now being in his seventies he was still lean and fit.

'Follow me.' Was all he said.

'Yes sir.' Was all I said.

Fateful coincidence

I had been in town two weeks earlier. I'd gone shopping for a woollen jumper and a pair of new shoes. There was a branch of M&S in the town, and I knew I could get both there. I hated shopping, but when necessity came calling, I had little choice. I had nobody else in my life to do it for me. Having got this chore completed I found a local pub, I entered, deciding to at least get some pleasure from the trip. I bought a pint then took it to a quiet corner. I like to observe, watch human behaviour in all its forms in action. My name is David Austin, I'm 43 years of age. I live alone because I never found anyone, I had wanted to share my life with. Girls never interested me. They seemed to avoid me which suited me fine. I must have put out adverse vibes although it wasn't something I did deliberately or even knowingly.

Now men were different. I had few friends; any I did have I tended to keep at arm's length. I guess I am what most will describe as a recluse. I have a very mundane and boring job. I work in an accounts office which I send out invoices and receive money in. I chase up late payment and I produce monthly financial reports for my employer. That is pretty much my day. I've never had a relationship in my life, but I am attracted to other men. I look at them in a way they never look at me. It was like that at school. The changing room before and after games and PE. Naked boys in the showers dancing around when the cold water was put on after hot. Another sadist posing as a teacher. That is when my fascination with a rather bizarre subject started; the day I saw a boy's bare bottom with several vivid red stripes equally spaced across both cheeks. I stared. I couldn't take my eyes off those marks. I counted them, or I tried because he wouldn't stand still. I counted six and I wanted to look closer, even to touch them.

A loud cheer went up as an unruly group of men were celebrating. It wasn't clear what. There was a man seated alone nearby and a shiver went down my spine. My thoughts went back to the shower, to that boy with his plump bottom covered in raised welts from a recent caning. I realised I was looking at the man who had put them there. It was clearly him. He had aged, but then so had I! He still had that look of menace about him. A man capable of making a boy wet himself with fear if he visited him for the wrong reason. He looked up, our eyes met. He frowned; I could see his mind working. A slight nod told me all I needed to know. He had recognised me. He should, I crossed his path often enough. The noise erupted again and I could see a look of annoyance break out on his face. Then he rose to his feet.

Initially I thought he was going to remonstrate with the group. Demand they turned down the volume, but it soon became clear he was moving in a different direction. He was coming to me.

'David Austin?' He asked. He stood waiting for my answer.

'Yes sir.' Despite the passing of 27 years some things never changed, and one was earned respect.

'Do you mind if I join you, that group have no consideration for others.' I couldn't turn him down, could I? Did I even want to?

'No sir, I welcome some company.' I have no idea why I said what I did or the opportunities for expanding the conversation that presented.

'Being alone is no fun, I know to my own cost.' I wasn't sure what to say. What came out of my mouth seemed rather lame.

'I agree sir.'

'So, David Austin, what have you been doing since you left school?' I shrugged; I knew anything I said wouldn't take long.

'Nothing special, I work as an accountant. Other than that, I don't do much. I came to do some shopping today and I dropped in here for a drink. I shall soon leave and head home. Find something to do.' Banford took a sip of his drink

'Sounds very much like myself. We could drink up and head out into the countryside and find a quieter pub, then you can tell me everything.' I was shocked. Why on earth would he wish to do that. Spend time with me, someone most found totally boring.

'I don't drive sir; I came here on the bus.' Banford put his drink down.

'Excellent, we can go in mine.' He paused. 'What do you say?' I realised it was an offer I could hardly refuse. Although for the life of me I couldn't see why I'd been chosen.

Five minutes later I found myself strapped into the front passenger seat of a large Mercedes saloon, a car I can barely imagine ever owning. Then there was the minor issue of not ever having learned to drive. Something my erstwhile headmaster picked up on.

'Did I hear right, you don't drive? Is that you don't choose to drive, or you have never bothered to learn? He asked after a short period of silence.

'I never bothered. I have a cycle, and I use that quite often; I never go too far when I do. When I need to travel further, I go by bus or train.' Banford glanced across then gave his damning verdict.

'You couldn't be bothered at school either, no wonder you haven't made more of your life. You can see why I caned you several times, never for bad behaviour but always because I felt you never tried.' I wondered now about the wisdom of joining this man for company, especially as I was to be the butt of his criticism. He wasn't done, what he said now came as quite a shock. 'I kept a record of every boy I ended up caning. It was quite a list. I chose a selection of boys who never came to me, to see if dealing with some boy's shortcomings versus those I never had cause to deal with made a difference academically, and even then, what were their comparative outcomes. I strongly believe you need more than qualifications to progress in life.' He paused and slowed down turning into the car park of a picturesque country pub.

'I sense you are trying to tell me something sir.' I urged him on. If he had some revelation up his sleeve I needed to know soon.

'My findings did suggest those that were never in trouble were self-motivated people and by and large they have done better in life than those I took a cane to. Sadly, even the regular, albeit infrequent use of the cane on you Austin had little effect. You are a stick in the mud.' I was starting to get a little peeved at the constant criticism.

'Is there anything you don't know about me?' I finally asked.

'Not a lot, I'd seen you around and I intended approaching you. Then when I saw you earlier, I could not think of a better opportunity. Besides it got me away from those morons. Let's go inside.' He spoke like it felt I was being given an order.

'Yes sir!' I'd always been submissive and in the case of this man I knew I'd always be so.

I was sent across to find a table in a quiet corner. He said we needed to have a frank and honest conversation. I wondered what that meant or even if I could now avoid it. I faced a five mile walk back to my home and it had started to rain. I felt trapped, like I was his prisoner. He returned with a large glass of mineral water with ice and a slice of lemon. He took his seat.

'What did you hope to become after you left school, surely you had a secret ambition, what held you back.' I shrugged. Something else he picked up.

'A shrug isn't an answer.' He rebuked.

'I don't have to take this!' I responded.

'No, you don't.' He paused briefly. 'There is nothing keeping you here, if you don't want to engage in healthy debate you can leave or go sit somewhere else.' I looked around. There was plenty of space.

'I think you'll find I came with you, so, if I leave, I'm faced with a long walk home in the rain. It feels like you planned this!' I replied.

'That is utter nonsense. You said you had nothing better to do, that you found living alone rather lonely. I didn't force you to come.' He answered immediately.

'I sense I'm being picked on. Singled out for criticism.'

'I'm just pointing out that you are lazy and need to show more urgency, exert more energy. That is what holds you back.' He wasn't wrong but I didn't see any means of climbing out of the hole I'd dug for myself over nearly 30 years. Banford looked around, I sensed he was checking to see if anyone was taking an interest in two men of differing age seated together in earnest conversation. 'Let me explain,

160

it might take a while, but it will give you something to consider later, when I return you home.' Now, that got my interest.

'When I left the teaching profession, I kept all the records of administered corporal punishment at the school you attended of which I was its head. You won't be surprised to know the list was long. I was kept busy!' I looked at him.

'Many at the school said you enjoyed it sir.' I replied, still feeling that sense of subservience to a man who was revered.

'You would be correct in that assumption too. I did enjoy thrashing a boy's buttocks, sadly covered. At the private school I attended boys were not so lucky, they were required to strip. Attend wearing just their underwear which would be pulled down just prior to the application of the cane and often the birch! Imagine that, Austin!' I cringed, I couldn't, but the thought had my sexual arousal increasing.

'That is harsh sir, if you don't mind me saying.' I responded.

'I agree, few returned after a dozen strokes, but some did. I took note of those that did, and I concluded that many of them came back because they needed to.' I was puzzled.

'Sorry, why did they need to?' I knew the answer, but I felt I should ask, play the naïve idiot I suspected he thought I was.

'Most returned because they couldn't keep out of trouble but there was a hard core, half a dozen who engineered their return.' I found the adjective used interesting, I felt that disguised another adjective which if used instead might illuminate a dark objective.

'I'm not sure I follow sir?' I answered unconvincingly.

'I think you do Austin; in fact, I know you do.' He still didn't spit it out.

'I'm not so sure I do sir?' I sensed frustration growing in the large man.

'I'll spell it out, they found a way to return because they enjoyed it too!' I closed my eyes. I sensed he knew an awful lot more about me than I realised. 'I spoke to the boys, and they went back because they enjoyed it! Some for the inflicted pain, others because they liked to test themselves, put their endurance to the test. I knew that and the more often they returned the harder they were thrashed.' He took a sip of his drink then brought matters forward thirty years. 'With that knowledge I knew which boys found their way back to me for repeated punishment. Those through just pure wickedness which could never be beaten out of them, to those who engineered their return.' He looked at me and I cringed because I was about to hear the most buried truth of my whole life. 'Boys like you, Austin.' I didn't reply. I'd been found out, something I'd carried around for 27 years was exposed. 'So, when I retired, I studied those repeat punishments and made a list, probably 50 boys. I looked at their offences and discarded those who were just plain bad. I checked them through. Each and every one of them had brushes with the law. Some a lot worse than mere brushes. A quarter have spent time in prison. That left about 20 boys and you Austin are on that list. I checked out each including you. Most possibly overachieved, maybe had a point to make. I then focussed on 5 who did not and like we are today; I engineered a meeting just like ours. I found out something very interesting.' He paused, it felt like he was still enjoying sadistic torture. 'Each of them either took their need for corporal punishment into adulthood or those that did not wished they could, but their timid nature held them back. Like your timid nature is holding you back from admitting this right now!'

162

Outed too!

I sat struggling with my greatest fear. Being found out. Holding onto a terrible secret which would destroy me if it ever came out.

'You say you engineered our meeting today, how was that possible. How did you know I'd be in that pub earlier. You were there when I arrived, you couldn't possibly have known I'd be there?' I asked rather timidly.

'You are a creature of habit Austin. I've frequently been in town, I've seen you go into M&S, it's where you always go to buy clothing. Most often when you leave, you dropped into the same pub, even took the same seat. All I had to do was enter, take a seat and wait. True to habit, you arrived, that noisy crowd gave me the perfect excuse to suggest leaving. That was important because I'm sure you would have got to your feet and fled, had we stayed put?' I knew he was right; I would have been gone and later regretted it.

'So, you brought me out here as a captive audience, knowing I couldn't leave. You had it all worked out. So, I imagine the big question now for me to ask you is what do you want? You obviously have some ulterior motive?' Banford smiled.

'I have a proposal to make. One you can accept or reject.' I listened.

'I can only refuse, go ahead – ask?'

'It's simple, I have two other ex-pupils from the school you attended, where I was your headmaster, who visit me. They often come together. They come for corporal punishment; quite a step up from what you received at school. There are no rules when they visit me, other than those I apply. I wondered if you'd like to visit me. Of course, you'll be alone the first time, but if all goes well afterwards and you'd care to return, all three of you can attend together and I'll deal with you all, one after the other with each of you present while I carry out the punishment.' He stopped at this point. I was stunned and flabbergasted by his suggestion; in fact, I was staggered by everything that had happened since I had looked across at the lone man, seated in the town pub I'd visited after my shopping trip. What I couldn't take in was the certain feeling I'd been set up and now I felt under pressure to make a decision.

'To be honest sir, I've no idea what to say to that.' He smiled.

'You haven't said no.' I knew that was true. He had guessed right about me wondering about seeking out someone to punish me. I felt it had to be a man, but how to find such a person was something I had long considered too. Even so, the man seated nearby? I had revered him; I'd been terrified of him too. True I had done things to ensure I'd been sent to him for punishment, but while his thrashings were searingly painful I realised visiting him now was a huge step up into a different league.

'I need to sleep on it sir, it's a huge ask and it's not something I dare take lightly.' Banford nodded.

'A very wise move. I'm working out another schedule. You can come and watch, but I'll need to seek permission of the two people in question. One you knew quite well. The alternative is you just come and experience the sort of punishment I have in mind. It will be a hard caning; you'll be stripped naked and restrained. It'll be like something you've never experienced before.' I felt a shiver run through my body; it was certainly fear but there was something else too. I shuddered when I realised it was excitement.

'Can you take me home please; I need time on my own to think about this.' I requested, starting to prepare to leave.

'You haven't finished your drink.' He replied looking at me direct.

'I don't feel thirsty.' I answered rising to my feet.

'Sit down, I'm not done yet.' I complied; my drink was pushed closer. I got the message and picked up the glass. 'I've really unnerved you, haven't I?' The question suddenly felt like the understatement of the year. I suddenly felt very emotional, and tears filled my eyes.

'I'm terrified of you sir; I always have been. You are inviting me round to your house to be stripped naked and flogged. I'm not sure I can take that level of brutality, so being unnerved is the last word I'd use to describe how I feel.' Banford sat back.

'You'll certainly cry once I start on you Austin, or should I start calling you David.' I noticed a change in his tone, a clear reduction of aggression, a kinder tone.

'I prefer David sir; I've not been called by my surname since I was at school.' The next question pushed me back.

'Are you gay, David?' I was shocked by his directness. I'd never been asked that question and to be honest I didn't know the answer.

'I don't know sir; I've never had a situation arise to find out.' Banford nodded.

'Do you masturbate.' I closed my eyes, the question seemed rather loud. I opened them and looked around, seeking a tell on someone's face which might suggest he'd been overheard.

'Yes sir, I do.' I kept my answer brief.

'What do you think about, women? Do you think about a woman, making love. Imagining her body? Have you ever seen a naked woman and looked at her body, her breasts,

166

her vagina, do you imagine entering her? Is that what you masturbate about?' I was starting to struggle with the direction the conversation was going. It went further. 'Has my description given you an erection?' He leaned over and placed a large hand in the centre of my lap. 'It hasn't, but if I leave my hand here and start talking about me getting your penis out and stroking it, feeling your balls......' He stopped. 'Ah! That got some interest!' He removed his hand, but the damage was already done. 'We will stop at a remote wooded area on the way back. We'll get your penis out and let's see how hard you get; I will masturbate you. I think you'll let me and then I think we'll have our answer.' He stood; I remained seated this time. 'I'm leaving David, so, unless you are planning on walking home, I suggest you leave with me.' He strode off leaving me in his wake.

We drove and as with anyone who knew his way around the narrow lanes in a very countryfied area he turned off and headed to a copse, wooded part which loomed larger as we got closer. There was a gravelled clearing which was clear, but I felt only due to the incessant rain. We stopped.

'In the back – now!' Banford spoke in his commanding voice. I hesitated. I looked at a man who showed now compassion in his cold eyes.

'What if someone comes past...?' I asked nervously.

'They won't; get in the back or I'll leave you to walk home from here.' I realised I'd have to get out to make the positional exchange. So, deciding there was little point in delaying further I opened the door, exited and quickly found my way to the rear seat where I now sat and waited for my tormentor's arrival. His transfer was just as swift and soon he was beside me.

'I'm not sure....' I started to plead but it was dismissed, ignored.

'Shut up, undo the belt of your trousers and slip them down, your underwear too.' I knew better than to argue, besides I was getting aroused. Something he would soon see.

'My word that is a fine erection David, I think we are getting closer to the answer we both seek don't you.' Banford then blew my mind, leaving me digging my fingernails into the leather seats as he leaned down and took my erect penis into his mouth and started to suck. He pulled me around, gripping my bottom, where his fingers crawled deeper until a finger found my anus. He pressed harder seeking entry.

'I'm going to cum sir.' I called out in alarm as the feeling of my rising climax started its unstoppable journey. He pulled away; his mouth wet. I could see he was aroused too. He now gripped my cock and taking a large tissue from a handily placed box nearby he started to masturbate me. I started to groan. Nothing could stop what was about to happen and when it did my whole body convulsed as the eruption came in several waves before the end came. I was spent, but he wasn't finished. I found myself dragged over his lap, my bare bottom uppermost. He then started to spank me, it was hard, it hurt, and his large relentless hand was like a paddle. I cried out, 'Owwww!' But this seemed to spur him on. Then it stopped. He pushed me off into a heap, got out of the car and moved once more to the driver's position.

'Why did you smack me?' I asked. Still shocked.

'For not telling me a truth you have always known! Tell me David, how many girlfriends have you had – ever!'

'None sir.'

'Exactly, no boyfriends either?' He then asked.

'It's not something I thought I should make a fuss about. I always suspected but I never did much about it.' I replied, which was true.

'Well, you know now!' Get dressed.

I'm home now. I'm still flushed and shaken by the experience. Banford left, telling me he wanted an answer later that evening. His spanking hurt, God knows what a caning from him will feel like. I made dinner and poured myself a glass of wine. I wasn't sure where all this was heading, yet I was strangely excited. I hadn't felt this way in years – if ever! I knew I could ring and say no, leave my miserable boring life where it was, or I could ring a sadist and engage in a sadomasochistic act and possibly engage with others, just like myself. I made a decision I rang.

'Good evening, sir, I've made my decision. I'd like to visit you.'

The exchange was brief. I was given an address to attend the following Saturday at 2pm, that was it. I was hooked.

Facing my fear.

I left in plenty of time. The last three days have given me much to ponded over. While I always had my suspicions about Mr Banford, I never knew his first name, that he might be gay, I now had none at all. I knew something else; I was too. There was something else. He'd mentioned two ex-pupils from the school I attended who visited him for punishment. Both men appearing together and witnessing each being punished in sequence. Apparently, he had said I would know one of them. This meant that person would also know me!

Now, I was travelling to Mr Banford for my first real punishment since leaving school. I often wished I'd taken up driving. I realised how easily Banford had controlled me when I had met him. Once I'd got into his car and driven me out miles into the countryside on a rainy day, taken me to a country pub for a more peaceful chat, I was then his virtual prisoner. I could still escape but not without the dual hardship of a long walk and the further ordeal of being soaked by pouring rain. The word "ordeal" was on my mind now as the bus I was on had reached the stop where I now had to get off. The route to Banford's house was then walking distance and as I reached a road with its name displayed, I looked up at the expensive detached homes on either side. It made my property minuscule by comparison.

Banford lived in a large double fronted property which was massive for his needs. That presumed he lived alone. I walked through two open gates and headed towards the black front door. Banford's Mercedes was parked outside. I was certainly at the right house. I noticed security cameras placed in different locations which gave me the uncomfortable impression I was being observed.

'Good afternoon, David, come inside. You are on time, I like punctuality.' I rang the doorbell, and the door had been opened shortly afterwards. I was greeted in a friendly way, to my relief.

'Thank you, sir, I've always believed in being on time.' I replied as I passed the much larger man. After closing the door, he led the way to a door leading off the hallway. There was a staircase to the left I assumed I'd soon be climbing, although it was equally likely there might be a cellar area, he had converted into a torture chamber, somewhere screams of pain would go unheard.

'You found me then?' Banford opened the conversation after instructing me to sit.

'Yes, I caught a couple of buses, then a walk from the bus stop.' I replied.

'You understand why you are here?' Another question, one I felt hardly needed answering.

'Yes sir, I have come to be punished.' I replied.

'Indeed, you have, and you most certainly will be.' I felt the first shiver of fear trickle down my spine. He got up and walked over to a cupboard where he withdrew a cane around one metre in length. It had leather binding at one end. He brought it back and handed it to me. It was heavier than I imagined. 'I shall use this cane, it's a great deal heavier and thicker than the one I was required to use at school. There I was restricted. Everything had to meet certain requirements. Here, there are no such restrictions either in terms of what I am allowed to use or the maximum number of cane strokes I was allowed to apply to a naughty boy's trouser covered bottom.' I looked up at the man who seemed to be relishing my discomfort. After a long period of silence where I found myself lost for words he continued. 'I intend giving you 12 strokes with this cane, this will be administered to your naked buttocks.' That did make me shudder.

'Yes sir, that is a lot!' I mumbled.

'It's a start, let's see how you get on. I won't hold back.' I had no doubt of that truth. The cane was taken from me and placed some distance away. 'Stand up, remove your jacket and hang it over that chair. He pointed to the one in question. 'I shall now strip you.' He spoke again moving closer. My shirt was unbuttoned, pulled out of my trousers and eased off my shoulders. Next my belt was loosened, my trousers unbuttoned and allowed to drop to my ankles. 'Step out, hang your trousers over the same chair, folded of course. Then remove your shoes and socks.' I did as I was requested, before returning just wearing my underwear. I was now erect, and his hands started to fondle the bulge which made me harder still. He slid his hand down the front of my pants and a finger traced the wet tip. 'I see you are aroused. I will soon cane your ardour; I'll make that droop with the cane you were holding.'

'Yes, sir.' I replied as my pants were pulled down to my ankles.' I stepped out of those too and folded them neatly. I resumed my position.

'Part your legs, wide.' I did as I had been requested, but a snapped 'wider' had me shuffling my feet to obey. 'Now bend over, let's have a good look at you.' I bent over and I felt my buttock's part and cool air flow over the one place I suspected he really wanted to inspect closely. A finger placed at its centre removed all doubt. 'Stay in position I have something in mind to even up the ordeal you face in a short while.' He got up and returned to his seated position directly behind me. I couldn't see much from my upside-down position looking up directly from below. He unscrewed a tube

172

which I suspected was lubricating gel. That was confirmed when his finger transferred a generous amount to my anus. I could then hear something being removed from a box he'd brought with him. 'Do you know what a butt plug is?' He then asked.

'Yes sir?' I replied a little too quickly which suggested eagerness.

'So, you own one?' I was then asked.

'No sir, I just know what one is.'

'You have not had one inserted then?' I shuddered when I realised I soon would.

'No sir.' I felt his finger smearing the gel around my anus, I shivered.

'This butt plug is one which is suitable for punishment. It doesn't have the normal rounded end but two thin strips which prevent it being lost, but tucked away out of reach so my cane won't strike its end. It is a very special butt plug which is connected to this little black box through a wire I will connect. While you are being caned, I will send certain sensations deep inside you. I will also connect this little harness to your penis. It has the same properties. As I thrash you, which is the pain element of your punishment, this will create a balance of pleasure. I rather think you are in for an experience you will never forget.' I then felt something smooth pressed against my anus. I was told to relax which I tried to achieve. The object was pressed harder, and I felt it entering me, my sphincter stretching to where it began to feel painful. This continued until it reached a point where the rest slid in deep until I felt something touch which I knew was its deepest point of entry.

Next minute, hands were at work between my open legs I felt something being slid around the erect shaft of my cock, it felt elasticated which I presumed prevented it sliding off. He

173

seemed to then connect wires before he sat back. 'Let me demonstrate.' I felt nothing immediately, then a tickling sensation deep inside me made my knees buckle, this was joined by a ripple around my penis which caused it to become more erect than before. Then the sensations changed. Prickling took over, then a scratchy feel. I found myself groaning and another sensation took over. I was being masturbated. Then it stopped. Wires were disconnected, my bare bottom gently patted. 'Now for the pain part. You will receive twelve strokes of my cane on your bare skin. – up you get. Follow me.'

I was led to the stairs where Banford stood back and invited me to pass. The inserted plug felt strange, it didn't hurt, and it wasn't intrusive, I felt it more as I moved up the staircase with the wires dangling gave a strange ticking sensation. I was aware he was following me and partially so that he had a full view of my unmarked bottom, a situation I knew was soon to change. At the top I waited until he caught up, he stroked my cheeks as he walked past, and we travelled down a long corridor. Banford then stopped by a door to the left which he opened and stood back; it was only then I was aware he was holding the cane I'd handled earlier.

'Inside please.' He invited me. I didn't hesitate even though fear of the unknown featured much in my thinking. Facing me as I entered was a padded bench which I sensed I would be laying across very soon. 'Stand in front of the bench.' He instructed me.

'Yes sir.' I replied meekly. I looked at the bench which had an absence of straps. I noticed there was a shelf running along the front with two semicircular pieces cut out. I could soon see its purpose which was confirmed when I was invited to step over and stand legs apart with my lower parts placed in the areas designed to keep my legs apart and which prevented any backward movement.

'Lean over and stretch forward.' I did and a bar was swung over which now prevented me from rising. I could neither move forward or back and with no restraint at all, I was effectively held in a punishment position with nowhere to go. My arms remained free, but any hope of my hands covering my unprotected bum was virtually impossible. I now knew I was completely trapped, and Banford could now do whatever he pleased. 'Well David, you are here, and your moment of truth has arrived. I'm going to offer you the opportunity to leave now. I need you to think very carefully about staying, but equally so, leaving? Taking the latter first, if you do leave there will come a time on your journey home, probably when you are seated on the bus, when you will regret leaving, you will know something you have considered experiencing all your adult life has been spurned. You will never know how you might have felt afterwards. It's unlikely you'll never get this chance again. Do you understand what I'm saying?' Oh my god I did! That sense of failure. The coward from my schooldays arriving back to haunt me.

'Yes sir, I do understand.' Banford picked up the cane which he swished close enough to my bottom I felt the draught.

'On the question of staying that is also something you need to think carefully about. Once you agree, there will be no going back. You will feel excruciating pain and no matter how hard you beg me to stop I will not until I have carried out the sentence, I have awarded you. Do you understand that?' I closed my eyes as I thought that through too. His canings at school had hurt. These were half the number of strokes and applied through two layers of clothing. This was going to be administered on my bare skin! I took my time, which he allowed me. Then I replied.

'Please proceed sir. I'll never forgive myself if I walk away and this is long overdue. It's something I've thought seriously about for over twenty years, it is literally now or never sir.' I realised I had just sealed my fate.

'Let's be quite sure.' Banford replied. He came to face me, and I looked up at the man from my prone position. He continued. 'Why are you here?' I wasn't sure why he'd asked; he knew why.

'I've come to be punished sir.' I replied, looking down and averting my eye contact.

'You will be. Do you understand how you will be punished.' I realised he was intent on dragging this out.

'Yes sir, I am to be caned.' I answered.

'You are and you will be judicially caned. Do you understand what that means?' I knew all too well it's meaning.

'Yes sir, it means I will be sentenced and the punishment carried out under restraint without mercy.' I could barely believe I was saying this.

'Has your punishment been explained?' I closed my eyes again, all I wanted was for him to start, get it done and over with.

'Yes sir, I am to receive twelve strokes of the cane you showed me.' I assumed that was it and he'd move to my unprotected rear.

'How hard will those strokes be applied?' I wanted to scream. 'GET ON WITH IT!'

'Hard sir, very hard!" I shouted.

'Very well, now all you need do is to ask me to cane you.' I knew the man was a sadist, but this pushed it into a new level. I wondered what to say. I was aware he'd moved behind me and the cane was now placed across my bare cheeks. All I had to do was to give my instruction to commence. The man had pushed the decision firmly in my direction. I just needed to tell him to start. I took a deep breath before speaking.

'Please cane me sir, I deserve it.' Then I felt the cane lifted at which point I clenched my buttocks ready for agonising pain. Nothing happened; I let my cheeks slacken, then I felt pleasure instead. My penis grew erect as waves of pleasure gripped its shaft, then deep inside me something stirred which made a shudder run down my whole body. I relaxed and drifted into a state of ecstasy. I closed my eyes and groaned as the exquisite feeling continued. I waited for the pleasure to cease; I mumbled something incoherent. I wanted this moment to carry on for ever. I knew it had a finite period before I climaxed, aware I'd spray the floor with my cum. Then it stopped as suddenly as it had started and just as I was about to adapt to a sense of normality, a loud swish and crack filled the room and my whole rear end erupted in searing pain. I cried out.

It's over now. I'm lying face down on Banfield's large king-sized bed. My bottom is raw and painful and covered in thick welts. I received a second stroke which caused me to emit a shriek of unbearable pain. I was about to call out and beg him to stop but just then the sensation of pleasure returned. My penis grew erect just as other sensations deep inside me took the edge off the pain. I felt a finger rub the tip of my penis out of which precum oozed. I realised I was weeping now while another hand gently stroked my back. My mind was becoming confused, especially when the pleasure stopped, and the vicious cane lashed me twice more. Four strokes and still eight more to come. This continued. After the twelfth had been savagely inflicted there was no pleasure to follow up. I was untied and helped to my feet. I was lifted over a strong male shoulder and carried to the bed where I now lay. I was still sobbing. I was cleaned up. Blood had been drawn where strokes had crossed each other's path. Now I lay while my bottom was gently rubbed and with me urged to part my legs the butt plug was removed and replaced by a finger which now explored and eventually probed.

Renewed acquaintance

Banford dropped me home the following morning. I was thankful I hadn't had to travel back as I had arrived on public transport. I spent the night in his bed, but nothing happened. The caning was a painful experience and despite the 'pleasure', it never really felt more than what it was – harsh punishment. I had a light snack before leaving, I wasn't sure if I'd return and that was how things were left. I was sure, once the still continued pain subsided and the vivid evidence of what had taken place faded and finally gone away, I might feel differently. I made coffee and I was standing, leaning against the kitchen worktop rather than sitting when my phone rang. I could only imagine it was Banford, possibly checking I was okay, but the number calling wasn't him.

'Hello?' I answered.

'David Austin?' The voice I didn't recognise enquired.

'Yes, who is speaking?' I wasn't used to telephone calls. I'd had a few from Banford but any others were cold callers asking about loft insulation.

'It's Andy Jameson, we knew each other from school – remember?' I did remember and we'd been close friends. We'd parted company after we'd left school, and we hadn't been in contact since.

'Of course, I remember, it's a lovely surprise. How on earth did you find me?' I couldn't bring myself to ask, why now, what made you think to contact me – what do you want?

'A mutual acquaintance gave me your number, he felt you'd might be interested in meeting up, for old times' sake?' I was even more puzzled now.

'To be honest Andy, I don't have many friends, although you did use the term acquaintance which isn't necessarily the same thing. Can I ask who that person is?' I waited for an explanation.

'Does Mr Banford ring a bell?' I felt a cold shiver run down my spine. The early conversation I'd had with Banford came to mind. "I'm working out another schedule. You can come and watch, but I'll need to seek permission of the two people in question. One you knew quite well...." Surely not, it can't be?

'Oh my god it's you, he said I'd know someone who visited him, I couldn't imagine who, is it true?'I asked next.

'Yes, it's me, did you know Derek Casey?' The name rang a bell. I remembered his name but he wasn't a friend, not even an acquaintance or someone I ever recall speaking to.

'Not really, I've heard the name but that's all, does he go too?' I had to ask.

'Yes, we both go together, Banford rang me a short while ago, he said you'd be joining us next time, he gave me your number, which is why I rang.' That news shocked me, I wasn't sure I was even in the mood to make that decision, I was feeling pretty raw about the event of yesterday and not ready to even consider returning.

'Hold on Andy, I'm not sure I'm ever going back. He gave me such a thrashing yesterday. I've just had a look in the mirror, I can't believe what I saw!' There was a period of silence, then a request.

'Can I come round; I think I'd prefer we discuss this face to face rather than over the phone?' I looked around, my home was tidy and respectable, I had nothing else planned, and it would be good to catch up.

'Yes, why not, it'll be good to see you again, catch up, although I never imagined it would be through something like this.' I gave him my address and he rang off.

I'd just been to the loo when the front door rang. I'd had another look at my bottom and the effects of Banford's cane looked even more stark, with the markings showing a blackness from its bruising effect. I opened the door and the person I'd previously known as a boy stood facing me. He'd changed with age but the basic person I knew still remained.

'Hello Andy, come in, what a lovely surprise.' I greeted him. He walked past and I showed him into a back room I rarely used. I made tea and brought it in. 'That was one hell of a shock, you ringing out of the blue.' I sat down gingerly. It was noticed.

'So was Banford ringing me to say he'd just dropped you home after a visit and you might need a call!' Andy replied, then added. 'Looks painful - was it?' I smiled rather sheepishly.

'You could say that. I'd visited him in his office at school a few times but to find myself naked in that contraption he uses to keep someone in position while he flayed my arse was on a different scale.' I replied, sipping my tea.

'How many?'

'A dozen, I've never experienced pain like it. He spoke of me returning and joining you and presumably Derek too.' I paused before adding. 'I'm not sure about that!' His own reply was a shock.

'I'm not sure either, the last thrashing he gave me went too far. That was a month ago and I'm still marked. I swim to keep fit and I've had to give that a miss.' I slowly shook my head.

'Meeting him after 27 years was quite a shock. It seems he'd been taking an interest in me for a while and him being in the same venue was not entirely a coincidence. He'd noted my habits and got himself into prime position to pounce. I got rather sucked in.' Andy nodded recognition, I suspected

181

he'd been enrolled into a sordid meeting of like interests in the same way.

'The same happened to me, he just turned up as I was having coffee in a local restaurant and made it look like he'd bumped into me by accident. You know what a forceful character he is, well it was hard to say no!' I then asked a question which would also apply to me.

'It sounds like you've had enough, so how do you plan on turning him down next time he contacts you?' I asked.

'Same way as you, I guess. I'll just have to say no!' I thought that might be easier said than done.

'I don't see Banford as the sort of man to take no for an answer.' There was nodded recognition of that.

'He can't force us, I'm not sure about Derek; I suspect he rather enjoys it rather than in my case enduring it.' I never knew Derek, so I was in no position to have an opinion, but his description of why I went, and I was guessing him too, was perfectly described. Andy put his cup down and then made an extraordinary request.

'Can I see your bum? I have seen it before but a long time ago. I'd like to see your marks.' My eyes opened wide with shock. I thought about it briefly, I rather wanted to see his, or what was left after a month anyway.

'Okay, but I'd like you to do the same?' I asked to which Andy nodded. We both stood and unbuckled our trousers. I noted Andy had a stiff erection inside his Y fronts and now feeling rather self-conscious I did too.

'How do we do this; do we just drop our pants or does one of us make the first move?' Andy shrugged.

'I could pull your pants down, then after I've looked, you can pull mine down. I guess I asked first.' I liked that idea.

'That sounds good.' Andy moved his hand down and gripped my erect cock as he moved behind. He let go and then tucking his fingers in the waistband elastic he eased it down over my still burning bottom. My pants then slid down to join my trousers, I stepped out and waited.

'Those do look painful.' Andy remarked once the previously covered area was exposed to view.

'They were, still are! He put me over this bench but even though I wasn't restrained, I still couldn't stop him doing that. I realise now he could have gone on and on.' I replied and I felt Andy's fingers tracing the welts with his finger.

'Did he insert that vibrating plug and put that thing round your cock?' I nodded, I felt myself getting erect, something Andy noticed.

'Still turns you on though, if you were caned for getting erections, it failed.' We both laughed.

'Can I see your bum now?' I got up while Andy undid his trousers and let them fall.

'Do you want me to pull your pants down. I've never done anything like this before.' Andy seemed surprised.

'Never? You're what 43? You've never been with a guy before?' He asked.

'No, you're the first if you take Banford out of the reckoning?' I replied.

'Did you sleep with him?' I didn't speak but nodded.

'Yes, he did some stuff, but it didn't go as far as I'd expected.' I replied.

'Did you know he's impotent?' Andy replied. I could clearly see he wasn't.

'How do you know?' I asked, it didn't seem a matter that Banford would want anyone to know.

'You spent a night in bed with him, did you ever see him erect?' I hadn't which was true, it also seemed odd the only sexual approach had come from him, and I had wondered about being penetrated which I wasn't.

'No, but does that mean anything?' I asked.

'It does when I saw a book in a side cupboard covering the subject of male impotence.' That certainly felt more conclusive. I now looked at Andy's buttocks which still showed the marks from a brutal caning.

'My god, how many weeks ago did he do that?' I found myself asking.

'Over six weeks. I got two dozen. He said it'll be even more next time. I can't do it David.' I touched his still heavily bruised cheeks.

'I'm certainly not going to risk getting anything close to that.' I replied forcefully.

'That's easier said than done. Wait till he calls you. I think he only contacted me to encourage you to obey, should you get cold feet.' I quickly dismissed that.

'He can't force us; I'm certainly going to refuse. My arse is never going to look like yours!' I sat down and Andy joined me. We both had erections.

'He films the beatings you know.' That was a revelation, but not totally surprising.

'Oh my god, really. That's creepy, kinda intrusive. He never said.' I replied.

'You'll never find out until he asks you to return, and you refuse.' Andy replied.

'I think you just said he blackmails you?' Andy nodded.

'That's the situation I'm facing, either return or he'll put my last caning up on social media. He knows who my employer is. He'll know yours too David.

'I haven't refused yet.' I replied.

'Just pre warning you.' I just shrunk. I hadn't thought. I just didn't imagine him caning my arse could become so public.

184

'So why are you here - why now?' I asked, a sour taste starting to form in my mouth.

'Certainly not because of Banford. Okay he gave me your telephone number, but I wasn't given any instructions. I think he just wanted us to regain contact, possibly with one eye to what he might be planning in the future. I'm short of friends, I just thought I'd contact you, old times sake. Nothing more.' I wasn't sure I believed him, but one thing was true. He had as many friends as I did it seemed. Two thirds of fuck all is still zero. I got dressed. I wasn't sure what to say now.

'So, what are you hoping for. Is today a one-off or were you hoping for more?' I asked.

'I'm not here for sex, if that's what you are thinking. We were good mates once, we were both lonely at school, neither of us made friends easily, so it was pretty inevitable we'd gel. Seems little has changed since, so yes, I am hoping for more, but not what you're thinking.' I just stared back.

'I wasn't thinking that, Andy. Until Banford got my pants down and started playing with my cock, I'd never had any contact with anyone before. I've got no friends so I'm in the same boat if I'm honest.'

'You doing anything Saturday?' Andy asked.

'I'll have to check my diary. It was blank this morning, so I guess I'm free.' I replied.

'Fancy coming round to mine. We can get a takeout, then catch up. Stay over even, I've got a spare room.' I looked at Andy who had an imploring look on his face. One which suggested he needed company as much as I did.

'I'd like that. I can't remember the last time I went anywhere, taking my visit to Banford aside. We left it there. For some reason it didn't seem the time or the place to continue now, so it was left until Saturday to move things along or more likely not.

Saturday came. It was so unusual to be preparing for an evening out. This was an invite which was a first. It had been a surprise meeting Andy again after such a long time. I had found it surprising that he'd led a similar life to myself. He was always more outgoing than me at school and I'd never imagined he was gay; was he? I now realised I was which was a relief to finally know. I had procrastinated long enough over the subject and if Banford hadn't forced the issue I probably still wouldn't know. I'd found Banford's recordings of the punishments meted out worrying. I assumed we'd be easily identifiable. I hadn't given the possibility he'd have a camera in that room a second thought. Now, I was to live on borrowed time, waiting for the invitation for me to attend a three-way session of corporal punishment. I imagined once it arrived and I refused, I'd then suffer the threat of exposure. I hated bullies and Banford clearly was one. I thought about my vulnerabilities. Who could Banford out me to? Certainly, I wouldn't want people at work to know, but who else? I'd ask Andy his position, who would he dread knowing?

I showered, I wanted to turn up clean and smart. It felt like a date although I'd never had one. I had no idea what to wear. My range of clothes was limited to the workplace. I couldn't turn up in a suit! I had a pair of jeans I'd recently bought; in fact, it was that trip to M&S which had brought me into contact with Banford. The bright side was that it had inadvertently renewed my friendship with Andy. I'd wear the clothes I'd bought then. I left at 4pm with my arrival time set for 5pm, I soon caught a bus and headed off the short distance to Andy's home.

'Come in, you are very punctual. Like me, I'm a stickler for being on time.' I was led into a comfortable lounge in what

186

was a house not too dissimilar to my own. Thankfully, Andy didn't live in a mansion! 'Beer, okay?' He asked, I nodded that was just fine. He returned fairly quickly with a bottle and glass, and I was handed several take-out menus which ranged from Chinese through to Pizza with Indian the other option. 'When you live alone a takeout is handy, I'm not a great cook – you?'

'My neither, I don't get take outs that often, I just cook the basics.' I replied, looking through the Indian menu. We both chose from that menu and Andy rang the order through.

'That must have been as big a shock for you as it was for me when Banford approached us?' Andy asked.

'Yes, it was.' I then explained what happened and how I'd been trapped into being driven into the countryside and unable to return except on foot in pouring rain.

'Did he invite you back for a good hiding?' I nodded.

'I'm dreading him making contact, do you think he will?' I asked.

'Definitely, what will you do if he does?'

'I might tell him to go to hell.' I replied.

'Call his bluff?' Andy suggested.

'To be honest Andy I'm not sure he could do much harm. I could threaten him with the police.' Andy looked wide eyed.

'I'd say that is pretty high risk.'

'I can't take a caning like you had; I have to say no.' Andy nodded.

'I was on the edge of reason last time; he'll go even harder next time. I can't go either.'

'Perhaps we make a stand together?' I suggested.

'We can try, thank you.' Andy came up to me and put his hand behind and gently squeezed my right cheek. I was taken by surprise. 'You don't mind me doing that do you?' He asked.

'Not at all.'

'Is there anyone in your life, someone close?'

'No Andy, there never has been.' I confessed.

'Never, nobody ever?' He asked with surprise.

'Nobody, no. Okay Banford played with me, made me cum, masturbated me, but before then the only person who has ever touched me was my parents and the occasional doctor.'

'Would you mind if I touched you?'

'No, I'd rather like that actually.' There was a ring on the doorbell.

'That'll be our food.' Andy got up. He placed a hand in my lap and felt my cock as he stood. 'Don't go away.' He smiled. Oh my god, where was this going?

Our take outs were laid out on the table when Andy invited me into the kitchen where he'd laid out the meal. He'd warmed two plates, and he'd opened a bottle of Shiraz and put out two glasses. We got started.

'Sorry, I'm a bit forward. I've had a few relationships but nothing too serious. I hope I didn't shock you.'

'No, surprise maybe. I need someone to make the first move because nothing would happen otherwise. I'm pretty much a virgin Andy.' I replied.

'Would you like to lose yours tonight?' He asked. For me, I couldn't think of a better time.

'I'm never going to lose it otherwise.' I replied. I could see want and need etched on Andy's face, he'd stopped eating.

'What about corporal punishment, we both clearly have retained that need. I don't want to return to Banford, but the need won't go away.' I hadn't thought of that, but he had a point. It was something I'd kept compartmented away for decades but Banford had reawakened it and putting the genii back into its bottle wasn't going to be easy with the marks covering my buttocks as a reminder.

'I guess I go back to how I was before I made the mistake of visiting Banford. Of course, I've thought about it over the years, I've overcome this by watching videos and masturbation. It lonely though and although effective in terms of keeping the lid on things, not very satisfying.'

'We could do it to each other. Could you do it to me because I'm pretty sure I could to you.' It was something I'd never considered.

'I really haven't thought about it. I'm not sure about doing what Banford does, hurting someone to that degree. I think I could smack your bottom, but using a cane or paddle? I don't know.' Andy changed the subject.

'We could clear the wreckage away and take this conversation next door see where it leads to?' I liked that idea.

Fifteen minutes later we were seated next to each other on the sofa. Andy suggested another beer and as it looked likely I wouldn't be going home to my place tonight, I joined him. Eventually he took the initiative.

'Can I touch you?' I wasn't sure where, but I didn't mind.

'Sure, if you want to.' I replied.

'Would you stand in front of me?' I nodded and got up off the comfortable sofa and stood in front of Andy who remained seated. I was now erect, and he saw my bulge.

'Are you excited; you look as if you are?' He reenforced his question but stroking my erection through the bulge in my jeans. He then unzipped me and ran his hand inside gripping my erection.

'That's nice.' I responded.

'It would be even nicer if I can get it out.' He added. I shrugged. He then undid the belt on my jeans, then a single securing button which loosened them, a single pull and they slid down to my ankles. I looked down and my erection was now only restricted by the stretched material of my Y fronts. 'I always liked looking at your cock at school David. Obviously, I couldn't touch it then. You weren't so big then either.' Andy now teased the tip which caused my erection to stiffen even more. 'Is that nice?' Andy asked what a bloody stupid question under the circumstances was.

'Yes, very much so.' I answered, aware my climax might not be far away. 'If you keep doing that, I'll cum!' I panted.

'Then I'd have to punish you, wouldn't I?' He continued.

'I suppose you would.'

'Shall I unveil him?' He then asked.

'Looks like you plan to doesn't it.' I was shaking, needing a pee as it turned out. Andy pulled my pants down by hooking his fingers either side. He pulled my erect cock down, bending it by forcing my pants down without easing myself out. Then, it cleared its own path and on its release my penis sprung back upwards and after coming to a stop it remained very hard and erect. I watched as he teased its tip, pulling his finger away and leaving an ever-stretching string of pre-cum.

'You are an excited boy, aren't you?' He looked at me, stroking the underside of my erect cock. 'What on earth am I going to do with you?' I just looked back.

'Anything you want Andy.' I needed to cum, but I sensed Andy had other ideas. His hands reached round to my welted cheeks, and he pulled me in. I was moved forward, and his mouth opened and clamped round my cock before he started to suck. I could feel his tongue working on my leaking tip in particular. I knew I was going to cum. 'Andy, I need to warn you, it's coming, and I've gone past the point of stopping.' Andy was too busy to reply, but instead he pulled my cheeks apart and an intrusive finger sought out my anus. That did it, my knees buckled, and I filled his mouth with cum!

An hour later we lay naked and entwined in his bed. We'd taken what had happened in Andy's comfortable lounge to the bedroom. In the rush I'd left my jeans and pants on the lounge floor, making the rest of the journey just wearing my shirt which I quickly stripped off. Andy didn't delay either and soon he was stripped of his clothing too. I'd cum, he hadn't, and his sap was on the rise. He knew how he wanted to finish and climbed over me, presenting his hard cock to my mouth, while at the same time offering his parted cheeks to my gaze. He soon gorged on me again, making my own flaccid member rise again from the dead. His own cock was dripping excitement, and I then did something totally new; I took him into my mouth and remembering what he'd done to me I followed suit. I'd never tasted a man's seed; I had little time to expel his penis before he too came in a rush of rhythmic spasms. I swallowed; it was gone.

'Do you have anything to get back for?' Andy asked as we sat at the breakfast table the following morning.
'Not a thing, no cat to feed, nothing, what about you?'
'No, I usually go out at some stage, but we don't need to. We can always go back upstairs and resume, shower together. I loved what we did last night. Maybe we can step it up, I'd quite like to cane you, then kiss it better?' I shivered at the thought, a diverse mix of dread and arousing pleasure.
'You keep a cane?' I asked.
'I've had one for years. I knew this old guy and he was clearing the decks, not wanting his family to find out about

his hidden vice. He gave it to me. I've tried self-flagellation but it's quite hard to give yourself an effective cane stroke. Besides, I shouldn't be able to regulate to force applied. What do you think, I won't do a Banford on you?' I was still marked but mine were fading. When Andy was kneeling over my chest with his parted buttocks in full view he was still marked too. More dark bruising from the flogging Banford had given him. I questioned the wisdom of adding more, even whether I could, but I was quite aroused at the thought of Andy caning me and what would happen after.

'I need a shower.' I announced.

'Me too, we could do it together, wash each other's naughty bits.' I laughed at Andy's description, but the idea appealed. We'd finished. Andy explained the way to his shower room. I entered, I removed my clothes which was now becoming a habit and seeing a mirror I turned to examine my bottom. It has a few fading bruises, but nothing to prevent a visual display of what Andy would be adding later, although when that would be I wasn't sure. I decided to wait for Andy to join me. He arrived and seeing me started to undress. Soon he too was naked. I looked at his bum, deciding the beating Banford had inflicted was far worse than mine which I realised had been half of what he'd received. He was still heavily bruised, and I could see why he didn't wish to opt for even more next time. We got in the shower together, once the temperature was up to create a decent level of steaming hot spray. We both used the shower gel, not just for ourselves but to work it into each other's skin followed by hair shampoo. We cleaned each other's bits, bearing in mind where our mouths would very likely be quite soon. Then, Andy got out and holding a large fluffy towel he invited me in close and dried me. 'Go back to the bedroom. I want you lying over the pillows I've placed at the foot of the bed. I want you nicely in position for when I return.' I nodded my agreement and set off.

My hair was still damp as I walked along the staircase landing to the room I'd been sent to. On entering a number of pillows had been piled on on top of the other centrally at one end of the bed. I was already naked, so I walked over and standing on tiptoe, I bent over to provide the appealing target I knew Andy required. I hadn't seen the cane he professed to own. I lay and waited. Five minutes went by, I suspected this was a deliberate ploy. Then I heard footsteps and something else. A cane was being viciously swished. I knew then he wasn't joking.

'Mmm, that's nice, I'm looking forward to putting some nice stripes on that, what do you say, 10 or a formal 12?' I wasn't sure it was a question, so I remained silent. 'Well, no answer suggests you've opted to leave that decision to me, I'm a sticker for tradition so I'll make it for you – 12 strokes David.' I didn't think two strokes would matter here or there in the scheme of things.

'As you wish Andy.' I answered.

'As you wish – sir!' I was reminded.

'As you wish – SIR!' I emphasised the operative word. I lay their waiting. I didn't clench my cheeks; I had no idea if he'd just lash the cane down without warning or whether instead, he'd measure it across my buttocks first. Banford had, but hadn't he aroused me first by switching on that electrical device which had placed me in a false sense of security. This felt worse. I lay waiting in as yet painless but mentally agonisingly suspense.

'I know where your mind is David. You're wondering if I'm just going to lash your bottom with no warning or whether you'll feel this first.' At that moment the cane tapped my bottom twice.

'It is unnerving yes, there is part of me that wants to scream – just get on with it!' I replied.

'I'll decide when I cane you, David. Open your legs.' I wasn't sure why he'd asked but I complied. I then felt the cold shaft of the cane being rubbed along the length of my erect penis before it then moved position and lifted my balls, sliding deeper before withdrawing. They dropped down into place. The cane went missing then before I felt its smooth rounded end sliding between my cheeks, then stopping at the centre of my anus – surely not. It was then removed and once again I wasn't sure where it had moved to without looking over my shoulder. Andy was playing with me.

THWACK!

'Oh my god that hurt!' I gasped, instinctively moving my hand round to ease the sting on my right buttock in particular. The cane was sharply brought down to urge it away.

'You don't touch your bottom David.' Andy spoke sharply. I was about to apologise when the cane found its mark once more which caused me to cry out. I then lay, closing my eyes as ten more strokes rained down, each with a brief gap in between. Then it stopped and Andy, kneeling beside me, removed the cap from a tube of soothing cream and rubbed it liberally into my welted cheeks.

'Have you decided what you're going to do when Banford gets in touch, assuming he will?' I asked. He had finished with my cheeks and was now stroking my anus with a gel coated finger having asked me to once more part my legs.

'Yes, I have a plan. He will be in touch, not immediately, he likes a nice blemish free bottom. He's thrashed enough to know how long it takes to achieve that, assuming someone doesn't do some redecorating in between. He patted my bottom to make his point.

'Like mine?' I suggested.

'Yes, yours will take a week or so, but if he's true to form he'll be contacting us in about a month's time.' That still didn't answer my question.

'So, what will we do, I can't return. Not if he decides to step it up?'

'Let me put my plan together, I don't want to share it. You may not agree but when he does request a visit, we should go, you have to trust me.' I wasn't sure about this at all but I felt I had little choice.

'You said you were a virgin; do you want to do anything about that?' Andy asked me next.

'I'm not sure what you mean.'

'I'm sure you do.' I felt his finger enter me and slide in until his knuckles rested against my cheeks.

'You mean....?' I never finished, his finger was withdrawn, and he urgently patted my welted cheeks.

'Up you get, I want you kneeling, head down legs really wide. I want you to offer yourself like you mean it!' He got off. I was hard, he was even harder. I'd never been fucked but I knew there must be a time when the opportunity to change that arose.

Resolution

Andy was correct in his timescale estimate. Banford did make contact. A letter having arrived which suggested a meeting at the end of the current week. A Saturday; as he put it - a non-working day, to attend an event which would go deep into the night. No need to get up early the following morning, unless attending church, which he knew was pretty unlikely, for anyone wishing to go. I called Andy and he too had received the same neutrally worded letter. Nothing that could possibly suggest any threat if we failed to attend or could be used should we decide to take it further.

Andy and I had continued seeing each other. He came to me, and I went to him. There was no further caning; spanking yes, which we both engaged in prior to our now routine, hot and dirty sex! Andy fucked me that first time. Entering me and masturbating me at the same time while he worked his magic at my rear end. The next time we reversed roles, another first for me, but one I was now becoming expert. We liked each other's company too. It wasn't all 'filth and depravity' or so we called it jokingly. I wondered if Derek Casey had received a letter from Banford. Andy suggested it was almost inevitable he had.

On the day of our visit, we both showered, Andy caught me twisting to take in a rear view of my pristine bottom, vowing it would still be so after the visit, but added he couldn't guarantee it remaining so later that evening. That didn't bother me, I just didn't want Banford to be its cause.

On arrival, Andy having driven us both, he remarked that Derek Casey was indeed there, or at least his car was parked nearby. Banford was at the door. He seemed in a typically flamboyant mood, almost arrogant, a predator having selected his prey and expecting to gorge on what had presented itself to be consumed. We entered together.

We followed the large man up a flight of stairs and into the same room where Banford had all the means of satisfying his sadism. 'Here he is, turn round Casey, you know Jameson, perhaps you are not so familiar with Austin.' Derek Casey, who I had seen but never conversed with, turned round, keeping both hands firmly together on his head. He was naked. I could see he also had an erection. If Banford's intention was for me to introduce myself, it failed.

'You may remove your hands Casey, let me introduce you to Austin.' We looked at each other, I could see he was deeply uncomfortable. I wasn't sure if the expectation was for us the shake hands, if it was, this failed too. I nodded, he did too, that looked as far as it was likely to go. Banford took centre stage once again.

'I have brought you failing boys together again for another dose of corporal punishment. This time you are to be birched. 30 strokes each!' My penis had been erect but fear made it droop and withdraw. Banford looked in our direction. 'Casey is stripped and ready, I need you boys naked too. Birching is always applied to bared buttocks; I prefer my boys naked for such applications.' I looked at Andy who shrugged and started to undress. He'd asked me to trust him, so I started to undo the buttons on my shirt. Andy quickly had his shirt removed. I then noticed he wore a thick gold chain round his neck. It had a circular medallion hanging down. It was new, I hadn't noticed it before. Banford noticed it too.

'I don't allow jewellery; you'll have to remove it.' I continued to undress as did Andy. He placed his clothes on a pile with his shoes on top. Andy draped the necklace over his shoes, the medallion dangling. We were now both naked.

197

'Casey, you know the drill, position yourself.' I stood near Andy who seemed more concerned about his chain. I assumed he feared it falling and in the confusion that followed he might lose it, perhaps forget it in our haste to leave? Derek Casey positioned himself so his lower legs fitted in the rounded section which would position his legs apart. He leaned forward, at which point Banford trapped any upward movement of his body with a restraining wooden bar. Once again, it's purpose solely to prevent backward or upward movement. Derek Casey was effectively restrained for flogging. 'You will each witness each other receiving the birch. I wonder which one of you will scream loudest.' I sensed Derek Casey was already weeping. Andy had assured me I wouldn't be beaten; I would leave Banford's home unmarked. I now had my doubts. 'Have you anything you wish to say, Derek?'

'No sir, except, please don't be too harsh.' He replied.

'I'm never harsh dear boy, only just.' He turned to look at us. 'I hope you two are watching and taking note, this will be you very soon.' Banford walked to the rear of the room. There was a large circular container which contained a liquid I later found to be a strong brine solution. He pulled out a bunch of rods tied at one end with bindings. It dripped liquid which he cleared by swishing the birch through the air, sending a spray of water through the air which landed on Derek's naked back. He advanced on his victim, taking position at his rear and to one side. He took the birch with its spread ends and touched it several times across Dereks stretched naked buttocks. I watched as he flinched and whimpered with fear. 'I'm now going to flog you Casey, 30 strokes of the birch rod, scream and beg for mercy, nobody will hear you except for those in this room.' With that Banford raised his arm and brought the vicious implement

198

down hard with a loud swish and thud which pushed Derek forward such was the force applied.

SWISH

Derek's whole body twisted and contorted, he wasn't secured, he could move but he couldn't protect himself as Banford moved position and lashed his buttocks a second time. Derek screamed in pain, begging Banford to stop. Banford moved once more, positioning himself ready for another withering stroke. At this point Andy stepped forward and intervened.

'Stop it you sadistic bastard!' He snatched the birch from Banford's hand and hurled it into a far corner. 'Undo him, David.' Andy called to me, surprised and shocked by his actions.

'How dare you Jameson, you'll get a lot more than thirty strokes when I have you over the bench. Leave it!' He barked at me.

'Ignore him David, we are all leaving.' Andy called out.

'Not until I've flayed the insolence out of you, and you've cursed your own mother for giving you life!' He moved forward menacingly. Derek was free and I was helping him up. His buttocks were seeping blood after two strokes, it would have been raw after thirty.

'Watch us, there is nothing you can do to stop us!' Andy replied, standing his ground.

'Oh, but I think I can, you dare not leave, that is if you don't want your previous visits shared on social media, to your employers, your families and your friends!' He replied harshly.

'Fine, go ahead, see if we care.' Andy moved closer now. 'Thing is Banford we've all got a hard on. You haven't, you can't because you can't get it up anymore, can you!' Banford didn't reply he just stood furiously staring.

'Get out, all you. Get out of my home. I'll make you all pay for that remark.' Banford then left the room.

'I wish you'd done that before he used that hideous thing on me!' Derek spoke. Wiping a tear from his eye.

'Sorry, but I had to let him start. I'll explain later.' With that we got dressed. We left the house together and Derek agreed to follow us back to Andy's house.

Once there, we congregated around the kitchen table. Andy got three beers out of the fridge. He'd just taken his seat when his phone bleeped, indicating he'd received a text message. He got his phone out when my phone sounded too and before I could barely respond, Derek's phone did the same. Andy opened his message

'It's from Banford, I suspect your messages are from him also.' I checked and indeed mine was.

Most urgent - read and respond!

This was my text message title. I opened it.

'You left earlier in the most unsatisfactory manner. Reply within 30 minutes, indicating you will return by 8pm this evening and take your punishment in full, plus extra for your insulting behaviour or face the consequences.

Banford.

We confirmed we had each received the same message. None were left in any doubt as to the 'consequences' referred to.

'Oh god, I know what he's planning. I'd better go back. I can't have what he filmed made public. I'll be ruined.' Derek spoke, rising to his feet.

'What do we do, he wants a reply? What should we say?' I asked.

'Simple – Fuck off!' Andy replied.

'We can't do that. Putting that in a reply will only make things worse.' Derek added to his earlier dismay, remaining on his feet.

'Sit down for God's sake. He won't do anything, or not if he has any sense.' Everyone now looked at Andy. He obviously knew something we didn't.

'How can you be so sure?' Derek asked. He'd sat down but he was still obviously shaken. Andy undid a button on his coat, then feeling around his neck removed the chain with its hanging attachment. He felt in his coat pocket and removed a flat device the size of a mobile phone. He then searched around further and pulled out a cable.

'In my line of business, I have access to surveillance equipment. This pennant is actually a camera which includes a microphone. With any luck if I plug this into my phone we can first hear, then see everything which took place in Banford's house from the moment we entered until we left.' Derek looked alarmed.

'Including my whipping?' He asked

'Including your whipping Derek, sorry!' He replied. He switched the unit on, and the screen went blank initially, then with the sound turned up the early exchanges could be heard.

'So, me supplying you with Austin's telephone number has brought you together. Come and meet Mr Casey who is already upstairs and waiting.'

201

Banford's voice could be clearly heard. The trio listened, then the screen came to life when Andy had removed his shirt.

'I don't allow jewellery; you'll have to remove it.'

Everyone remembered that comment too. We all remained clustered around the phone watching events unfold, right through to the withering first stroke and Derek's vain attempt to move his arse out of harm's way. Then when the section Andy had waited for appeared.

'Oh, but I think I can, you dare not leave, that is if you don't want your previous visits shared on social media, to your employers, your families and friends!'

Andy waited briefly after shutting down the phone and turned to the duo. 'That my friends is raw blackmail, plain and simple. No ifs or buts!' He announced. I looked at Derek who just shrugged.

'I wouldn't argue with that. But how can we use it, he's threatening to out us later this evening?' He asked.

'It's very simple. We reply, starting with 'Fuck-off' Then I send this video with a clear message, he has one hour to withdraw his threat and delete his evidence, otherwise this record of what happened today will be handed to the police. Have you a better solution?' I looked at Derek again who felt the suggestion held water. We left Andy to work on his phone and two minutes later he placed it down and waited. We waited several minutes. Ten went by, fifteen, it looked like Andy's plan had been rebuffed. Then a reply came. It wasn't what we'd expected but its underlying message was what they had hoped to receive.

'Cowards, resorting to underhand tactics to avoid what you all deserve. Under achievers all of you, especially you Jameson. I will let you off this time. Do not contact me again.'

Banford

We all let out a huge cheer and Andy went to the fridge to bring out three more beers. Derek held up a warning hand.

'I'm driving, I'll give it a miss.'

'We can't possibly allow you to drive home after what Banford did to you.' Andy once again took the initiative. He looked over at me.

'I agree.' I replied simply.

'You need aftercare.' Andy added further.

'I guess I'm outnumbered.' Derek replied. I was glad he had decided to stay. I didn't know him from before, but I sensed we'd all formed a group bond, created from adversity.

Six months later I had moved in with Andy and we'd become lovers - I guess. It was hard to even think about the life I'd endured and in a perverse way, I had Banford to thank for that. The first night we'd all come together saw us engaged in a remarkable threesome, something I'd never imagined in my wildest dreams ever being part of. Derek became a close friend to both of us and he defied the expression "two is company, three is a crowd". We were never bothered by Banford again. Sadly, or for him anyway, he never learned from threatening people to visit him. Unbeknown to us, we were just part of a larger group he had visit him. Broken into groups of three he had created a conveyor belt of sadistic abuse which eventually went too far. He threatened one reluctant member of the group with his nasty brand of blackmail and this person refused to buckle and went to the police.

Banford was headline news, splashed in lurid detail across the tabloid press, or at least the ones which specialised in scandal. We created our own little sadomasochistic group. Andy and I role played. He was naturally dominant anyway, so I am his sub. Derek joins us and in a much less vicious and unfeeling way, a form of Banford's regime does briefly operate when Derek forms part of the group and Andy wields the cane, or whatever implement we agree to use. It's the group aftercare sessions which follow which is the bit we most enjoy. Penetration on a mutually enjoyable scale happens to seal the climax of the evening – literally.

'I sold my home. I did let it for a while until Andy and I decided we were compatible. Neither of us wishing to rush into a relationship which might have ended in failure. Most of all we were friends and as friends we'd visit the pub together, often joking about what we'd do if Banford was there and decided to join us. The last we heard his huge home had been put up for sale. He became ostracised and the butt of jokes in every pub. He had gone, disappeared into the ether, never to return and cause us any threat or be a reminder of our past as mid-teen boys who attended the same school.

I changed jobs. Thankfully, with Andy and to a lesser extent Derek's help, my self-confidence grew. My self-esteem increased and I was able to see myself in a better light. The boy, who then became a man didn't need to seek punishment for existing, for being someone who only deserved inflicted pain as a reward for getting through each

204

day. Much as I detested Banford and what he'd put me through, I knew I was in that dark void long before I met him, and he recognised that within me. The predator seeking weak prey and finding it.

I'm preparing dinner. I cook a lot. Derek is coming over and I think we'll both go to bed later with sore bottoms. Andy is in a strict mood tonight and as soon as the food is consumed and everything is cleared away, a bottle of wine maybe two, now only fit for recycling, Andy will disappear and reappear as Mr Johnson, our headmaster and tell us to follow him to his office when our evening would only then have just started.

The Castigation

The corporal punishment training of a young man....

By

Sam Evans

The Advertisement

I'm an experienced ex Headmaster looking to provide much needed discipline in the lives of young deserving men of minimum legal age (18) to a maximum age limit of 25. The next stage is to meet and discuss your needs and my terms in the form of an interview. There will be no further correspondence after first contact. A healthy BMI is essential. Show proof of this in terms of weight/height. The meeting will terminate without this information being available. I am firm but fair and I can tailor a session towards your needs so that it's as effective as possible. I look forward to your detailed response which must be a minimum of 1000 words.

I pressed send and with a whoosh my advertisement in Castigatio, went live. What came back was in the lap of the gods. I realised the wording was blunt and uncompromising, a take it or leave it approach. That had been deliberate. I knew the vast majority of submissive men would take one look and sneeringly reject its tone, move onto the next with a muttered comment. Possibly, even an expletive. Those were not my target. I wanted someone with sufficient intelligence to read between the lines and be attracted to the author of those words. The age range was crucial. I am 62 years of age and the person out there I am seeking is looking for someone very special to meet their needs. Quite simply described – me!

I know I'm arrogant, but only to those I despise. The young man who has yet to read my advert will not see me as such. He will see me as the father figure who has been missing in his life. I sense I will excite him. I will resonate on his wavelength. The young man I seek will be very shy, inexperienced. A virgin in every way. He will be submissive and certainly gay. He will be masochistic too. I know precisely what I'm looking for and if this advert fails to attract him, I will wait until it does. I'm very patient. There is one certainty. The man I seek, this boy, exists. He is out there, he will come.

I'm in town now, shopping and I live alone, I always have. I am retired having been a head teacher at a large London comprehensive. Times have changed, discipline has gone. Behaviour now compared to when I started teaching is laughable. Even in those days things had become rather lax. Certainly, in my Father's Day, schools were ruled with a rod of iron, too harsh my father said. I dread to think what he'd make of behaviour now. A group of boys jostle past, there is no point admonishing them. At best I'll get a mouthful of abuse, at worst threatened with a knife. I check my watch, it's nearing midday. I can't be too long because I have a visitor arriving at two. A young man of 23, a regular. He realises he needs my attention and when he leaves around five, he'll be sore. He is one of several young men who visit me. They know the rules. They write their shortcomings down a week in advance of arrival, knowing I will read this in detail. They know on arrival they will be subjected to corporal punishment. The recipe is simple, they all know what to expect when they arrive. I was caned at school, pretty much everyone I knew was at some time or other. You stepped out of line and that was the end result. Some thought that activity engendered a need which then extended into adult life, I never subscribed to that theory, and it didn't answer why young men contacted me who would never have experienced such treatment.

I'm back at home now. I've made a quick lunch, then with thirty minutes to go I open up the room where everything will take place. It was a bedroom, in fact it has a bed inside, but this one isn't for sleeping, it's for restraining young men. With wrists and ankles fitted with Velcro restraints, each with securing rings attached they lay over a padded raised mound to position their bare buttocks for downward strokes of the cane and occasionally the birch rod. This has one key advantage over the padded bench which sits adjacent to the bed. Being right-handed, the implement being used tends to favour one offered cheek, the other cheek gets less attention. Obviously, I can alter my position to avoid any hint of favouritism but having the victim tied face down over the mound allows me to merely walk around to the opposite side and punish from that position instead. I can move up and down too and apply strokes diagonally, criss-cross even. Oh, trust me, a boy is well and truly flogged in that position. It's the bed for young Jason today. It does have a downside however, nothing is perfect. Most of my boys like to be penetrated. The horizontal position means they have to be de-restrained first before entry, while those retrained over the horse, legs already parted will just need their tight hole lubricated and then penetrated whist held in position. Jason isn't keen, so I'll just clean him up, wipe the blood from his lacerated buttocks and send him home thoroughly chastised. He'll leave tearfully, with a gentle slap on his raw behind, with a reminder he will need a refresher in 30 days. 50 strokes today. Five batches of ten strokes with sexual arousal at each interval. All these men come because it turns them on sexually, some will scream and howl, but living in a large house without close neighbours means their ordeal will not be heard. Lying flat is slightly more difficult although the design of the mound ensures my hand can reach their penis which will go from soft, (after a batch of strokes) to rock hard (ready for the next batch). On completion and aftercare. Jason will be rolled onto his back and expertly brought to climax.

Everything is ready, I close the door to keep it warm and as I descend the stairs the doorbell rings. Jason will be standing nervously on the doorstep, he will be invited in and told to go upstairs. He knows the routine, visit the toilet, then enter the room, strip naked and wait for my arrival.

The Reply

My name is Thomas Riley. I am 19 years of age. I am currently at college studying computer science. I guess i consider myself rather shy. I don't make friends and any I do have are male. I am gay. I live at home with my parents, and I spend most of my time in my room. Many will think I live a very sad life, but I am happy, I'm quite content with my own company. I've just arrived home and tonight I plan to browse the contact adverts on Castigatio, which specialises in men seeking other men to engage in corporal punishment. Being shy and submissive my interest is in receiving, not giving. I obviously cannot accommodate, so I could only ever visit. So far, I've only ever looked and wondered. I've never visited anyone or ever received corporal punishment. Even so I get erect even thinking about it and given the right person, I'd be tempted to meet them. I had replied to adverts. All, barring a few, received aggressive responses. Men, who claimed to know exactly what I needed, then proceeded to tell me in excruciating detail. I wasn't sure if those were genuine or men getting off on writing sadistically to someone, they knew was young and vulnerable. This wasn't what I wanted. I replied to some, less aggressive replies, saying thanks for replying, but no thanks. I still got further responses, being called a fucking time waster. I wasn't interested in just going to be thrashed. I wasn't even sure I could take a beating. I needed someone I could meet, get to know, and be eased gently into whatever activity we both chose to engage in. Most of all, I needed to explain. To explain in writing because I was too shy to explain in the spoken word. No, all were very precise. I would need to visit them and engage in whatever they had described.

I ate my evening meal. I shared my day's events with my parents who then left the table to avoid missing the evening soaps. They watched all three, recording one which they promptly watched when the others had finished. Television was their life; weeknights were taken up with soaps while at weekends it was gameshows or idiots shut away in some phoney jungle setting being annoying. It was little wonder I spent most of my leisure time in my room. I'd lock my door for privacy, and I'd strip. Then select caning porn on my laptop. Most featured women but some had men, being caned by men, often dressed as a strict headmaster. I loved ritual. The offender stood before the man, head bowed, being admonished. The 'boy' being told he'd be taught a lesson, this time, he'd be required to bare his buttocks, more often than not be required to strip naked and with legs parted told to bend over.

I'd be erect now and I'd start to masturbate. Slowly, waiting for the cane strokes to commence. I didn't want to finish one event before the main event had started. I loved to see a young man's bare buttocks, legs parted so his balls were very visible and dangling down under their own weight. Often, even before taking position, the boy's tent pole erection would be noted. Often the cane would be placed underneath that stiff penis and lifted to emphasise it had been noted. 'We'll soon remove that young man.' The head would boast, he was rarely not true to his word! The camera would be placed behind the victim, his parted cheeks exposing his secret exit. That thrilled me most because I was so aroused by touching my own. I shivered at the thought of mine being touched but even more so at the thought of being penetrated. A finger or some object, not of great size I might add. Dare I even imagine an erect penis sliding inside

213

to its full length then being pumped in and out slowly – deliciously.

The cane is being measured now. A second camera is focussed on the 'boys' face. I see him flinch and tense as the cold length of bamboo touches his bare skin. Then TWACK! That same face screws up in pain and moving onto the rear camera a thick red stripe appears across both cheeks. Now a cry of pain and I sense the youth tries to rise but is advised not to unless it was to be repeated as the other would no longer count. I was mesmerised. I was erect, my cock standing up hard with its veins standing out. I looked again as the second stroke strikes barely an inch away followed soon after by a third. The 'boy' is crying now. Is it real? An actor obviously, but are the tears authentic? Surely even actors in this type of film production feel pain. I realise now I wish to be that person, but could I withstand such pain. Twelve strokes are completed, and the victim is told to stand, then move to a corner as directed by the pointed cane. Hands on head, legs apart! Not to even consider touching himself, to rub his bare bottom to ease the pain. I'm looking at those welts, I've seen each one delivered, I'm masturbating and I'm starting to feel the first signs that the end isn't far away. It's building and now it's gone beyond the point of no return. I grab a tissue just in time as I cum. Again, and again I eject my seed until I'm spent. The urge has gone now, and the door handle of my room is being tried.

'One minute I'm getting dressed.' I called out and quickly climbed back into my clothes. My mother calls out that they are heading to bed and to say goodnight. I return the words and settle down. I'm less aroused but not so that my main goal of browsing through Castigatio is missed. As that was my main goal for the evening, I now selected the website and settled to view.

I look every week; this enables me to just view the most recent posts. I never go beyond the first dozen posts. I almost groan as the first six were just the same, certainly the same messages. Aggressive with the same likely response if I replied. I was about to give up when I spot one which bucked the trend. For a start it was a long post and whoever had written it seemed able to string words together far better than most. I started to read and as line by line was completed my interest grew. Dare I suggest my excitement too?

"I'm an experienced ex Headmaster looking to provide much needed discipline in the lives of young deserving men of minimum legal age to a maximum age limit of 25."

I shivered. The man's description reminded me of the video I'd recently viewed. I was on the bottom end of his age limit too, but would I be too young for him? I was barely of legal age, by one year. I read on.

The next stage is to meet and discuss your details in the form of an interview. There will be no further correspondence after first contact. A healthy BMI is essential. Show proof of this in terms of weight/height. The meeting will terminate without this information being available.

The next part really appealed. Most demanded I turned up at their home, or if I accommodated, to invite him to mine. This advert meant I could meet this person first, and on neutral territory too. I was puzzled by the next line. It

215

seemed the Interview would be a one off and final. Any further discussion removed. I'd have to think about that, but it was a minor downside when others rarely offered anything whatsoever. The next part made me smile. I'd have to show my BMI. I knew this would pose no problem. If anything, I could benefit from adding a few pounds. Proving this would not be difficult either. I knew my height and weight, I'd just had to go online and put the numbers in. I was getting excited about following up this post. Moving on....

I am firm but fair and I can tailor a session towards your needs so that it's as effective as possible. I look forward to your detailed response which must be a minimum of 1000 words.

The last part added a cherry on the top of the cake. I could discuss my needs and most of all the final part, I could write in detail about me and explain exactly why I was applying to meet. I knew it was late, I also knew I had to go to college the following morning, but this was what I'd been waiting for. I'd never sleep knowing I was being given this opportunity. I made a drink and started to write.

Reaction

I slept well. I always did after meeting one of my boys. Jason left three hours after arrival sore but like me, sated! I usually saw at least one young man a week, I had another visiting the following week, after that a break. Last evening, I met with friends and colleagues from the education system which at one time employed me. It's changed a lot since my day and I'm glad to be away and rid of it. We all met for dinner and the wine, followed especially by the brandy which later flowed, added to a pleasant night sleep. I'm in the kitchen now. It's the main hub of my home and I spend a surprising amount of time there. I've made tea and while I'm here, before I dress, I can log on and check my mail. It has been a day since I posted my advert and like an angler, I like to see if my bait has been taken, even a nibble! Mail is a rich mixture today. A lot which should be in my junk box, then some which has ended up there hardly junk at all. I note the special account I use for Castigatio has a single reply. I didn't expect an avalanche because of my wording. Those unsuitable will not understand, this being my reason. Only the right person will understand. I check through the rest first, I'll leave the best, (hopefully) until last.

I top up my tea, I open the mailbox, and I see I have received an email from a Thomas Riley. Well, Thomas Riley, let's see what you have to say for yourself. I open the message, and my excitement grows immediately – it is LONG!

Dear sir,

My name is Thomas Riley. I am nineteen years of age, and I am a student studying computer science. I read your advertisement with great interest, but mainly because it gives me the opportunity to explain myself in depth. You state one thousand words, i hope that isn't a maximum because I have a lot to say and much of it will be difficult to express. Thankfully I can write it down because otherwise I doubt, I could tell you with the spoken word. I will describe myself as a boy. One who is immature for my age. I doubt I have developed much emotionally beyond the age of fourteen. I was bullied at school, and I hated having to expose myself to others. I am referring to the showers after games and physical exercise. I often sensed this was planned humiliation. I used to look at other boys and see their penises nestled amongst a nest of bushy pubic hair. Mine by comparison was puny and stood out because my own pubic hair was so sparse.

See, I've written close on 200 words and said very little.

I looked and on the surface that was true. But what I sensed I was reading were the outpourings of a troubled young man desperate to talk to someone. My heart beat faster now because I'd always yearned to meet someone like this. A blank canvas, somebody, unsullied by human contact of the wrong kind. A boy (I'd noted what seemed to be a certain age, possibly a preferred age even?) I'd read up on so called daddy and little relationships, was this possibly what he was expressing in ignorance? He, seeking the guidance from and older man, firm discipline within a loving relationship? Was this in fact what I was seeking myself?

218

Another source of humiliation was far away from the gymnasium and the shower block. It was each and every day, knowing girls were of no interest to me other than as a casual friend. Other boys did, however. But hearing the crude homophobia expressed by other boys I shivered with dread at the thought they would find me out. I had seen one boy almost driven out of the school by bullying. I didn't want that. I am digressing. It's late and I am now going to make a confession. Thirty minutes ago, I watched a porn video of a boy being caned by his headmaster. I watched him strip naked and then with legs well apart he bent over and offered his bare bottom to be caned. I became very aroused. I saw he was erect too, his penis standing upright, his balls hanging down between his legs. His cheeks were parted, and I saw his secret place. Then the caning commenced. 12 hard strokes, each one landing with a loud crack. The boy cried out in pain. I wondered how that must have felt. You see Sir, I don't know because I've never experienced it myself, so, how could I know. As the final strokes landed, I climaxed. There, I've told somebody at last. I hope this is what you hoped to hear.

Oh my god it was. Here was a total virgin in every way. Never caned, probably never slapped or even spanked, but I sensed as I read on, he will say, that he needed to experience what that naughty boy received. I think this was my main hope, when I placed my advert, that someone would reply, a totally, willing innocent. Someone, who over time would submit to being caned just as he had described in his scenario. Another thing too, he was gay, or I sensed he felt he was. Was this young man, just what I was seeking. I know I haven't finished reading his reply, I doubt I'm even halfway through. But what I've read feels like that same angler seeking out a shy but wily fish. One that would need care to hook. After netting, to be treated with equal care before being released, unscathed but with greater experience. I need to read on....

The thing is sir, I want to be that boy visiting the headmaster. But I don't know how to achieve it, I'm hoping you might be able to help. I've written to several others but the replies I have had, have been very aggressive and I sense all these men wish to do is inflict pain. I need far more than that. I saw the boy in the video slowly strip, I'm torn between having to do this or to be stripped, item by item by...... You? This boy didn't undergo a detailed, intimate, physical inspection. Is this what you might carry out. I've read how those being judicially flogged in bygone days were physically examined and passed fit for punishment. I'd like that. Another thing, would I be subjected to a harsh caning on my first visit? I'm unsure if I can even take it. Which leads me to ask whether I'd merely bend over for you or whether I'd be restrained? This thought excites me as much as it does terrify me. The fear of things being done I cannot prevent.

My god I can't believe what I am reading. It is like I'm reading a script I then suddenly realise I have written myself. It poses all the questions I hoped would be asked, maybe some I hadn't expected. Our first and only preliminary meeting was going to be very interesting. This reply was ticking every box, I just hope he wasn't going to tell me he was overweight, because that would sadly be a game changer. I continued.

Sir, I am 5 ft 6" tall, I weigh 9 stone. That means I have a BMI of 20.2 which is slightly below mid-range. My parents say I need to add a few pounds. I know you said I have to prove my BMI but you can see for yourself when we meet that I am slim. I trust you will wish to meet me. I'm not sure what more I can say. Your opening words speak of seeking a man of legal age, which I am and below 25 which I am also. I feel I need discipline, but I also need affection. I am gay, so I realise what this may entail. I have never been penetrated but with certain precautions and care I'd like to experience this also. You speak of tailoring a session to my needs. I feel the videos I watch and duly masturbate as I watch, are those I'd like to emulate, me as the errant teenager and you as my strict master. I know caning will hurt and I'm sure I'll scream and cry. I hope afterwards I'd be held and cuddled, my sore bottom treated. What we do afterwards I'd leave to you, so long as when I leave, I am contented and happy and wish to return at the earliest opportunity when once any marks have gone. I'm not sure if there is much more I can add. I suspect I might not have met the 1000 words you demand. If I have not, I apologise. I must leave something to discuss when we meet, assuming you wish to. I don't see the point in padding this out to meet an arbitrary margin. I feel I have answered your advert fairly and made an effort in my reply. I look forward to meeting you,

Sincerely yours, Thomas Riley.

I sat back. I was stunned. I hadn't expected that! Even the arbitrary figure of 1000 words was of no importance. Okay, being picky he's supplied 903 words, but even half that number had more than met my expectations. I'd certainly wish to meet this young man, but I realised I'd have to treat him with kid gloves. This shy little mouse was hoping I'd be unlike anyone else he'd encountered on Castigatio. I certainly wouldn't be treating him like all the others who had passed through my hands before, even as late as yesterday with 23-year-old Jason. I decided to shower, shave, and tidy myself. This would give me time to think about my response. I didn't think it should be long and detailed. That would be reserved for when we met. I knew the venue which would be ideal. It had a quiet corner where over lunch or as he was a student during weekdays, an evening, we could talk openly in private. It might become emotional, so I'd have to take care this meeting would not be misconstrued.

I'm back downstairs now, I have decided on my approach. I write it down and having read it through again several times I press send. Now it's just a case of waiting, just a simple yes, to say he'll be there and what time and day will suit him best. Meantime I'll have to wait, won't I!

Meeting?

My phone pinged while I was in class. I got a sharp look from my tutor; it should have been turned off. I had sent off my reply to the Castigatio advert late into the night and having checked my phone before I entered my class, I'd had no response at that point. I had pinned so much hope on that posting, it seemed to have everything I desired, as a result, concluding I'd never see another that good, I'd call it a day if I got no reply. Maybe I was expecting too much anyway. The ping signalled the arrival of something, maybe an email, more likely just a text. At the first break I'll check. I'm excited and as a result I've become distracted. The lecture ended. I pulled myself together eventually and I didn't allow my lack of concentration become destructive. I apologised to the lecturer about my phone and said I'd be more careful in future.

In the college canteen I bought a coffee, I sat alone which was quite normal and decided to finally check my phone. There was indeed an email and from one I'd not received before. Who was Charles Warden? I opened the email and with a coffee in my free hand I started to read.

Dear Thomas,
Thank you for your very full and detailed response. It was exactly what I hoped for. As a result, I would like to meet you for lunch or dinner at the Grosvenor Inn, at Redbridge. The venue is close to both the bus and train station. There is a quiet area towards the rear where we can talk in complete privacy. Thinking of your college I offer you the choice. You give me a date and time of your choice and I will book it. The BMI comment was more of a hint

about the appearance of the person I meet, I accept you fit ideally into the category I am seeking. Please make this arrangement soon.

I await your earliest reply,

Charles Warden

Wow! I thought. So that is the man who wrote the advert I responded to. Of greater importance, he wants to meet me. I wasn't sure what to think? Of immediate importance was deciding when was best to meet. Part of what attracted me to the advert, albeit a small part, was the strong likelihood he'd be within easy striking distance for travelling. He was just a short bus ride in fact. Now, all I had to do was decide to meet for dinner, which suggested an evening, or lunchtime which would entail a weekend meeting, probably Saturday. Evenings were best I felt, and they could be very soon, a matter of a day or two?

I was due to attend my next class, I needed to decide. I got my phone out and typed my reply.

Dear Mr Warden,
Thank you for your reply. Dinner is best for me. Any evening even tomorrow is fine. 7.30 would suit me. I can catch a bus to the Grosvenor Inn. I look forward to your early reply.

Yours sincerely

Thomas

I decided simply using my first name would display a degree of intimacy and friendship. I hoped Mr Warden wasn't overly formal. I pressed send. I got up to leave, I left the canteen and was heading to my class when my phone pinged. I just caught the message as I was about to turn my phone off.

Tomorrow is fine, 7.30 sharp. Dress smartly,

Charles.

I smiled; he had replied in the same informal vein although his message about dress code suggested formality applied at the Grosvenor Inn. I just had time to reply. Fine, see you then, before turning off my phone and heading to my class.

I got home early the following afternoon. I'd told my parents I was going out the following evening which surprised them. Was I meeting a girl? They asked. I said it was a get together from college. I knew my parents harboured a faint hope of marriage and possibly grandchildren. That was never going to happen. I thought about formal dress. I owned a single suit. My parents had bought it for a wedding we had attended. It hadn't been worn since. I feared it might not fit. What then? I had smart casual clothes, but would they meet the requirements Charles Warden had laid down. I didn't wish to turn up for an important, no vital meeting, and disappoint him.

I showered. I looked at my body later as I dried myself. There was certainly no spare flesh on me. I turned and looked at my bum. I sensed that was going to be a part of my anatomy which could see much focus if we pursued this friendship beyond dinner. Even tonight? Was it possible? I turned and viewed my front. I found I was erect, and I realised how quickly that had taken place. From those days when my pubic hair was sparse, it was now quite a bush. I knew it was the thing these days to keep oneself shaven, I'd been tempted but for whom? There wasn't anyone to get the razor out for although that may change. Would I if instructed to? You bet I would!

I set off at 6.30. An hour would be ample, but I wanted to be on time, not too early but certainly not be late! I told my parents I might be late and to not stay up. I had my key, and I'd let myself in. Thankfully, my suit still fitted. I wasn't blessed with a vast supply of ties, but I found one that matched the suit. With my black shoes polished to a shine and overcoat buttoned up, I called out goodbye and left the house, walking smartly to the bus stop ready to meet a man who was making an impression on me even though we'd never met.

The Grosvenor Inn

It's just gone 7, I always intended being early and certainly arriving before my young guest. Despite my age and obvious experience, I felt nervous. There was more than a hint of excitement too. It is early evening, and the main rush will come later, even so as I am shown to our secluded table it will be nice to not be subjected to stares from those who may find it strange to see two men of such diverse age seated at dinner. I order a gin and tonic and wait. At 19.25 a waiter appears; he is leading what almost looks like a schoolboy only this one isn't in uniform although the devil in me knows I have one in a wardrobe at home which will fit him perfectly. I rise to my feet and greet my guest who looks shy, and shell shocked.

'Good evening, you must be Thomas?' I extend my hand.

'Yes sir, I'm pleased to meet you Mr Warden.' He replied as the waiter took his leave. We shook hands and I invited him to be seated.

'Do you live far away?' I asked.

'No sir, a fifteen-minute bus ride.'

'That is fortuitous, I live thirty minutes away by car. I can drop you home later.'

'Thank you, sir, I'd appreciate that. I don't like being out late, public transport can be tricky at night, people aren't nice anymore.' Amen to that I thought. I decided to get started.

'So, now I have you here all to myself, tell me why you are here?' I saw the question strike home. I saw a tongue-tied young man unused to explaining himself.

'I tend to be better at writing things than speaking sir.' I smiled.

'You did too. So, what was so different to my advertisement to that of others you no doubt read before mine?' The waiter arrived which I assumed would give him time to consider his reply. I ordered a soft drink as I was driving. Thomas ordered a Coke. He left menus too. I knew what I wanted and left Thomas to decide. Then he answered my question.

'As I said in my reply you asked me to explain my needs. I tried to do that as honestly as possible. Nobody has ever requested that before. Those I read tend to be just telling me what to expect on arrival.'

'Which is?'

'Corporal punishment sir.'

'I inflict corporal punishment James. I made quite a mess of one young man's bare buttocks just a day ago. Fifty strokes. Is that what you are seeking?' I asked a question which I could see went home very quickly.

'I hoped what you offer sir is more than that.' I smiled at the open-ended opportunity his reply offered.

'You wish for more than fifty strokes?' I continued smiling, knowing full well what he meant.

'Oh no sir, I meant I hope what you offer extends to more than caning although I anticipate you will cane me.' I nodded slowly.

'You can count on that young man. Have you ever been caned?' He shook his head as he replied.

'No sir, in fact I can't ever recall being smacked. I certainly wasn't as a child by my parents, and they did not do it at school.'

'I see. So why do you watch videos of men being caned, while you masturbate too?' A question which had to be delayed answering as the waiter appeared to take their

228

order. Wine was offered but neither took up the offer. He continued when we were alone.

'It is a subject I've always found interesting. It excites me too sir.'

'Meaning you become erect?' James cast his eyes downward, I could see he was embarrassed.

'Yes sir.'

'You mentioned the showers at school. How you felt inadequate. Other boys having larger penises and pubic hair while you did not?' James nodded. 'Do you have pubic hair now?' I asked.

'Yes, sir, quite a lot. I've often considered shaving it off. It seems the trend these days.

'Don't, I will remove it. That would be my job. Do you understand?' James looked at me now.

'Yes sir.'

'How big is your penis, erect?' Another question I saw James become uncomfortable answering.

'Does that matter sir, unlike my BMI, you didn't ask this in your advert.'

'Of course not, hopefully I'll soon find out when I give you a very detailed examination. Would you like me to do that. Strip you naked and examine every inch of you?' I saw a shiver go down his body. 'You are erect now, aren't you?' I could see discomfort. 'Imagine we were not in a public place, would you strip for me if I demanded that of you, or would you prefer I stripped you – naked!' James remained silent. I could see he was shocked but even so, I couldn't imagine he was about to flee.

'Yes sir, it's something I've thought about often at night in bed.'

'Were you masturbating then too?' I decided I'd ease up now.

'Yes sir.'

'I cane boys who masturbate.'

'That is harsh sir.' He replied.

'It is a question I will ask once you arrive in my home. So, you'd better stop immediately thereafter. Assuming you choose to visit me. I will be in charge of your sexual needs after tonight. Well?' I could see he wasn't expecting that.

'I will try sir.'

'Wrong answer. Try again.'

'Yes sir.'

'Better!'

The food arrived which created a brief interlude. I could see he wasn't expecting my current questioning.

'Have I shocked you?'

'Not really, it is the sort of response I had hoped for, I guess it was a shock when it actually happened.'

'Everything you wrote in your letter ticked one of my boxes. I see you as a blank canvas, perfect for me to guide and mould as I wish. Almost every other young person I meet has prior experience, they have different expectations to someone like yourself seeking guidance, I can provide that. So, describe to me your needs and my role. If it helps, you fit precisely into the mould I have you fitting into also.' Once again James made no attempt to speak until he'd cleared his mouth.

'As I explained, I'm very shy and introverted. I struggled at school where I was bullied remorselessly. I need a mentor, I can be lazy, so that person needs to be strict, and I need to be made to toe the line. I have a father and mother but neither, especially my mother provided this guidance. Your advert suggests you can. I note you mentioned discipline and spanking. This fits into a lifestyle I have always wished to explore, but slowly and gently. I have no wish to visit a man who restrains me and beats me to within an inch of my life.' I was impressed by that reply.

'What if I tell you I'd restrain you for corporal punishment?' I asked.

'I'd fear that, but even now in the brief time I've known you I'd trust you enough to submit. I sense you are not seeking this to be a one-off event. Why would I return if you hurt me so badly, I'd never repeat it.' My words exactly, had I expressed them instead of him.

'Let me ask you a question you may or may not be interested in answering. Do you have a preferred age you wish you had been had you visited me in the past. It sounds like you needed a mentor in your earlier life.'

'Probably in my early teens. This is when my life at school seriously declined. This is when I wished I'd known somebody like you sir to help me with schoolwork but also to guide me, support me, encourage me. Give me sound advice. Those were seminal years, had things gone better then, the rest of my time at school would have been so much better. Happier too.' That was perfect a perfect response. I felt I could have been the role model he obviously lacked. I had another question, one which was pressing with the waiter due to arrive soon.

'Would you like to skip sweet and coffee. Get out of here and you come to my home and continue this? I can supply coffee and maybe something stronger to drink. We can get to know each other better and you can look around. I can drop you home, or you can even stay over. I have a spare bedroom, and I do cook a mean breakfast.' I saw surprise on his face.

'Really, I'd love that. I'll need to call my parents, let them know. I'll say I'm staying over with a friend. My parents fear

231

for my safety at night so they will be relieved. I didn't bring any pyjamas though or my toothbrush.'

'You will sleep naked in my home, maybe you'd like to keep me company? I'm sure I can find you a toothbrush, maybe it will sit next to mine for future visits.' The waiter arrived and I paid up. Then with me leading the way, we headed to my car which was parked outside.

Chez Warden

I couldn't believe the car I am invited to enter. I had little experience of driving, not owning or driving myself. My parents never owned a car either. My father owned a motorcycle, and my mother sat on the back. This was a different world. It was a Mercedes, and the seats were leather. I called my parents who were relieved I wasn't risking a late-night journey on a bus; they hoped I had a good time. I hoped so too, but I doubted in their wildest dreams what such enjoyment might entail.

On arrival at the home of Charles Warden we entered a large property through large iron gates which opened on command. Once inside they closed which sent a slight shiver down my spine. Did that mean I was now trapped. I was now his prisoner. Inside, I was taken down a long hallway which had a wide staircase heading up onto the floor above. I wondered where he punished young men who already visited him. I assumed I'd be going up there later when I headed for bed. Further down I could see a large kitchen but to the right an open door which led to a comfortable lounge.

'Would you like a drink, something stronger than a Coke?' Charles asked me as soon as I was settled.

'I don't drink sir; I've only ever had Coke or soft drinks.' I replied.

'You haven't been in the home of a strict, older man before either, have you James, so this can be another first.'

'What do you recommend?' I asked timidly.

'I can pour you a small whisky or a brandy, maybe something less alcoholic, like a beer?' He then suggested.

'I'll try a whisky, in for a penny, as they say.' I left it there and watched as my host went to a cabinet and returned shortly after with two identical looking drinks.

'I take mine neat, but I can get some ice. He asked.

'Thank you, sir, that would be nice.' I waited while he left the room, returning shortly after with a container I assumed contained ice cubes. He dropped two into my glass and took a seat beside me.

'Well James. You are here. Is there anything you'd like to say or do, or would you prefer leaving me to drive the agenda?' That didn't take long to answer.

'I'd like you to sir, I have no idea what to suggest?' I replied.

'Do you wish to just talk; we could watch a movie, or I can create some activity?' I'd spent a long time considering whether to reply to Castigatio advertisers. I had now found someone who seemed on the same wavelength as me. We had talked, talked plenty and I'd written plenty. I certainly didn't want to watch a movie. I wanted action.

'I'm in your home sir, I'd like you to take charge of me. I trust you enough not to proceed with anything I don't like. Please take charge, it is what I hoped for.'

'Very well, stay there, I shall be back soon.' Charles rose to his feet and left the room; I sat there wondering what he had in mind. Finally, he was back.

'Come this way.' Charles spoke, his hand outstretched directing me out of the room. I was then directed into the kitchen. I didn't reply. I was nervous but very excited I was erect too. On entry a large wooden table dominated the room, it was totally clear except for a large towel which had been laid out. There was shaving equipment nearby, a tube which was labelled KY Gel and beside this a metre long cane which sent a shiver down my spine.

234

'Take your clothes off. Fold them neatly. Leave your underpants on. I will remove those when I'm ready.' I couldn't believe those words. I'd heard them endlessly in my dreams or when I had quieter moments. My erection grew. I hoped I wouldn't climax.

'Yes sir.' I replied. I removed my suit jacket and hung it over a nearby chair. My tie came off next which I was thankful to lose. I slowly unbuttoned my shirt and removed it, again folding it neatly and placing it on the chair seat. I leaned down and undid my shoelaces. After removing my shoes and socks which I placed side by side under the chair, I unbuckled my belt and allowed my trousers to slide down to my ankles. I stepped out and folded them placing them over my jacket. I was watched throughout. All that prevented me from nakedness was my underpants. I looked down and realised I had a tent pole erection which stretched my pants forward.

'I see you are erect?' I could hardly say no!

'Yes sir, I'm sorry.' He picked up the cane which he viciously swished through the air.' I visibly cringed. He used the cane to touch my erection through my underwear fabric.

'I can see I'm going to have to deal with that.' I knew what he meant by "that".

'Yes sir.' He sat down and beckoned me forward until I was a mere touching distance away. His hand came up and he stroked the tip through the material. There was a small wet patch where I had leaked. He grasped the elasticated waistband and looked inside.

'Nothing puny about that Thomas although I think I need to pull these down to be sure.' My underwear was lowered. I stepped out of them, my erect penis springing up and sticking straight out at the end.

'Thank you, sir.' I replied. Relieved my penis met with his approval.

'Not sure about this though!' He grabbed a tuft of pubic hair and tugged it.

'I'm sorry sir, it won't happen again.' I replied nervously.

'I know, I intend shaving you quite soon. Let me check the other side. Turn around'. I turned.

'Yes sir.'

'Part your legs wide – wider!' He commanded. I shuffled my legs apart, then even wider still. I hoped my feet didn't slide and create a nasty situation. 'Now bend over, let's see if I need to take my razor anywhere else.' I shivered. I'd dreamed of this moment, to expose myself intimately, totally to another man.

'Let's have a look between these shall we?' I felt his hands pull my buttocks apart almost to the point of being painful. 'No anal hair, I've had some boys who have, I tug them out with tweezers!' I shuddered at the very thought. 'Mind you there is some hair on your cheeks and your perineum needs cleaning off. You've a very nice bottom, I quite look forward to smacking that later.' Oh my god I couldn't believe what was going on, I felt so aroused. 'What's this I see?' I. Felt a finger touch the tip of my penis and encircle it, I looked up and saw a long string of mucus dripping down which was gathered up and brought to my face. 'Well?'

'I'm sorry sir I'm excited.' I stammered.

'I should say so. Let's get you up on the table.' He finished the sentence by giving my bottom a sharp slap. I got up and clambered onto the table, waiting in a kneeling position until told which way he wanted me. 'Lie on your back, I'll have you kneeling afterwards.' I moved, turning over and lying flat on my back, looking up at the ceiling. Mr Warden then fetched a spray can of shaving foam and a brush and liberally covered my bush of hair, working it in with the brush. He made a start with the razor. 'Far better than watching online porn and masturbating I hope?' He asked.

'Oh goodness I'm not sure anything I can think of beats what is happening tonight sir.' I replied. There was no reply, just deft strokes with the razor, periodically washing the razor in a bowl of water leaving my bushy pubic hair floating on the surface. For the next few minutes, the shaving continued, my legs were lifted and opened, and I was moved around so that everywhere accessible from the front in that groin area was devoid of hair. Them I was turned over and told to kneel with parted legs. I was gently slapped to make them wider. Then shaving foam was squirted on my unmentionable place before being brushed around and further down. The feeling was sensational and my erection, which had never subsided returned even harder.

'Have you ever been penetrated?' He asked, touching the place of entry that I'd always associated as a place of exit.

'No sir.' I replied.

'Have you penetrated yourself, a finger perhaps, something you might have purchased or even found that might fit?' I was very conscious of the lewd position I was in, what I was displaying to a virtual stranger. Then again, I'd imagined doing just this in my quiet moments as my hand encircled my penis and I slowly masturbated.

'I've touched myself there sir, but while tempted I've never gone any further.'

'But I sense you'd like to?' He asked.

'Yes sir.' He started to shave me. He ran the razor over the surface of my exposed cheeks which were stretched tight like a drum skin. My cheeks were pulled open, and the razor run between and then to an area between my crinkled vent and my balls. The sack of my scrotum which hung down had been

237

gently shaved at the front, now he turned his attention to the rear. Then, finally he announced I was as hair free as I was as a newborn baby.

'Stay in position.' He requested, not that I was planning to move. I noticed he reached out for a tube marked "KY Gel" he unscrewed the cap and then squeezed a generous amount onto my bottom. I shivered. 'Okay young man, I'd like you to relax.' I shivered, not just with the coldness of the gel where it was but also at the prospect of what I knew he was about to do.

'I'll try sir, but it's difficult.'

'Stay still, you have a very nice little bum James and I'm about to stretch your sphincter. That is the tight muscle I have to penetrate. Just close your eyes and enjoy the sensation. I murmured my pleasure as his finger smeared the gel around the area in question and then I found that same finger seeking the centre of the exit point. Then a little pressure which started to become painful. A slap on my right cheek was followed by a sharper instruction. 'Relax'. I let my whole-body droop as his finger finally overcame the tight ring of muscle and slid in deeply.

'Oh my god, that feels so forbidden sir!' I called out.

'Well, it most certainly is, you naughty boy.' I smiled as I thought about our previous conversation and me meeting him much earlier. I imaged the forbidden nature of the activity he was now engaged in, had it occurred then. Thankfully, that situation hadn't arisen. His finger started to move slowly back and forth, in and out while another hand worked on my cock. A finger was encircling its slippery tip. I realised I would cum soon and if I did, it would be explosive, almost violent. I sensed he knew this because his finger was withdrawn, and he then washed his hands under the tap.

'Off you get.' The request was backed up with a hard slap which made me wince. 'Follow me, it's time you visited the punishment room.' I shivered, unsure if this was a mere viewing or somewhere more sinister and that slap was just the start.

The Room

I woke the next morning James lay on his front, asleep and from the peaceful expression on his face he looked contented and relaxed. It had been quite a night. The covers were pulled back exposing his buttocks, I stared at the single, thick red welt which was visible across the centre of both cheeks. I'd brought tea up, having carefully extricated myself from his clinging grip. I could see, despite the contentment now, redness under his closed eyes, evidence he had been crying. He stirred and slowly opened his eyes.

'Good morning, James. I've brought tea in bed. You slept well, once you got off, how's your bottom, sore?' I asked, knowing it had to be.

'Yes sir, it still hurts a bit, more when I move, I'm lying on my front to avoid it chafing on your sheets.'

'A sensible move, sit up and drink your tea, you'll have to think about getting up soon. I can drop you off at college or near your home. I guess there will be questions asked of I drop you outside your door?' James shrugged, he said he didn't mind, just so long as he could return soon.

I was at the bend in the stairs the previous evening after having left the kitchen I led James up to the room where I punished young men of similar age, although at nineteen he was currently the youngest who visited me. I looked back down and saw this attractive boy following me. He was naked and he looked much younger, but thankfully legal. It was James himself who had used the term "forbidden", it could so easily have been, with him using that word as he looked back up at me while my index finger was inserted deep inside. I had waited for him to catch up. Normally when young men visited, I sent them directly upstairs fully dressed

240

to strip and prepare. James was already naked from the deforestation which had taken place in the kitchen. He'd had his vent penetrated too, but only by my finger. He didn't know, but he had something much thicker and longer going up later. He was tight, I relished feeling that band of muscle around and gripping my erect cock. He passed and I smiled when I saw the red hand mark. I couldn't resist giving that cute little bottom a good hard smack! Maybe not this time, but possibly next time, I'd have him over my knee for a good hiding he wouldn't forget!

'Come inside.' I had opened a door further along the landing passageway and turned on the light. It wasn't bright, it wasn't meant to be. It was intended to create an atmosphere of menace for all those entering for the wrong reasons. I wondered if walls had memories. If they did, they'd hear the swish of canes and the very recognisable sound of flexible bamboo striking bare flesh and the sounds of pain being expressed – again and again. Even a wall would lose count of the number of times that combination of sounds had been repeated over recent years.

'Oh my god, is this where……?' He didn't finish.

'Yes James, this is where my young men come to be punished. It will be your turn next time. Have a look around. Today is purely exploratory for you. Something to reflect on tonight as you lay in bed.' James came in and moved over to the bed. He gripped the metal frame and looked first at the leather mound over which victims lay, then at the fixing rings and their attached chains. I walked over to a nearby cupboard and removed a Velcro fixing strap with its sprung clip, identical to that on the end of a dog's walking lead. 'These are connected to wrists and ankles and connect to the four corners of the bed. The naughty boy about to be caned or birched, lays face down over the mound whose purpose is

241

obvious.' I now pointed to the caning horse which stood adjacent to the bed.

'So, the mound presents the victim's bottom for downward strokes while the bench is for sideways strokes? I assume I'd be restrained on the bench also?' James asked.

'Both have advantages over the other, can you see the pros and cons of each?' James moved around both, I noted his erection wasn't evident now.

'Not really, both just offer a different means of restraining the victim. Whichever is chosen, I imagine both have one common purpose. To hold the victim in position so the intended target remains still. Both will still offer unimaginable pain.' I nodded my agreement.

'Yes James, that is very true. But let me demonstrate.' I went to the cupboard and selected a stout dragon cane which I swished through the air. I saw fear on James's face. 'Bend over the horse!' James looked back shocked.

'But I thought you said next time?' I smiled.

'I did, this is to explain one key difference. Don't you trust me?' I asked.

'Y.. yes sir.'

'Then get over that horse – NOW!' I replied sharply. James tiptoed and hopping up. He then lay over the top and stretched forward, placing his arms near to the ringed fixing chains. I moved to the rear and opened his legs to align with the rear chains would secure his ankles. 'Now the disadvantage. 'I walked to his rear and lifting the cane I stretched my arm and touched its cold surface to his right cheek. 'As you can see, because I'm right-handed there is the constant preference to strike this cheek and not the left one. As the cane lands it will compress that buttock and if there is flexibility, it will wrap around to the sides of that fleshy part. Okay, I can change position like this and strike both cheeks centrally, but the end of the cane will always dig into that buttock and eventually break the skin. You will bleed.'

'What is the advantage sir?' James asked. I put down the cane, moved directly behind and pressed my finger on his spot.

'Do I need to spell it out?'

'You can penetrate me while I'm still restrained?' I patted his bum.

'Yes James, you can go to the top of the class. Down you get. James clambered down I then pointed to the bed, with its sheet covered mattress and leather raised mound. 'Over you get!' Another command which James obeyed without question. I pulled his arms and legs into a crucifix position then picking the came I tapped the furthest cheek. 'So far so good, I give you six strokes with me standing here or.' I moved around to the other side I did the same again but now the furthest cheek.

was the other buttock. 'I give you six of the best and hey presto, both cheeks are equally caned. I can cane across centrally or I can move up and down either side and give diagonal strokes also. Any thoughts?' I watched James rise to his feet and stand equally between both.

'I imagine there is no problem with the first method if you are ambidextrous?' James answered smartly with a self-satisfied grin on his face.

'Be careful young man, otherwise I might bring my decision forward a few weeks!' I paused and asked a question. 'Which would you prefer?' James looked at both.

'The horse I think, I like the advantage it offers.' I smiled.

'Now that presupposes you are ready to be penetrated. Do you think you are?' He smiled.

'That could depend on you sir, how big you are?' I wasn't ready for that question.

243

'Well, maybe it's time to find out but first you must do something for me. There is a good reason for this although you may not be sure immediately.' I saw puzzlement on his face.

'What can I do for you sir?'

'Bend over feet apart and touch your toes.'

'What now sir?'

'No, next week! Now, when do you think I mean.'

'But…'

'Bend over NOW!' I pointed to where I needed him, he stepped forward and after parting his legs he leaned forward and took up the classic punishment position. I moved until I was behind him and to my left. I tapped his taut buttocks twice, then leaning back I brought the cane down hard centrally across both cheeks. There was an immediate reaction of pain. A scream, followed by crying. I moved forward and picked the boy up, throwing him over my shoulder like a trophy. I left the room, turning off the light and took him to my bed.

'Why did you use your cane on me? I wasn't expecting this, and it came as a huge shock when it happened. I know it was just a single stroke, but it hurt so much. I screamed the house down.' James had taken up position next to me against the headboard I saw him wince as the thick welt on his bottom scraped across the bed sheet as he pulled himself into position.

'In the relationship I hope we have started to form, it is my job to provide affection, guidance and support. I sense you have rarely expressed your emotions, and I doubt your parents gave you comfort and affection when you cried. That you shouldn't cry – men don't cry! Well, men do cry, even I cry from time to time. I suspect it is years since you shed tears, well you certainly did last night, I saw to that, and I held onto you and let you cry yourself out. You cried yourself to sleep James.'

'I did didn't I and I've only just woken up, what's the time?'

'It has just gone six, we have plenty of time. Drink your tea.'

'I'm wearing the same clothes as I wore yesterday, will anyone notice?' James asked as we headed to his college in my car. We'd eaten breakfast as I suggested James think about what had happened since meeting at the Grosvenor Inn yesterday. We had become known to each other in every way and James had a very visible souvenir across his backside he'd be able to reflect on for a week or two. He was still a 'virgin', penetration awaited him still. Once I'd taken him to my bed and he'd cried himself to sleep, it seemed cruel to disturb him. I imagined the sleep he was in was one of the deepest he'd had in years and while I enjoyed touching him, he didn't disturb. We'd discussed next time and how that might differ from this time. He said there was no question of him not wishing to come again and he said he'd hoped it would be sooner. I'd refused. I said he needed weeks, not days to think long and hard about next time because he'd be placed under restraint, and he'd face a dozen strokes next time followed by penetration whilst held down, none of which he could prevent no matter how much he begged me to stop.

I stopped short of the college. I saw hordes of young men and women of similar age entering the modern college. I told him to keep in touch and he left the car. I could see he was

245

tearful as he left and as he walked away, he turned several times and at the gate he waved before disappearing.

Make your mind up time.

I'm home now. Today was hard with my mind elsewhere. There was no looking at porn, or if I did, I couldn't masturbate. Mr Warden had fitted a cock cage which prevented access, it was strapped round my waist and tucked behind my balls. It isn't uncomfortable and I'm managing. The fixing has a seal which if broken will show I removed it. I've been warned against doing this. A threat of a severe birching awaits me should I offend. Of course, I can, but I could never return and face that. He'd birched a boy of 23 called Jason recently and he showed me a picture of his raw buttocks! Masturbation apparently is now his job as is shaving too. Even an erection is hardly possible. The leather cage is a tight fit when flaccid and if I become erect it would squeeze against the rough leather inside which has rough edges, as I found to my cost. It became very painful. As a result, I avoid anything that can create an erection. Mr Warden says young men my age shouldn't masturbate anyway and it's proving too painful to do otherwise.

As instructed, I'm giving Mr Warden an update on my day, I am to continue to do this until he plans to invite me over formally. Each week I am to summarise how I feel about the next visit which will centre around discipline and corporal punishment. I have been told to start tonight and tell him how I felt things had gone and whether my expectations had been met.

Dear Mr Warden,
Thank you for dropping me off at college today. It has been hard to concentrate at times and as a result I have been constantly taken back in time to when I first arrived at

the Grosvenor Inn. You were older than I expected which pleased me. I needed my father figure to be mature and able to inspire confidence and be worthy of respect. In that regard you overachieved my expectations. You quickly put my mind at ease – thank you.

I didn't expect to return to your home and what we did there left me beyond even my wildest dreams. I've never been comfortable displaying my nakedness, but I felt comfortable undressing in front of you. I loved being inspected and of course the shaving routine was sublime. I have found it strange walking around hairless; my smooth skin rubs constantly, and it is an odd sensation. I was surprised that afterwards I didn't really wish to dress. It felt so natural walking around your house naked.

Your upstairs punishment room was an unnerving experience. Seeing that bed and your punishment horse brought home to me where I am heading now, and I appreciate the huge step up this lifestyle offers. I wasn't sure at first whether it would work but later, especially after you hurt me and I cried, I did go back to a much earlier age when I needed to release my emotions and found I could not. You made me cry and once you offered comfort and support, holding me close, I found the floodgates opened and I couldn't stop. Thank you.

Thinking ahead I realise next time things will be different. I realise my own needs reflected the videos I used to watch. I can't describe how I wish to present myself and what I have so often felt the need to explore. To do so will make me erect and that now is a very painful experience which makes me sore. I'll stop now because I'm expanding within the tight confines of that leather cage. I will end by stating I am still on course to visit you and submit to all you described.

Thank you for taking care of me. Nobody ever has before, well, not like you did.

Yours sincerely

Thomas Riley.

I pressed send and it was gone.

Three weeks have passed, and I am hoping Mr Warden will invite me to visit and stay over. Evenings have been so different. Long gone is endlessly watching porn. I have climaxed several times, but these have been nighttime, wet dreams. Involuntary climaxes. As usual I hardly see my parents. We sit down for meals but that is pretty much as far as it goes. I heard my phone ping as I arrived but as dinner was being served, I decided to check later after we'd eaten.

It was a message from Mr Warden inviting me to visit at the end of the week. Arrive Friday eat at the Grosvenor Inn, return and at 10pm, submit to 12 strokes of the cane. Saturday would be recovery and sexual activity and the following day; Sunday I'd be returned home. I wasn't sure quite how to react. Everything seemed more of the same, except the caning. I'd had just a single stroke. But a further 11? Could I honestly take that many, one single stroke had been painful beyond description. The thing is though, I'd be under restraint so where was the choice? There was none. Of course, there was but that meant turning Mr Warden down.

249

It meant also missing out on everything else which was a turn on – an experience on steroids!

I lay in bed later; despite all efforts I was aroused, and my penis had expanded inside that tight cage. The more aroused I got, the more it grew, and the pain increased accordingly. My cock was getting sore with chafing against its deliberately designed rough interior and exposed stitching. I imagined some Chinese woman working in a regional sweat shop making these without a clue to their intended use. I was sure I'd be carefully inspected once it was removed. Hadn't Mr Warden not only warned me off masturbation but advised me to sterilise my thoughts too. Was this to be proof I had failed and had the cage not prevented my hand gripping my cock and carrying out the forbidden act I'd have succumbed to that too. I'm sure he would have asked that question. 'Have you masturbated James?' I could never have lied. He'd have seen through my lies. That created a dilemma. Mr Warden intended caning my bare buttocks. But why? Then again to mitigate his sadism, why was I going there knowing this was my fate? I would submit to him, willingly strip naked and quite voluntarily climb up onto that horse. I'd done this already when he demonstrated the pros and cons of its use. I'd compared it to the bed frame nearby. I'd lain over that too. The only difference this Friday at just before 10pm was that no securing straps had been used. That would certainly not be the case soon. If be secured to a point where I'd be unable to move a muscle. He'd have my bare bottom offered at a perfect height and he'd lean back and with great force lash the cane down on my bare skin. Ouch! That cage was really hurting now. Then it struck me, no pun intended. Why was I getting erect at such a thought. The masochist within me a perfect foil for a sadist.

I left the house just after 6pm. This time I took a small overnight bag. I explained I was meeting some friends and as before my parents were pleased to see me get out. It was so rare and yet this was the second time in a month. I caught the bus, and I arrived just before the appointed time I was due to meet Mr Warden. As before a waiter took me to my table and he stood, holding out his large hand to greet me.

'Good evening, James, I like punctuality.' I'm sure he said the same thing last time too.

'Good evening, sir, I've looked forward to meeting you again.' I replied.

'Even bearing in mind what I plan for you at 10 this evening?' A good question, one I wasn't sure how to answer.

'Not that no. I don't think anyone should look forward to being caned sir. I'm not sure how anyone can relish enjoying pain infliction to that degree, but I do see it as a test of endurance and one I must overcome, get past in order to move on.' He smiled.

'I enjoy inflicting pain James. Even though I will damage your adorable little bottom. I like to imagine the mind of the recipient. Fear and trepidation. Some boys start to cry before I even start. I look at the bottom in question and decide where to place my first stroke. High and work down or in the sweet spot, the crease where the swell of the buttocks meets the top on the thigh. It is considered the most painful place. A starting stroke there instead and move up. I sometimes alternate. High then low, moving down and moving up until the centre is reached. Diagonals too. A lot depends on how many strokes have been awarded. I'll decide at the time when I have your buttocks stretched over my horse.' I couldn't believe the conversation taking place. Other diners seated a respectable distance away making small talk while Mr Warden was discussing flogging me!

'How have you got on with the cock cage? I imagine you are looking forward to its removal?'

'Yes sir.' His question was somewhat of an understatement.

'Are you erect now?' I looked around the restaurant, quite sure in the knowledge nobody else seated had been asked such a question. 'You are, aren't you! Was it my earlier conversation?' I nodded.

'I am sir and I'm getting sore.' I replied.

'So tonight, hasn't been the first time, has it?' I shook my head. 'We discussed sanitising your mind James, you are incorrigible. I plan to inspect you soon. I'll be able to tell how many times you have lapsed. Imagine if I hadn't fitted the cage, how much semen would have ended up in tissues.' My thoughts too. 'Did you bring the homework I requested?' I nodded.

'Yes sir, do you wish to see it now?'

'Yes, of course. Hand it to me.' Just then the waiter arrived. He took a drinks order and left menus. I handed over a folded sheet of regrets, misdeeds and matters I needed to atone for. I had a good idea why he had requested it and he then confirmed it, but not until we'd chosen our food orders.

'So, you regret your time at school. Why?' The first question. I placed my hands together on my lap and answered.

'I was bullied sir, I mentioned this in my initial reply.' I replied.

'You did, but that was then, and this is now. I'm asking the questions, and you will reply are we clear?'

'Yes sir.'

252

'What did you do to stop that? Lots of children get bullied, but they don't hate school or fail to achieve. Some even work even harder to rise above the bully.

'Nothing sir, I just accepted it.'

'You did, I imagine you blame your parents because the next regret was having the parents you have, so it's their fault?' He asked next.

'It would have helped if they had supported me or encouraged me more sir.'

'I'll take that as a yes then!' The waiter arrived and took our order. He then continued. 'You mention being bored at work; you regret not having a better job?'

'It is very mundane and repetitive sir.'

'What was your ambition, the perfect line of work for you?'

'I don't know, I've never really given it a lot of thought.' I saw him raise his eyes to the ceiling. I knew he was annoyed.

'That reply rather sums you up young man. We will return to these later when your bottom is bare, and I am flexing my cane. Let's see if I sense a change of heart when I've put a dozen stripes across your arse!' The conversation ended abruptly which was timely with waiters arriving with our meal.

253

Moment of truth.

'Come inside James, shut the door, it costs a fortune to keep this place warm' I snapped. I saw reluctance on his young face which had grown as the time for him to face his worst fear drew closer. He came inside and shut the door. 'Go upstairs and strip. You will remain naked until you leave on Sunday.' I saw terror in his eyes now. It had now dawned on him what lay ahead. He didn't delay, he knew just two options lay open to him, obey, or leave. I closed down everything on the ground floor. Other than making tea of coffee later, anything and everything that was about to unfold would now take place upstairs. Everything was ready in preparation for the main event which was now an hour away. On arrival in the bedroom, James was naked. His clothes were folded neatly he was standing by the bed.

'Turn around.' I instructed. I moved forward and crouched, looking at his bottom for any evidence of the single cage stroke I'd lashed across both cheeks a month earlier. There was none. Just pristine smooth cheeks which I knew were unlikely to remain this way very soon.

'I checked myself everyday sir, the mark was pretty much gone by the end of the week and day by day any sign of it had gradually disappeared. I imagine it's going to look a mess quite soon.' I wasn't sure if that was a question. If it was, he'd assumed right.

'Okay James let's be very clear what is going to happen tonight. In less than an hour you will be caned. I plan to use your homework task as the basis of your punishment. You will feel pain which is unknown in your experience. When you replied to my advertisement, you knew very well this moment would arrive in your life. If you did not or you feel you've misunderstood or made a mistake, I now invite you to get dressed and leave my home. I can provide the father figure I sense you feel you have never had, but I made it clear my methods are a mixture of support and affection with discipline. That discipline is instilled into you with corporal punishment. I've never hidden that from you. I gave you a single taste of what that entails, and you didn't take it well. That event is to be upgraded twelvefold.' I stopped and waited for my words to sink home. 'I now plan to leave you to contemplate. I'm going to the punishment room down the corridor. In fifteen minutes, you will either be dressed and gone, there is an envelope with £50 inside to get a taxi back to your home, or you will join me where the act of corporal punishment will take place. The choice is yours.' I went to withdraw.

'What about this?' James stood pointing at his cock cage.

'Just remove it. The fixing just pulls apart, but it breaks the seal. Just leave it. It was very nice meeting you James but now you must decide. It is your moment of truth.' I turned and without another word I left.

I'm in the room now. I've left James to consider his next move. Part of me hopes he will leave. I'm fond of the boy and deep down, I don't want to leave his bottom welted and bloody. Then again, I hope he comes and faces what he knows deep in his heart he must endure. He'd watched enough videos of boys receiving worse and he'd admitted masturbating as he watched it unfold stroke by stroke. Five minutes have gone, perhaps he has too, or if not, he will soon. I look at the horse, leather topped, it's sturdy front legs shorter than the rear pair. Everything designed so whoever is strapped down tightly is placed with the target area I seek to welt, and stripe is placed at an ideal height and angle. The cane I intend using is leaning against a nearby table and on top the tube of KY, with which to smear onto his tight vent for the final part of the deed. An unopened condom is nearby. The rear legs of the horse are wider than the front, adjustable too. I will widen them when the act of penetration is reached.

Most who do not understand will wonder why I plan to beat a nineteen-year-old boy with a cane. Surely it is an act built upon hate. Those will not understand the needs of the perpetrator or the victim. James met me as a result of an advert placed in a magazine whose sole purpose, its very existence rested on men seeking other men to engage in the act of corporal punishment. The act of castigation. I'd placed the advert, James, seeking a particular man to satisfy his needs chose me. Obviously, the situation he is facing now is deciding between fantasy and reality. Those who watched the same videos he did should wish to be one or the other. The person suffering or the person inflicting that suffering. Few watched such videos in a neutral position. The next hour, assuming it took place, wasn't about being the father figure he sought, love and affection, a supporting role. This would come later when a broken and sobbing young man would be untied and carried to my bed. My sheets would be smeared with streaks his blood by morning and our mixed seed would also stain my sheets. After washing, they would be hung on the line or being dried in the tumble driver before the sun set the following day. This was sadomasochism starkly portrayed.

The door opened and James walked in. He was still naked. He didn't speak, he just walked over to the horse, climbed up and placed himself voluntarily across it, thus inviting me to secure him.

'You decided then.' I made doubly sure, a stupid question I know but still an essential one.

'Yes sir, I've come this far. The alternative is to return home and sit masturbating while I watch this act carried out. I need to endure it and afterwards to feel proud I took it and came through the other side. Secure me sir and carry out my punishment.' I picked up the securing straps. I took his nearest wrist and fixed the Velcro tightly. I then clipped it to the ring on the short length of chain. I did likewise on the other side. I moved to the rear and fixed an ankle the same way, pulling his leg outwards to where the leg of the horse defined how parted his buttocks would be during punishment. With the other leg secure too, I fixed a waist strap, further straps fixed to the horse to secure knees and upper arms. James was secure. He was erect, he had removed the leather cage, I leaned down and grasped his cock, noting it was quite sore. He'd be sore elsewhere soon. I noted too the tip of his cock leaked slippery precum too. It was dripping in a long string. I suspected that might stop soon. I picked up the cane. I swished it several times through the air.

'We will now discuss your time at school, then your parents and finally your lack of ambition. That James neatly breaks the punishment into three. That by my calculation is four strokes each.'

'Yes sir.' A tiny voice muttered a reply. I detected almost a sob. I knew as the punishment progressed; I would be competing with much louder cries of pain as the act of atonement continued.

'You were not a success at school, were you?'

'No sir!'

'Whose fault was that, James?'

'Mine sir.'

'Correct!' I raised the cane and lashed it centrally across both small but plump cheeks. THWACK There was a scream of pain.

'Aaaeee!' then uncontrollable sobbing.

'You were bullied too weren't you.' He continued screaming so I shouted louder. 'WEREN'T YOU!'

'YES SIR!' His cries subsided just slightly.

'Did you take any action to prevent it from happening?'

'No sir!' THWACK! I continued. We covered a surprising amount of ground and there was loud interaction from both sides, despite his screams as the punishment continued. My first central stroke has formed into a thick red welt and another at the highest point I intended going was joined by another on his sweet spot. That created the loudest scream of all. I stood back and looked at my artwork. A central line and two others either side with plenty of room to colour in the white spaces either side. A painting, consisting of many colours but unfortunately for James his would consist of differing shades of the single colour – red! After four strokes we moved onto James's parents, his relationship with them and what he'd done then and since to make them proud. The spaces either side of centre were filling up and I congratulated myself on my accurate spacing. Mind you, I'd had plenty of practice and as James couldn't move the target area, any shortcoming was entirely my fault. After the eighth stroke and just four more left, we got to the subject of ambition. This was the one area where I intended making a real difference. The bullying which I'm sure still took place, would be resolved by him enrolling in a martial arts class, maybe taking up boxing too. That would soon be arranged. His parents could yet see a change in him but not until his attitude changed towards who he was and where he wanted to be in life. We covered this next.

'You have a little blood leaking from the sixth stroke young man, we have just four to go. Let's discuss where you wish your life to go shall we?' There was no reply, so I lashed the cane low, just colouring in a space which needed filling. That woke him up, even though he was hardly sleeping. I knew he was merely surviving.

'Please stop, it hurts so much pleeeze!' He begged, especially the imploring length of the final word.

'Soon, we need to discuss your future, I need a commitment from you that by this time next year you will be a changed man with an assured future, and you can be proud of yourself.' Again, no reply.

THWACK! 'YES SIR!' That got a response I had two more strokes. James's bottom was covered with a pattern of welts. The pattern was uniform. Two central welts, one at the top and another at the bottom of the target area and three in the two spaces between. Ten strokes. There was no room for the others without disturbing the uniform pattern. I decided two diagonals would finish the event perfectly. I moved well to one side. And raising the cane high above my head I lashed it down harder than any preceding stroke. The reaction was incendiary. The scream almost unbearable.

'Well, is that a yes, that you will be a much better, successful, and confident person this time next year? I raised the cane, and he saw me.

'Yes sir!' He cried out in between the screams. I moved position to the opposite side. I planned to strike his buttock downward at an angle this time leaving his buttocks looking like the Union Flag.

'LOUDER.'THWACK!

'YES SIR' 'AAAAEEEE!'

I brought a bowl over with warm water, I squirted disinfectant spray onto several sore looking places. Nothing very serious, just where those last two strokes had left him a little raw and this would take a week or two to heal. I bathed him and his howls gradually subsided. I dried him with a towel and moved onto the next part. I opened the legs of the horse to maximum and looked at the boy's secret area. Looking at his ravaged parted cheeks and seeing that crinkled entry point aroused me further.

'You will learn gradually that is is about pleasure as well as pain James, you've just had the pain, now some pleasure awaits, or so it should be?' I wasn't sure James quite knew what I had in mind, but he wasn't in any position to argue, and it wasn't until I'd removed the cap of the tube of KY gel and squirted a generous amount onto his tight hole, he had a clue. I smeared it around then placing my finger centrally, I inserted my index finger fully until my knuckles touched his raw cheek. I put on a condom after dropping my trousers and underwear, I liberally smeared gel onto my erect cock and lining myself up and gripping his shoulders I fully penetrated him in a single movement which brought out another cry of pain. I started to enjoy him, deep and almost exiting, I increased the force and frequency as I continued and as I felt myself starting to climax, I slowed right down until I finished. As I had pleasured myself, my arm had reached up between and I was masturbating him. I felt his climax reach almost at the same time as my own. He cried out, but this time not in pain! The deed was done and as I pulled out, I saw his own seed smeared in long splashes on the floor below where he lay still restrained. I realised to many this would be the ultimate act of depravity, perversion, but I had no doubt by morning James would view this as the most exciting and satisfying event of his young life.

Epilogue

A year has gone by. So much water has flowed under that bridge which was my life and that of Charles Warden my mentor, often lover, disciplinarian, and most of all loving father figure. I've just moved into my own apartment with Charles's support. We decided together I shouldn't live with him, that might have raised awkward questions with my parents who were nervous about me moving out of the family home anyway.

I remember waking up the following morning after that savage but beautiful evening. The beating was harsh, brutal some might say. I had been a virgin, but I certainly didn't wake up one. Mind you I wasn't when I went to bed either, carried there sobbing by Charles. I was so sore, the spray disinfectant to clean up several areas where those last two diagonal cane strokes had broken already welted skin did nothing to ease my cries, then I felt something pressed against my bottom and with the help of two hands gripping my shoulders, something long and large slid in between my parted cheeks. In and out he pleasured me, then his hand came round and perhaps the most exciting experience of my life then started when he masturbated me, my climax coinciding with his almost to perfection. He took me again later, waking me from a fitful sleep. He needed me, so this time, I knelt open legged for him to take me. I came again too. Then unbelievably, he demanded more of me at dawn and unsurprisingly, when he laid me on my back and worked on my cock, I sprayed his sheets still more. We went for a drive later, walking along a riverbank where I saw the brilliant colours of a kingfisher for the first time, a brilliant flash of blue and green as it stood and stared back defiantly from the safety of an outstretched branch. Going home the following morning was an emotional affair after yet another night of unbridled sex, where Charles enjoyed me yet again.

I am now a different man at the ripe old age of twenty. Charles enrolled me in a club which specialised in martial arts. I was taught judo and surprisingly I took to it naturally. It included weight training, and my body has since bulked up. Boxing was a bit of a shock to the system, but after suffering a bloody nose on my first bout of sparring I enjoyed returning the compliment soon after. I wish I could meet those who had made my life a misery during those awful years starting in my teens. My confidence grew too. I no longer felt the same about computer science either. I am not a nerd, and I didn't really fancy what had become my self-imposed isolation from human interaction I'd needed before. I had the necessary qualifications to study medicine and Charles booked me into medical school. I am thriving. I've met men and women on my course, and I seem popular and attracted to both sexes.

Charles remained my port of call on sexual matters and he kept me trim. He urged me to go on dates which I'm still considering. I do sense my time with Charles in its current form is changing. He said he doesn't see more seasoned young men now. He was so proud of the progress he had made with me, so he plans to mentor other young men who like me a year ago needed similar help to that which I had myself received. Initially I panicked, I felt like a fledgling bird perched on the edge of the nest flapping my wings. Ready to fly but fearing that moment of launch. Charles with the bird theme in his sights said I now had to soar with eagles, my period of nurture, albeit late in life, was at an end. I had to make of life what I could. He explained others awaited his help. I would still meet him but in another context altogether. He explained he had slightly reworked his original Castigatio advert where he had lowered the age specifically to 18-20 years and he'd had several responses. I feared I'd be jealous; he was so known to me and I of him. I was a perfect fit for his cock which I also sucked while he did mine in that perfect position featuring the numbers 6 and 9. Then my growing maturity took hold. Just as my life at been, just before I met Charles Warden, totally barren, such that I had to move on, I had to move on again now and let another shy, introverted young man, bullied, and feeling worthless meet Charles Warden at the Grosvenor Inn and start his process of rehabilitation into a life he wouldn't otherwise know existed. He too would visit Charles as I had done. Hopefully, if Charles had chosen well, picked a young man of substance, he too could grow, just as I had.

The English Vice

By

Sam Evans

Copyright © 2012 Sam Evans 2022

The Meeting

James knew the pub well. He'd often visited in the past but not for a while. He was meeting someone for the first time and the venue had been his suggestion. One-week earlier James had been scanning through an on-line contacts website, one which specialised in male BDSM. James was submissive and scanning through the lists of those seeking a Dom while others sought a sub, he'd spotted one post which seemed to match his needs.

Strict master seeking a male submissive under the age of fifty to receive corporal punishment in the form of caning. No time wasters. Can accommodate.

There was a location plus a box to click to make contact, so James had pressed it and replied.

Dear sir, I saw your advertisement and feel I might be someone who fits the profile of person you seek. I am 46yrs of age, so I meet your age criteria. I feel the need to be punished currently so I hope you may consider me suitable. I live in the same county, and I am able to travel. Sincerely James.

James pressed send and the reply was sent.

Two days went by and there was no response. It seemed time wasters were not restricted to those who replied to advertisements, those who placed then could be too, although why felt beyond him to understand. Perhaps he hadn't explained more, again, perhaps the man hoped for someone far younger despite fitting within the age range he'd set. He browsed through the adverts again but saw no other that fitted his greatest need – location. If true, the man lived in the man lived in the same county, he could accommodate too. He'd often travelled long distances in the past, but this appeared quite local. James shrugged. He'd look again in a few weeks. See if something caught his eye.

He'd arrived home from work after a frustrating day. He'd made tea and seated himself in the kitchen. His laptop was close by, so he powered it up. He checked his mail and noted there was an email waiting to be read using the address he only used for BDSM activity. He couldn't think of any other reason why he'd had a reply so surely it had to be? He clicked the box and there it was. He had received a reply. James opened the email.

Dear James, thank you for your reply. You indeed do fit within the age range I seek. I'll keep this brief as I do not engage in lengthy exchanges. I see you appear to live locally so to ensure we have similar expectations, meet me for lunch at the Admiral Nelson pub in Wheatchester on Friday at 7pm. I will be seated towards the rear of the pub so we can discuss your application in detail with privacy. Ask for Mr Burrage at the bar. They will point me out. Don't be late. Confirm your attendance.

That was it, no name at the sign off. The reply was very direct and to the point of coldness. A shiver went down James's spine. Who was he about to meet and was this possibly a step too far?

Four days later saw James with the pub in question in full view. He'd entered the car park, and one car stood out, a magnificent Bentley Continental GT. There were other cars, two BMW Minis, other German makes too, plus a Jaguar. James realised his rather commonplace Ford Mondeo, a company car, looked rather out of place as he parked and looked over at the expensive line up, wondering if one of those belonged to the man he was about to meet.

Inside, the pub had more of a buzz about the place than he remembered. The bar was large and standing back he stopped and looked to see if a lone man stood out amongst the groups of people meeting up for a night out. None did, but then the bar ran deep, and it had a dog legged extension which left a whole area out of sight. James recalled the instructions in his reply, one was the be punctual which he had been, but the other was to ask the barman to point out a man by name.

'I'm looking for a Mr Burrage, I was told to ask at the bar, and you could direct me to him.' James asked meekly. There was immediate recognition, and the man came round and led the way. James followed with the bar employee turning a corner at the back end of the bar which explained why a man seated alone at a remote table, away from the main area had been out of view. Reaching the table James was introduced and before leaving the pair to make their acquaintances he asked James what he'd like to drink. James normally would have ordered a pint, but seeming his host was drinking what appeared to be a glass of sparking water with slices of lemon floating on its surface he asked for similar. Then he found himself alone with a man who until then was only known to him by a few carefully chosen words.

'Well, don't just stand there gawping, take a seat.' Burrage spoke.

'Yes Sir, I assume you wish me to address you as Sir.' James spoke as he made himself comfortable.

'You assume correctly. I like formality almost as much as I like punctuality. You were on time so if we meet on my terms, I won't need to add a further six strokes of the cane to your bare buttocks!' James was taken back, not only by the vehemence of the reply but by the volume in which it was spoken. James looked in alarm fearing they conversation being overheard. 'You seem alarmed, are you concerned about being judged? If you are, I fear it's rather late? The management of this pub are well aware of my sadistic tastes, and they will have seen many others before you. If this is going to work, I suggest you relax and engage with me. Otherwise leave. Do you understand?' James wanted to explain his needs were very personal, something he wished to remain private and certainly not broadcast across a busy pub. He decided to give a simple reply.

'Yes sir.'

'Good, so let's talk about your reply. I note you are forty-four years of age; it is just within my age criteria. So why do you have a desire to be punished?' Again, the question was put to him in a voice which James wished had been softer, quieter. The large man, James estimated was over six feet in height with greying hair that was slightly too long, then sat back and waited for James to take the stage.

'It's a need Sir, one I've had for a long time. I've never had great self-esteem, and I've never felt I was good enough. I've often felt a failure and I need to be punished for existing, for being inadequate, for being who I am.' James decided that was enough for then. He felt if Burrage needed more he'd soon ask.

'Do you enjoy pain because I certainly get huge enjoyment from inflicting it.' James looked at the man's large hands as he gripped a glass which has long drips of condensation on its outside from the volume of ice on the inside. Just then a waiter appeared and placed a similar glass in front of James who tried to imagine the flat of Burrage's hand smacking his bare bottom or gripping a length of bamboo.

'No sir, not enjoy. I do like to challenge myself to endure pain.' James replied, once the two men were alone again.

'I like that answer. Personally, I think it's strange to enjoy pain, I like stoicism too. I sense I am being challenged. It urges me on to break the person who is providing that challenge.' James could imagine that; he looked into the man's cold blue eyes and saw very little pity. 'When were you last beaten.' Another question.

'About two months ago. I had been visiting an older man, but he has become ill. I fear the arrangement may be ending. I thought I could turn my back on this need, but I find I cannot. This is why I contacted you sir.' James wondered where his would-be tormentor would take the conversation. The next question was no surprise.

'Describe your beating. In detail of course. I like detail.' James sensed Burrage was enjoying the conversation. He wondered if he had an erection even half as much as his own.

'I'd visit a flat in west London. I'd remove my clothes and attend a small bathroom where I'd go through a hygiene ritual before being taken to his kitchen where I'd be shaved. I'd then wait until he was ready for me when I'd be taken to a small room, secured face down over a bed frame and I'd be caned. It was very painful.' James left it there.

'I'd expect It to be. There is a tipping balance between recreational spanking and serious corporal punishment. Would you say you fit into the latter description or the former?' James quickly answered that question.

'Oh, the latter most certainly. I've had this need from my school days but as I've aged the need to continually go one step further has increased. It is a vice, an addiction. Something, no matter how hard I try I cannot walk away from permanently.' Burrage took a sip then continued the conversation.

'You mention the word vice. There is a term for corporal punishment called the English Vice. There is the suggestion that something that started in Victorian times or much earlier, created from the public school system through to the brothels of women who provided a service to the upper classes was exported across the world. The British Empire upon which the sun never set.' He paused to let his words take root. 'You sound just the sort of man I need to challenge but I should warn you, very few who visit me ever return. Does that worry you?' James could imagine but he hadn't been put off yet.

'I think that has to depend on why sir. People can be put off for a host of reasons.' James didn't head for the most obvious cause of non-returning but chose to leave that point open. Burrage shifted position. It felt like a point had been reached where a new direction had to be taken and now was that moment.

'At this point, I will have weighed up the person I'm seated with. I have these meetings to avoid fantasists and time wasters. Once I have decided to continue, I take the meeting to another level which in essence means we leave here and I take you to my home, which is close by. Once there I will give you a little taster of what to expect should you visit me in earnest. How do you feel about that?' It was an interesting question, and one James hadn't expected.

'I wasn't expecting that Sir, but if this is your wish and it helps dispel any notion, I'm wasting your time then I'm more than happy to follow you to your home.' Burrage didn't move. James had expected him to stand and prepare to leave.

'We will travel there in my car which is parked outside. Once the brief visit is over, I will return you here. Approximately three quarters of those who come for this preliminary visit decide to back out. I'm most interested to see if you will add to that list or join the quarter who arrive later for the main event.' James felt his stomach lurch as the cold, matter of fact way the words had arrived. He wondered how much worse a beating from this man could possibly be from that which he'd suffered before. He knew there was only one way to find out.

'Sounds okay to me Sir.' James replied. Not sure he believed the words he'd just spoken. Burrage rose, he walked ahead with purpose and as James passed the bar, the man he'd met originally, leaned forward and beckoned him closer.

'Good luck!' He spoke softly before withdrawing. James didn't reply, watching Burrage walking out through the door. James glanced one final time at the man who returned a knowing smile. A look which suggested he'd made the journey himself.

The Venue

James exited the pub, looking round the carpark to see which of those parked outside Burrage would head for. To his astonishment he headed towards the Bentley.

'Don't just stand there, get in.' Burrage snapped at James who stood in awe looking at a car he knew he could never even think of driving, let alone owning. The seats were made of thick leather and the whole interior had that distinctive smell of opulence. They headed off noiselessly with James now wondering what sort of house the man owned as well as what his description of a 'taster' meant. 'Nervous? You look it and you should be.' Burrage broke the silence after about a mile. They were heading deep into the countryside and for James into the unknown.

'Yes sir, very.' James replied to which there was no reply.

After another mile or so a high wall appeared. Further along were gates which opened remotely. Burrage drove in and in the wing mirror James noticed the gates closed behind them. A short distance further, the car drifted silently to a halt and without further delay Burrage got out, leaving James to follow. Ahead was a large imposing house with steps leading up to a black painted door. The man opened up and stood to one side to allow James to enter.

'Follow me.' Burrage spoke in a commanding voice which didn't sound like a request. They continued until a door was reached which the host opened. James followed. Once inside, James found himself in a large living room. There was comfortable seating centred around a huge television. There was a fireplace too which James could imagine would be useful on a cold night. He cast his mind back to a previous location he'd visited, a first-floor flat which in total could almost fit into the room he was in. 'Please wait here I have to fetch something; I won't be long.' James found himself alone. He saw a wall which featured a large bookcase, it was stuffed with books. James always felt a lot could be said of a person by his taste in books. James walked over and checked the titles and authors. Nothing stood out. Burrage was obviously an educated man, a successful one too. James had expected to see books on the theme of sadomasochism but found none. He could imagine finding such literature somewhere, but it wasn't evident in that room. James walked over to a large expanse of glass which looked out onto gardens he imagined needing a gardener to maintain. He was still immersed in thoughts when the door opened. Burrage had returned and James eyes immediately focused on something he held in his right hand – a cane.

'I promised you a taster, come closer.' James felt his stomach lurch. The cane looked heavy and was a metre long. It looked brutally painful. James moved nearer and finally stood and waited in silence for the large imposing man to continue. 'I now intend giving you six strokes with this cane. I normally require the recipient to strip but as this is just a test, you may remain clothed. Remove your jacket.' James hands were shaking as he undid the single button which held his coat together. He slipped it off, then folding it neatly, he laid it over the arm of a nearby sofa. Burrage walked forward into a clear area which had more than enough space to carry out the act about to take place. 'Step forward.' James obeyed and moved to a position indicated by the cane pointing to a spot about eight feet away. 'Part your legs then bend over and touch the floor, I assume a fit man like you can do this?' James didn't reply. He imagined Burrage preferred actions to words. He walked forward and parted his legs. 'Wider, I like cheeks parted, even more so without clothing.' Burrage barked.

'Yes Sir.' James widened his stance which made the act of touching the floor much easier.

'Let's test your resolve shall we – six strokes!' With that Burrage took a position to James's left and he measured the cane none to gently across his stretched trousers. James felt the sting and winced. Another painful tap followed. There was brief silence in the room before a loud hissing swish and a THWACK which sounded like a pistol shot. There was nothing to feel immediately, something which James was used to, but soon what followed started to burn and sear and increase to a level he was finding hard to cope with. He knew immediately his period of inactivity was catching up - fast. He waited for the second stroke which didn't come any too soon. James knew this sadist was an expert, delaying the caning to ensure every nerve tingling degree of pain would be felt before it was added to

THWACK!

The second stroke caused James to move. His feet shuffled slightly, and he knew he'd uttered a sound. 'You felt that didn't you, just imagine it on your bare buttocks because if you return, that is what awaits you.' Another stroke lashed down and this made James cry out. The caning continued, slowly, painfully and remorselessly. Then, after the final stroke, James was told to stand. 'Loosen your trousers, let's have a look.' Burrage spoke as he took the cane and leaned it against the wall. James loosened his belt and let his trousers drop to his ankles. 'Take them off altogether, let's have a proper inspection.' James stepped out and folding his trousers laid them beside his coat. He stood facing Burrage, now very conscious of his erection pushing out his pants. 'What's this then?' The man remarked, fondling the bulge with his large caressing hands. He gripped James's penis and walking away led him to the sofa where after taking a seat he spoke again. 'Place your hands on your head and keep them there, I wish to see how excited you are.' James stood in front of the man who sat facing an erection he was about to expose. Without further delay Burrage raised his hands either side and pulled on James's underpants forcing the fabric hooked over his penis to work its way past causing the stiff member to bend under the downward action before suddenly springing back upward and coming to a rigid halt. Burrage let go of the garment which then slid to the floor. 'Step of of those and remove your shirt. Let's see you totally stripped.' James obeyed in silence as Burrage watched. 'You are excited aren't you!' The man noted a wet slippery mucus start to form a string at the tip of James's cock. He ran a finger round the open end which caused James to shudder. Burrage then moved it around in a circular action. 'Are you enjoying this?' He then asked.

'Yes sir, very much.' James's voice was shaking with excitement.

'Have you heard of "aftercare", James?' He then asked.

'Yes sir.'

'Have you always received it after punishment?' Another question which James quickly answered.

'Occasionally sir, but generally no.' He answered.

'That is very remiss of those in charge of your welfare. Even six of the best over your trousers deserves my attention and should you decide to return for the full experience you will have aftercare taken to a level in line with the severity of your punishment.' James was getting very aroused especially when Burrage's hand slid deeper between his legs and gently grasped his balls.

'I'd like that sir.' He replied. Burrage picked up on the response.

'You'd like what James, the aftercare or the full experience.' James felt his arousal starting to become a problem he would soon have no control over as his penis hardened and rose considerably to stick out at right angles to where he stood.

'Both Sir.' He replied.

'I hope you are not going to climax; we will certainly go to the next level if you do, I'll let you calm down!' Burrage removed his hand and slowly, gradually, the tension started to ease. 'Turn around.' James turned and exposed his blazing cheeks to his tormentor. Soon, exploring fingers traced the thick red welts which covered both cheeks. 'You took your thrashing well; of course, you had the protection of your trousers and underwear which won't be the case next time.' Burrage then placed his hand high up between James legs, pressing outward in a way which predicted his next request. 'Part your legs wide and bend over.' James knew precisely why, and especially what he was about to display.

'Yes sir.'

'So, I take it when you say "both", you plan to return?' The next question was asked as James felt his buttocks open to expose his anus.

'Yes sir, if you will permit me to.' James answered

'I see no reason to refuse, in fact I rather like what I see James. A red striped bottom which has nice thick raised welts equally placed apart. Obviously, next time the distance between them will be far less, simply because there will be a lot more than six cane strokes applied. Does that worry you?' James mischievously chose to return Burrage's early comment.

'The distance between the stripes or the greater number?' Burrage, grabbed James's dangling balls and squeezed them, causing James to cry out in pain.

'Enough of your lip young man, you know precisely what I meant.' The grip was quickly released to James's relief.

'I fear the caning sir. Who wouldn't?' He quickly replied in case the man staring at his most intimate parts chose to grab him again.

'Surprisingly, I'm looking forward to your visit. Previously, most who did arrive here will have left by now. Some before the caning even started. I noticed you winced when I tapped your bottom a little roughly, but I've had grown men cry out in pain even at that stage. Few reach this point, most will have fled, but you didn't, did you James - why is that?' James felt a finger encircling his anus.

'Oh my god that is so nice.' James murmured in a wavering voice. He looked up between his parted legs and watched as Burrage squeezed clear liquid gel from a tube and he closed his eyes as it was applied deep between his cheeks.

'You didn't answer my question.' Burrage pressed, while his finger deposited slippery gel onto his anus, pushing at its closed centre until it was inserted.

'Because I wanted you to cane me Sir, because I want you to cane me next time too, because I want you to hurt me!' James cried out almost falling backwards in his attempt to force Burrage's finger deeper still.

'The anus has a function James, but I'm only interested in how many people have done this to you and in particular if you've had more than a finger inserted?' Burrage asked as he slowly started to work his finger in and out rhythmically, almost withdrawing completely before pushing slowly back until his knuckles touched the inside of James's soft hairless cheeks.

'Once or twice Sir; the thing is I'm unsure of my sexuality, I've never been in any form of relationship so I can't say if I'm gay or straight.' James was struggling to hold himself together now and his breathing was becoming erratic as pleasure started to overwhelm him. Burrage stopped and patting James's right cheek indicated that the period of pleasure was over.

'I think you are certainly gay; a straight man would have been protesting by now, but you were actually pushing back on my hand.' Burrage paused and rose to his feet. 'As it appears you are planning to return, its best you see exactly what I have in mind, once you see it, you may change your mind.' Burrage then led the way with James following behind feeling very vulnerable due to his nakedness. They left the room and continued to a door further down the hallway. Burrage opened it and stood back to allow James to pass. The void ahead was in total darkness which was transformed by the flick of a light switch. Facing were stairs which led down into what was obviously a cellar area. 'Straight down, obviously what takes place down here requires a huge degree of privacy, like you were earlier, it's not something I advertise to my guests.' James didn't answer but instead, supporting himself by holding the banister railing, he continued down into the bowels of the earth. At the bottom, Burrage slid past and reaching for the handle opened the door. Once again there was darkness facing, but as with entering the expensive Bentley, a familiar smell of leather assaulted his senses. Burrage reached up and put on the light and all was revealed.

'Oh my god!' James couldn't believe his eyes.

'Shocked?' Burrage asked. The room was small, the walls were lined with wood which was stained dark to create a feeling of age. Otherwise, the room was bare, with the only other feature in the room a leather topped bench with straps attached to its stout legs.

'It's very stark and I don't have to spend too long wondering what that is for.' James moved his head towards the main feature which he realised was bolted to the floor.

'You will be strapped to that next time James, as you are – naked.' He let that sink in. Then he raised the stakes. 'Twenty-four strokes of the cane - hard strokes. Almost certainly you will bleed!' Now James knew what had taken place upstairs was nothing to what he would face down in the room where he stood.

'That is harsh Sir.' James replied wondering if he had the resolve to take such a brutal beating.

'It is all that is on offer James, this is the point when the very few who make it to this room, often choose to leave and never return. This is your moment of truth James, but of course you don't have to decide right now; let me leave you down here, to get a feel for the place. Please turn the lights out when you leave, I'll be upstairs. Join me when you are ready.' With that James found himself alone.

Upstairs, James found Burrage seated holding a glass of what was unmistakably whisky when he returned. He wondered how he might be returned to his car or even drive home himself if he joined the man in an extended session.

'Well, are you any closer to making a decision?' Burrage asked as James walked to his clothing and made to dress. The man noticed. 'I like you naked James, come and join me then we can talk more.' James stopped, his erection had returned and that had been noticed too. James walked closer and deliberately stood facing the seated man. He moved closer still so his dripping member was inches from his would-be tormentor's mouth. Burrage placed his glass down and raising his hands gripped both marked cheeks and pulled

James forward taking his wet tip within licking distance. James was uncircumcised so transferring his hands to James's erection Burrage pulled back his foreskin and took the bulbous end into a willing mouth whereupon he sucked while his tongue wiped the end clean. James groaned. James felt his arousal growing and called out in alarm.

'I'm going to cum if you continue.' Burrage ignored the plea, his fingers pulled James's buttocks apart and a finger was inserted into his anus. James felt his climax building and was reaching the point of no return when Burrage stopped just in time.

'It's called edging James, but you will already know that!' With that he sprung to his feet and pushing James over the sofa edge opened his legs wide before kneeling behind. He pulled James buttocks apart and leaning forward brought his mouth down and his tongue in particular sought his sticky anus. James felt so aroused and now a tongue was working in an unexpected area. It went up and down deep along his perineal area before returning. Becoming frustrated, Burrage made a suggestion.

'Do you need to return tonight, why not stay. I can drop you off after breakfast?'

'I'd like that Sir.'

'It's Ralph, James, shall we?' Burrage stood, picking up the whisky and two glasses, he was about to lead the way when he moved over to the other side of the room and picked up the cane. 'I haven't finished with you just yet!' James smiled nervously and followed his host to the stairs.

Morning

The following morning James woke. The sun was shining outside, and he suddenly realised he was naked and not in his own bed. He turned and looked to where Ralph Burrage had slept but that place was empty. He sat up and made to shift position but winced as his sore buttocks scraped the sheet. There was a mirror facing so he rolled over and inspected himself and was shocked to see the raw looking stripes which now covered his bottom. He glanced over at the cane which had been used again the add to the marks he'd had created soon after arrival. In two places that soreness had become more than red stripes and when James looked back at where he'd lain there were thin smears of blood transferred to the bedding. He was sore elsewhere too. His anus burned and looking over to the bottom of the bed he saw the cause, a rather large looking butt plug which had been inserted. His penis was sore too from further oral sex and masturbation. He'd certainly climaxed then, and any further edging was replaced by further demands on his sexual stamina. Just then the door opened, and Ralph appeared in the doorway carrying a huge tray on which a light breakfast had been prepared. He was naked too.

'Good morning young man.' James rather liked the welcome.

'Good morning, Sir.' James decided to maintain the formality.

'I assume you are not rushing off?' He asked.

'No sir, I don't work weekends. If I was at home, I'd be thinking about getting up. I had nothing on today so I'm in your hands really, it's a long walk back to my car if you cast me out into the wilds. I have no idea where this place is.'

'I'm sure I can entertain you for a while longer.' Ralph put the tray down on the bed and noted to position James was in. 'I see you have been inspecting your backside, let's have a look.' James rolled over onto his front. 'I see you have a couple of overlaps.' He sat down and ran his fingers along freshly made welts pressing down on the points where rawness was obvious. James winced. 'I thought I'd give you another six but bare this time. You squealed but otherwise you took it well. Have you thought about returning and possibly when?' James had and he had an announcement to make.

'I will return, I'd like to return but I would like to suggest a change to your plan?' James probed, turning over and sliding up to the headboard where he sat legs apart.

'I hope you are not going to suggest wearing shorts. From now on it is full, hard caning on your bare buttocks, twenty-four strokes. I will not compromise on this.' James took a mug of tea that was offered. Ralph placed the tray between them and sat back too and waited to hear James explain.

'I want it bare; I want it to hurt. I'm not bothered about the number of strokes or being retrained while I'm beaten. The problem is the venue.' He paused but continued before Ralph could react. 'When we first met, you were very cold and formal. I didn't know your name was Ralph, a name I like. You brought a cane up here and you used it just as hard as downstairs. I enjoyed the experience, not necessarily the pain but the ritual of corporal punishment. When I come next time, I want the event to be very real, but I don't want to have to be immersed in the sinister feel of that dungeon downstairs. Flog me here in this room. Please don't ask me to endure that room.' There was brief silence.

'That is no problem, we can do it in here, or there is an adjoining room where I can bring the caning bench. Do you object to being strapped down to that?' James quickly dispelled any concerns over that.

'Not at all. I have been tied spreadeagled to a bed and my wrists and ankles secured so being beaten while restrained is nothing new. If anything, it adds to the event. I feel I am being punished which is the whole point after all.'

'In that case it's settled. One reason for the room downstairs is the noise. The screams and shouting from men under huge duress is something I like to contain but you are more of a grunter and squealer, so I have no fear of anyone passing wondering if murder is being committed behind my walls.'

'I think it will take a couple of weeks for these to heal, would the end of the month be, okay?' James enquired.

'That suits me fine. I have to go abroad next week, I'll be away for a week, I believe the last day of the month is a Friday so come for a very lively weekend.' James picked up a piece of toast which after agreeing the date he started to eat.

After breakfast both men lay together. James quickly formed a new erection despite climaxing three times during the night. Again, his foreskin was pulled back and Ralph sucked him deeply. After climax Ralph suggested they showered together but before that he announced a surprise.

'Have you ever had a herbal enema?' James looked up in surprise.

'No, should I have?' He replied jokingly.

'It's good for you, it certainly wakes you up, fills you with newfound vigour!' Ralph wasn't laughing, he'd finished breakfast and got off the bed. 'Let's have you in a kneeling position so you'll be ready for when I get back.' James realised Ralph was serious, so putting his tea and plate aside he turned over into a kneeling position and stuck his bottom out in readiness. Ralph then left the room, returning with a

286

jug of coloured liquid and a contraption mainly consisting of red coloured rubber tubing. 'Part your legs and get your head down.' He commanded. James obeyed, his cheeks parting exposing his anus which Ralph then liberally smeared with gel.

'I can't believe I'm actually letting you do this, what's in that liquid?' James enquired.

'This enema is two litres of warm water which is infused with camomile tea, but you can infuse crushed garlic, coffee, even yogurt.' James laughed.

'Yogurt! Now you are joking!' Ralph assured James he most certainly was not before smearing his anus with gel and pushing in the bulbous end of a section of smooth white tubing.

'I most certainly am not joking, are you ready?' James looked back at Ralph and nodded to which his hand squeezed a soft ball like section which started to pump liquid inside him.

'Oh god, that feels amazing, how much do you plan to insert?' James asked as the ball pump was squeezed again.

'The full two litres, then we will carefully transfer you to the toilet, you'll think you can hold it in, but nature and gravity will ensure you cannot, no matter how hard you try.' Another squeeze and a slightly uncomfortable bloated feeling started to grow. Ralph started to massage James's abdomen as it started to fill the pumping continued until the full two litres had disappeared. Ralph took a wad of tissue and after carefully withdrawing the tube he pressed the pad against James's anus before taking his hand and encouraging him to press down. 'Let's get you to the toilet, we haven't got long believe me!'

Later, now fully dressed James sat in a spacious kitchen drinking coffee. Clean, inside and out, James realised it would soon be time to leave. It had been a remarkable twelve hours. He looked at the clock realising this time the previous evening he'd never met the man seated opposite. Now, all those hours later he knew his body, his most private and personal parts were known to a man he now knew as Ralph. As he sat, he could still feel the soreness from the thrashing he'd received, knowing also in a couple of weeks he'd return for more and a similar experience of extras too. James sipped the strong dark liquid and had a question.

'Why do you enjoy inflicting pain?' It was a simple question he knew couldn't be answered by a simple yes or no.' He looked at a sadist and waited.

'Why did you enjoy me inflicting pain?' James wondered if he'd avoid answering it and had almost predicted the reply.

'Sorry, that is not fair, I've already explained because you asked me that question in the pub. I expected more.' James took a risk, a submissive criticising his Dom.

'I only enjoy one aspect of sadism, caning. I like the philosophy behind it. A plant, grown in a far-off land which has been carefully selected for someone like me to inflict pain. I enjoy it's feel, it's weight and flexibility. When I use it, I like the sound it makes, the swish and especially the sound as it strikes soft fleshy buttocks. I then like to stand back and witness the reaction from the person I have struck, to not only see and hear their reaction but witness the damage it has caused. I really enjoyed caning you James because you wanted me to hurt you, and you fought back with a resolve to not let me win. It then becomes a competition. I try harder and you in turn fight harder too. I'm looking forward to the next round where I'll certainly put your resolve to the test.' James had another question.

'Have you been caned, placed on the receiving end of what you dish out?' Ralph smiled.

'I was at school once or twice. In general, I was a good boy. So, my only contact with school discipline was witnessing its use at my school in the showers after PE.' He left it there.

'So, your only experience of pain infliction is one way?' Ralph nodded, looking back and wondering where the conversation was heading.

'Of course but isn't that the case with all sadists. They enjoy hurting others, not being hurt themselves?' James smiled. He finished his coffee and remained silent. Ralph had a question now. 'Are you suggesting I should be caned? You are not offering to carry it out, are you?' James wasn't sure how to reply.

'I hadn't until you put the idea into my head, but maybe you need to find yourself strapped down to your bench and have a dozen strokes across your bare arse. You will then know how painful it is.' Ralph frowned.

'You are offering aren't you, is the reason for me being under restraint a sense you feel I couldn't take a beating such as I administer?' James wasn't sure if Ralph was going to volunteer and kept his reply as neutral as possible.

'I'm not offering at all. I merely asked you a question. As for being restrained, your choices become rather limited once the beating starts. You are then at the mercy of another person who has the power to carry out the sentence or decide to stop. It's a huge psychological power exchange. I think you should consider it sometime and yes; I will gladly cane you, but only on condition you are strapped down and I am in control. I think you'd learn a lot about yourself.' The conversation ended at that point and James prepared to leave.

An hour later James entered his home and closed the door. He'd left the evening before, filled with trepidation and nervous anticipation. Now, after a huge high, the opposite feeling had taken over, a complete anti-climax. He went to his bedroom, deciding to change into more casual clothing. He stripped and turned, shocked at the dark stripes which covered his buttocks entirely. Just then the phone rang. He sat on the bed and answered it.

'As you kindly gave me your phone number, I thought I'd ring you and check you got home safely?' Ralph's distinctive voice was at the other end of the line.

'Yes, thank you, in fact I was just admiring the marks on my bottom!' Ralph laughed.

'It'll have a distinctly different pattern next time James. Don't they say these days, less is more? I think I can definitely turn that expression on its head, more will definitely be more!' James couldn't even start to imagine how his rear end would look after double the amount of caning at Ralph Burrage's hands.

'You are a sadist Ralph, but I'm not complaining. I really enjoyed the experience and the next two weeks won't come quickly enough.' Ralph changed the subject.

'I will submit to you James. Surprisingly, I've long thought about my position, but I didn't wish to submit to a stranger. I don't think we should mix the roles next time, let's enjoy that together in a traditional sense, but maybe the following week you drop by and give me what you feel I deserve. My only fear is I prove I'm a coward and I never can revert back to my role as the dominant figure I know you need in your life.' James let that remark sink in before he replied.

'A sadist cannot be a masochist, Ralph. Whether you take the beating well or not is immaterial. I'll admire you for finding out how painful the beatings are you inflict. I don't wish to be a Dom Ralph, I'm a submissive man and we make this work perfectly because we get on, I feel I'm your friend

290

already and I feel a huge sense of anti-climax now it's over and we have parted. I just think, finding out will add to what you do, perhaps understand limits a little more because you have been there. I suspect you may feel the need for occasional refreshers, just to keep the balance in perfect equilibrium.' James stopped, fearing he was going too far.

'I'm going to miss you too. Take care and enjoy your day.'

The Return

The next two weeks dragged by. Each morning before work, James checked his buttocks in a mirror and saw a gradual reduction in markings. By the middle of the second week only the faintest evidence remained of the beating he had sustained. His thoughts now focussed only on the next visit which was on the evening of the following day. His work as a graphic designer had suffered as the date of his arrival neared and as a result, he decided to take the Friday off, realising his mind would be elsewhere most of the day.

He had an email from Ralph waiting in his email inbox when he woke the following morning. He was returning later that day and suggested James came earlier for dinner. He lay in bed a while thinking about later, his arrival, how Ralph would react, his mood and in particular the caning he'd receive and most of all where it would be carried out. As always, prior to a visit, doubt started to grow, the biggest of which was his pain endurance. James always feared next time would be different to last time. Okay he'd had doubts last time too and these had proven to be unfounded, but what if next time something radical had changed and when that first stroke had lashed his bared buttocks, and the pain was at a level he'd never experienced before? What then, strapped down and totally helpless. James looked at his penis, erect and hard, even thinking about the worst possible scenario was arousing him. He knew that helped because the more aroused he became the greater his need to be caned grew too. Then another thought. What if having secured him to the punishment frame, now hopefully deployed in the bedroom or nearby, Ralph masturbated him to a climax first. That when he picked up the cane and took position behind him, James knew he was spent for the foreseeable future, or certainly during the period where two dozen indescribably painful strokes of his vicious cane rained down on his exposed naked bottom. James looked at his cock, expecting that fear to cause his ardour to drain away and become a soft limp sausage, but it hadn't. If anything, he was harder, stiffer and leaking fluid. He was up for the task and despite his fears, looking forward to the visit. Normally he'd masturbate and let his mind imagine the scene arousing him, that he'd grab some tissue just in time to catch his climax which would leave him satisfied and thinking about anything but what had previously excited him so much.

James showered, he dressed in some old clothes and carried out chores he'd put off for weeks. He had laundry to wash and then iron. He had a light breakfast, unable to eat much due to a familiar sensation in the pit of his stomach, that of the opposing sensations of excitement and trepidation. As always, the hours dragged by, he knew what he was going to do later was weird and irrational, the act of someone not quite right in the head, being driven by sexual need. After lunch he went out, deciding to go into town, then returning in time to shower again and put on more suitable clothing. He smiled as he sat outside a high street coffee shop. He watched people going about their business and wondered how many of those had similar plans to his own. He often watched people, looking at their clothing covered bottoms and wondered how many showed markings from a recent spanking or perhaps as in his own case something far worse. He wondered if there was a common tell, some feature or behaviour which was a giveaway. A young woman walked past wearing a pair of indecent shorts, her displayed cheeks certainly needed a spanking but hers where clear, white and totally unblemished. James then thought of his desperation before having met Ralph, who was playing on his mind far more now. Two weeks earlier he would have cut some thin rods from a nearby apple tree and lying curled and naked on his bed he would have self-flagellated, whipped himself until he drew blood. But wasn't that self-defeating, as the pain grew or the damage sustained became a problem, wasn't he in control? Wasn't he the person who decided when enough was enough? Wasn't that the difference now because he had someone who was removing that choice, taking away that decision when to stop and replacing it with his own? Wasn't that the real buzz, the part James loved and hated equally but yearned for all the same?

Getting out of the shower later, James walked to the full-length mirror and gave his buttocks one final inspection. Yes, he could still see the faintest of traces from his last beating and there were still two slight blemishes from where blood had been drawn but he knew these showed up more when his skin was wet and once, he was dry and settled into clothing those marks would fade still more. He shaved and looked down at his pubic area where he was becoming shaggier. He wondered about taking some cream to that place and turning up smooth, but as Ralph hadn't complained or given instructions as to how he should attend he left it and now pondered over what underwear he should choose. As he went through his drawer, deciding what to put on and selecting a further pair for the following day, he even imagined going without, surprising Ralph as his trousers dropped to his ankles? Deciding he knew nothing about his newfound friend or his ability to cope with the unexpected he found a tight pair of Calvin Klein full underpants, something Ralph would have to pull right down if he wanted to see his bare bottom.

After leaving and climbing into his car, James let the satnav take him the fifty or so miles to Ralph's spacious home. He'd made similar journeys before and like this one he was growing more nervous as the miles ticked by and his destination grew nearer. This time the stakes seemed greater. Of course, he was nervous about the promised twenty-four stroke thrashing he'd receive but there was more this time. Unlike before, there was promised intimacy, something he'd always either shied away from or found missing in earlier activities with Dom's he visited. The worst were those who were cold and sadistic, carried out the thrashing and then had shown him the door. Some wanted more than James had permitted which always made him wary of being restrained. Ralph was different, he not only wanted to be pushed to his limit and even beyond, but he loved what he'd done to arouse him sexually and he sensed this time it would be far more

The high walls came into view a quarter of a mile away. There was something both comforting, yet sinister about being enclosed. The feeling of security knowing what was about to happen between two consenting adults would not be witnessed but balanced by the fear of being trapped, escaping the house but knowing he was still unable to escape. He entered through gates which opened automatically as he turned in and as before closed behind him. He sensed his arrival was being monitored. James pulled up and stopped, he looked up at the house he was about to enter with certainty no plans to flee, in fact he couldn't wait to enter and get on with whatever proceedings his awaiting host had planned. He got out, not bothering to lock up he walked up the few steps which led to Ralph's front door which opened before he had a chance to announce his arrival.

'Good evening, James, do come inside, so you found me then.' Ralph was at the door, seemingly in wait behind it ready to welcome his guest. Gone was the rather formal, even severe clothing he'd worn at the pub the first time. Now he was in light casual trousers and an open necked shirt. He wore so socks on bare feet which were fitted into a pair of brown slip-on shoes. He stepped back, allowing James to pass and after closing the front door Ralph leaned in and gently kissed him on the lips while his right hand went due south and felt the growing bulge in his trousers. 'It looks like you are already having naughty thoughts, and we haven't even started the evenings activities.' He was closer still now and his other hand went around the back and caressed his buttocks. 'I trust these are pristine, I do like a blank canvas to work on.' The hand now went deeper and grasping one cheek squeezed it rather harder. 'You have a beautiful bottom and I'm looking to reacquaint myself with its features after we have eaten. I hope you are as hungry as I am?' It was a question which was becoming increasingly hard to answer. Had Ralph suggested skipping food and getting on with more carnal pleasures he would have jumped at the idea, but any further escalation was curtailed with a sharp smack on both cheeks and then separation. 'I'm sure you'd like a drink, shall we?' Ralph walked away, his own bottom plump and full with James viewing it, wondering if he'd ever thrash it as the previous conversation had suggested.

They entered the same room as before, but instead of James being directed towards clear space to taste the cane he followed Ralph to a large sofa where he was invited to sit down. 'An aperitif?' Ralph asked.

'A sherry would be nice, an Amontillado would be great if you have one, nice and dry.' James replied as he sat and crossed his legs.

'My exact choice too.' He replied heading for a small cocktail cabinet where we spent a minute pouring two drinks into appropriate glasses before returning and placing himself enough distance away from James to sit around facing him but still close enough to lean forward and place a hand halfway up his thigh. 'I'm very tactile as you can see, I trust you don't mind a rather obvious approach?' James smiled.

'I sense your approach is nothing to what it will be like later, so of course I don't mind; I wouldn't be here otherwise.' Ralph laughed gently.

'Oh, you have no idea what I have lined up for this evening's entertainment, but after we have eaten, which reminds me I must check. I'd say we are about thirty minutes away from retiring to the dining area. I'll be back, feel free to explore.' With that Ralph stood, but not before his hand slid all the way up until it touched James's full erection which was squeezed gently. 'I'm looking forward to me own exploration, but not just yet.'

Alone, James stood. He'd already viewed Ralph's book collection which unusually told him nothing about the man who owned it. There were no photographs either, photos of himself past or present, a photo perhaps of parents long deceased. James wondered if Ralph's invitation to explore meant he was free to leave the room and go further, enter through closed doors and see beyond their exterior. He picked up the glass and decided to look upstairs, in particular to see if his choice of venue to be severely caned later was his preferred option. At the top of the stairs there were numerous rooms, he knew he wouldn't have long and his absence would soon be noted and even possibly in alarm in case Ralph's idea of exploration had been solely to the room he had left, would then come looking for him. James chose the one room he wanted to check and on opening it he found

297

to his horror there was no caning frame on show. His heart sank as he realised the awful cold dungeon in the basement was where the act was to be carried out. Then he remembered Ralph mentioning an adjacent room which he sensed was further along the corridor. He left the bedroom, closing the door as he'd found it. Moving along to a door the shortest distance away he opened that and there, centrally placed was the wooden bench with its padded top. There was a table upon which lay an assortment of tubes containing unknown substances, even a small container which he sensed contained salt. There was a lemon sliced too. It didn't take James long to realise the significance of both, together with an assortment of smooth, round pointed objects with only one purpose, that of insertion. There was a book too, which James picked up and opened. There were photographs inside which turned him cold. Numerous buttocks marked and bloody. Previous victims of Ralph Burrage's sadism.

'You found it then?' A voice from behind startled James out of his fascination as he leafed through the pages of raw savagery. James closed and returned the book and faced Ralph who stood facing him. 'When I said feel free to explore, I meant anywhere. So, I'm not surprised you came up here and you didn't go downstairs to see if the bench was still there.' James didn't reply immediately but when he did, he kept it brief.

'Thank you, that was appreciated.' Ralph quickly responded.

'The thrashing will hurt just as much and as you can see from the photographs; I have no intention of taking it easy.' James looked at the two items lying on a plate, wondering if he should ask why they were there. He cast his mind back to the rawness of numerous male buttocks and tried to imagine their use on top of the brutal flogging each had received.

'Dinner is served James. This can wait until we have eaten.'

Downstairs, James was seated when Ralph appeared with dinner which he announced with a flourish was garlic chicken cooked in a rich white wine sauce to which cream had been added. It was served with rice and a selection of vegetables. Ralph opened a bottle of chilled Chablis and filled James's glass. For the next minute there was silence before James spoke.

'Where did you learn to cook like this?' He asked.

'Well, I could say I attended a French cookery school in London where I was taught by an internationally renowned chef, or I could just tell the truth and say I bought a cook-in-sauce from Waitrose.' James smiled.

'So, I've been under the impression my host was a gourmet chef when all the time you just put chicken in a casserole dish and poured over the sauce. You'll tell me next the rice was boil-in-the-bag and the vegetables were pre packed and just needed dropping into boiling water?' Ralph pointed his fork at James in mild censure.

'Are you being one of those food snobs and you'll tell me you could tell the difference?' James took a further mouthful of food which he swallowed before speaking.

'So, you normally avoid cooking at all costs?'

'I eat out a lot, but I cook simple meals, you?' Ralph replied.

'Very much like yourself.' James was keen to discuss something far more important than their limited culinary skills. 'Did you leave that album of photos on view just for my benefit, can I expect my bloodied buttocks to be added?' James asked directly.

'I wanted you to see them yes, so you know what to expect, as for photos, no.' He paused but before James could ask him why not he explained. 'I like you, James. I sense you like me too, very few will even try to understand a sadomasochistic relationship, but you are here knowing full well what we will be doing soon and when it is all over, I'm sure there will be no regrets on either side and we will do it again in the fullness of time. They were fleeting trophies which if things go to plan, I will destroy. I will have no need of a photographic memory of your buttocks after I have thrashed them because I know I will frequently see them marked and otherwise.' He stopped and tossed the ball into James's court, waiting to see how he responded.

'The salt and slices of lemon, I assume you weren't planning those for shots of whisky or vodka?' James smiled and waited.

'You don't miss much do you, you didn't mention the stiff little brush next to those items either. Yes, I will squeeze those slices, just a teaspoon full of juice mixed with salt to form a thick paste and I will brush that into all your rawest spots. If the caning doesn't make you scream this will.' James shook his head.

'You have a vivid imagination to match your sadism Ralph, you really do think you are going to break me don't you.' Ralph nodded his head slowly.

'Yes, James I do, the thing is it won't be the pain which will break you, although it will certainly add to the words, I will speak softly in your ear which will have you crying like a baby. But brushing your raw spots is not just about pain.' James had a confused look on his face. 'Let me explain, you've no doubt heard the term; to rub salt into the wound, this means often to make matters worse. However, salt has been a long-used disinfectant to prevent infection. It uses the

300

principle of osmosis, but let's not get into detail, but it also hurts as does the citric acid. I will wash it off after you have suffered for 30 mins standing in the corner with your hands on your head. I will be standing behind you with a heavy strap should your hands move from their placement. Now that really will hurt – lemon cheesecake, courtesy of Marks and Spencer?' Ralph curtailed the conversation and stood to start clearing the table.

James found himself alone while Ralph left the room to fetch the sweet, he promised coffee too. He thought back to a remark earlier "I will speak softly in your ear which will have you crying like a baby." He seemed pretty sure of the outcome of what words would achieve that and this created a sudden feeling of nervousness. After a minute or two Ralph reappeared with a tray upon which we're two plates of cheesecake, a carafe of coffee with cups and saucers, while under his arm was a long round, brown paper covered tube.

'I have a present for you James – open it.' Ralph handed over the parcel over then placed the tray down.

'Do I guess what it contains, it's rather obvious.' James reacted lifting the parcel which had little weight.

'That obvious, yes?' Ralph replied as he pressed down the carafe plunger and laid out the cups ready for filling. James didn't reply, but instead picked at the end of the parcel until it opened before tipping it up and allowing the contents to slide out. James grabbed the handle end of a new cane one metre long. It was as round as a finger.' James felt a shiver run down his spine. 'I thought you deserved your own special cane, in fact it should have your name etched on its side, just for your exclusive use. How do you take your coffee?' James couldn't believe the casual nature of the conversation. It felt like they could have been discussing anything rather than the serious nature of what lay ahead as soon as food was consumed.

'Milk and no sugar please Ralph.' James decided to join in the spirit too as he searched and indeed found his name. Ralph was almost through his sweet and James put the cane down and caught up. Coffee was poured and soon consumed, and a period of silence fell over the room while both men sat looking at each other with each waiting for the other to make the first move. Ralph broke the silence.

'I noticed you were unshaven last time; have you removed your pubic hair or shaved your hairy arse?' Ralph asked.

'No sir, you never specified whether or not you wished me to, so I left things as they were.' James replied wondering how his host would respond.

'Perfect, because I plan to shave you front and back, I'm going to treat you as an errant schoolboy at an age where hairiness would not have been an issue, so I think it's time to conclude events down here and reconvene upstairs. So, if you are finished, leave me to clear things away and load the dishwasher and I'll see you in the punishment room. Strip and find a convenient corner, stand against the wall and put your hands on your head and wait for my arrival – go.' James stood, leaving the cane lying on the table.

'Yes sir.' He left with Ralph standing watching him intently until he disappeared from sight.

Corporal Punishment

James entered the room with its overpowering scent of leather he knew came from the bench at its centre. He knew very soon he'd be secured to it and thrashed with the cane he'd been holding minutes earlier. He wasn't sure how much time he'd be given to strip, so he didn't delay. He undid his shirt and slipped out of it, neatly folding it and placing it on a nearby chair. He removed his shoes and socks, then undoing the belt to his trousers he soon found himself just wearing a pair of Y fronts. The instruction was to strip, so he removed these too. As always, he felt vulnerable, but also excited mixed with a degree of fear. The thought of finding himself unable to take the promised beating always played on his mind, but even so he found a corner in which to stand, moved towards it and placed himself there, finally putting his hands on his head as he'd been told to do.

He waited several minutes before the door opened and Ralph entered. He carried a tray of shaving equipment which he placed on a table then coming closer he crouched down to inspect James buttocks. 'Open your legs.' He asked softly but firmly. James obeyed. Fingers then pulled his cheeks apart, then those same fingers inspected their plump contours. 'You have healed well, just a couple of blemishes. Turn around, let's see if you are excited.' Ralph was teasing, knowing full well what he'd find when he checked. 'Oh! You are an excited boy, it must be the thought of the caning you are about to receive, but before that we must deal with this!' He tugged at the thatch of pubic hair which encircled James erect penis. Ralph stood and taking a large towel from a nearby drawer he laid it over the bench. 'Up you get, let's deal with the business end first, kneel on the bench.' James found it ungainly to clamber up, but he did. He parted his knees as far as he could then lowered his head until it rested on the leather top. James heard the familiar sound of soapy foam being squirted, then he shivered as this was transferred between his cheeks and deeper down along his perennial area up to his scrotum. More foam was spread to both cheeks. It felt cold, but this didn't affect his erection which was stronger than ever. 'I'm going to treat you as an errant schoolboy James, boys of that age are not hairy and besides your skin will be softer so the marks I leave will show their redness much earlier too.' James just closed his eyes and Ralph got to work with the razor. For the next few minutes, the implement found its way into every nook and cranny with frequent washings in a bowl of warm water which now showed unwanted hair floating on its surface. Then another towel was used to wipe the shaved area clear of soap. A single smack indicated work was complete and the remaining side was next for treatment. 'Let's have you on your back, this side will need more work.' With that James shuffled round until he found himself looking up at the ceiling.

'I was going to shave Sir, but I wasn't sure you'd approve.' James spoke for the first time since Ralph's arrival.

'You'd have been correct too. This is my job, and I'd have been annoyed to find you'd made such a decision without my agreement. You'd have been given extra punishment for that.' James replied simply and meekly.

'Yes Sir.' Foam was applied to the main bush of hair around the stem of James's penis which remained erect. This soon came off in large tufts. More was then applied to his scrotum which was carefully shaved. Next, gripping his penis firmly Ralph added more foam and cleared the whole area until James was as smooth as the day he was born. Ralph then slowly started to masturbate James, first pulling his skin back before placing his penis in his mouth, teasing the wet tip with his tongue and sucking hard. 'Please sir, you are making me cum!' James called out frantically before Ralph stopped.

'In that case you'd better make sure you control yourself otherwise you will be caned with a limp cock, and you certainly won't like that!' James blanched at that thought. Ralph continued. 'We will try a really cold caning one day, I'll put a wet towel in the freezer and wrap it round your bare bottom for thirty minutes then gave your bottom a stiff caning - you'll certainly feel that!' James shivered at that prospect; his buttocks felt cold enough now. 'Off you get, I forgot I left the cane downstairs, so go and fetch it while I clear away your hairy mess!' A sharp slap across both cheeks got James moving as he clambered down.

James walked naked down towards the stairs. It felt so decadent walking through Ralph's home in total exposure, especially as he was heading off the fetch an implement which would soon be used to inflict pain – on him. He reached the hallway and glanced at the front door. He wondered how many other men had walked through that door; how many bare feet had walked the same strip of expensive carpet. James shrugged, he didn't care, he knew the man upstairs liked him and he was in vogue, so nothing else really mattered. The cane lay on the table where he'd placed it. The wrapping had been cleared away which put a lie to the suggestion the exclusion of the cane was not an oversight but a deliberate act. James was always meant to fetch the cane and bring it back for Ralph's use.

Ralph was waiting as James returned, handing the cane to him immediately on entering the room. Ralph placed the cane down beside the study frame which James looked at with trepidation as it now featured large in his thinking. He looked at the attached straps he knew would soon secure him, knowing that once held in place he'd have to take the severe caning Ralph had promised.

'Well James, when you first met me in the pub everything was always going to lead to this moment. I notice your erection has drooped so I imagine the significance of this moment is not lost on you. But I feel I should offer you one final chance to stop this, I like you James and it won't affect our friendship. If at this late hour you wish to call a halt to proceedings, get dressed and return to more comfortable surroundings you can choose that option. I need to know but your decision has to be final because once you are strapped down you will receive twenty-four of the hardest cane strokes you will have ever been given, that is of course unless you choose to return for more. So, what is it to be?' James knew he now had a choice to make. His gremlins, those tiny but loud voices which spoke in each ear were prominent now. "Don't, it's way too much, leave it, you don't have to put yourself through this, it's insane. You won't be able to cope! He'll rub salt and lemon juice into your bloody welts! The man is a sadist on steroids – what if he keeps going? You don't know him – walk away!" Another opposing voice took a different view. "Go for it, you'll never forgive yourself! You've never walked away, imagine how you'll feel sitting downstairs, or more likely making excuses to leave, if you don't carry this through, endure it and feel proud when it's over. Remember those quoted words *I hate the thought of being caned, but I'd hate even more the thought of not having been caned!* Do you really want to face the prospect of walking away, the thought of wimping out and not having been caned? You can, YOU MUST!

'I wish to proceed Sir. I've come this far and self-flagellation, which is what I've had to resort to, is a very lonely act. I need the warmth and comfort of company afterwards and I cannot achieve that alone. I'm ready for your punishment.' Ralph smiled and with his right arm creating the invitation he replied.

'In that case, please place yourself over the frame.' James stepped forward and lay over the top, whereupon Ralph pulled him forward so his feet were clear of the floor. Starting at his ankles he secured each to the stout rear supports, pulling his legs apart to match the stance of the frame itself. He then secured two thigh straps pulling them tight to prevent any movement whatsoever. He did likewise at the front-end, tightening straps round his wrists and upper arms. Two further straps, almost unnecessarily, secured his torso also. James was held in place and he was now fully committed to the task ahead regardless of choice. Ralph wasn't finished. He took the album of photos James had viewed earlier and placed them on the floor in full view, he then lay the cane on the floor to add to the fear now creeping into his being. 'I now plan to leave you for thirty minutes James to think through what you've chosen to do. I have a surprise, I recorded the sounds from one of those thrashings, the young man didn't take it well as you're about to find out. Ralph then left the room, with the hideous screaming of a man at the end of his endurance filling it with sound.

James couldn't believe the sadistic invention of Ralph Burrage. He was staring down at pictures of bleeding, torn skin. He was hearing screams he hoped he wouldn't be making himself. He wanted to walk away, to turn his back. Maybe the self-flagellation wasn't so bad after all. Then the sound stopped. He realised this was all part of the process of mental torture. To see and hear what was soon to happen to him, then silence! Wasn't that even worse; to know the clock was now counting down and this deliberate, interminable wait was all part of the plan to break him. "I will speak softly in your ear which will have you crying like a baby." Hadn't that started already, he was starting to feel his emotions rising and he was trapped, unable to move an inch. He started to panic. What if he didn't return, that he was to be left overnight, the following day. He'd wet and foul himself. What if Ralph had a stroke? A heart attack or had fallen down the stairs – what then.

'Ralph, are you there?' He called out then repeating it louder still. He closed his eyes and felt tears squeeze out and roll down his face, one tear dripping onto the photo below. The sudden rush of cold air indicated someone had entered the room. 'Is that you Ralph?' James called out in panic.

'Who on earth did you imagine it would be other than me.' He walked around and looked down into James's tear-filled eyes. I see you have been crying, I said I'd break you, there will be plenty more believe me.' Ralph then leaned down and fitted a blindfold. 'This isn't a visual experience, James; this is all about what you hear and especially what you feel.' James really felt panic now. He struggled against his bonds and soon found it was a fruitless talk.

'You didn't mention blindfolds, I'm not sure I want to do this!' James spoke in a nervous voice filled with emotion.

'You made your choice and for the next hour you will atone. You will be broken piece by piece and wish you'd never been born. His words were backed up by the sound of a cane being sharply swished through the air which ended without striking bare flesh. 'So, let's make a start. First, tell me why you answered my advert, what did you hope the achieve?' This wasn't going quite as James had expected but he imagined Ralph had a plan.

.

'To meet a strict but friendly dominant man. Not a woman. I knew one once, but she died and despite her saying I shouldn't attempt to replace her, I found that was impossible, so it had to be a man.' James wasn't sure whether or not that was a satisfactory reply.

'So, does that mean only a man can satisfy your total needs or was it just impossible to replace her?' Ralph followed up.

'Nobody could replace her, male or female.' James replied wondering where this was going and uncertain how long the discussion would continue before his caning started.

'Tell me how you would describe yourself as a pupil at school?' The question put to him had just radically changed direction.

'It's hard to say, it was a long time ago Sir.' James replied without realising he was about to have one uncertainty removed. There was a loud swish and THWACK! Suddenly his lower end exploded in an unexpected sea of pain. 'Aaahh!' James called out, completely caught off balance.

'One thing you are going to learn James is when I ask a question I expect an answer – right!'

'Yes Sir, sorry sir!' James called out feeling disoriented by his loss of visual perspective.

'If I didn't have questions to ask, I'd plug your ears too, so you wouldn't hear a thing either, just feel the pain. Let's try again. Describe the sort of boy you were at school, tough, weak, strong, a weakling? A wimp!' He followed the question with another lashing stroke which made James cry out.

'I wasn't strong sir, I was a coward, yes, I was a wimp!' James replied quickly, he had desperation in his voice now.

'Your father didn't think much of you did he which is why you are really here isn't it James!' A terrible memory was lingering now like a dark cloud, what did Ralph know, if he knew more, how did he find out.

'I don't know what you mean sir, I'm not sure how to answer the question.' Two more strokes landed which had James crying out in pain.

'You really are your own worst enemy. I found out you had a major issue with your father just after your sixteenth birthday. You should be careful what you write down, what you share with others because it can return and bite your arse!' James knew where the conversation was heading now.

'I was told I was a failure, that I'd never be any good!' James's voice broke with emotion as he recalled his humiliation.

'It's not nice to feel worthless, is it?' Ralph pressed.

'I am worthless, why do you think I'm here!' James's admission created silence, only occasionally broken by the sound of him weeping.

'Four strokes and I have you in tears, you didn't expect that did you?' There was only one answer he could give because it had never happened before.

'No sir, but you've got inside my head, I've never felt these emotions before.' Ralph ran his fingers along the four thick raised welts which ran across the centre of both buttocks.

'I'm now going to give you six strokes, that will take you nearly halfway, we haven't even started to open your floodgates.' James started to get upset at the thought as panic replaced any degree of stoicism. He screamed when the first stroke landed, followed by five more at regular intervals. At the end James was emitting one continuous howl.

'I am beginning to wish I'd done this downstairs where most of those who have preceded you have screamed the place down too. Let's try this instead.' Ralph went to the pile of clothing and selecting the folded pair of underpants, stuffed them into James's mouth which reduced the sound level considerably. 'Now we cannot converse which means I just have to flog you instead.' Ralph then walked back and taking the cane firmly in his hand continued the beating with eight further strokes leaving just six more. He waited until the howling had reduced to a whimper then removed the garment from between James gripped teeth. 'You are a naughty boy at heart aren't you, that's why you are here isn't it?' He asked softly stroking James's hair with affection.

'Yes sir!' James decided just to give a simple reply.

'Your bottom is bleeding, the question on my mind is whether to finish the caning or not. What would you like me to do?' James, thought of the obvious, then decided against it.

'I'm hardly in a position to make that choice Sir. That is for you to decide.' Ralph went to the table and selected a tube. He squeezed a short length of clear substance which he transferred to James's anus. He then inserted a finger which caused a sudden relaxation.

'No matter how hard I cane a naughty boy they all like this!' He slowly started to pump his finger in and out. Then with his other hand he sought James's penis which was already becoming erect.

'You are supposed to be concentrating on your shortcomings as a man, for which you are being severely caned, so why are you getting aroused?' James wasn't sure how to reply. Should he admit to his growing enjoyment, which was becoming more evident as time progressed, or avoid the truth and suggest confusion. He knew Ralph would spot a lie.

311

'Because despite what you did, I cannot help myself when you do what you are doing.' He replied.

'Correct answer, so as a result I am going to defer the promised remaining strokes and release you.' Ralph unstrapped his victim, leaving James lying over the bench. 'Stay in position for a minute or so and when you feel you are ready, join me in the bedroom for your aftercare.' James watched as Ralph walked out and left him alone with his thoughts.

Aftercare

Ralph was naked and patiently waiting on James's arrival in the bedroom. A towel was laid out on the bed which he laid across face down. Ralph offered him a glass of chilled wine which was received gratefully by him rolling over onto his side and sitting up.

'Are you all right, I'm beginning to regret upsetting you so much. That emotional release seemed a long time coming.' James nodded.

'It has been Ralph, pretty much thirty years in the making. I've never been that upset in my life before.' James replied softly. 'It's strange, in a very odd way, it wasn't the beating which caused that emotional meltdown, it was the combination of that together with being reminded of a four-year period in my life filled with humiliation and failure. Yes, I did fail but that was an inevitable combination caused by poor teaching and my lack of self-esteem. It's easy to blame others but I needed help and there was nobody around to provide it. The teacher, the one person who should above all others helped me understand refused to. That, and my father's indifference left me in a lonely void. Of course, I've succeeded since but my self-esteem, that sense of worthlessness has kept me company ever since.' Ralph who was sitting nearby stroked James bare leg as he responded.

'You brought your unwanted friend here didn't you.' James nodded. 'Let's now agree we have left that person in the room you have just vacated, shall we.' James repeated his acceptance with a further nod of his head.

'I'll try sir, I want to make a fresh start even at this stage in my life.' Ralph was ready for that.

'I will beat you regularly James but not like that again. I needed you to get that period in your life out of your system.

I will dismantle the frame and store it away so that room isn't a constant reminder for you to go and visit your past. You will never be restrained again, from now on you offer your bare bottom for me to cane out of desire, not retribution or atonement. Who knows, I might offer you mine to beat also.' He placed his wine down and held out his hand to take James's glass. 'Time to lie down and let's sort out the damage.'

James lay down he felt Ralph's hands move to his blood smeared buttocks. He now feared more sadism, the painful salt and lemon juice mix being rubbed into the most raw and sore looking areas, but instead another tube was selected, and this was rubbed into those places instead. It still stung but nothing to what he'd feared would happen.

'I was expecting something else; this is much nicer.' Ralph was sitting legs apart over James legs and his reply seemed sharp.

'I can soon mix something else if you'd prefer!' James was quick to reply.

'No, you're doing fine, carry on its soothing.' Ralph then explained.

'The salt and lemon mixture was never intended for use. It's like so much that happened next door, it's about playing with your emotions. I dragged up your past, your traumatic childhood. When we met and after it became clear we would meet again here and take what happened before much further I did some research on you. Do you recall writing an article about damaged childhoods?' The penny dropped. He'd written a blog and added it to an open discussion taking place on the web. He realised now that Ralph had found its author and what had taken placed in the next-door room had been carefully designed.

'Oh my god, of course. I wrote that ten years ago. I was pretty open then about sharing experiences in my life and as you say, it can come back and bite!' Ralph was now massaging his buttocks and ensuring the soothing cream covered totally.

'The idea about use of that mixture was taken from an article I read about slave whippings in the southern states of America. Slaves were hung by their ankles and flogged with the overseer's thick heavy strap. This quickly stripped the skin and to add to the pain a mixture of crushed chillies, pepper and lemon juice was smeared on by a boy slave using a wide stiff brush. The flogging continued of course. You did think I meant it though, didn't you?' Ralph asked.

'I did, it certainly sent a shiver down my spine. I much prefer what you are doing now.'

'I think I can improve on that though, up you get, onto your knees I want to taste you.' Ralph pulled up on James's hips which helped bring him up into a kneeling position he then felt a hand push down on his shoulders which meant his head now rested on the bed. He realised where Ralph was taking this and with his bottom in its most prominent position James parted his legs and opened himself ready for attention. He felt his cheeks being pulled wider apart and then the sensation of hot breath like a warm summer breeze wafting over his anus. When the tongue licked across its now flattened and stretched surface he shivered, his penis hardened just as a hand gripped it and squeezed before starting a movement which could only have one end result.

'You'll make me cum, it won't take long if you continue doing that.' James panted, feeling all manner of sensations building in his groin.

'In that case you'd better tell me when the sap is rising because I will need to catch that. I'd hate to have to cane you for messing on my bed!' Ralph replied not letting up on his masturbation technique.

Another minute went by and James knew his time was close and rolled over to put immediate closure on Ralph's actions. 'Lie on your back, let's bring you off in style.' James turned and lay flat, looking up at the ceiling while Ralph leaned across and pulled two, man sized tissues from a nearby box. He then sat next to James's hips and leaning on his elbow grasped his penis and continued the up and down movement slowly. All the time he retained eye contact.

'Where does this go now Ralph?' Ralph didn't answer immediately but concentrated on arousal.

'I hope you don't mean what I'm doing. I'm making you cum and I expect it to be pretty explosive!' Ralph smiled. James knew he'd ducked answering the real point of his question.

'I mean us and you know full well what I mean.' Ralph nodded.

'I know what you mean James. When I placed my advertisement, I had no idea I'd meet someone like you. This has changed everything.' James was struggling now as his arousal was reaching the point of no return. He called out in panic.

'I'm coming!' Ralph stopped. The rising sap stopped too.

'I was speaking, your climax will have to wait!' James felt his urgency waning. 'As I was saying meeting you has changed everything. I was expecting to cane a few young men, but I hadn't expected this, but I'm afraid this is probably going to be your final visit.' The words delivered hit James like a bombshell.

But why, what has changed. I thought we were really hitting it off?' Ralph started the activity of arousal. James was reluctant to proceed until the issue just raised had been

316

settled. 'Please Ralph, this is amazing, but I need an answer.' Ralph didn't stop but started to increase the pace again. James gave in, unable to concentrate.

'I think we are hitting it off, I think we are amazing together, but I don't want you to visit, I want you to stay!' James's look of astonishment was being quickly overwhelmed by something on an unstoppable path.

'I'm afraid even if you stop now, you're too late this time. If you don't want a mess on your bed, you better be ready to catch this!' Ralph sat back and really milked James's cock.

'I changed my mind, I want to watch this, see how high you can spurt. I'll bend in in your direction slightly so most of it ends up on you.' With this he slowed the pace until by looking down at James he could see his climax was on its way and as James's breathing increased and he stiffened Ralph speeded up his pumping action until after arching his back, his penis spurted a stream of white fluid several feet into the air whereupon it splashed its warmth over his chest with one spurt narrowly missing his face. Ralph continued and more spurts followed; then still more until despite further attempts the pump had run dry. James rolled over sated and exhausted.

Ralph lay next to him and their lips met. They kissed but softly. There was silence for a while until Ralph broke in. 'Well, is this your last visit, do you plan to continue your singular life or join me here?' He asked. James had his answer ready.

'Do I seriously have to answer that?'

The Retired Headmaster

Corporal punishment – dark
and dirty....

By

Sam Evans

1

I'm back. I've just returned from an extraordinary meeting; one I couldn't imagine ever taking place. One which now left me with a lot of soul searching to do before I could make any decision moving forward. Today had started like any normal morning, it was weekend, and I'd got up in a leisurely fashion. Normally, had it been a workday, I'd have been out of bed an hour earlier ready to jump on the treadmill called work. I'd showered and headed downstairs to make a simple breakfast, my name is Harry Brown, I'm 40 years of age, I live alone and for the record, I'm gay. I'm not sure why that fact was important to share; possibly, more so having met the person who was now central to my thinking. He was gay too which tied up a lot of loose ends which had left me wondering years earlier in my teens when I have first encountered him.

I'd just finished eating. I'd loaded the dishwasher, and I was wondering how I was going to fill my day. That was solved instantly when the phone rang.

'Hello.' I replied. I never gave any more information to incoming calls until I knew who was calling.

'Harry Brown?' A male voice asked.

'Yes, who is calling?' I asked. There was so much annoyance with cold calling, and I was always wary before I have too much information away.

'It's Gerald Trent, I'm sure that name rings a bell?' Oh, my God, it rang a peel of bells. A voice from my deep and distant past, one I'd last heard at the tender age of sixteen, a voice I have never expected to hear again.

'It does sir.' I answered showing deference to a respected figure who figured frequently in my time at school – my headmaster. One question now prominent in my thinking was very simple. What did he want? He removed the need for me to ask.

'I imagine you must wonder why I am calling.'

'Yes, of course, how can I help you?' I asked in reply.

'It's more a case of me possibly being able to help you, Harry.' I sensed a cat and mouse game was in play.

'In what way sir?' I asked my own question in reply.

'Could we meet for lunch. I feel this will enhance our discussion. I think it will be preferable to us going back and forth with questions and answers over the telephone. Any conversation is better conducted face to face.' I agreed silently.

'Where did you have in mind and at what time?'

'The Horse and Groom pub in town, say 1pm?' He asked. I had nothing else planned. It would give me something to do. Besides he seemed to suggest there was a benefit to me personally by us meeting, so I agreed.

'I'll meet you there then?' I answered somewhat uncertainly.

'Until then, goodbye.' He answered and rang off.

I didn't have far to travel and set off at 12.30. This allowed me to arrive in plenty of time to avoid being late. Punctually was a virtue instilled in me since childhood and it had nothing to do with the person, I was setting out to meet. After he'd rung off, I made coffee and took it outside to a table set up on my garden patio and as I sipped it, I couldn't help but wonder why this man wished to meet up with me again. The last time was eventful in that it hadn't worked out quite as well as I'd hoped. I had been in trouble and was sent to the headmaster, Mr Trent. That meant one thing – a good caning! I'd been reading a book on corporal punishment, especially that which related to its use in the educational system over the years. It was liberally illustrated, a few archived photographs, but mainly pen and ink drawings, depicting boys at the receiving end. Those bending over in the traditional way while a man in a schoolmaster's cap and gown administered the cane or sometimes the birch to often bared buttocks. I'd get aroused and often masturbated while I imagined myself adopting such a position to Mr Trent. Now this same man wanted to meet me, and I was minutes away from finding out why?

I knew the pub well. It was probably the best-known drinking joint in town, it was large and had plenty of seating. I assumed Mr Trent would arrive before me. I sensed he'd want to maintain control and by arriving early he could dictate seat position and be prepared for my arrival and not the other way around. Entering, I wasn't wrong, I saw the familiar figure in the far distance, so I made my way towards him.

'Hello Mr Brown, it's Harry, isn't it?' He opened the conversation as soon as I appeared on his radar.

'Yes, sir.' I answered formally. He'd always called me Brown previously and adding a Mr to my name seemed a likely compromise. Even so, I wasn't ready for the informal, over friendly use of my Christian name, or at least not until I understood why he'd suggested meeting up.

'Take a seat, someone will be along for our food order soon.' I noticed he hadn't ordered a drink for himself so I assumed that, together with my own, would be fixed at the same time. I sat at what was visually a small table and waited nervously for him to make the first move. 'Do you recall the last time we met?' Of all the questions he could have asked, the one he had was not what I hoped he would ask.

'I think we both know when that was sir.' I replied without answering his question.

'You'd better remind me.' He quickly responded. I knew he was trying to make me uncomfortable.

'I'd owned up to a serious misdemeanour, something which took place off school premises.' I left it there.

'Ah yes, I remember now, but that merely covers the offence, not how you presented yourself.' I knew he'd mention that. I was being toyed with.

'I think you know what happened sir, you do not need me to remind you.'

'So, you are a mind reader too. How do you know what was going through my head.' He backed me into a corner. I now had a choice. To tell him what he clearly wanted to hear or rise to my feet and leave.

'I turned up, somewhat under dressed sir.' I looked around nervously, fearing being overhead. Mr Trent didn't reply immediately. A young female waitress appeared and was approaching to presumably take our orders. As I was driving, I chose a soft drink. I noticed he did likewise. Food consisted of a sandwich and once again Mr Trent did likewise. Then she was gone, and I awaited his reply.

'Yes, I do recall the event now. Not only was I still reeling from a boy owning up to something which would affect the reputation of the school, a pretty much unheard-of event I might add, but once I had you in bending position it became clear what you were wearing, wasn't going to offer you much protection.' He paused and our eyes met. 'Perhaps you can re-enlighten me as to why you arrived like that?' I felt the increased pressure being applied.

'I've been fascinated by corporal punishment all my life sir. I knew I was to be caned and I wanted to experience it as boys did at private and public schools where the rules that were applied there were far more relaxed.' Mr Trent smiled.

'So, you really wanted your bare bottom caned, didn't you?' He asked an almost rhetorical question.

'Yes sir.' There was no other reply I could give.

'I quickly knew. I was sure when you adopted the bending position. I could see every pimple on your backside showing through the frayed and worn fabric of your flannel trousers. Then, when I applied the cane, the sound was different too. I knew something was up and confirmed when a raised welt formed through the thin fabric too. Did it hurt?' He then asked.

'Yes sir, your canings always hurt but this felt much more raw - Sir.'

'If you recall I asked you what you were wearing. You struggled to answer because you'd been rumbled, found out – correct?' I nodded, again looking around to see if anyone was taking an interest in the exchange. 'Are you aroused by this conversation? What I mean is, are you erect?' I was, I nodded. Mr Trent then moved his hand beneath the table and I was shocked and surprised to feel a hand touch my leg and move upwards. I almost panicked especially when he asked the next questioner. 'Undo your belt and loosen your trousers.' I was aghast and looked back wide eyes.

'What here?' I replied quickly. He looked around theatrically.

'I can't think of a better place, can you?' I could. I could think of a million other places. I still hesitated and when the young waitress appeared with our drinks order the hand was withdrawn. He waited until she had left before continuing. 'Just so you understand Mr Brown, I'm gay too. A straight man would have brushed my hand away.' Something I'd wondered about Mr Trent had just been made clear after twenty-five years of waiting.

'Yes sir, I am.' I answered his question. There seemed little point in denying it.

'In that case you won't mind me feeling your penis will you.' I stared back into his cold searching eyes.

'I don't think it's appropriate to do it here sir.'

'So, where are you planning to show me your cock?' He continued.

'I wasn't sir, or at least not until about a minute ago.'

'Undo your belt and loosen your trousers. I want to feel it now.' I moved my hands down and obeyed his command, doing it in a way that wouldn't be noticed. On completion I rested my hands on the table. He now repeated his earlier searching act, reaching the band of my underpants before pulling it open and moving his seeking hand to find its destination. It was found and his fingers closed around my erection, with his thumb moving to its tip where he felt it in a circular movement. 'You are aroused aren't you. This suggests you still need the cane applied to your bare buttocks, is that correct?' I was too breathless to reply. I nodded. 'I was tempted that day. To ask you to drop your trousers and expose your bare bottom. But, with my secretary just on the other side of the door, it was way to risky, I'd have loved to give that taut bottom of yours a couple of cane strokes – bare! Even that would have been a risk. The sound of a cane on bare skin has a very different sound and Mrs Price had heard enough caning noises and their reactions to know the difference. I might have invited you to my home. Strict rules wouldn't have applied there. Unfortunately, my wife was housebound. I couldn't even wait for her to go out for the day and invite you round. It was impossible.' He released my cock and withdrew his hand. Normality was restored and I discreetly secured my trousers again. I was lost for words. 'You must be wondering why I asked you to meet me here today?' He then asked.

'Yes sir, I was an unexpected surprise.'

'Sadly. Three years later, after you'd left school, my wife passed away. I checked to see if you might with to accept an invitation to visit me but when I looked, I found you had left the area.'

'I'd gone to Manchester sir. I got a place at university.' He smiled.

'Ah, that would answer it wouldn't it.' He paused. 'Would you have accepted my invitation then?' It was a good question.

'Yes, sir.'

'In that case, assuming you still feel the same, I'd like to invite you to visit me soon.' That was a shock. I now had a question of my own.

'How did you find me sir. This isn't where I used to live, so how did you end up ringing me this morning?'

'Quite by chance dear boy. I do not live around here or where I used to reside either. I came here on business, and I saw you coming out of the bank yesterday. I searched for your name on telephone listings and there you were. It then just took a simple phone call.' I shook my head in amazement – the coincidence was astounding. Our food arrived. We ate during a period of silence. I was still erect and knew I'd be masturbating once I got home. It felt like my mind was being read because once again the suggestion he now made blew me off course.

'Once we have eaten, we could find a secluded spot and I'll give today's proceedings a happy ending, what do you say?'

'My god, how do you keep doing this to me sir?' I asked.

'Do what?'

'Press all the right buttons.'

'Did I press them before when you were fifteen, even younger?' He asked.

'Yes sir, you always have. I'm in awe of you, excited and terrified in equal measure.' I replied.

'So that is a, yes?' He didn't ask for further explanation but sought confirmation I would accept his immediate invitation, while deciding on another offer later.

'Yes sir.'

Back home now, masturbated and sated, my bottom sore from a hard bare bottom spanking, carried out on the back seat of his large limousine, I was seated with a neat scotch whisky calming my shattered nerves. Going over Mr Trent's knee was one thing, offering my bare bottom to a proven sadist was quite another. I had to think this through.

2

I decided to give it a few days. Meeting Mr Trent had been a bit of a shock to my system. Nearly 25 years had passed since that brief moment in time where I wouldn't have hesitated. Gone without a second thought. Something else occupied my mind now. Mr Trent had come out, he was gay also, and I doubted this was a sudden event. He'd have been gay when I was fifteen and had I gone to see him then, I doubt whether me being underage would have stopped him engaging in a forbidden act. Caning an underage schoolboy would have only been part of his crime, other things too and the list wasn't that long. I tried to imagine how I would have felt afterwards following the conclusion of his abuse. This focussed my mind to the present which made me wonder if I'd wake up the following morning after a night of perverted debauchery and have similar feelings of regret, shame, feeling used and left dirty and rejected. I wasn't stupid. Beside the caning and the vivid welts on my buttocks, there were limited options available to him. A woman had two main entry points for penetration. Assuming my mouth was taken out of the equation, I had just one! He'd made me cum and that was explosive. I loved him doing that, but I also knew I'd have to earn the right to climax and he'd drive me hard to reach that point. Then again, when I did masturbate, what was foremost on my mind as the sap started to rise. Being fucked and beaten? Was my real fear that of having no experience of either and was that the main reason for my hesitancy?

It was Thursday. The distraction to my thinking was becoming a problem. I couldn't get this decision to make out of my mind. He'd suggested a Saturday. The act carried out into the night and Sunday to recover – accept aftercare as he described it. I wasn't sure what that word meant, but I assumed the word was self-explanatory, after the event and care applied. That seemed something to look forward to. I realised I was now procrastinating, so I took the bull by the horns and called his number from my work desk.

'Trent!' He barked. I sensed my call might have jarred him out of an after-lunch nap. He sounded grumpy.

'It's Harry Brown sir.' I introduced myself as the caller.

'Well? Have you decided? It's taken you long enough!' He was grumpy, which didn't bode well.

'I've decided to take you up on your offer. Could I come this Saturday?' I asked.

'Are you sure? I don't want you changing your mind at the last minute. I don't like time wasters!' Was that how he saw me?

Saturday came and with it, butterflies, and cold feet. I was making a far-reaching decision which might be the most exciting thing I'd ever done or the biggest mistake of my life. I'd lain in bed thinking about this choice most of the night. If I went, what if the memories of his school canings had moved up to scales, I could never even hope to reach. Then again, if I changed my mind, chickened out, he'd probably never engage with me again and my need of him to take me back to my teens would be lost forever. Obviously, I was scared, terrified even, but I knew I had to face this or potentially regret my cowardice for the rest of my life. I left around midday; the journey would take around an hour and I set Mr Trent's postcode into my satnav and left. It was just an overnight stay, so I only took a few items, notably clean underwear. My toothbrush too. The journey passed without incident. In fact, my mind was so engrossed in what lay ahead I didn't remember much about the journey at all.

Finally, having arrived in a leafy suburb, the satnav instructed me to turn left, then when I reached a large double fronted house, I was informed I had reached my final destination. Those words seemed to have an extra significance today which sent a huge shiver down my back. There were gates which exposed a gravel driveway leading up to the expensive looking house which suggested Gerald Trent had done rather well for himself. I entered and followed up to the house itself, I parked up next to his expensive car which I recognised immediately.

'You made it then. I did have my doubts whether you'd turn up. Come in.' Mr Trent moved back and allowed me to pass. He closed the front door. Locked it and removed the key. I realised I was inside now and the only way I could escape was by retrieving that same key or him unlocking the door to allow my exit. 'Come through.' I followed him into a large comfortable lounge where I was directed to an armchair where I sat.

'I thought a lot about coming sir. I realised finally if I did not, I'd always be left wondering.' I replied.

'Wondering what?'

'What I should have experienced all those years ago would have felt like? How well I would have taken the beating I desired?'

'It's amazing the number of people who seek to relive their childhood experiences of corporal punishment Harry. It was unfortunate I couldn't offer you that experience outside the school. Sadly, as I've already explained, by the time this was possible you'd moved to Manchester. Still, as the expression goes, better late than never – drink?' I nodded. 'I have a beer?'

'That will be fine sir.' Trent left the room. I didn't get up to have a closer look, but there were photographs dotted around the room. Some ornaments too. Everywhere, screamed order and everything in its place. I doubted there was a speck of dust anywhere and I suspected a cleaner came in each week. He was back.

'It's a large house to rattle around in alone. Having said that, I could never imagine sharing it with anyone else.' I wasn't sure why he said that because I certainly had no wish to live with him. A brief but painful visit was all I sought.

'You mention the number of people, I have to include myself in that number, who visit to relive that moment in time, but doesn't the same apply to those who carry out the punishment?' Trent smiled.

'But of course. I often think about the number of boys and older men I've thrashed over the years. I always thought, a man visiting me would be coming to relive an actual event. On that basis, those people like yourself would gradually die out and not be replaced by those who never experienced corporal punishment. Yet, I have numerous young men visit me who never experienced it. I think we can safely put that myth to bed, don't you.' I agreed but he hadn't really answered my question.

'I do yes. But what is your motivation? While mine might be considered an unhealthy addiction, how would you describe yours as the person administering the punishment.' I watched as he deliberated on how best to reply.

'Mine is as much an addiction as yours Harry. Obviously, while I was an active head, I couldn't expose a boy's bare buttocks to be caned. Obviously, the number who come here to receive corporal punishment who do not expose themselves is zero. I rarely cane a covered bottom other than to warm up that man's bottom to more serious attention later. I'll let you into a little secret. There was a small room next to the school showers and changing room. I had the key and on Fridays I worked in there. But I had a view into where you boys changed, and I used to visit and enjoy seeing the results of my work. I saw you on several occasions.' I was shocked. The sadist was a perverted voyeur too. 'The games and PE master, Mr Peters liked to slipper wet naked boys in the showers. I'm sure you remember?' I took that to be a question.

'Yes, while it never happened to me, I was certainly aware he was doing it.'

'I saw him do it from my secret vantage point. He never knew. Of course, I could have got him in a lot of trouble but then I'd have to admit my own peeping Tom activity. Obviously, I wasn't going to do that. Nothing like thrashing a nice wet bum!' I saw half a smile appear on his face. A rarity.

'Did anyone know or ever find out about your secret viewings?' I asked.

'Not to my knowledge, but who knows or frankly cares. It doesn't apply now. I can see the results of my canings almost instantly.' I continued drinking my beer until Trent stood and invited me to follow him out of the room to where food had been laid out.

An hour later, full, and somewhat lightheaded after drinking wine on top of beer, Trent stood and announced it was time to get started.

'What is the plan?' I asked nervously.

'The main event is this evening but for now it's worth being nostalgic and giving you a reminder of life when you attended school. Follow me.' Trent walked out of the room with me trailing in his wake. We returned to the living room where we'd started earlier. Once I was inside, the door was closed, and he walked the length of the room and brought back a long cane at least a metre in length. Remove your jacket, you won't need that. Hang it on the back of a chair. I did so, maintaining eye contact throughout. 'Do you remember that last time I caned you?' He asked.

'I could hardly forget sir; it left its mark in more than one way.'

'Yes, if I recall, had I invited you to my home and you would have come, am I right?'

'Yes sir, in fact for a week or so I used to pass where you lived. I got it into my head that had you seen me I would be invited in. I didn't know about your wife - I'm sorry she was ill.' I wondered if I'd been seen.

'I saw you on more than one occasion. Had I been able to, I would have had you inside like a shot. Given you a good dose of what you needed.'

'That would have been great.' Trent flexed the cane.

'Bend over part your legs and touch your toes.' I was stunned. I could barely believe what I was hearing.

'What here, now?' I asked.

'Of course, now! I certainly don't mean next week or even tomorrow!' I took a step forward and bent over. 'I said open your legs.'

'Yes sir.' I complied. I saw him walk over to my left and then I felt the cane touch both cheeks before he tapped it down firmly a couple of times. It stung. Then he moved forward, and his hand came between my legs seeking my firm erection.

'I'm glad you find this exciting. It'll be nicer later when you are stripped naked, and I can feel you properly. But, at this stage I require you clothed.' He released me and stepped back. I felt the cane tap the stretched material of my trousers and having expected more teasing, I was unprepared for what then happened.

THWACK!

'Oh god! Jeez that hurts!' I reacted as pain like I'd never felt before engulfed my rear end. My hands immediately moved to touch where it continued to hurt.

'Hands away, you know the rules. Touch yourself again and that stroke won't count. Get back down.' I stopped the rearward movement of my hands and moved them back. 'A bit of a different level to what I used to give when you visited me before I imagine.' He wasn't wrong.

'Yes sir, I don't remember your canings to be that painful before.'

'You're a grown man now Harry. In those days I had to abide by rules, you were still considered a child. Now you are an adult and those who visit me must expect adult punishment. Remember you get it bare later and I will really lay those strokes on believe me!' I did and suddenly the folly of making this trip became vividly clear.

THWACK!

I cried out in pain as the second stroke landed very close to the first. One thing I did remember was his accuracy. I'd go home and find the six strokes plainly visible over an area of just over two inches wide. Welts not touching but hardly showing any visible separation.

'Four more Harry, you'll get a lot more tonight. You won't sit easily for a week!' I believed that too. After the six were delivered, as promised I stayed in position. The cane was placed leaning against the wall and Trent returned and stood behind me.

'This is the bit I enjoy most after I've caned a clothed bottom. To view my work. See if my accuracy has been maintained.' I felt his hands move round to the front of my waist and the belt of my trousers was unbuckled. My trousers were pulled down. 'This is like opening a gift-wrapped present don't you think? I had no means of easy

334

comparison. I knew I was hurting, burning across the whole surface of my bottom. Next his hands attached to the elasticated waistband of my underpants, and these were pulled down too and my shirt lifted. 'Mmm, now that is a sight for sore eyes Harry, even though it is your bum that is sore. I can't wait to thrash your bare bottom. I'll certainly extend that marking considerably.' He ran his finger along the welts while his other hand went between my legs searching for my erection. 'How does this feel?' He asked.

'Nice sir, very nice.' I answered breathlessly. He then slowly masturbated me.

'And this?'

'Even nicer sir, but don't do that too long, I'm pretty close!'

'You'll get much more later, after eighteen strokes on the cane across your naked buttocks!' I was shocked.

'Eighteen, that is a lot bare, I'm not sure I could take that clothed sir?'

'I think you've gone soft in the intervening years Harry. When you were in your mid-teens at school, and I had invited you into my home I don't think you would have had the doubts you are showing now. Why is that do you think?' I didn't consider the question difficult to answer.

'Life sir? At that age we have no experience, it's easy to imagine anything. I've moved on, seen the reality of life.'

'Yet you are here, and you have cane welts on your bottom, have you moved on?' It was a good question.

'I can't answer for how I might have seen things over twenty years ago. It never happened. A lot changes in twenty years.'

'This aspect of your life obviously hasn't. Do I detect a sudden change of heart, that perhaps, the brutal reality has suddenly hit you and you've got cold feet about pursuing this any further.' He'd asked the critically important question.

'I don't think I can stay down and take 18 strokes bare sir.'

'I do not expect you to. That is why you will be restrained. Strapped down to my punishment bench.'

'I'm not sure I can do that; I mean allow you to.' Trent remained serious.

'I think you have some very serious thinking to do Harry. I have a room set aside for you in case you choose not to sleep with me afterwards. I suggest you go up there now and consider very carefully your next step. But bear this in mind. You have an unfulfilled desire you have waited twenty-five years to enact. You came here after giving our recent meeting some serious thought. You must have known you were not coming here to go over my knee for a smacked bottom! You will have to consider two options. You decide to continue, in which case you will present yourself naked at 7pm in the downstairs lounge when I shall escort you to the punishment room to receive eighteen strokes with that same cane across your bare bottom. Alternatively, you pack your things and leave.' He left that to sink in and I didn't attempt to fill that gap. 'One thing I can assure you of Harry, is you will drive home full of regrets, knowing we will never meet again and no matter how hard you try you will always wonder? What if I'd stayed, gone through with it and come out the other side, definitely scathed. That is as certain as night and day, but at least you will know. The alternative is you never will. That's it Harry, no more to be said. Pull your things up and follow me, unless you wish to leave now?' I was so unsure what to do. I certainly needed time to consider my options. The list of pros and cons was short. In fact, they were starkly obvious. Trent moved away while I pulled up my pants then reached down for my trousers. I followed him out of the door and upstairs.

3

I woke with a start. When I arrived and was shown into a small bedroom with a single made-up bed, I suddenly felt overwhelmingly tired and soon fell asleep. I frantically looked at the bedside clock and saw it was well past six. I realised I hadn't thought through the decision I knew I had to make. Time was pressing. I thought about his summing up. It felt like I was a juror, having listened to a judge clarify the evidence. Removing any uncertainty or confusion so I could reach a verdict based entirely on the evidence alone. I knew I only had two options open, and they were starkly different. Chalk and cheese. He'd just given me six of the best across trousers and underpants and that had hurt unbelievably. Why had it felt so starkly different to when I was at school? Was it just as Trent had said – I was an adult now, there was no strict rules and guidelines to follow in his house. I then wondered about being restrained? Strapped down helplessly within a sadists home. Deep in the bowels of a large house where my screams would be unheard. He'd be free to do anything he wished, and I couldn't prevent it. That was the deal breaker. It was all about trust. What if he was some predator, luring men to an uncertain fate. He might be a serial killer, after all, who would miss most of his clients? Most were single men, living on their own. Who would miss me? My neighbours were transient. I didn't know any, and they were gone after a week. I'd be missed at work. But I had no friends or colleagues. I never met up for after work drinks, get togethers. It would be assumed I'd moved on. I had another ten minutes. I was clothed, I could leave it another few minutes. How long would it take to strip and present myself for justice?

I now thought of the other option – that of leaving? He'd starkly laid out everything I needed to consider. I'd always regretted I hadn't visited him as a boy. What would he have done? He'd have stripped me naked, or more likely ordered me to strip. Like now, I'd have found myself trussed up like an oven ready chicken, bend over head down. Legs secured apart. My bare bottom exposed and vulnerable. I imagine I'd have whimpered as I heard the rattle of the cane being selected from the many, I imagined he kept stored in a cupboard. My heart would miss a beat when he swished it dramatically through the air. Maybe feeling the drought, knowing how close he was to its target. Then finally it's cold feel as it was measured across both plump bare cheeks. How many strokes would he have inflicted even then and surely, I'd have screamed in pain as the cane landed with a loud THWACK! What was different then to now? Only that I'd be missed! Time was up, I had to decide.

'You wish to leave?'

'Yes sir!'

'Can you give me your reasoning?' He then asked.

'Cowardice sir.' I admitted fear had overwhelmed me.

'What was the main factor in reaching your decision?'

'Being restrained sir.'

'So, that suggests a lack of trust in me on your part?' He went straight to the meat of the issue.

'I realise it looks like that, but it's not just that, it's more a practical issue?' I lied.

'Really, explain what you mean?'

'What if you just died, had a stroke. Became too ill to release me? I could be here until someone eventually broke in to find me tied up and helpless. It could be days, weeks, months even.' I explained. It wasn't the real reason, but it would suffice, it was perfectly feasible.

'Years more like, I imagine they'd find our skeletal remains!' He laughed. I didn't find the response remotely funny.

'I sense you are clutching at straws Harry. We both know the real reason. You think if I restrain you, I will abuse the trust you placed in me. All I could do was to reiterate my plan, then you had to decide. It seems you have, and I must express my disappointment in you. But I respect your decision and now I must ask you to leave my house.' This wasn't how I wanted this to end, but the reality of the situation dictated by the path I had chosen to follow, meant there was no other alternative.

'Yes sir, I'm sorry.' Trent held out his hand and I stopped to shake it as I passed. He came forward and unlocked the door.

'I'll keep the offer open for six months. That will give you plenty of time to think about your decision. However, like all offers, it is for a limited period, and you have rejected what was on the table. If you should return it will be on much less advantageous terms. Next time it will be thirty strokes! There will be additional activity you may not relish, more BDSM related. Medical play too, such as enemas!' He was certainly right about that. I was wavering now but kept my face and body language under control to give a neutral impression.

'I hear what you say sir.' I chose to leave it there. Trent opened the main door, and I stepped out into the bright sunlight. It felt like a great burden had been lifted. He'd gone back inside, clearly angry. I walked to my car and sat inside. I felt emotional and burst into tears. I'd bottled out at the last minute, realising though, had I stayed, my buttocks would already be sore and brutally abused by now. I pulled myself

340

together and starting the car moved off, under the watchful gaze of a man viewing my departure through a window in an adjacent room.

Three months went by, and I'd moved my life on again, albeit slowly. I'd driven home and sat in my bed sit flat pondering over my decision. After I left, I realised as I reached the bottom of Mr Trent's road of affluent houses, had I stayed it would all have been over by now. It was 7.30 then, and even if he'd delayed the punishment by one minute between cane strokes, I'd be in a different place; very likely in his bed! I'd waited for that moment for so long, desperate to relive that moment as a fifteen-year-old when something I'd thought about to the point of yearning could have happened by didn't. Now, years later I had faced it. My thoughts went back to that bedroom where I had to make a final choice. Instead of quickly stripping my clothes off and rushing downstairs and presenting myself. I had failed. Come up short, been found wanting? Wasn't this why I'd never succeeded in life, always been risk adverse? Now, months on, that wrong choice still followed me around, the regret I hadn't just manned up and accepting my punishment and then enjoyed Trent's attentions. I still had three months to return. But wouldn't I be faced with that same moment of truth once more? Would I be able to overcome that same fear next time, would my final decision be any different? Night after night I'd struggle with myself. That same repetitive conflict.

I had considered visiting another Dom. For goodness' sake, there was plenty to choose from. Castigatio, the on-line contact site was full of them. Men seeking submissive men to visit. To relive visits to the headmaster's study. Spanking, the

341

slipper, the strap and finally the cane. Bare of course! How else? What if I did, what was I facing then? Making the acquaintance of another different man. Surely that was even worse. I knew Trent, the devil I was familiar with, while anyone else would be a total stranger. It was Friday, my favourite day, especially in the evening, having finished work and two days away from the mind-numbing office to relish. I'd got home, I was preparing dinner when my doorbell rang. This was most unusual. When was the last time that had occurred? I left what I was doing and answered the door. A man of similar age to myself stood looking back at me.

'Harry Brown?' He asked.

'Yes, how can I help you?' I asked.

'I think we have a mutual friend?' He answered, leaving me quizzical.

'I have no idea who you might mean?' I replied. I didn't have any friends, let alone one I shared with a total stranger.

'Could I come in, it's a little sensitive and not something to discuss on the doorstep?' That was a big ask, I wasn't ready to invite anyone in, especially a total stranger. 'Does Gerald Trent ring a bell?' Just the name was enough. I stepped aside. We walked through into the lounge; I offered the as yet unnamed man a seat which he took.

'I know Mr Trent, what is this about?'

'My name is Thomas Clarke, I've known Gerald for over ten years, more like twelve. We both know what he does so we are on common ground. I used to regularly visit his home for him to administer corporal punishment. He'd contact me and remind me it was time for me to atone. When I hadn't heard from him recently, I contacted him, only to find he had stopped.' I listened unsure that this had to do with me.

'So, how does that decision bring you to my door?'

'I think you know damned well why. Anyway, I visited him, and I saw a very changed man. A man who had lost his spark, his energy. He then explained how during a visit to this town he had met an ex-pupil at a school where he was its head teacher. He mentioned your name, Harold A Brown. Nothing more, just a name. He told me how you'd willingly visited him to engage in adult, consensual corporal punishment, namely caning. He went onto explain you had a history which unfortunately had not been fully explored, dare I say fulfilled. He assumed you wished to experiment it to the full but when the moment of truth arrived you turned it down which was your right to do of course, but the reasons given deeply upset him.' He stopped and passed the baton back for me to continue the conversation – if I wished of course.

'He wanted to restrain me. I wasn't prepared to allow a man, a known sadist, that control over me. I feared what he may do while I was so vulnerable.' I decided there was no point in sugarcoating the pill. It was the truth.

'Gerald has been doing this to me for a decade. It's ritual as much as anything. He is a very honourable man, very much from the old school – my word is my bond. You questioned his integrity and your ability to place your trust in him. He was so hurt, so insulted, he started to question whether others felt this way – even me?' He stopped again and sat staring back waiting for my response.

'I'm sorry, it was how I felt. I was in his home, I had to present myself naked and allow him to completely incapacitate me. There was the issue of my vulnerability in the event he had a heart attack, suddenly died on me – what then?'

'He mentioned that too. He said you offered that feeble excuse first as the main reason, but he knew there was far more. He knew deep down; the real reason was one of trust.

343

He couldn't get past that, he still cannot.' I started to feel resentment. I had someone arrive out of the blue and make me the main cause of a brutal and sadistic man hanging up his cane! Taking retirement.

'So, he sent you here to see if I'd change my mind?' I asked.

'Gerald has no idea I am here. I left, annoyed and resenting something I needed had been summarily removed from the shelf as it were, and I had been given a name and a town. I don't think for one minute he expected me to follow this up, but I went online and found the address for a Harold A Brown on the electoral register. Here I am.' Indeed, here he was.

'So, can I assume the purpose of your visit was to update me, inform me how by my choice, one he made clear I could make, a man was so offended he turned his back on his activities – that I'm somehow at fault? Or is there more you haven't got to yet?'

'You were offered a choice, there is no denying that. On every visit I am offered that same choice just before he secures the straps holding me down in position. You questioned his trust. That is what this is about.' I was confused. It felt like there was more.

'Why do I get the distinct feeling you haven't told me everything?' I ventured further.

'You are surprisingly astute, of course there is more.' I shrugged. 'I'm here to offer you a way back.' There it was. After all that soul searching over the weeks that followed my departure, I was going to be given the means to return, assuming I wanted to.

'Please explain.'

'It's simple. I act as a middleman. We both visit together that day. I am as it were your chaperone. I accompany you

344

and it is my responsibility to look after your welfare. I won't be present in the same room; I'll no doubt be in his comfortable lounge but I will hear proceedings. I'll be there to ensure he doesn't exceed his remit, I will also be there to release you in the event of his sudden, unexpected death, unless you fear I might also die!' I knew sarcasm when I heard it. 'Anyway, think about it. Don't make a snap decision. Here is my card. If you decide to take up the offer, let me know.' He rose to his feet, ready to leave.'

'Sure, you won't stay for tea?' I asked.

'No, I came for a reason. You know why now; the rest is up to you.' He walked towards the front door and without another word spoken, he left.

4

A further week went by. I'd put Thomas Clark's card on the front of my fridge with a magnet and glanced at it endlessly. My troubles continued. I had these two gremlins on my shoulders, one each side and each whispering their different positions into my ears left and right. One spoke. "Come on, stop procrastinating. You know you've got to go sometime! The sooner you do it the quicker your inner conflict will pass – what are you waiting for!" As soon as my brain had flopped over to that thinking, the other ear was invaded by a different view. 'Stay put, don't go. You can't take the beating he's proposing. He's upped it; hasn't he gone from 18 to 30! You couldn't take the 18, you struggled with six and you had two layers of clothing then? What chance have you with 30 bare, and despite Thomas Clarke's reassurances, he's only there to deal with excess and bereavement. He won't see thirty strokes in the same light as you will. Stay away!" This had been going on a week. I tried spinning a coin. It came up supporting the first position. Best of three? I tried again. The coin fell heads again. It was looking ominous.

The big issue was, I was being slowly consumed. Eaten alive painlessly. It wasn't plainly obvious, but I was finding this thinking was starting to affect my ability to work. I'd already had a query from one of my team. 'Are you alright? You seem distracted, you don't usually make mistakes?' I'd been found out. I had to shut this down. I suddenly realised, even if I chose not to proceed, these same nagging doubts would remain. I was trapped. I couldn't refuse. I knew the only way forward was to contact Mr Trent. Explain how sorry I was to doubt his integrity and to throw myself at his mercy.

I made another decision too. This was between Gerald Trent and me. I didn't want a middleman holding my hand. I'd make a sensible suggestion and leave it there. I'd deal with this matter tonight.

'Thomas Clarke?' I asked.
'Speaking.' Came the reply.
'I've made a decision.' I announced.
'Really, that is excellent news, or at least it will be if you've made the right decision.'
'I've made the only decision which will give me long term peace of mind.' I responded to his remark.
'Which is?'
'I will return to Mr Trent's home and take his punishment.' There is was out.
'What if you change your mind?' A good question.
'I can't move forward unless I do, I can't keep putting off the inevitable. I'm in constant torment by not attending, so I have no choice, I can't continue as I am.'
'I think it's the right decision. Get this sorted out and we can all move forward.' He then asked the big question. 'When will you go?'
'Friday, that is the day after tomorrow.'
'Oh, that's a bit soon, I'm not sure I'm free on that day, evening too.' I had a swift response to that.
'It won't be a problem, Thomas. I don't want you there. This is between Mr Trent and me. I'm informing you of my intentions, then, you can check on Saturday that we are both in rude health. If you hear from neither of us, you'll know something is wrong and you can investigate.'
'So, you will contact Gerald yourself, you don't need my assistance?' He asked.

'No, Thomas, I appreciate your offer as a means of solving this problem, but I have to do this myself.' There was a brief silence.

'If you're sure.' He checked once more.

'I'm sure, thank you for your help anyway, I think your visit made he think harder about my options. I'm sure things will return to where they were once, I have settled matters with Mr Trent.'

'I wish you well, goodbye.' Then he was gone. I hoped I hadn't upset him, offended him because he wanted to act as a kingpin in a tricky negotiation. I decided to make tea and then sit calmly and contact the man who was causing me such mental turmoil.

'Trent.' A familiar voice barked his response to my phone call.

'It's Harry Brown sir.'

'What do you want?'

'I think we need to talk sir.' I answered.

'I think we've done all the talking that is likely to be fruitful don't you?' The response wasn't quite what I had hoped for.

'I would like to visit you and for you to punish me severely. I had a visit from Thomas Clarke, he told me you are very upset by me questioning your integrity. I deeply apologise for making you feel that way. I'd like to make amends.'

'Very upset, I think that description hardly starts to describe how I felt, still do in fact.' His voice had a slight quiver. I could hear the emotion in his voice.

'Even more reason I should come and seek atonement.' The words were out, spoken. There was no coming back from this. Everything now depended on his reaction and whether my offer would be accepted.

'What, you come here, play silly games and when you were asked to come to the fore, to stand up and be counted, you ran for the hills like the coward you are. How do I know you won't get cold feet and run off like a frightened boy again?' I gave him the only honest answer I could.

'You don't sir, but I can't get any peace of mind. Needing what you offered and distancing myself from its fulfilment is driving me insane. I'm in mental turmoil sir. I know the only way I can move on and be at peace with myself is to allow you to carry out what you planned to the full.' He didn't reply immediately.

'But I might drop dead, I might allow my inner sadist to get out of control. These were the issues associated with restraint. You will be strapped down to my punishment bench and what I have previously described carried out to the letter.' I had my reply prepared for this too.

'Thomas Clarke offered to come with me and wait away from the action. To remove the issue of your first description and ensure my safety was assured. I turned him down, although he will phone us both the following day to check on our welfare.' Again, a silence. I had no idea how he might react.

'That sounds a reasonable compromise under the circumstances. I have no objections to him being here if it reassures you further.'

'No sir, this is something only we can resolve.'

'When did you wish to come?' It felt like he'd relented.

'If it's convenient, this weekend. I arrive Friday and return Sunday?' I suggested.

'Arrive at 8pm, come for dinner.'

'Thank you, sir. I will arrive at that time, and I will fully submit to you in every way,'

'Damned right you will – goodbye.' The phone clicked, he'd rung off as suddenly and abruptly as Thomas had before him.

I realised as I went to bed that night, I'd set in motion events I might still live to regret. I slept naked and I felt my erection which had been full and hard throughout my conversation with Trent. He was miffed and still resentful over the implications of my decision to leave his house. I was lain on my back so I eased my hips upward so I could run my hand over the surface of my bottom. It was smooth; I knew if I checked it in the mirror, it would be unmarked, hardly a blemish except for a mole on my right cheek. I sensed in two days' time it would look very different. Covered by thick welts, possibly bloody too. I knew I had to pay a price, and I suspected Trent would put more effort into the caning. Still, the decision was made, the deed was set to take place on Saturday.

5

The time ticked down. Always, as it did, the minutes and hours dragged. Thursday night was worse by far as I lay in bed with an erection which just wouldn't ease off. Normally I'd masturbate, but I couldn't this time. I was relying on my sexual arousal driving me to Mr Trent's front door. To release my ardour would be like taking a pan of simmering milk and placing it elsewhere on the stove which would start the cooling process instantly. I couldn't ease off. I had to be hot and needy, I had to be kept that way throughout, even while the cane was raining down on my bare skin. Friday morning came, I showered, soaping every nook and cranny. I would do this again later before setting off on the hour-long drive to Trent's spacious home.

I thought of Thomas. I know he was seeking what I was still dreading. Okay, I resolved to go through with Trent's sadistic and perverted plan, but perhaps he was accustomed to it and all I was doing was replacing that opportunity from him to me. Something else had occurred to me, something that I had and few of Trent's regular clients did not. I had history. Trent had been caning my buttocks since I entered my teens, that special one at fifteen, just before my sixteenth birthday. We had made a connection during that caning. He'd admitted under different circumstances, that caning would have been carried out with my trousers around my ankles, my underpants sitting on top. My buttocks bared. Had he not been married I would have been invited back to his home and with school punishment rules thrown out of the window something far more severe and this followed by forbidden acts of a sexual nature taken place. I knew that too which was another reason I had made my decision. Gerald Trent liked me; I think it might have even gone further than liked. It

351

had with me before, it had even that day when I had skulked out like the coward I was. I couldn't really forgive myself now because I realised after it was too late, my guarantee of safety was always assured. I suspect he even loved me and would wish me to return again and again and maybe one day, eventually, not leave at all.

It was what else he planned to do which was keeping me erect, even at work. I left on time. I didn't go to the usual after work get together. I rarely went anyway. I needed to get home and shower, decide what to wear and when all was complete, head to where he lived. I set off, I showered and shaved. I was hairy down there, but I wasn't sure how Trent wanted me. At least, if he liked his boy's hairy, I wouldn't disappoint by arriving smooth. Obviously, he could remove hair but not grow it instantly. The journey was straightforward. Most traffic headed in the opposite direction to that which I travelled. With about five miles to go the butterflies started to flutter. I was getting nervous now. I kept my eyes on the road and listened to the voice on my satnav. I'd only travelled this journey once, but it was already familiar. The voice told me to turn left and immediately I did so, I saw the house ahead in the far distance. I turned the satnav off; I knew the way.

'Good evening, Brown, come inside. You are punctual which I like. Tea, coffee, or something stronger.' Trent had arrived carrying a glass. I wasn't totally sure what it contained but it wasn't wine. I suspected a double malt, probably expensive too.'

'A glass of red wine would be nice.' I'd put a few essentials in a small overnight bag which I dropped in the hallway before following him into the lounge I'd been in last time. Looking round I noticed prints on the walls, all of which depicted scenes of corporal punishment. Over the fireplace was one entitled "Kissing the Gunners Daughter" it showed a boy sailor, his buttocks bared, being birched while strapped over the breach end of a ships cannon. He poured the wine and returned handing me the glass.

'Envious?' He asked, seeing me transfixed by the image.'

'Not really sir. Those were different times.' He nodded and remarked they were certainly harsher, but people lived within clear lines of acceptable behaviour then and knew also there were consequences for breaching them. He remarked about the behaviour of schoolchildren and how many things that happen in modern life would have been crushed in his day. I'd spent time under his regime, so I was able to confirm this.

'So, you made the journey then. I trust you do realise what awaits you. I hope you are not going to run out on me this time.' It was a question of sorts.

'No sir, I've not had a pleasant time since I left, and I deeply regret the impression I left you with.' I saw the man's eyes water. I knew how deep my mistrust had been received.

'You have now idea Harry. Did you know I stopped, and you are the first person who has entered my home since. You knocked the heart out of me because you mean a lot to me. I suspect the feeling is mutual.' My earlier conclusions were borne out by his confession.

'It is sir. My deepest regret is we never followed up that which started in your study that day. I realised when we met again, nothing had changed, especially when I entered your home. I just panicked; I wish to put that right tomorrow night.' Trent placed his hand on my leg and moved it up until it reached my bulge.

'I see you are erect. You are having a hard time aren't you!' He fingered the contours.

353

'I am sir.'

'In that case why don't you put your wine down and strip. I'll take your clothes and lock them away. I'll leave the car keys out on the table but, in the event, you choose to leave before I'm finished with you, you'll have to go home naked – do you understand?' I did and I smiled thinly at the clever trap he had just unveiled.

'I'm not planning to leave sir.' I half-heartedly protested.

'I'm pleased to hear it but I'll still have your clothes if you don't mind. I'll still have them even if you do. My home, my rules. Now get your clothes off; the lot!' I wasn't going to argue, so I stood, first removing my jacket. I handed him my car keys which he placed on the low table in front of us. I then unbuttoned my shirt before removing that too. I started a neat pile of folded clothing and soon my trousers were added too. I sat and removed my socks. This just left my pants. 'Come here, let me pull those down. I've wanted to do this for twenty-five years!' I stood in front of Trent who looked at my tentpole erection. 'You are excited aren't you.' My cock stiffened as he stroked the tip which had left a circular mark where it had soaked through the fabric.

'I am sir, I've been like this on and off since I left three months ago.' He looked at me.

'In that case I need to inspect the cause of this bulge. Place your hands on your head.'

'Yes sir.' I replied as I complied. First, I watched as he pulled the elasticated waist out fully and peered into the area which had opened.

'My word, you are quite a big boy and that is some erection.' I didn't reply but continued watching as he then drew my pants down until they fell by gravity to my ankles. 'Step out, turn your back, and pick them up. Don't stoop, I wish to see how flexible you are.' He instructed me. I looked

354

at his request very differently, he just wanted a quick look at my bum!

'So, this is what all the fuss is about, your glutinous maximus, otherwise known as your buttocks! I really should have seen this part of your anatomy 25 years ago, but of course your bottom would have been far less developed. Yours are pear shaped which I rather like. It denotes someone who walks a lot, sits a lot but doesn't over exercise. I'm not very keen on walnut cracking cheeks Harry.' He finished by slapping my right cheek.

'I'm on my feet a lot. My place of work is half a mile from my home and I do not use my car because I prefer to walk. That's the only exercise I get, I'm certainly not enrolled in my local gym.' I hoped that answered any questions he might have wished raised.

'Right, upstairs for you now, not the bedroom this time. There is the bathroom at the end of the corridor. In the shower, plenty of shower gel between those cheeks and I want you back here for a very full and detailed inspection.' I questioned the need.

'I had a good shower and did everything you are requesting just before I left to come here?'

'I don't care what you did then, I want you to repeat it here, now get moving!' I was sent scurrying on my way by a much harder smack across both cheeks this time. It hurt.

'Ouch, that stung!' I complained.

'You'll get another one if you don't move your arse. Get going.' He raised his hand, but I dodged out of the way quickly.

In the shower I found plenty of different shower gels to choose from. I picked one at random and squeezing the container I pooled a quantity into the palm of my hand

355

before spreading it in the area I was told to focus on. I didn't wash my hair again. I knew where Trent planned his attack and that's where my effort was concentrated. After drying I didn't powder myself, he obviously wanted me au natural and that was how I presented myself. I noticed my clothes were missing. On the table wine glasses stood filled.

'Ok young man, stand with your back facing me, part your legs wide and bend over.' My prediction was correct. I'd wanted to do this for a long time. It appeared he had too. 'When we last met at school, I imagined you naked and in this position at my home. How would you have felt about that?' I shivered.

'You seem to have the uncanny ability to read my mind sir, I was just thinking the same thing.' He parted my cheeks still further and ran his finger up until it stopped on my anus.

'Thinking about this?' He encircled my crinkly spot.

'Yes, exactly there sir?' I replied.

'Have you ever been penetrated?' He asked.

'Only by my own slippery finger and things I inserted.'

'Would you like to be penetrated?'

'Yes sir, very much.' I took a deep intake of breath when another hand caressed my balls and felt for my penis which was grasped.

'Shame, I'd rather like this inside me, but as you realise your total submission to me renders that impossible.' I did get that. 'You will share my bed tonight and you will be penetrated, you have my word on that. Stand up and turn around.' I obeyed and stood in front of him open legged, my penis erect and now oozing long stringy drips of mucus which Trent caught before they reached the ground, licking them from his capturing finger. Then slowly, he turned me and forced me over his knee, jamming a leg between mine to separate my cheeks for individual attention. 'I'm afraid it's a

356

bedtime spanking for you Harry. Then, before I could even get used to the idea he started on my right buttock. He had a hand like a paddle, and it stung like hell!

'Ouch sir!' I cried out in pain. The attack was ferocious and increasingly painful. A score of hard smacks continued that exposed lone cheek. Then after turning me, he started on the other. Then in a final flourish he spanked both before ordering me back up onto my feet.

'Upstairs, I'm going to shower. When I return, I want you kneeling in the centre of the bed. Spread the towel and kneel on that. Make sure your legs are well parted and place the tube of KY next to you. I want to see those burning cheeks as soon as I enter the room – understood?' I did and I ran off quickly clutching both burning cheeks.

I waited in position for ages it seemed. I heard water running as the shower room had an adjoining door to his bedroom, effectively making it an en-suite. My cheeks hardly stung now but emitted instead a glowing warmth which I found arousing. My erection was beyond further description. I was turned on like nothing I'd ever experienced and the man about to join me, presumably taking advantage of what I openly offered, was about to fuck me!

'Nice, very nice Harry.' He spoke behind me, suddenly. I had my eyes closed and I had imagined just feeling his weight on the bed and his own erect cock touching my anus as the first sign of his arrival. Wantonly I thrust my bottom out still more, an inch closer to his advancing member. 'Let's make sure entry is nice and smooth shall we.' I felt something cold smeared around between my cheeks and then after he presumably smeared gel on his spear, he lined it up and gripping my shoulders pulled himself inside me until I felt his bare skin touch my stretched buttocks.

'Oh God, that feels so good!' I called out.

'You needed this when you were a less hairy 15 yr old. Which reminds me, I'll be shaving you tomorrow.' I didn't mind that at all. He started to fuck me, and I sensed his breathing getting faster, heavier, as the tempo increased. Soon his hand came round and gripped my cock. He started to masturbate me, slowly at first but soon we were both at the same tempo. I felt a shiver. The first signs my ending wasn't too far away. He wanked me harder and still faster then as we both felt the same rising sensation, I reached the point of no return and with us both reaching a screaming climax together I sprayed the towel again and again before we collapsed in a heap – spent!

6

The sun bright and shining on my face woke me the following morning. I knew by the time this happened again the following morning my forthcoming ordeal would be over. I felt sore. My bum, from the sustained spanking and my anus from being penetrated several times during the night. One thing for sure, Trent had energy aplenty. The plan, after breakfast, was to visit the punishment room where I'd be taken tonight. I wasn't relishing that! I had to be shaved then given an enema. Mr Trent said it was all part of a judicial punishment ritual. It was the first time he'd used the "J" word. I had looked it up. "Pertaining to judgement in courts of justice or to the administration of justice" I think in this case the word administering, was a more accurate description of what was to take place and while the only court involved was that of the court of Trent, being restrained would mean it would be carried out ruthlessly and to the full.

'Good morning, Harry' Mr Trent greeted me shortly after he'd got up and slipped away, his own muscular buttocks on display as he left. He returned shortly after with tea on a tray which meant he'd been for more than a pee in his brief absence. He wasn't erect, I'd be surprised if he was after the work out, he'd given my anus the night before. 'Looking forward to later?' He asked a rather crass question.

'Not really, would you?' I answered in the only way I could.

'Probably not under the circumstances, still after a light breakfast you can see where it will all happen later.' I was looking forward to that even less! I'd finished my tea and went to get out of bed, a firm hand stopped me.

'Haven't we forgotten something?' I looked back quizzically.

'No, I can't think what that could be?' I answered innocently.

'We forgot one important detail last night.' He ventured.

'Really, what is that?' He didn't reply but instead, dragged me back as prey, he placed both hands under my bottom and lifted my growing erection to his now open mouth. 'Oh my god....' I called out as he drew me in deep his lips sucking hard beyond my swollen head. I started to get really aroused now and wondered if I climaxed now, my beating later would be further torture? Was this more of Trent's plan to offer love one minute then break me in pieces the next. Thankfully, I never found out because he stopped. I'd never been sucked off before and Trent dropped me back down on the bed, smiling back.

'Let's shower together, save water!'

Mr Trent was an excellent cook. I had a full breakfast of eggs and bacon, a sausage perfectly cooked too. There was toast and marmalade to follow, and this was washed down with strong Italian coffee. He was dressed. I remained naked in submission. I had grown used to being unclothed or I was until Trent told me to hang the washing out of the rotary airer some distance from the house.

'I can't, your neighbours will see me!' I bleated.

'Of course, they will. They are used to my visitor's doing chores. You're not refusing, are you?' I wondered how he'd react if I did.

'Don't they say anything?' I asked.

'Occasionally, they comment on the marks on naughty boy's bottoms! They'll be very interested in yours tomorrow when you bring the washing in. Apparently, there is no rain forecast tonight so you can leave it out.' The casual way he responded was worrying. Reluctantly, I emptied the spun washing into a laundry basket and as I was used to hanging out my own clothes to dry, I had no issues with the task. The only issue I did have was rather obvious as I left the kitchen and headed outside with Trent standing hands on hips watching.

Once back inside I was told to check the post box on the wall just outside the house. This meant giving the neighbours on the opposite side of the road more than they bargained for. Either Mr Trent had tolerant neighbours or as I suspect he didn't give a shit!

'Okay Harry let's have a little look inside a room just down the corridor, I'd like your opinion. I rather suspected I knew what would be inside and I wasn't wrong. The door was thick. The room had no windows, and it was airless. I suspected it was soundproofed and containing entirely the activity that went on in there. When the light was turned on my heart stopped albeit briefly. Except for a cupboard at the far end the only feature in an otherwise empty room was a padded bench with one purpose only, that of strapping a victim down for corporal punishment to be inflicted. It was on stout legs, the ones at the rear spread wider than those at the front. The purpose obviously to ensure the legs of the victim were open. Straps were fitted to secure ankles, thighs at the rear and wrists and forearms at the front end. The padded leather top sloped down too which ensured the buttocks target area was raised to prominence. 'You will be strapped down over that at 8pm tonight – any thoughts?' I had plenty but I saw little point in sharing them. My fate was sealed it would appear, and if I was to become part of Gerald Trent's life in future, I had to endure what he had planned.

361

'Not really sir. It wasn't quite what I imagined, if I'm honest it is far more sinister than I expected.'

'You can try it out, hop up and stretch out. I'm told it's very comfortable even though what happens afterwards is not.' I couldn't see any harm. It might ease my worry if I tried it for size. I moved forward leaning up over the waist high start of the padded section. I now found myself looking down at the floor below where the word "REPENT" was emblazoned. The area was stained, and I realised it could only have come from tears and dribble, sweat too from the sufferings of countless victims over the years. It felt odd knowing my bare skin against the leather surface just added to so many who had come before. Thomas Clarke no doubt? What worried me most was my feeling of vulnerability. The natural way my legs opened to follow those stout rear legs meant the cheeks of my buttocks opened too and Trent was already exploiting this by fingering my anus and hanging balls. I was erect again, but I suspected my ardour would soon diminish once I found myself secured for real and his cane was being measured across my arse!

At four Trent arrived and I was shown into the kitchen. Where I had eaten breakfast was now transformed into a place of practical use. A towel was spread on the top and shaving equipment stood on the table surface. I was told to mount the table and spread my legs. I did so, resting my head down on my forearms. I heard shaving foam being ejected from a spray can and then it's cold feel as it was spread over and smeared between my cheeks. Next the scraping sensation of a replaceable razor as my hairy bottom and all between were depleted back to smoothness for the first time since my birth.

362

'I doubt you were very hairy at fifteen were you, Harry?' Trent asked as he continued.

'No sir, other boys were but I was different. I even had just a few straggly pubic hairs then too.' I recalled those moments in the shower room when some boy's maturity stood out like a beacon against my immaturity.

'You made up for it since though.' He remarked. I certainly had.

'Yes sir. It happened in my twenties, a sudden spurt of manhood. Hair sprouted from nowhere.'

'I want to take you back twenty-five years Harry. Have that hairless fifteen-year-old back ready to cane his errant bottom. It will give me immense pleasure.' He was pulling my cheeks apart now and shaving their insides. His finger encircled my anus but stopped at insertion. Once completed he spoke again as he wiped my now smooth skin with a towel. 'Let's have you on your back now, let's clear your considerable thatch.' I loved Mr Trent's choice of words. Twenty minutes later I was done. The towel he'd already used now cleared any traces of soap away and that whole area now felt chilled with my insulated covering removed. I was still erect, and Trent kissed the tip of my penis.

With two hours to go, I tried to eat but found it a struggle. I feared being sick during the forthcoming ordeal. I feared something else too. Losing control elsewhere but Trent had thought of that and once I'd finished at the table I was instructed to go to the bathroom and wait. After ten minutes Trent arrived with a mixed variety of equipment. There was a stand in the room already, similar in nature to that found in hospitals for connecting a patient to a drip. The rest was a concoction of tubing and a bulging bag of liquid. I'd never

363

had an enema before, but I realised quickly this was about to change.

'Down on your knees, part your legs and get your head right down, just like I placed you for shaving.' I complied. I knew my whole being had been taken over and everything that would happen now was out of my control. I knew I could get up and leave, demand the return of my clothes but that would only take me back to where I was when I had arrived the night before. Things were unbearable then, I didn't wish to return to that situation so my situation, while not ideal, was voluntary.

I wasn't sure what he was doing. I know he'd moved the stand, and I sensed he'd clipped the bag of liquid high above, then I felt searching hand around my bottom before my cheeks were parted wider and my anus lubricated with a generous blob of cold slippery gel. I didn't speak, I just closed my eyes. I knew what an enema consisted of and soon the nozzle of something smooth and round was inserted. It had a bulbous end, presumably to prevent it slipping out and my sphincter had to be overcome to allow it entry. 'Relax it'll hurt less if you do!' He suggested, as if he knew from personal experience. It was totally new to me. With this inserted I waited until a strange bubbling sensation announced the introduction of something liquid. I started to fill up and this gradually became more uncomfortable until it even started to hurt as this extreme bloating sensation took all my resolve to endure. Then, after I felt it would never end, I was instructed to stand and with my legs wide apart to hold the liquid in. Trent placed tissue on the floor, promising to add to the thirty strokes I was due if I released even a single drop. The liquid pressing down was becoming increasingly unbearable, in fact virtually impossible to hold. Then to my relief he left the room, calling out as he left. 'You can release now, I want you downstairs in the punishment room when you are done, take your time.' I didn't need any further telling. I moved quickly, sat down, and let nature take its course.

7

Finished, I washed myself in preparation to returning downstairs and entering the room where I had no doubt Mr Trent would be patiently waiting for me to arrive. This was it, the moment of truth. Everything that had gone before had led to the event about to take place. I wondered how many others had made the same trip from the upstairs bathroom after the ritual had been carried out up there. I imagined he had a tried and tested pattern of events, and I'd just fitted neatly into it. Hadn't he joked almost about neighbours commenting on the welts on bottoms of those collecting or putting out washing. Almost as if it was a regular event, which I guess it was. I wondered if it was to be my marked buttocks going on public display tomorrow morning this time.

'Come in.' Mr Trent saw me hovering by the door, fearful of entry.

'Yes Sir.' I replied nervously.

'So, the time has finally arrived albeit after twenty-five years. Be it the innocence of youth had that fifteen-year-old been standing nervously instead.' I realised now this would have been the same circumstances had I visited his home then as I yearned to at the time. All pure fantasy of course. The reality was something very different.

'I've often thought of that eventually sir, the reality feels very different now.' I looked over at the padded bench. There was a minor addition since I was here last, lying across its top was a metre long cane, one I had already become acquainted with then I was clothed.

'Okay Harry, time is up. I promised you a good caning and that is what you are getting.' I closed my eyes briefly as I took his words on board.

'How long will it take sir?' I asked.

'Thirty strokes, 15-20 seconds between each stroke. Around 8-10 minutes.' I visibly shrank. That wasn't long in any other context but regular pain infliction at intervals over that length of time felt like induced torture. It was his way of prolonging the agony.

'That's a long time Sir.' I pleaded.

'I spent a long time recovering from the hurt of you lacking trust in me. I need you to repent and suffer just like I did. I want you to feel each and every one of the thirty strokes I'm planning to inflict. Cry out in pain after each so I can hear you atone. Believe me 8-10 minutes isn't nearly enough time, I'd like to make it longer, but I'm in a generous mood so don't push me.' I got the message and decided to button my lip.

'I'm sorry sir!'

'Not as sorry as you are about to be.' Trent moved to the bench and removed the cane which was obviously placed there for effect 'Mount the bench please.' A shiver ran through me as I realised, like the condemned man mounting the scaffold this was it. Like the trapdoor that victim would stand on, the bench was its replacement. The only difference I would survive or at least I hoped I would. I'd baulked at 18 strokes, now an extra 12 had been added. 10 minutes of hell awaited but at least I'd been promised aftercare – whatever that was.

I took a deep breath and stepped forward. There was a shallow step with I mounted. I moved forward slightly before the bench halted my forward momentum, I stood up on my toes and leaned forward, stretching as far as I could as the downward curve of the bench leaned me down at a surprisingly acute angle. Trent got to work immediately. Pulling my right leg apart to align with the associated stout leg. A strap was placed around my ankle. Another fitted around my calf while a third secured my thigh halfway up. He then repeated the other side. I didn't expect my legs to end up so far apart and my shaven smooth cheeks parted stickily to expose goodness knows what. The cool air which now wafted through the now vacant hairless space felt cold and a shiver ran through me. He moved to secure my waist and gave my bum a playful smack as he passed.

'I'll photograph that sight, Harry. Before and after. I'm so looking forward to putting some lovely stripes on your beautiful bottom. Shame it wasn't a long time ago but then I'd have had to be rather more circumspect, bearing in mind your age. Your bottom was half the size to that which it is now also. More to stripe under the guise of maturity. Enjoyment awaits!' He laughed. Enjoyment for him, uncertainty and bowel loosening fear for me, although that likelihood had been removed too. He now moved to the front where Velcro wrist straps were fitted before short but stout chains were attached the rest of my arm was left free. Another torture? Allowing my arms some freedom, but not enough to interfere with the activity going on at the rear end with my exposed and vulnerable bottom was left high in the air ready for anything my strict dominating master wished to do. I looked down at the sign REPENT. I'd viewed it earlier but then I was just trying out his bench for size and feel. This time it was for real and that was just how this word felt. Trent picked up the cane and swished it viciously through the air several times as he made his way back to where he planned to perform his sadistic retribution. I felt the cane tapped across my bare cheeks and I instinctively flinched, pulling them in tight. Then it began.

One Month Later

I'm still at Gerald's home. I moved in two days later. I'm settled in a relationship for the first time. The event in Trent's punishment room was my first and last. I screamed my lungs out from the first until thankfully the last, the thirtieth stroke was delivered. I was told halfway through I was bleeding which didn't help. Incredibly it wasn't the pain that created my screams, or it wasn't after about one third of the punishment was delivered. Certainly, the first six were, the pain was excruciating, and I let my suffering out so the world, had they been listening, could hear. No, it was guilt and his constant reminding me why I was there and how he, a man who had harboured feelings towards me since boyhood, felt by my not trusting him that day when I'd walked out. He made me pay.

Afterwards he untied me and carried me over his shoulder to his bed. I was lain on a towel and my bottom was cleaned up. He used an ice cube to ease the swelling from each raised welt, then he rubbed arnica cream onto the whole damaged area. I was soothed and aroused, then I was lifted onto my knees, legs planted wide apart and with a large blob of gel smeared where it mattered, he entered me, masturbating me while he fucked me and both of us climaxing together. I was then tightly hugged and eventually I fell into a fitful sleep.

Gerald continued to entertain men in his room. I never went in there; I have no intention of entering again. That was his secret vice which he used to punish men he'd known for years. He says it is never sexual other than sending those who visit him home with a happy ending. Thomas Clarke visits, I keep out of the way. I watch standing back looking through net curtains at the arrivals. They follow Gerald to the room and an hour later, sometimes much less they emerge and leave, I don't need to know the details of what takes place, it is sadistic and brutal and some who later leave are visibly upset. Gerald has what I can only describe as a couple of sissy boy clients. Both who come separately, are effeminate and Gerald explains they only come for a good over the knee spanking which he administers with his hand, followed by masturbation. They bounce in but walk out far more circumspectly. I leave that part of Gerald's life to him and play no part in it.

I still receive the cane. I am a masochist after all. Mine is administered in the bedroom where a cane is kept. I am beaten naked, how else, bending over the end of the bed. It becomes a very sexual act, one which generally ends up with me being fucked and masturbated to a climax. When I am needy, I don't ask to be beaten. We have agreed a secret signal which is to use a particular mug when I bring tea up in bed. It's kept just for this purpose. Gerald knows I have a need and that night to expect six of the best. I'm erect too, when am I not, and while this might not be enough on its own to signal, I have another need, bringing tea up in that particular mug tells the true story and what I can expect that night.

Moving in wasn't a hard decision. The severe beating drew a line under the past and all was forgiven if not forgotten. Our life together is blissful, the neighbours have got used to me being around although I no longer hang out the washing naked. They never get to see my marked bum either. They do see the comings and goings of his other clients although it isn't as frequent as it might be imagined. I often think back to how it all started back in my school years and what might have happened had I visited him as a fifteen-year-old boy instead of a forty-year-old man. But then of course I'll never know, it might have happened but didn't. All I focus on now is what did happen and our future.

Visit our Website

https://www.texshirebooks.com

About the Author

Hello

I'm Sam Evans, writer, father, and grandparent. I've travelled around quite a bit, both for work reasons and pleasure. My main interest now is as a writer. I have met a lot of people throughout my life, and I like to write about both my own experiences and those I've met along the way. I've written two books which reflect on a conversation I had about early life. One was during the latter stages of school and then later in life when a dark event which took place followed that person into adulthood. It was a difficult period in that person's life, and it describes an obsession which will be carried for ever. It was hard to describe and even harder to put into words. Much of the narrative in these two books are based on true events, although names are changed, and some parts were added to make the story more readable. More books will follow on equally challenging themes.

About Texshire Books

https://www.texshirebooks.com

Welcome book lovers to our website! We are a group of indie writers working together to promote our books as well as support other independently published writers

On our pages you will find full length novels as well as short stories. We like to say we write books with an edge! An edge to what? An edge of kink, an edge of sadism, an edge of mystery, an edge of romance. Our books aren't everyone's cup of tea but if you like your books a little more on the extreme side, if you like books which don't shy away from difficult subjects such as rape, racism, or domestic abuse then you are in the right place. If you like books with lots of dirty, kinky sex, or a touch of sadism then you are definitely in the right place!

Many of our books explore DDLG, Dom and Sub relationships and BDSM. If you are in the DDLG community and are looking for books to help you or your little enjoy little space, we offer adult fairy tales and colouring books.

We hope you visit our site shown below. Please be sure to subscribe to get all our latest news and updates

Printed in Great Britain
by Amazon

57911044R00208